Allie Spencer is an author with many strings to her bow. She gained a BA in English and Related Literature and an MA in Medieval Studies before reading for the Bar. She completed pupillage in London with a leading set of family law barristers and then joined a firm of solicitors as a matrimonial specialist.

She is the author of four novels: *Tug of Love*, which won the Romantic Novelists' Association New Writers' Scheme prize for the best debut of 2009 and was shortlisted for the 2010 Melissa Nathan Award for Comedy Romance, and *The Not-So-Secret Diary of a City Girl*, *Summer Loving* – also shortlisted for the Melissa Nathan Award, and *Summer Nights*.

ALLIE SPENCER

Save The Date!

arrow books

First published by Arrow Books, 2013

2 4 6 8 10 9 7 5 3 1

First published in Great Britain in 2013 by
Arrow Books
The Random House Group Limited
20 Vauxhall Bridge Road, London, SW1V 2SA

www.randomhousebooks.co.uk

Addresses for companies within The Random House Group Limited can be
found at: www.randomhouse.co.uk/offices.htm

The Random House Group Limited Reg. No. 954009

A CIP catalogue record for this book
is available from the British Library

ISBN 9780099579977

The Random House Group Limited supports the Forest Stewardship
Council® (FSC®), the leading international forest-certification organisation.
Our books carrying the FSC label are printed on FSC®-certified paper. FSC is
the only forest-certification scheme supported by the leading environmental
organisations, including Greenpeace. Our paper procurement policy can be
found at: www.randomhouse.co.uk/environment

Typeset by SX Composing DTP, Rayleigh, Essex
Printed and bound by CPI Group (UK) Ltd, Croydon, CR0 4YY

For Chris

Acknowledgements

As ever, this book feels like more of a team effort than anything I could have achieved by myself and I owe all those involved a deep debt of gratitude. To begin with, huge thanks go to my editor Gillian for her astute insights and guiding comments, to Teresa my agent, and to everyone at Arrow who has supported this book on its journey to publication. There are also many enthusiastic friends who helped, commented and gave generously of their knowledge along the way (you know who you are) and I owe a particular debt to Cas Smeaton who not only read and commented on the book at various stages in its development but whose dog, Arthur, plays such a large part in the novel itself. Huge, huge thanks also go to Vicky (aka VM Whitworth – go buy her books!) for her help with the Italian translation and I also owe the fabulous Dr Joanna for her input re: martini-making. Finally, though, thanks and much, much love to my family who have (yet again) graciously put up with me spending so much time with made-up people – I love you xx.

Mr and Mrs Dudley Westfield Request the
Pleasure of the Company
Of
Ailsa Stuart
At the Wedding of their Daughter

Jessica Morag
To

Mr Justin Chilmark

At
Hotel Santa Lucia, Tuscany
3rd June and the week preceding
RSVP

sheilandud@youmail.net

Reasons not to go to cousin Jessica's wedding:

1. It takes up the whole of half-term
2. It's a thousand miles away
3. I'm busy at work
4. Nick
5. Nick
6. Did I mention Nick?
7. I get airsick
8. When she was fifteen, Jess threw a shoe at Auntie Sheila in a tantrum and it hit me by mistake
9. Auntie Sheila drinks too much
10. Nick
11. Uncle Dudley is beyond obnoxious
12. Nick

Reasons to go to cousin Jessica's wedding:

1. It's in a posh hotel in Italy
2. Emma thinks it would be a good idea
3. Um . . .?

Chapter One

The gold-embossed wedding invitation sat almost unnoticed in my kitchen for a good month or so, festering behind the kettle, an (empty) fruit bowl and an out-of-date, half-eaten malt loaf.

In fact, I almost entirely forgot about its existence.

It sat there; I ignored it – and both of us were more than happy with that arrangement. Until one Friday, when me and my best friend and flatmate Emma slithered home after midnight, on the wrong side of a few mojitos.

We'd just walked through the door when my phone bonged loudly, announcing an incoming email.

'Wassat?' Emma stood in the living room doorway, swaying gently. 'And – oooooh, Ailsa – did you know the floor is moving – like, in waves?'

I rummaged through my bag, unearthing the lids of long-dead lipsticks; remnants of claggy tissues and three boiled sweets covered in fluff.

'I'm not sure it is,' a moving floor seemed unlikely, but in my mojitoed-up state it wasn't something I could dismiss outright. 'What about the hall? Is that like it too?'

With slow, deliberate movements, Emma looked round, while I located my mobile and peered at it: the screen was sliding disconcertingly in and out of focus.

'You're right! It is . . . but side to side rather than up and down,' she breathed, 'wowzers.'

I squinted even harder at my phone and read aloud: 'You must come you have to come you must.'

Emma, who had been looking first at the living room floor, then at the one in the hall, stopped and stared at me.

'Come where?' she asked. 'I'm here already.'

'No.' I squinted at the phone again, just to be sure. 'It's what the email says: *You must come you have to come you must.*'

Emma frowned.

'Why are you speaking like Yoda?'

'I'm not; I'm reading you the email.'

'Well, who is it from, then? Apart from possibly Yoda.'

I peered again at the screen.

'I don't know, they haven't signed it and the name in the 'sender' line just says *sweetbabe305.*'

'Do you know anyone called *sweetbabe305*?'

'Of course not, it's a ridiculous name.'

Then I paused.

'Emma, do you think it could be from Nick?'

Emma slithered down the wall onto the floor. I watched as she swayed gently from side to side, in time with her imaginary floor-waves.

'Don't be silly,' she murmured. 'Nick wouldn't set himself up with an email account called *sweetbabe305*. If he wanted to get in touch he'd use his own name *and* he wouldn't do it at half past twelve on a Friday night.'

'He might be using the name to lull me into a false sense of security. Or he might be drunk,' I felt I currently had expert insight into this. 'People do all sorts of strange things when they're drunk.'

'It's not compulsory, sweetie.' Emma collapsed further onto the floor. '*You're* drunk and you're not trying to email anyone.'

There was a certain, inescapable logic to this. Emma suddenly stopped swaying and looked serious.

'Ailsa,' she said softly, 'do you want it to be Nick?'

A large, awkward lump appeared in my throat and I felt my chest contract painfully.

I'd walked out on Nick and our life together three weeks ago after a particularly bitter row. He was half-Scots, half-Italian, had a body that your average Greek god would have killed for, and did his best to scratch a living as an artist. Unfortunately, art – rather like crime – doesn't pay and I ended up bankrolling the bills for both of us. While this was sort-of okay to begin with, I soon heartily resented Nick and his refusal to take our finances seriously. Finally, after swearing blind that he hadn't been spending money behind my back, I found a court summons for a loan he'd run up without telling me. In some ways it was good, because it meant I could deal with the debt before the court did – but it was also the last straw.

If I remember that evening correctly, I'd thrown a frying pan at his head, yelled that if I'd wanted to spend my life with an unbearable selfish pig, I'd have moved in with my Uncle Dudley, and walked out of my own beloved little flat. When I walked back in a week later, he'd disappeared. Emma moved in with me to help pay the bills and I'd changed my phone numbers and systematically ignored his attempts to make contact. I was devastated, yes, but I also had my self-respect – and

7

I was not going to spend the rest of my life terrified the bailiffs were going to turn up and cart away my hard-earned possessions.

Bong! Another email.

'*Tell me that you will be there totes life and death.*' I read.

Emma tried to walk over to the sofa but instead fell head first into an armchair.

'Trickly,' she remarked, removing her face from the scatter cushions.

'You're not wrong there,' I replied. 'Someone – who I now think probably isn't Nick – wants me somewhere. But I don't know where. Or why. Or when. But apparently it's very important.'

'Like I said – trickly,' slurred Emma solemnly.

Bong! A third appeared. I pressed 'open' as fast as my mojitoed fingers would allow.

Btw, it said, *it's Jess. Can't tell you any more until I see you all top secret and hush hush laters.*

'Mystery solved,' I said, navigating carefully across the floor and settling myself on the arm of Emma's chair. 'Well, sort of solved – it's Jess and she wants to talk to me about some sort of top secret life or death thingamabob.'

Emma's eyes fluttered open.

'Jess? Remind me.'

'My cousin. Wedding. Posh hotel in Tuscany. All expenses. Invite in the kitchen behind that mouldy Soreen.'

Emma sat up and blinked at me.

'All expenses? Posh hotel? And you need to *think* about it? Jeesh, didn't they teach you *anything* at university? Particularly after the money you've had to shell out on

Nick and his fecklessness; it's the only holiday you'll be getting this year.'

This was true. Nick and his fecklessness had been very expensive.

'Yes, but—'

'No buts. You'll get to sleep in a luxury pool, swim in a luxury room, eat champagne and drink lobsters and – and – what's not to like?'

I put my mobile down onto the floor and then rolled off the arm of the chair to join it. Emma was right – the laminate *was* moving: in a gently undulating, soothing sort of way.

'You know what's not to like,' I said. 'Nick. Again.'

When you see it like that, on a page, it seems so simple. Nick.

One syllable, phonetically uncomplicated, four little letters.

N-i-c-k.

Weddings.

Italy.

Nick.

Emma reached down and fished for my hand. My right hand. The hand that wore the ring Nick had given me – white antique gold set with three tiny pearls – and which, despite the fact we were well and truly over, I hadn't been able to take off.

'Nick isn't going to be there,' she said firmly. 'In fact, it's the last place on earth you are ever going to run into him. He doesn't even *know* Jess, does he?'

I tried to shake my head but I couldn't because I was lying on the floor and there was no room for manoeuvre.

9

Instead, I laid my cheek on the varnished boards and their coolness took some of the sting out of my over-flushed face.

'It's a family wedding,' Emma continued. 'Jess is obviously desperate for you to go and, even if she wasn't, I don't see the problem. You'll be surrounded by people who love and care for you – or, at least, seeing as it is *your* family we're talking about, people who share some of your DNA and don't actively wish you any harm.'

Bless her, she was obviously trying hard to make it sound an attractive prospect.

'Go,' she said. 'Forget Nick and have some fun. You never know, the man of your dreams might be there; and if you *don't* go, you'll never meet him and end up dying loveless and alone – and then you'll be sorry.'

'I don't think people can be sorry after they've died,' I pointed out. 'And anyway, Gary asked me out for coffee the other day – you never know he might be the man of my dreams.'

Emma rolled her eyes.

'If Gary's the man of anyone's dreams I'll eat my hat. In fact, seeing as I don't own a hat, I'll go out and buy one specially and eat *that*. '

I was just about to defend Gary's honour when there was another loud, email-induced bong that reverberated across the floorboards, into my jaw and my teeth and up through my nasal cavities.

Life or death remember? Are you coming?

It was Jess with a long-distance, cryptic demand for action.

I rubbed my exhausted face with my hands before

10

pressing 'reply'. A blank page sprang onto my screen. To accept or not to accept, that was the question. Hmmm . . .

Looking forward to it, I typed, *speak when I see you.*

Then I pressed 'send' and promptly passed out on the floor.

Chapter Two

It was dusk on the Monday before Jess's wedding. My taxi rounded the final hairpin bend on the wiggly road leading up to the Hotel Santa Lucia, sending a cloud of dust billowing up behind it, and launching me and my suitcase across the back seat at Warp Speed Nine. The driver briefly indicated left (probably to show off, rather than out of concern for other road users) before heading at full throttle through an enormous stone archway.

I was exhausted. As well as a day spent travelling (not to mention arguing with the baggage check-in people over the weight of my suitcase), I'd had a job interview the day before and spent a lot of energy bombing up and down the motorway to Newcastle. It was a job I very much wanted, a promotion, in fact: deputy head of a brand-new school in a leafy suburb that, come September, would be full of apple-cheeked children, eager to sit at my knee and absorb my outpourings of wisdom, a far cry from the antiquated, leaking, Victorian school-come-prison-camp that I currently dragged my bones to on a daily basis.

I pulled my phone out of my bag to see if there was any news yet – damn! No connection.

Never mind.

I was here to get away from work as well as from Nick. There would be plenty going on in a luxury hotel to distract me.

'Is here,' the driver shouted, slamming on the brakes and sending me crunching into the back of the passenger seat. 'Is hotel. Is thirty euro.'

I blinked, reattached my left shoe to my foot and extracted my right hand from the ashtray.

'Is hotel,' the driver insisted loudly. 'Is here. Is thirty euro.'

I don't know what I'd been expecting in the weird Venn diagram overlap of 'Italian hotels', 'my crazy family' and 'places I am not going to bump into Nick' – but it certainly wasn't this. The building in front of me was massive and was configured into a giant 'L' shape. It was four storeys high, with an imposing crenellated tower looming over its rows of mullioned windows – although the seriously wonky angle of some of them indicated that the floors inside had probably never met with a spirit level. Wisteria and bougainvillea jostled for space on its walls and, around the corner, I could just make out a vine-covered terrace lit by honey-coloured lamps. However, the most spectacular feature by far was the roofless ruin of an ancient church standing a slight distance from the main site, the ragged remains of an enormous rose window hanging from it like a battered crescent moon.

Blimey.

I was staying *here*?

'Is hotel. Is thirty euro. You get out now,' the insistent voice of the cabby brought me back to earth with a bump.

'There,' I said, scrambling out of the cab and thrusting what I hoped was an appropriate amount of currency through the driver's window.

I couldn't drag my eyes away from the edifice in front

13

of me. It was insanely beautiful but also rather spooky in a way that made me think its management team probably included the Addams Family. Right on cue, an owl hooted and a loud Mancunian voice behind me said: 'Do you want me to take that suitcase for you or what?'

I think both my feet left the floor.

'Sorry,' apologised the voice, 'that should have been, "Do you want me to take that suitcase for you or what, *madam?*" It's only my second day here.'

I swallowed, drew the breath of life into my lungs and felt my adrenalin levels slowly return to normal. Behind me was a stocky young man with stubbly red hair wearing a claret-coloured waistcoat.

'Don't do that again,' I begged. 'Or rather, I mean, "don't make me jump like that" not "don't ever talk to me again".'

The young man grinned and heaved my suitcase out of the cab.

'I think you jumped all by yourself – well, maybe with a little help from the owls and the Scooby Doo architecture. I'm Liam, by the way.'

'Ailsa Stuart,' I replied. 'I'm here with the wedding party. The Westfields? Jessica, the bride, is my cousin.'

Something strange happened to Liam: the jovial smile froze on his lips and his eyes took on a strange, glassy quality. Then he shook his head.

'Sorry,' he said, 'it's fine. I mean – they're fine – I mean—'

He was trying to be polite.

'It's all right,' I said gloomily, 'I grew up with them. I know what they're like. Look on the bright side – we're

14

only here for the week and there are support groups available to help you recover afterwards. Or maybe that's just something I tell myself to make myself feel better.'

Liam grinned again and ushered me across the gravel car park towards the ornate main door. We pushed our way through the revolving glass and I found myself in a reception area so large you could have fitted my entire apartment block into it and still had space for the Happy Shopper and BP garage next door. Marble pillars rose up from the gleaming floor like tree trunks, supporting an enormous expanse of white stuccoed ceiling; while the walls (also marble) glittered and shone as the light from ten full-sized chandeliers bounced off their polished surfaces.

It looked more like the check-in area for an upmarket afterlife than any hotel reception area *I'd* ever seen.

I followed Liam as he wound his way through a tastefully arranged mish-mash of antique chairs, designer sofas, potted plants and coffee tables, before ending up at a highly polished wooden counter, behind which sat a girl in a claret-coloured suit. Her blonde hair was swept up into a severe-looking bun and she had a suspicious expression on her face.

'Your name, please,' she said.

Despite the fact I had Liam standing beside me clutching a suitcase, it was clear from her tone that she regarded me as someone more likely to be asking for a job scrubbing out the hotel toilet bowls than in need of a room. She knew instinctively that the Hotel Santa Lucia was not my natural habitat.

Professional Intimidation.com.

'Ailsa Stuart,' I replied as loudly as I dared, 'you are expecting me.'

The girl narrowed her eyes in a way that clearly said I was the last thing she was expecting.

'The wedding party,' Liam explained. 'The Westfield block booking.'

'And could you tell me which room Jessica Westfield is in, please?' I asked, thinking that I might as well investigate the meaning of Jess's life-or-death emails sooner rather than later.

The girl raised her nose even further in the air, rummaged under the desk and pushed a key card towards me.

'You are in A-one-one-three,' she announced, superiority dripping from every syllable as she spoke. 'It is in the Michelangelo wing. Miss Westfield is in B-twenty-seven in the Donatello wing.'

She paused.

'And there are no pets allowed.'

This was a rather random statement.

'I don't have any pets,' I replied.

Because I didn't.

The girl didn't bother to respond verbally but instead raised an eyebrow and stared, very hard, at a spot on the highly polished floor just behind me. I followed the line of her gaze and there, looking happily up at me, was a small dog. It was a dirty white colour with a large splodge of brown in the middle of its back and another slanting down over its right eye that gave it a piratical air. As I stared at this apparition, it pulled its lips back into something that could only be described as a doggy grin and wagged its tail.

'It's nothing to do with me,' I said, turning back to the girl and pocketing my key card. 'I've never seen it before in my life.'

The dog behind me gave a small whine. It sounded disappointed.

The girl sighed.

'Breakfast is between seven and nine in the dining room, lunch is served from twelve and dinner from seven-thirty,' she intoned, sounding as though she was reading from a script with which she was very, very bored. 'An extensive range of luxury extras is also available – please see the brochures in your room for further details; and remember to charge all hotel goods and services to the Westfield account by swiping your key card at the various hotel paypoints. That is all.'

I nodded; then, checking that Liam still had my suitcase, I picked up my handbag and prepared to leave, but I was not getting away that easily.

'Excuse me!' the girl behind the desk stopped sounding bored and became indignant, 'I have just explained – you cannot take your dog with you.'

And she wrinkled up her nose as though a particularly unpleasant smell had wafted up her nostrils.

'He's not my dog,' I repeated, more loudly this time, and followed Liam in the direction of what looked like a marble-coated lift.

At the sound of my voice, the little dog jumped to his feet and wagged his tail; but, before it could trot along behind us, the girl pinged a bell on the desk and a burly man in a claret-coloured concierge's uniform swept in and scooped the pooch up. The dog growled and wriggled but

17

the concierge was unmoved. He deposited it outside the revolving door.

'It ees the one who has been bothering chef,' he announced. 'Chef says if ee see 'im again, he will put him in the lasagne.'

I didn't really give the incident any more thought. I stepped into the lift, Liam pressed the (gold-plated?) lift button and up we swept, leaving my stomach behind somewhere around the level of the first floor. We were regurgitated out onto a landing covered from floor to ceiling with dark wooden panelling and Liam led me along a winding passageway to an unassuming door, bearing a brass plate with 'A113' engraved onto it.

'I'm afraid you're stuck over here on your own,' said Liam. 'The rest of your lot are in the Donatello wing. But maybe that's a good thing.'

He winked.

'Thanks,' I said, taking out my key card, 'I'll manage from here.'

I fumbled a note out of my purse and pressed it into his hand. He nodded his thanks and I slid my card through the lock and shouldered open the heavy oak door.

My room turned out to be large – disconcertingly so – containing a four-poster bed, an enormous chest of drawers and a pair of armchairs. On the far side of the room, a writing desk and a drinks cabinet-cum-minibar flanked a pair of French windows opening out onto a balcony.

There was a pile of glossy-looking brochures lying on top of the cabinet and I wandered over and began flicking through them. As well as the expected flyers for local tourist attractions, there was one offering bespoke gourmet dinners for up to fifteen people cooked by my own private chef and served in my room; another advertising a special discount rate for racehorse ownership from a local stables; and one urging me to hire my own Learjet for the duration of my stay.

The phrase 'different world' wafted through my brain. Uncle Dudley must be doing spectacularly well, I thought, to even think of paying for a place like this for his daughter's wedding. While it was fair to say he'd always had a taste for the good things in life, my uncle by marriage was far from being the Alan Sugar of Droitwich Spa. He was the chairman of Sidebottom's, a West Midlands microbrewery once owned by my mother's family. There had been monumental unpleasantness when my Granny Sidebottom died and the shares had been inherited lock, stock, and barrel by my mother's sister/Dudley's wife, Auntie Sheila – who had then promptly handed over the running of the company to her husband. I was a little hazy over the details, but my memories of the time mainly involved my mother exploding with fury at being cut out of the brewery and refusing to have anything more to do with Auntie Sheila.

I carefully replaced the brochure. Even if Sidebottom's was raking it in, I didn't think Dudley would be happy about me chartering my own private aircraft for the week.

Then I saw *it*.

Next to the Learjet advert was a card with scalloped edges and gold swirly writing.

You are cordially invited to an evening reception in the Noel Coward Room, it informed me, *black tie, dancing, champagne and canapés.*

And it started – oh crap – ten minutes ago.

I pulled off my creased travel clothes, threw on a gorgeous, fluffy, complimentary hotel bath robe and ran into the bathroom. As I turned on the shower, my eye caught a row of little bottles and packets lined up on the shelf in front of me.

Mmmmm . . . really? Jo Malone?

I picked up a particularly lovely looking tube: face mask.

Yup, after a couple of hours on a budget-price aeroplane, I could definitely do with a face mask and look – this one only took five minutes! I could pop it on, have my shower, and then rock up to the first gig of the week looking like an actual, living human being.

Result!

I stared at my travel-worn reflection and began smoothing the deliciously scented paste over my skin.

'Nothing bad is going to happen this week,' I informed my mirror-self. 'I will return to Scotland relaxed and refreshed. This is going to be the first week of the rest of my life and, after the time I've had recently, I bloody deserve it.'

Right on cue, an all-too-familiar scratchy, lumpy feeling at the back of my throat appeared but I did my best to ignore it. Nick was a thousand miles away and hadn't tried to contact me for three months. It was over. What I needed to do was come to terms with that and move on.

Or perhaps, maybe, *think* about *beginning* to move on.

Baby steps, Ailsa; baby steps.

There.

With my mask applied, I rinsed my hands off under the tap and opened the shower door but, before I had a chance to take off the robe (which was so soft and warm I was fast beginning to love it as a mother does her newborn child), there came a knock on the door.

'Turn-a your bed down?' called a female voice from the corridor outside. 'And would you like-a complimentary luxury chocolates?'

Complimentary luxury chocolates? Totally my favourite sort.

'Just a moment,' I called back, remembering that I was slathered with white nectarine and honey face mask, 'I'm not really—'

But it was too late. My door opened and I heard a noise that sounded like an excited bark. Deducing that chocolate-delivering, bed-turning, hotel staff did not, in the usual course of events, make barking noises, I came out of the bathroom to see what was going on – and was met by the sight of a young woman wearing the Santa Lucia's claret-coloured uniform hurtling floorwards at great speed.

To avoid colliding with either her or her large basket of complimentary luxury chocolates which was also airborne, I stepped backwards – and promptly tripped over something small, furry and fast-moving. The small, furry, fast-moving thing ran over to my open suitcase where, after a lot more barking and some growling, it re-emerged gripping something between its teeth.

'*Mamma mia!* Eet ees a dog!' cried the girl. 'You must not-a have the pets in-a the hotel!'

'It's not my dog,' I cried, trying to scramble to my feet but slipping on a box of pralines and falling back to earth with a bump.

'What 'as eet got in eet's mouth?'

21

I made a second attempt to get back on my feet, only to be foiled again – this time by some caramel Brazils.

The dog had stopped barking and was now making growling-chewing-type noises. It was fully occupied with an object clamped between its sharp little teeth . . . something pink and cylindrical and oh-so-very-familiar.

I just couldn't quite put my finger on what it was.

I squinted at it again – and the penny dropped.

A hugely embarrassing and cringeworthy penny that made me go hot and cold just thinking about it.

'Oh buggerfuck!' I lunged at the dog, which dodged neatly out of my way like a rugby forward avoiding an opposition tackle, 'it's got my tampon holder. Quick – grab it! Don't let him have it!'

The girl, who had been picking up little boxes of complimentary chocolates, leaped into action, but the dog again sidestepped all attempts at capture and made off through the still-open door.

'Get it!' I yelled, already off in hot pursuit.

Down corridor after corridor, staircase after staircase, we chased the little dog who, despite the shortness of its legs, couldn't half move. Doors whizzed past me, oak panelling flew by, occasional tables decorated with vases of flowers became a blur. I, however, barely noticed the scenery; every atom of my being was focused on getting my hands on the canine from hell and wresting my sanitary products from its slobbering jaws.

We hung a left, a right, another left, pounded down a flight of stairs, along a corridor, down another flight of stairs, *another* corridor – and then through a set of double doors and into a large room. The dog paused, looked around and, for one tantalising moment, was almost within my grasp—

Then it shot forwards, right into the middle of a group of people, where it growled loudly and shook the canister with all its might. It burst open and little fluffy white tampons hailed down upon us.

Slowly – very slowly – I looked up.

Staring in frozen horror back at me was a sea of faces. From somewhere at the back there was a single, solitary snigger of laughter – then more silence.

This is bad, I thought; this is just about as bad as it can get.

But I had bargained without my canine friend's capacity for chaos.

The dog was playing with something on the floor – jumping on it and growling. Then it barked, yelped and threw the item high into the air. As if in slow motion, it flew across the room, followed by about twenty pairs of eyes, before landing – plonk – in the glass of a woman standing nearby and expanding rapidly with a loud fizz.

That was as bad as it could get.

I closed my eyes and decided that if I died now, it would probably be for the best.

The dog trotted over, laid the remains of the plastic container solemnly at my feet, sat back on its haunches and looked expectantly up into my eyes.

'And this is Ailsa, my niece,' the familiar voice of my Auntie Sheila cut through the horrified silence. 'So glad you could join us, Ailsa. And – is this your dog?'

'No,' I replied, straightening my bathrobe in a vain attempt to give myself back a little dignity, 'it's not.'

There was a truly ghastly pause.

With nothing left to lose, I took a glass of champagne from a tray held by a nearby waiter, downed it in one and walked out of the room doing my damnedest to hold my head high.

Chapter Three

I needed to hold it high again the next morning when, as I walked into the dining room, silence once again fell like a guillotine blade across the room. I smiled at the starers, gritted my teeth, and then made my way over to a free table outside on a little terrace, conveniently screened off by a lemon tree in a pot and some trailing vines.

It worked.

As soon as I was safely out of sight and it was clear that I was not going to provide any more sanitary-based entertainment, everyone turned back to their newspapers, menus, smartphones or whatever it was that had been occupying them before my arrival.

Liam silently materialised by my elbow and placed a tiny, steaming cup of espresso on the table: it must be some sort of mind-reading trick they teach staff in posh hotels, I decided – strong coffee was exactly what I needed.

I took a sip.

It was delicious.

I rolled it round my mouth and felt the smooth, smoky taste ping off my tongue before I swallowed it.

This was good, I told myself; this was the life I should be living. Single estate espresso on a terrace in the morning sunshine while the Mediterranean glimmered blue-green nearby. Not that other rubbish from last night involving tampons and dogs and face packs.

'Can I have another one of these, please.' I turned to Liam who was hovering discreetly next to one of the lemon trees. 'And some food – I'm not really fussy what it is, just as much as you can carry, as soon as you can.'

Liam grinned and went off to do my bidding.

I closed my eyes and sighed deeply.

The dog/tampon nightmare began to lose some of its intensity.

I exhaled and allowed the warm summer breeze to wrap itself around me and soothe away some of my tension. Not just from the previous evening, but from the days and weeks and months before.

Emma had been right; a week off would do me the world of good.

A week of peace and quiet and—

'EEEEEEEEEEEEEEE!'

I leaped out of my seat and looked around.

For a moment, the only sound was the wind wafting through the lemon trees and the sea lapping soothingly against the rocks on the shore: Nature at her most chilled.

I picked up my cup and put it to my lips and—

'Eeeeeeeeeeeee!'

Cup, coffee and any hope of undisturbed peace and quiet came crashing down to earth.

It wasn't quite a scream, it wasn't quite a cry. Drawn out, high-pitched and ear-meltingly loud, it was the sort of noise that posed a serious risk to the ear drums of anyone in the vicinity – and there was something horribly familiar about it.

Pushing back my chair, I walked over to the edge of the terrace and peered into the garden beyond.

Immediately, I spotted Auntie Sheila and a woman in a bright red suit who seemed to be following her. Auntie Sheila was moving slowly and carefully and had her hands on her temples, while the woman in red strode along purposefully. They looked for all the world as though they had lost something.

'Jessica!' the woman in red yelled. 'Jessica! We need to sort this out NOW. JESSICA!!!'

Auntie Sheila winced as the decibels ripped through the air. I suspected she had had a rather heavy night.

'Jessica, darling,' Auntie S's voice was soft and pleading (although that probably had quite a lot to do with her hangover), 'Jessica – this is very important. We need to talk.'

'EEEEEEEEEEEEEEEEEEEEEEEEEEEE!'

Another, even louder, scream tore through the tranquillity of the Italian morning and both Auntie Sheila and her scarlet-suited companion shuddered.

'Go away!' A young female Brummie voice floated up from somewhere on my left. 'I hate you. I hate all of you. Go *away*!'

'Listen, darling,' Auntie Sheila gripped her temples even more tightly; she was clearly suffering. 'There's nothing I can do. You're just going to have to come to terms with it.'

'I don't *want* to come to terms with it. I don't care if there is a baggage handlers strike at Gatwick – Justin's parents will get here somehow. I know they will. I don't *want* to make any other arrangements. This is *my* wedding, Mummy. *My wedding*. What bit of "my wedding" do you not understand?'

I didn't actually hear the stamping of a petulant foot at this point, but I bet it happened anyway.

'This is a *family* wedding, darling; and it's very important for Daddy and me that everything runs smoothly.'

'It will run smoothly – if you don't keep on trying to *ruin* everything.'

'We're not ruining anything, darling; if you'd only be sensible and—'

'EEEEEEEEEEEEEEEEEEEE!'

There was a final, high-pitched onslaught, followed by the sound of someone running as fast as they could in the opposite direction.

Then, mercifully, silence.

I sighed. This was exactly what my family were like: more drama, shouting and overreaction than an omnibus edition of *EastEnders*. It was one of the reasons why I'd moved to Scotland; I slept better with an internationally recognised border between us. Thank God I wasn't like them.

The lady with the red suit walked over to Auntie Sheila. I noticed that her talon-like nails were exactly the same shade of blood-red as her clothes.

'So?' she asked. 'What are we going to do?'

She said 'we' in a way that clearly meant 'you'.

Auntie Sheila slumped down onto a nearby bench and reached into her handbag. She popped two white tablets out of a blister pack and swallowed them, waterless, with an enormous gulp.

'Just go ahead,' she said. 'Dudley will go mad if we don't. Write it down in the itinerary that if Justin's parents don't get here in time, Charles will sit on the top table.

God only knows why Dudley wants Charles up there; but he does and that's an end to it.'

The woman in the red suit produced a clipboard from somewhere and began scribbling furiously.

'The next thing is the peonies,' she said. 'I need to know what to tell them about the peonies. The suppliers have been on the phone twice this morning.'

Auntie Sheila lifted her feet carefully onto the bench and lay down, covering her eyes with her hand.

'I'm beyond peonies at the moment,' she murmured weakly, 'I'll think about it later. Right now I need – ah – a little rest.'

The red-suited one tapped her pen loudly on the clipboard and Auntie Sheila winced.

'Mrs Westfield,' she said tartly, 'this is not the time for having little rests. This is the time for thinking about peonies.'

Auntie Sheila did not reply. The woman paused for a moment and then continued.

'Well, if you won't talk about the peonies, then perhaps you'd like to discuss the hand-tied bouquets – do you want them hand-tied using string or twine? And do you want the twine to be string-coloured, or the string to be twine-coloured; or would you rather leave the artisan look behind entirely and go for—'

Auntie Sheila waved weakly in her general direction.

'Please,' she said, a thinly veiled air of suffering in her voice, 'please just go away.'

The red-suited lady did a bit more pen tapping. Auntie Sheila responded with a bit more wincing.

'Well, when can we reconvene? I have to get the final order to the florist by midday, the twine and string people need to know by nine a.m. tomorrow – and we still haven't even *begun* to think about the ice sculptures—'

Auntie Sheila's hands returned to her temples: she looked as though she was trying to stop her head exploding.

Which might very well have been the case.

'I tell you what, Veronica, *you* decide. I'm sure you know best – after all, this is what you do for a living. You go and talk to the peony people, and the string people and whoever else you feel you need to chat to, and then come and find me when you've made the arrangements.'

The woman in red sighed heavily and stalked off towards the hotel, leaving Auntie Sheila alone for some quality time with her hangover.

Show over, I turned away from the railings and looked at my table. In my absence, a plate of bacon, eggs, tomatoes, mushrooms and sausages had appeared. Next to it sat a silver rack containing delicate triangles of toast, a plate of Danish pastries and a fresh cup of espresso.

I made short work of it. As I ate, I wondered why weddings always brought out the worst in people. In fact, marriage in general seemed to have that effect. Maybe there were the odd few peeps (with odd probably being the operative word) who were genuinely happy to be manacled together with the matrimonial handcuffs – but then again, maybe they were just very good at pretending.

The scratchy lump materialised once again in my throat. For a moment I thought it must be a renegade piece of toast and swallowed hard, but it refused to budge. In fact, it got worse, and itchy pre-tears began to crowd into my ducts and congregate at the back of my nose.

This was not good.

It was worse than not good – this was exactly what I'd hoped to leave behind on the tarmac at Edinburgh Airport.

I pushed back my chair, picked up one of the remaining Danish pastries, and made my way down a flight of stone steps that led from the terrace into the gardens. I would go to the pool, the private beach, the spa – anywhere that would take my mind off Nick, weddings and relationships in general.

My route took me along a gravel path that led past the main entrance of the hotel. As I did so, I happened to glance in through the glass doors towards reception and got the shock of my life.

There, at the desk, stood a figure: tall, dark-haired and broad-shouldered. I couldn't see his face – but then again, I didn't need to. Everything about him was totally, completely and one hundred per cent familiar.

I couldn't breathe.

I couldn't move.

I couldn't speak.

This was it – I'd finally gone stir crazy and started seeing things. There was no way – as in *no way* – this could be Nick.

And, yet again, there was no way that it could not.

I knew not only the pitch of his shoulders, the back of his neck and the size of his feet, but the rise and fall of his breathing, the weight of his gaze: the very sense of his being.

I shut my eyes and willed the vision before me to disappear: but, when I opened them again, everything was exactly as it had been – the man still calmly signing a check-in slip and chatting to the girl. I stood stock-still, unable to move. Then, suddenly, the vision bent down to pick up a battered brown holdall that I had last seen sitting on top of my wardrobe three months ago and walked across the foyer in the direction of the lift.

The spell was broken.

With my heart beating so hard it felt as though it might burst out of my ribcage, I turned and ran down a shrub-lined path. I had no idea where I was going; I only knew that I needed to get away. The old fight or flight had kicked in and, for the time being at least, flight had won.

Through a grove of broad-leafed trees – across a lawn – past a pool surrounded by sunloungers – further, further – past some more trees – a funny, ramshackle hut – and then—

I reached the end of the line.

There in front of me was the sea: a pure, almost transparent blue, with the sun glittering on its millpond surface more brightly than a drag queen's eyeshadow. Away to my left was the sweep of a rocky little bay and, in the other direction, a sandy beach patrolled by a flock of noisy seagulls.

I ground to a halt on a piece of closely cropped, mossy turf that overhung the beach and put my hands on my knees, doing my best to catch my breath. I still couldn't believe what I'd seen, but the blood pounding in my head and the terror in my heart told me that my reaction had been real enough.

Even so . . . *it couldn't be; it just couldn't.*

Beyond my little promontory of turf, the rocky shoreline led, staircase-like, into the water. I slipped off my shoes and lowered myself down onto the sun-baked stone, sliding my toes into the clear water.

Oh, Jesus – Nick.

What the hell was he doing here? Had he followed me? Had Emma told him where I was?

And, most importantly, why had he come?

Because if it was to tell me about yet another debt he had forgotten to mention while we were together, he would soon be wishing he hadn't bothered.

My chest clenched.

Painfully.

What if it was? What if it was another huge, hidden loan? What if there was another court summons? With the address of *my* flat written on it in big, bold, scary legal type. Shit – what if I couldn't pay? What if he'd left it so late that the bailiffs were already pounding at my door; ready to tow away my car and help themselves to my laptop and Granny Sidebottom's gold locket? What if . . .?

For a second, the world around me went all wobbly and I found myself struggling to pull the air into my lungs. My hands shook and my heart pounded.

The day after I'd walked out on Nick I'd had my only full-blown panic attack. It had been a weird and completely terrifying sensation: a pain in my chest, my legs refusing to work and the absolute certainty that I was about to die. Luckily, it had happened in the staff room, not in front of the kids, and Emma (thank God) had been on hand to get me to a doctor – but it was something I was anxious not to repeat. The doctor had offered pills, which I'd refused, choosing breathing exercises instead to try and get my overstrung body to relax.

Breathe in . . .

. . . and out . . .

. . . and in . . .

Thank goodness. The chest pain started to ease and the pounding in my head died down a little; but my hands still shook like leaves in a Force Ten, endangering the Danish pastry I was still clutching from breakfast.

. . . and out . . . and in . . . and . . .

'Pssst!'

A loud and insistent whisper cut across my attempts at breath control. I turned round; but, apart from a couple of scraggy bushes a few feet behind me, there was nothing.

Cautiously, I looked back out to sea and did my best to focus on the lap-lap-lap of the water round my ankles and the cries of the seagulls on the sand below. Slowly, the knot of tension inside my ribcage unwound itself and my body began to climb back down from Code Red.

. . . and in . . . and out . . . and in . . .

My thoughts, too, became less panicked and more rational. Had that really been Nick in reception? It seemed very unlikely. Maybe I had imagined it. Maybe I was so stressed that I was projecting images of him onto total strangers.

'Pssssssssssssssst!'

My eyes popped open. This time I was sure it wasn't my ears playing tricks. Someone (or something) had definitely hissed at me. But who? A few rocks further along was a grouchy-looking seagull that bore an uncanny resemblance to my Uncle Dudley – but apart from that, there was nothing.

Except the bushes.

'Ailsa!' said one of the bushes loudly.

It said quite a lot about my state of mind that being hissed at by a plant actually made me feel less anxious than thinking about Nick; but it was true.

'Are you alone?' the bush continued in a penetrating stage whisper.

I nodded – trying to remember the correct social etiquette for those occasions when one is addressed by a piece of vegetation – before spotting the toe of a pink ballet pump poking out from underneath one of the lower branches.

'Jessica? Is that you?'

'Are you alone?' hissed the bush.

I looked round.

'I think so,' I hissed back.

Slowly and gingerly, my cousin (wearing white linen trousers and a pink and white striped T-shirt) clambered out from her leafy hiding place. She had grown up a lot since we'd last coincided (had it really been ten years? Ten *whole* years?) but she was hardly the blooming bride. Her figure was on the skinny side of slim; her skin lacked lustre; her hair was brittle and over-straightened, and there was a hollow, reddish quality to her baby-blue eyes that concerned me.

'Blimey, Jess,' I blurted out before I could stop myself, 'is everything all right?'

Jessica's eyes widened to the size of dinner plates, and she blinked. Twice. It made her look like an owl. Or, to be exact, a thin, stripy owl who looked as though it might be about to cry. The contrast between this and the screaming, hysterical fury of half an hour earlier couldn't have been more pronounced.

'Nothing's wrong,' she said. 'Nothing at all.'

I trailed one of my feet through the bath-warm sea water and little bubbles rose up from between my toes. Jess walked over to my rock and then stopped.

'Actually,' she said, 'that's not true; I'm feeling pretty shit most of the time but I'm so used to telling everyone how happy I am and how bloody wonderful everything is that it comes out automatically.'

She sat down next to me.

'Thank you for coming,' she said, 'I really appreciate it. I think you're the only sane person in this family – or at least you used to be. You haven't gone mad or anything recently, have you?'

I decided to take this as a backwards sort of compliment.

'Not that I'm aware of,' I replied. 'So, this feeling shit most of the time – has it got anything to do with that matter of life and death you emailed me about?'

Jess looked alarmed and leaned in towards me.

'Shhhh! Veronica – that horrendous wedding planner-Nazi woman – is on the prowl. She might hear.'

'There's no one here,' I reassured her. 'I promise – just you and me. I left Veronica back up at the hotel, she was on a mission to do with peonies if I remember rightly. Or twine. Or possibly string. But she certainly didn't have any plans to head to the beach.'

Jess opened her mouth, presumably to reply, but quickly shut it again and began to stare hard at my left

36

hand. I followed her gaze and saw that she was looking at the Danish pastry still clutched between my fingers.

Jess swallowed.

'Do you—' she asked with undisguised longing in her voice. 'Do you want that?'

I glanced at it. After fifteen minutes in my hot little hand it was looking rather battered and flakes of pastry were drifting gently down onto the rocks below.

'No,' I replied, holding it out towards her, 'why – do you?'

Jess's eyes lit up. She took it from me and began to tuck in as though this was the first solid stuff to pass her lips in days.

'Thank you,' she mumbled through a mouthful of Danish-y mush. 'You're a lifesaver.'

I watched, my bemusement increasing by the second.

'Did you miss breakfast?' I asked, remembering the hoolie in the garden.

Jess shook her head and swallowed the last of the pastry.

'Black coffee, fat-free yogurt and half a peach,' she whispered, running her tongue round her mouth in case there were any crumbs lurking that she hadn't yet hoovered up. 'I wanted a banana as well but Veronica told me I shouldn't overdo things so soon before the big day.'

I stared at her in disbelief, running my eyes down her minute little frame. I had seen stick insects that needed to watch their weight more than she did.

'But you're tiny,' I told her, lifting my feet out of the water and swivelling round to face her, 'there's nothing to you. They'll be taking the dress in at this rate, not letting it out.'

Jess gave her lips one last sweep of the tongue.

'It's not just the dress,' she said sadly. 'She keeps on going on about how the camera adds a good half-a-stone and that if I don't want to spend the rest of my life looking at my wedding photos and wondering who the fat girl in the tiara is, I'd better be careful.'

I was outraged: Auntie Sheila and Uncle Dudley were paying this woman good money to what – give their daughter some sort of complex about her weight?

Jess's face crumpled.

'Oh, Ailsa, it's horrible. There's no escape – every mealtime it's the same: "*Jessica, do you really need that dressing on your salad? Jessica, do you have any idea how many calories are in those shortbreads? Jessica, why don't you just starve yourself into an eating disorder and have done with it?*" She's even sneaked into my room to check out my minibar in case I've been going crazy with the salted cashews.'

She gave a sigh that came right up from the soles of her little pink ballet pumps.

'But you know what? The moment I get to that airport on Sunday afternoon, I'm heading straight for the first place I can find that sells muffins and I'm going to stuff my face. After that, it's chocolate – slabs and slabs and *slabs* of it – and then after *that*, when Justin and I arrive in the Bahamas, do you know what I'm looking forward to most?'

I didn't – but I got a feeling that it wasn't going to be the honeymoon suite with a queen-sized bed, her new husband and a 'do not disturb' sign on the door.

'Steak,' she replied (we were very close to actual drooling by this point), 'steak after steak after steak. I might even have it for breakfast. Steak and huge, thick-cut, greasy chips. And cheesecake. And breakfast – proper breakfast with bacon and eggs and sausages and fried bread and not a crappy fat-free bloody yogurt in sight.'

'But – she can't do this to you!' I cried. 'Tell her to sod off. Tell her to take her fat-free yogurts and half a peach and shove them—'

'Shhhhh!' Jess waved her hands at me in alarm. 'She'll hear you!'

'Good,' I replied mutinously, 'I hope she does – then I can tell her to her face to stop bullying you and get on with sorting out the seating plans or whatever it is she should be doing.'

Jess looked hopefully up at me.

'You haven't got anything else to eat, have you?' she asked.

I dug through the pockets of my shorts. Two toffees, one partially unwrapped, unfolded themselves from a crease in the lining.

'Here,' I said, handing her the wrapped one and keeping the other for myself, 'they're not terribly appetising but it's the best I can do at short notice.'

Jess smiled. A watery, uncertain smile – but a smile nonetheless.

'Thanks,' she said, unwrapping the toffee and popping it into her mouth. 'Look – I'm sorry. I didn't mean to vent at you. It's not your problem.'

'Vent away,' I replied, removing a small piece of fluff from my own toffee. 'I don't mind. But there must be something you can do, Jess. Can't you tell your mum and dad how miserable this is making you?'

Jess shook her head sadly.

'No,' she said. 'Pops thinks that because Veronica's the best money can buy, we have to follow her every word; and as for Mum – well, she just goes along with whatever Pops says. In fact, if Justin wasn't my own, true angel soulmate, I don't think I'd be going through with this wedding.'

'But if it's this bad, then you've *got* to say something.'

But Jess didn't hear me. The pain had left her face and had been replaced by a dreamy expression: I guessed she was thinking about her angel soulmate.

'Oh, Ailsa! The moment I saw him, I knew he was the one. He'd just started at Sidebottom's and Pops roped him in to play at the annual company golf tournament. He was wearing this yellow and green checked jumper and a pair of those funny little spiked shoes with tassels on them – I just couldn't stop staring at him.'

I'm not surprised if he went around dressing like that, I thought. Even on a golf course he'd be pushing it.

'Although,' Jessica breathed, 'even before then, even before we actually met, I *knew* we were meant to be together.'

'You did?'

This seemed a bit unlikely. *Before* they'd met . . . ?

My cousin nodded, her blue eyes wide and serious. She couldn't have been more earnest if she'd been teaching me open heart surgery or explaining what to do in the event of an emergency plane landing.

'Totes. You see, I'd been to see this *beyond amazing* psychic woman the week before the golf tournament and she told me that someone who I'd been in love with in a previous life was about to return and make a huge impact

40

on me in *this* life – and I'd know who he was because his name would begin,' she paused dramatically, 'with a "*K*".'

'But he's called Justin,' I replied, 'that doesn't begin with a "K".'

Jess smiled the smile of a girl about to brandish her trump card.

'Ah, but if he'd been born a girl, his mother was going to call him *Karen*! Don't you see? Justin and I were wrenched apart – destined to spend centuries searching the swirling void of time and space for one another before finally being reunited at the Mildmay Parva golf club. It makes perfect, perfect sense!'

Er . . . I was pretty sure this swirling void of time and space wouldn't be anything Brian Cox would go along with – but hey! It made Jess happy, so I wasn't about to knock it.

'That's wonderful,' I said as enthusiastically as I could, 'really, really lovely. I'm pleased for you and your, um, soul angel.'

Jess stood up and tucked a strand of blonde hair behind one ear.

'It's the only thing that's keeping me going,' she said, 'the wedding itself is unbelievably stressful. You wouldn't believe it, Ailsa; even without Veronica being a total cow, there's the endless paperwork: the birth certificates; the photocopies of birth certificates, the passports . . . but I love Justin and I'd do anything to be married to him. Angel man!'

Then she turned to me.

'Are you seeing anyone?' she asked.

The image of Nick – or at least, the person I'd

thought was Nick – standing at the reception desk not thirty minutes ago crashed into my brain and my chest constricted painfully.

'No,' I replied, looking down at my lap and trying to get the air in and out of my lungs. 'Not at the moment.'

Jess looked distressed. She crouched down beside me and slipped her hand into mine.

'Oh, Ailsa – don't worry. It doesn't matter if you haven't met him yet. Remember that your angel soulmate is out there – *right now*. You just have to trust the universe will intervene and bring you together.'

I bit my lip and focused hard on the lapping waves.

'That sort of thing doesn't happen to me,' I said at last.

'It happens to everybody,' replied Jess. 'If they truly want it.'

Out of nowhere, another image of Nick – this time wearing nothing apart from a broad grin – sliced through me and my heart turned over. The tension in my chest passed but the corners of my eyes went hot and prickly. Oh God – I didn't want to have sidestepped a panic attack only to burst into tears.

. . . and in . . . and out . . .

At that moment, however, the universe did intervene – only it was nothing to do with my soulmate.

'Jessica!'

From somewhere over by the hotel, the sound of a lesser-spotted wedding planner hunting down her prey wafted through the hot, heavy air.

'Jess-i-*ca*!'

Jess gave a little cry of despair and looked round wildly for escape.

'Don't worry.' I scrambled off my rock, 'I'll tell her I saw you going to the pool. While she's looking for you, why don't you slip off into town? It might buy you a couple of hours' breathing space.'

'Thank you.' Jess nodded. 'Thank you so, so much. I'll go and find Justin, maybe we can sneak a bit of one-on-one time.'

I patted her hand.

'Stay strong and think about the steak,' I whispered. 'And let me know when you want to talk about life and death.'

But she had already been swallowed up by the hotel shrubbery.

Chapter Four

I followed the braying sound of Veronica's voice and discovered her a few hundred yards away, standing underneath a huge cedar tree, clutching her clipboard and shouting into her mobile phone. I waited until she had finished shouting and rung off, introduced myself and told her that if she was looking for Jess, I'd just seen her heading in the direction of the pool. Veronica manoeuvred her lips into a very convincing impression of a cat's bottom and sighed heavily, before rolling her eyes and marching pool-wards.

Job done.

Whatever Jess's views on angel soulmates and past lives, she deserved an afternoon off.

I waited until Veronica and her clipboard were safely out of sight, then I slumped against the trunk of the cedar tree and got back to the main event.

Oh God – Nick.

What on earth was I going to do?

If I was wrong and it *wasn't* Nick I'd spotted, the answer of course was easy – carry on as intended with the swimming pool and the spa and the beach and the wedding.

But if it *was*? (Cue tightening chest and pounding head.)

Did I confront him? Did I ignore him? Or – and this was very, very appealing – did I simply pack my bags and get the hell out before he even realised I'd seen him?

The backs of my knees went sweaty just thinking about it.

One thing was certain though: at some point I'd have to go back to my room, even if it was to grab my suitcase and call a cab. Much as I would have rather sawn my own leg off than go back to the hotel and its environs, I decided I might as well get it over and done with as soon as possible. With a heavy heart and legs like lead, I turned and made my way across the turf towards the path.

As soon as my feet touched the gravel, I heard it: pitpatpitpatpitpat, coming along somewhere behind me.

I stopped – but so did the noise. I set off again and, almost immediately: pitpatpitpatpitpat.

I stopped and so did the noise. It was strange: like a very bizarre game of Grandmother's Footsteps.

I started walking once more, only this time, I did so backwards, keeping my eyes peeled for whatever it was that was following me.

Sure enough – pitpatpitpatpitpat – round the corner emerged a little dog; the same one that had caused all the havoc the night before.

As soon as it saw me, it barked happily. I, on the other hand, groaned.

'Not you again,' I said. 'You've caused enough trouble for one holiday. Go on – shoo! Go back to your own kind.'

But the dog didn't do as it was told. Instead, it walked up to me, sat down on the gravel and put its head on one side.

'I'm sorry,' I said, 'you might think you're being cute but that sort of thing doesn't wash with me. I'm not a dog person.'

I turned round and continued my route along the

path. The tell-tale pitpatpitpat sound struck up again. I stopped. Right on cue, the little dog stopped too. With a heavy sigh I turned round and kneeled down close to it, gingerly extending my hand. The little dog walked over and licked my fingers.

'Seriously,' I said, 'you do need to move on. You'd hate it here. The hotel staff have it in for you and my Uncle Dudley eats things like you for breakfast. You would be much better vamoosing off somewhere else.'

To encourage it, I pointed back the way it had come, but the dog was unmoved. In fact, it lifted a paw up and placed it solemnly on my knee.

A plea for help? I wondered. Was it trying to tell me something?

What's that, Lassie? The children are trapped in the abandoned mineshaft and the flood water is rising?

Then I got a little cross with myself for even countenancing the idea. Real dogs didn't *do* altruism and daring rescues; they did self-interest, petting and copious quantities of Scooby Snacks.

Tentatively, I reached out and ran my fingers under its ear. Its fur felt warm and soft but, to my surprise, I couldn't find a collar. I pulled the little pooch in closer and had a proper look – but I'd been right the first time.

'I see,' I said as the dog broke off to growl menacingly at a twig lying by the side of the path, 'this puts a different complexion on things, doesn't it? Are you a stray? Or have you simply lost your clothes and are running around naked?'

The dog jumped on the twig and threw it up into the air – rather as though it had been a tampon holder, actually

46

– before carrying it over and depositing it proudly at my feet.

'I appreciate the gesture,' I continued, 'but giving me a manky old stick won't change anything. The bottom line is that you are a dog: now, I do not *do* dogs and – worse than that – the hotel *hates* dogs. You've got to believe me, I'm really not the girl for you.'

The dog narrowed its eyes and threw a hard stare in my direction, making it look – just for a split second – like a shorter, furrier version of my sister Kitty. Then it stopped giving me evils and bounded off into the undergrowth, emerging after much rustling with another, larger, stick, which it placed next to the first one.

I smiled. I couldn't help myself.

'You're good,' I said, giving it a tickle behind the ears, 'you're very good. But it still doesn't change the fact that the hotel manager would rather serve you up as a puppy panini than let you over his threshold. Although,' I brightened as a thought occurred to me, 'if you could bite Veronica on the arse for Jess, there might be a steak in it for you.'

The dog's tail thumped hard on the gravel. It seemed to understand the word 'steak'. A bilingual dog, I thought, what were the chances?

I stood up. There ahead of me was the main façade of the hotel, the revolving doors through which I had recently glimpsed Nick (or his doppelgänger) glinting in the sun.

However much it terrified me, it still had to be done.

With the hugest effort imaginable, I put one leg in front of the other until I reached the entrance. I paused, turning back to look at my canine companion, who was standing a little way behind me, its eyes all hopeful and expectant.

The thought flashed through my head that I should smuggle it into my room and maybe give it a drink or something to eat – but reason got the better of me. What could I do for a stray Italian pooch? I wasn't the Dogs' Trust.

I swung round and walked in through the door, keeping my eyes peeled for strong-shouldered, dark-haired, half-Italian Scotsmen. To my enormous relief, though, the foyer was empty of Nick or anyone who looked like him. My shoulders relaxed and, even though I had no conscious memory of clenching them, I felt my fingers slowly uncurl.

Thank God for that.

I made my plan: I would run to my room, shove my things (and the complimentary Jo Malone cosmetics) into my suitcase and be off before Nick even knew we'd been in the same quadrant of the universe. I would deal with Jess and her life or death issues over the phone and I would email Auntie Sheila and apologise profusely for mucking up her seating plans. I couldn't spend the next week with shaky hands and a pounding heart waiting to bump into my ex.

It just wasn't worth it.

Escape in mind, I darted across the foyer . . . and ran slap bang into Auntie Sheila. She was looking an awful lot more chipper than she had done earlier and was accompanied by an arresting-looking young man with blond hair and blue eyes – not that I cared how arresting he was, I'd had enough of men to last me a lifetime.

'Ailsa, darling,' said the aunt, 'how are you?'

'Fine,' I said, hoping I sounded more convincing than Jess had back at the beach. 'Really, really fine.'

'Good.' Auntie Sheila beamed as though she had arranged this personally.

I took an unobtrusive step sideways, towards the foot of the stairs.

'This is Charles Chapman,' continued Auntie Sheila, 'he works with Dudley and Justin.'

The young man smiled in acknowledgement of this introduction.

'Lovely,' I smiled politely in return and took another step stairwards. 'Great. Hello, *Charles.*'

'I'm going to be seating you next to Charles at dinner tonight,' Auntie Sheila chattered on. 'I'm afraid that thanks to the baggage handlers' strike we are quite a small gathering. Justin's family may not be able to get their flights – so it's only us, a few close friends – and Charles here. I hope that's all right?'

'Great,' I said again. Her choice of words struck me as rather odd, but I was much too caught up with my own problems to worry about it. 'Um – Auntie Sheila – I'm afraid I'm not going to be able to make it for dinner. You see – you see – something has happened.'

Auntie Sheila looked concerned.

'Is it a problem with the hotel? With your room?' she asked. 'I'll get the manager – *Roberto*!'

'No, the hotel is fine. I've – I've just had a phone call from school,' I lied shamelessly, 'the school I teach at. Kids got in – well, when I say "kids", I don't mean the kids who should have been there; these are other kids – bad kids,

49

ASBO kids – and I have to sort my classroom out before my kids – the good kids – come back after half-term.'

To my left, the lift doors opened – and my heart leaped into my mouth. No, it was fine: no strong-shouldered, dark-haired men, just a little old lady.

Charles's eyes flickered over me. I got the feeling I was being sized up.

'That's terrible,' he said. 'When did you find out?'

'I got a message via the main desk, just now. I'm sorry, Auntie Sheila; I know how much this wedding means to you.'

My aunt sighed loudly as though my absence caused her personal inconvenience.

'You won't miss me,' I promised, 'I've barely even arrived.'

I was aware that Charles was still staring at me and that his gaze had become even more intense.

'Have we . . . ?' he began.

I knew immediately what he meant.

The tampons.

And the dog.

Dog/tampons. Tampons/dog.

My face flared up, hotter than a blast furnace. I really didn't have the emotional energy for this now.

Now? Make that *ever*.

'You know, Auntie Sheila, I really should – pack – I'll just—'

And I shot off across the marbled foyer before she could introduce me to anyone else.

Up on the second floor, I slid my key card through the lock and walked into my room. Pulling my suitcase out from under the bed, I threw in my dressing gown, my slippers and my pyjamas.

Then I stopped.

Winding its way in through the open French windows was a lovely breeze. It was cool and soothing and carried with it the tang of the sea. I closed my eyes and rubbed my face with my hands: wasn't this a huge overreaction? The phantom man with dark hair probably wasn't Nick. There must be hundreds – if not thousands – of Italian men who looked like him and, yes, who owned battered old holdalls; and, even if by some weird chance it *was* the one-and-only Nick Bertolini, shouldn't I be brave and bold and see what he actually had to say for himself, rather than fold up my tent and disappear off into the night (or the sunny Italian noontide as it actually was)?

Throwing a T-shirt back into its drawer, I stepped onto the balcony and allowed my eye to wander out beyond the lush green of the hotel grounds, across the orange-tiled roofs of the little town to the blue-green haze of the distant mountains. It was beautiful: tranquil and timeless – surely nothing bad could happen in a place like this?

A noise to my right made me look round. The French windows on the balcony next to mine had been thrown open and (through the branches of a large wisteria plant and, less attractively, a cast-iron fire escape) I could just about make out the outline of a man clad in a white, hotel-issue bathrobe. He turned, a coffee cup in his hand and—

'Jesus Christ. Ailsa?'

There was a shattering sound as the cup slipped from his fingers and smashed to atoms on the balcony floor.

I hadn't made a mistake: it had been him all along.

My knees went all funny and I had to grip the iron railing that ran round the edge of the balcony to keep myself upright. Only when I was sure I was not going to fall to the ground did I manage to articulate: 'Nick?'

Followed by: 'Oh, my God.'

And then (again): 'Nick.'

It was absolutely one hundred per cent Nick. No case of mistaken identity, no tricks of the mind. This was the original model, in flesh and blood and – the horror – standing not three feet away from me.

The man himself sat down with a thud on a wrought-iron chair placed conveniently nearby. I would probably have followed suit on one of my balcony's identical chairs, except they were less conveniently placed and I didn't trust my legs to make it that far. Instead, I gripped the balcony railings so tightly my knuckles turned completely white.

'Ailsa,' he said (it was a small comfort, but he looked about as shocked as I felt) 'what the hell are you doing here?'

The tiniest, tiniest spark of relief flew through me: he hadn't come to find me. My fears about debts and bailiffs and court orders might have been premature after all.

'It's a wedding,' I replied, unpeeling my tongue from the roof of my mouth, 'a family wedding. My cousin Jess – she's part of my family – it's her wedding. She's getting married. Here. I don't think you know her.'

Nick looked down at his feet. He was wearing brown leather slip-on man sandals. Sandals, in fact, that I'd bought for him the August before when Scotland had experienced an unprecedented heatwave and temperatures had rocketed into the high teens.

'No,' he said pointedly, 'I wouldn't know her, would I? You never introduced me to any of your relations.'

I swallowed. Hard.

'And you?' I asked shakily. 'What are you doing here?'

A shadow passed over Nick's face, or – to be accurate – *more* of a shadow.

'You already know,' he replied coldly. 'I'm helping Riccardo. One of his tour guides let him down and he needed someone to run a couple of historic art and architecture tours in Tuscany.'

'You didn't tell—' I began and then stopped. He had told me – sort of – ages ago, in the middle of a row. I just hadn't bothered to retain the information. 'Whatever. It doesn't matter. I'm leaving. I'll find somewhere else to stay while I wait for a flight home.'

Nick frowned.

'The girl on reception said the wedding party was booked in till the weekend.'

I looked down at my hands, which were still gripping the railing for dear life. I wasn't about to admit my hasty exit had anything to do with him.

'It's kids,' I began, 'kids have broken in at school and—'

Nick sighed heavily.

'No they haven't,' he said.

Even though I knew the 'kids' were a total fabrication, I was still instantly indignant.

'How do you know?' I demanded. 'Have you been there? Have you seen for yourself?'

'No.' He eyeballed me and my legs immediately turned

53

into a pair of those strawberry shoelace things I used to eat as a kid. 'But we both know that kids have broken into your school on at least three occasions since we got together – and each time it's been when you're trying to get out of something.'

I let go of the rail and looked down at my feet.

'Twice,' I said, 'I only used it twice.'

Nick brushed a fly off his bathrobe.

'Oh, aye,' he said, 'when your mother wanted to come and stay at Christmas, that was burst pipes. Not kids.'

I twisted my hands so hard, my knuckles cracked. *Do not admit defeat; do not say you are in the wrong.*

'Well, if you're going to be like this,' I said archly, 'I think it's probably for the best.'

I began to turn away and Nick ran a hand through his thick, almost-black hair. Nick's hair always looked as though a small creature of the woods was making its nest there, and today was no different, excepting the fact that a shaft of midday sunlight had fallen upon it, tingeing the middle section with a streak of raven blue.

'I'm sorry, Ailsa,' he murmured.

I turned back.

'Sorry for what?' I asked.

My heart gave a tiny, almost imperceptible leap. Was this it? Was he about to apologise for what he'd done – everything he'd put me through? Was he going to try and make things good between us?

Instantly, I beat my heart back down again. We had come too far for Nick's apologies to carry any weight.

'I mean,' his voice was almost completely emotionless, 'I'm sorry for you.'

54

'Me?' This didn't make any sense. 'What are you talking about? This isn't about me.'

He stood up, pushed his chair back and took a deep breath.

'So, no change there then.'

'Excuse me?' I walked back over to his side of the balcony and leaned so far out across the railings, I was in danger of flipping over the top.

'It's fine.' Nick turned his back on me and began to pick up the shattered pieces of his coffee cup. 'Don't let me keep you from your packing. Only, good luck getting a flight; there's a baggage handlers' strike on.'

And he disappeared off inside his room.

At some undetermined point during this last exchange, my original sense of 'Stunned Disbelief with a Hint of Annoyance' had segued into a full-blown case of 'The Outrage'; and along with 'The Outrage' came an overwhelming sense of déjà vu: it was as though the second Nick opened his mouth, I was whisked back in time to the last angry moments we'd spent together. Pressure started to build inside me and steam issued forth from my ears like a reflex action.

With my heart thumping, I ran across the room, out onto the landing and banged loudly on his door. It was flung open almost immediately.

'You still here?' he said. 'I thought you had a plane to catch. Super Teacher – off to save the world.'

'Oh, don't be ridiculous,' I snapped, 'I'm not going anywhere until you tell me what you mean. This is outrageous. It's *not* me. Even though I don't have the faintest idea what you're talking about I can tell you categorically that *it is not me*. Have you got that? It's not me. It's *never* me.'

Nick sucked his breath in with a hissing noise, making him sound like a bad-tempered snake. Then he threw a towel across his shoulder and stepped out into the hallway, slamming the door shut behind him.

'Really?' He stomped away down the corridor towards a flight of stairs. 'Is that right?'

'Don't you dare walk off!' I chased after him. 'I'm talking to you!'

Nick speeded up, taking the stairs two at a time.

'Well, maybe I don't want to talk to you,' he called back.

At the bottom of the stairs, he pushed his way through a set of glass double doors, letting them swing back in my face and missing my nose by mere millimetres. My Outrage levels shot up from 'Incandescent' to 'Positively Dangerous'. I followed and found myself in a tastefully decorated room with pictures of dolphins on the walls and soothing music coming from a speaker near a desk. This desk was manned (or, more accurately, womanned) by a slim, blonde-haired girl wearing a white short-sleeved coat. Nick, ten steps ahead of me, nodded in her direction and she smiled back; a flirty, simpery sort of smile. This did nothing to help 'The Outrage': I might have been at the point where I could have cheerfully murdered him, but I absolutely didn't want him trading smiles with pretty girls.

'Nick,' I called in my sternest, most teacherly voice, 'stop this *now*! You are to blame for all this – *you*. Do you understand?'

Nick didn't reply. Instead, he opened another door and disappeared.

'And will you *stop walking*!' I cried, preparing to follow him.

'No!' The woman behind the desk became very agitated. 'No! I'm sorry, miss! You can't go in there—'

But it was too late. I already had.

As the door closed behind me, I was enveloped by a vortex of pure, humid, heat. It made me choke and cough and, thanks to a cloud of swirling vapour, it was very difficult to see.

'Nick,' I called out into the steam, 'what the bloody hell do you think you're doing?'

About half a dozen faces snapped round and stared at me.

Men.

They were all men.

And they were looking at me in a very peculiar way.

The question, *why are there no women in here?* hovered for a moment in my brain before I dismissed it. I wasn't here to argue about the gender politics of the set-up, I wanted an answer from Mr Bertolini.

Through the tendrils of steam, right across on the far side of the room, was an unmistakable dark head. I marched over: a single-minded, one-woman panzer division. Nick had taken off his bathrobe and was sitting on a wooden bench wearing Not Very Much apart from a towel. My eyes skittered over his body – from the olive skin of his legs, up through his well-toned torso and across the broad sweep of his shoulders – trying to work out if anything had changed since I'd last seen him in the buff: a sort of lustful spot-the-difference exercise.

'I could,' he replied, 'ask you exactly the same thing.'

'Excuse me,' said the man sitting next to Nick, 'I don't want to interrupt—'

'Good,' I said, keeping my eyes fixed very firmly on Nick, '*don't* interrupt then. Nick – answer my question. Why do you feel sorry for me?'

Twelve pairs of male eyes stared first at Nick, then back at me.

For a moment it looked as though Nick was going to start yelling again but, at the last moment, his expression changed and sadness flickered over his features.

'EXCUSE *me*,' the man next to him tried again, but Nick cut him off.

'I'm sorry, Ailsa – but if you can't work it out, there's really no point in me explaining.'

This was getting ridiculous.

'Well, if you'd stop running away and talk to me, maybe I could work it out.'

Nick stared hard at a knot in his wooden bench.

'It's not me who ran away, Ailsa,' he said softly.

You know that thing – the one where you are so bound up with the hurt someone else has caused you that you forget you might have had a hand in it too?

And then they remind you.

And it's the truth.

And it hits you like a slap in the face?

Well, that moment was then – only I was so angry that there was no way on earth I was going to admit it.

'I only ran away because you *made me*,' I growled.

'So I put a gun to your head and forced you to leave?' he threw back.

'You behaved so atrociously that you gave me no other option!'

'EXCUSE ME!' The man next to him stood up. 'Do you realise that this is the men only sauna?'

Slowly – very slowly – I allowed my gaze to leave Nick's face and travel round the room.

The men only sauna.

Populated by men, all sweating profusely and wearing towels – apart from the chap on the end who seemed to have mislaid his and was resting a flannel over a vital part of his anatomy in order to preserve his (or perhaps my) modesty.

Oh no.

Oh *nonononono*.

Oh monkeyfucklebuggerchups.

'Yes,' I said, my face taking on redness of never-before-seen proportions, 'I do. Now. Thank you.'

'You'll find the door over there,' continued the man.

'Yes,' I said, taking a step towards it. 'Of course.'

I glanced back at Nick.

'Hope you get those kids sorted out,' he said.

I didn't reply.

Instead, I turned on my heel and walked back out through the wooden door, the last vestiges of The Outrage trickling from me as I went.

Naked men: nothing good ever came of them.

Chapter Five

I trudged back up the flight of stairs to my room with Nick's shot about running away burning deeper and deeper into my brain. More than ever, I wanted to chuck my worldly belongings into a suitcase and get out – but wouldn't that just prove he was right?

Well, he wasn't. He was wrong and I was going to bloody *show* him I didn't do running away. I was going to stay put, even if it killed me.

Which, if the rest of the week was as bad-tempered and shouty as our first meeting, it very well might.

With a gritty determination building in my soul, I rounded the final corner on the landing and saw, sitting on the mat outside my door, an all too familiar face.

No, not Nick (thank God) but the little dog. It said a lot about my encounter with Nick that I actually felt pleased to see it.

'How the hell did you manage to dodge reception?' I asked, sliding my key card through its slot and opening the door.

The dog gambolled in and made its way straight over to the bin, where it pulled out a sandwich wrapper. I furrowed my brow in a puzzled frown: who had been eating sandwiches in my room, I wondered, when *I* most certainly hadn't?

The dog stopped licking for a moment and stared hopefully in my direction.

I folded my arms.

'We've had this conversation before,' I said firmly, 'I don't do dogs and neither do the management of this hotel. You need to go and find your own people.'

The dog deposited the sandwich wrapper on the floor and pawed at it piteously. I remembered its lack of a collar. Maybe it was a long way from home, I thought – and its normal food supply.

I pulled a canvas beach bag I'd brought with me out of the wardrobe and set it down in front of the dog. The bag was lightweight and didn't actually do up, so I was sure its intended passenger wouldn't suffocate. I wasn't sitting here like a lemon waiting for Nick to get back from the sauna, I would take a trip into town, get something to eat, sort my head out and – last but not least – do something about the dog.

'In,' I said, pointing at the interior of the bag.

The dog sniffed it for a moment or two and then did as it was told.

'Now, be quiet,' I warned, slinging the bag over my shoulder and making my way back down the stairs that led to reception.

As I approached the foyer, I sent up a silent prayer to the Patron Saint of Dog Smugglers that I wouldn't be stopped on my way out – and I think it must have been answered. I spotted Auntie Sheila conferring with Veronica over by the entrance to the bar, but, thankfully, I managed to slink unnoticed out of the door.

I crept along the main path, across the car park and

out under the ancient archway that marked the entrance to the hotel grounds. Then, once I was clear of the Santa Lucia's sphere of influence, I lifted the dog out of the beach bag and popped it down on the pavement next to me. It trotted happily along at my heels as we made our way down the hill, without needing so much as a 'here, boy!'

Together we passed through an ancient gateway in the high medieval stone walls that embraced the little town and wound our way through a maze of cobbled lanes so narrow that I could reach out and touch both sides of the street at once. The houses lining these mini-roads were a complete jumble of shapes and sizes, their windowsills bright with terracotta tubs of red geraniums and their stone walls bleached almost white from centuries upon centuries of summer suns.

Gradually, the streets grew wider and the houses grander and more elegant, until the road opened up into a bustling market square, dominated on one side by a magnificent church.

A few metres away was a little café with a cheerful yellow awning over its door and a scattering of mismatched tables and chairs outside. The little dog ambled over and sat down under an empty table, its tail thumping the ground so enthusiastically that small clouds of dust were sent scuttering across the cobbles.

I hesitated. It had been a long time since breakfast and I was thirsty from my walk.

'Well – go on then,' I agreed, pulling up a chair.

'*Buon giorno, signorina!*' A smiley dark-haired waiter materialised soundlessly behind me. '*Cosa vorrebbe mangiare?*'

Oh blimey – now you're asking!

'*Un cappucino, per favore,*' I managed, dredging up a few phrases of Italian from the cobwebbed hinterland of my brain, 'and a salad – ah – *insalata?*'

Oh God, this was hard – and not just because I was as thick as two short ones when it came to languages. Italy and the Italian language were synonymous in my mind with Nick. His father was Italian by blood, although Edinburgh born and bred, and Nick himself spoke the language so beautifully that it made me go weak at the knees – as well as affecting a few other parts of my anatomy in quite a spectacular way.

Down at my feet, the dog yapped excitedly. The waiter crouched on his heels and tickled him under the chin. My canine companion rolled over and waggled its legs in the air, a big doggy grin plastered over its face.

'And for you, my friend?' the waiter enquired in English, moving the tickling activities to the dog's stomach. 'Something tells me you won't be wanting *pomodori e olive.*'

I paused. I knew what dogs ate at home – large tins of foul-smelling offcuts topped with crunchy, biscuity things. Would an Italian dog be more sophisticated? Would he demand veal steaks or *linguine al pollo*, all washed down with a nice Chianti?

'A bowl of water, please,' I began, 'and – well, what do you have on the menu for dogs?'

The waiter sprang back onto his feet.

'My mother 'ave been making a slow-cooked dish of beef since last night. I think it might be the thing to tempt the little guy.'

And, before I could say that I didn't necessarily want to shell out the price of a gourmet meal on a dog, he vanished, only to return a few moments later carrying a large cup of frothy, steaming cappucino and some freshly baked bread for me, together with a dish containing gravy and the most enormous bone I had ever seen in my life. The little dog fell upon the bone with a grateful growl and slurped noisily at the moist strips of meat still adhering to its surface.

I broke off a piece of bread and popped it into my mouth. The outside was warm and crusty, the inside soft and yielding. It was the gastronomic equivalent of a comfort blanket and somehow managed to make the upsets of the day seem a little less terrible. The waiter returned again, carrying a pasta bowl containing crisp green lettuce, tomatoes, huge black olives, moist green beans, golden-yoked egg and slivers of anchovies. My mouth began to water even before he'd put it on the table.

It's salad, sir, but not as we know it.

'*Buon appetito,*' he said with a grin that lit up his eyes.

I couldn't help but smile back.

I had a tentative prod at a bean-anchovy combo and popped it into my mouth. The saltiness of the anchovy and the fresh green of the bean – I'm not kidding, it actually tasted *green* – burst onto my tongue.

I'd be mad to go home to Scotland and leave all this.

Wouldn't I?

Bloody hell, Nick, why do you always have to make everything so difficult?

The dog stopped demolishing its bone and pawed sympathetically at my ankle. I gave it an absent-minded scratch behind the ear and pulled off another mouthful of comfort bread to steady my nerves.

The square was busier than before. The tables around me – and at all the other cafés nearby – had been taken, and the air was filled with bustle and chatter. A group of gangly teenagers sloped past exuding the air of disgruntled boredom cultivated by adolescents the whole world over. Underneath my chair, the little dog smacked its lips in satisfaction. For a moment, peace reigned supreme – before an ear-piercing shriek rent the air.

I turned round with a start, trying to peer through the crowds to see if someone had hurt themselves or – even worse – had had their bag stolen; but instead my eyes clocked Jess, with a face like thunder, stalking through the midday mob clutching her mobile phone. She didn't see me until she had all but tripped over my table and toppled head first into my salad bowl.

'Ailsa,' she looked amazed, 'what are you doing here?'

'Lunch,' I indicated my bowl of salad.

She gave herself a little shake.

'Sorry,' she said, 'brain all over the place.'

Pulling up the chair next to mine, she sat down. The little dog trotted over to her, its tail wagging as though it was hooking up with a much loved pal. My cousin patted it on the head.

'I saw your party piece last night,' she said affectionately, 'you're trouble, you are.'

'It's not my dog,' I said, wondering if I should just have the words printed on a T-shirt to save me the trouble of having to explain it every five minutes.

'Maybe you don't own it,' replied Jess as the dog rolled on the ground in front of her, 'but it might own you – have you thought of that?'

'No,' I said – mainly because I hadn't. I didn't like the idea of dogs choosing which humans they wanted to be attached to; it made life feel even more random and unsettling than it did already. 'Anyway, he won't be here much longer, we're on our way to the V-E-T-S.'

Jess stared aghast at me, mid-tummy tickle.

'You're not—' She paused. 'I mean you wouldn't have him, you know – *put down* – would you?'

Even though that hadn't entered my mind, a wave of guilt came crashing through me.

'No,' I said hastily, 'but I think it's a stray. I'm getting it checked out and handed over to the RSPCA or whatever they have here in Italy, that's all.'

Jess sat back in her chair and dropped her mobile into her bag.

'And you?' I asked. 'The last time I saw you, you were escaping from Veronica for a few stolen hours with your soul angel.'

My cousin picked a paper sachet of sugar out of a pot in the middle of the table and began to fiddle with it. She was – what's the word? – *twitchy*. She certainly didn't look as though she'd spent the past couple of hours being loved up.

'Justin wasn't around,' she said. 'In fact, I've only just got through to him on his phone. He says he's in a meeting. *A meeting?* We're supposed to be on holiday.'

She looked round for the waiter.

'*Prego! Scusi!*' she cried, clicking her finger imperiously.

66

I cringed. Was she going to give her order in over-loud, shouty English with embarrassing hand gestures?

The waiter made his way towards us, an amused twinkle in his brown eyes.

'*Un bicchiere de Prosecco, per favore.*' A stream of flawless Italian tripped from Jess's tongue and took me completely by surprise. '*E una grossa fetta di torta alla crema.*'

'*Certo, bella signora*' – the waiter winked and threw her a dazzling smile – 'it would be my pleasure.'

'Where did you learn to speak Italian like that?' I asked, as he trotted off to do her bidding.

Jess shrugged.

'Pops paid for me to have a term at this college thing in Rome. I just sort of picked it up. By the way, where did you get your sandals? They're epic.'

'Top Shop,' I replied, wondering if she'd even heard of the place, let alone been inside a branch.

But Jess's eyes closed in rapture.

'God, I *love* Top Shop! The clothes are so cheap you can just wear them once and then throw them away!'

I was taking a sip of my cappuccino at this point and had to concentrate really hard on not letting it splurt out of my nose. Presumably Sidebottom's 'Sidling Stoat' profits were well up. Take the words 'other', 'half', 'how' and 'live' and use them to make a well-known phrase or saying . . .

'Anyway, talking of soulmates, Ailsa,' Jess segued seamlessly into a complete non sequitur, 'did you see that chap who arrived at the hotel this morning? Crikey – tall, dark and handsome doesn't even *begin* to cover it.'

'No,' I said, popping an olive into my mouth and

thinking back. I hadn't seen anyone that morning apart from Nick, and he didn't count.

The waiter returned, placing a large slice of strawberry layer cake and a glass of sparkling wine in front of Jess. She tipped the glass in my direction.

'Cheers,' she said, 'I'm safe to eat. Veronica's busy terrorising the hotel kitchen staff. Anyway, this guy – crikey! He was hot. Hotter than a sunbed in the Sahara. And you tell me you're unattached . . .'

She waggled a large piece of cake at me to make her point.

My heart sank – even without Nick hanging around, my appetite for romantic liaisons was deader than a cremated dodo.

'Thanks but no thanks,' I said, 'I had a nasty break-up not so long ago.'

Jess grinned as though this was the best news she'd heard in ages and shoved the forkful of cake into her mouth.

'Well, you know what they say, Ailsa – the best way to get over someone is to get under someone.'

Bless her, she was trying.

Then, her face fell.

'Oh,' she said, 'but Mum told me you had to go home. There's an emergency at your school or something.'

'There were these kids . . .' I began and then stopped.

The kids had lost their allure. Thanks for that, Nick.

'You can't go,' Jess pleaded through a mouthful of cake, 'you just can't. I need you here.'

As she spoke, she threw a glance over her shoulder

and the atmosphere at our little table changed: it was as though the sun had gone behind a cloud.

'It's okay,' I said, wanting to put her mind at rest, 'it's – well, it's been sorted. I can stay after all – for a bit, anyway. But will you tell me what's going on? If you want me to help you with this life or death thing, you're going to have to tell me what it is.'

Jess heaved an enormous sigh of relief and swirled her Prosecco round in its glass. 'It's like this,' she began.

'Yes?' I leaned in over the table.

Jess hesitated.

'You won't be cross, will you?'

'No,' I was puzzled now – why would I be cross about a matter of life and death? 'I think I'll manage to stay calm. Go on.'

Jess sighed.

'All right,' she said. 'The thing is, there isn't a problem, well, nothing life or death, anyway; I was just desperate for you to come to the wedding. I know how awful things have been between our mums for years now, but I couldn't bear to get married with just Justin's folks and a few of Dad's work cronies gawping at me. I wanted my family here too – my flesh and blood. So, after a bit of screaming and shouting, I got Mum to invite you all and, when we didn't hear back, I sent those emails. I didn't think you'd turn up otherwise. Go on – hate me.'

She was absolutely right, I wouldn't have come. Immediately I felt like a real cow.

'Oh Jess,' I said, 'I'm sorry. If I'd known how much it meant to you, I'd have accepted straight away – but you know what our family is like: we're either at each other's throats or giving one another the silent treatment. Lion taming is relaxing and stress-free compared to one of our get-togethers.'

Jess looked at me earnestly.

'My mum and your mum perhaps – but not you and me, surely? I don't want this row about bloody Sidebottom's to affect us.'

I reached across the table and took her hand.

'It won't,' I said, 'and I'm sorry you felt you had to lie to me. However, I've got to say I'm quite pleased nothing of real life or death importance has actually happened.'

Jess threw another look over her shoulder and there was a pause, during which I felt the atmosphere at the table change subtly.

'Well,' she said, 'it's funny you should say that, but something *did* happen, about three weeks ago. Not life or death exactly but just a bit weird.'

'Oh?' I said.

Jess let go of my hand and scooped up another forkful of cream sponge.

'I mentioned it to my psychic, Serena—'

'The one who told you your future soulmate's name would begin with the letter "K"?'

Jess nodded.

'That's the one; and she told me that there was trouble brewing – specifically to do with money – but that someone would come from the south and lift my burdens from me.'

I opened my mouth to tell her that Edinburgh was generally considered to be in the north, but Jess continued.

'A few weeks back, I was at Mum and Pops's. Mum and I were off out to this spa for the afternoon. There's

70

a new body cream in from San Francisco that uses goats' placenta and—'

'Please,' I begged, putting a forkful of food back in my bowl, 'enough with the goats' placentas, I'm trying to eat.'

'Sorry – anyway, we'd just got into the car when I realised I'd left my handbag in the hall, so Mum gave me her keys so I could I let myself in – and that's when I overheard Pops on the phone. He was shouting – really loudly – that there was nothing wrong with Sidebottom's finances and that the Italian distribution deal for Sidling Stoat would go ahead as planned.'

'Oh?' Italian distribution deals? This didn't sound much like the chunky-knit, Real Ale world of Sidebottom's that I'd grown up with.

'Yes, it's Justin's baby. He persuaded this European distributer to take Stoat and try it out in a chain of Italian hotels. If it works, it could be huge – France, Spain, Germany even. I'm very proud of him – when he doesn't go rushing off to meetings during our wedding week, that is.'

Jess rubbed her eyes. She suddenly looked exhausted.

'Anyway, Pops was angry, Ailsa; really, *really* angry. I can't get what he said out of my head and it makes me feel a bit funny, even now. What should I do? I don't want to talk to Pops because he really hates it when people stick their noses into Sidebottom's business – he'd go ballistic.'

I pushed my bowl away and leaned over the table. Psychic Serena or no Psychic Serena, I reckoned Jess was stressing out over nothing.

'Look, do you think you might be overreacting a little? I mean, your dad was basically telling whoever it was on the phone that everything's okay – that there is no case to answer where the finances are concerned.'

'I don't know, Ailsa – I have this weird feeling. I mentioned it to Serena and—'

I held up my hand.

'I want to stop you there, Jess. I'm sure Serena comes highly recommended and can tell you all sorts of things about soulmates and people whose names don't begin with the letters she says they do, but let's look at the facts here.'

Jess nodded.

'Your parents live in a lovely house,' I counted off on my fingers, 'they have – how many foreign holidays a year?'

'Three,' replied Jess.

'Three foreign holidays and they're paying for this wonderful wedding. Do you think they'd be able to do that if there were any problems with the brewery?'

'No, I suppose not.' Jess sighed again.

'Good; and you said Justin is masterminding this deal with Sidling Stoat – has *he* mentioned anything to you about the accounts being a cause for concern? Or talked about moving jobs? Or – or anything?'

'No.'

'Well,' I drained the last of my cappuccino, 'there you are then. I'm sure it's all fine. In fact, it's better than fine – I think you're just anxious because this could be Justin's big break and you don't want anything to come along and mess it up.'

Jess smiled.

'Probably.'

She sighed again. This time with relief.

'All right, I'll stop worrying. Thanks, Ailsa – you're brilliant. You don't panic like Mum or yell like Pops, but there's still a bit of you in Sidebottom's, isn't there? It's always been a family firm at heart.'

I looked down into my empty cappuccino cup. A family firm, perhaps, but not my bit of the family. It was Jess who would ultimately reap the benefits of the upcoming Stoat invasion of Italy – but hey, I wasn't bitter.

Jess shook her head, stuffed the last of her cake into her mouth, then reached down and tickled the little dog who had finished its bone and was happily chewing through the handle of the beach bag. I picked the bag up and examined it – ruined. Never again would it serve as a vehicle for puppy smuggling.

'Hadn't you better be taking this little fellow to the vet's?' asked Jess.

The dog leaped to its feet and glared at me accusingly.

'Ssh,' I replied, rolling up the defunct beach bag and stuffing it into my handbag. 'I think it speaks English.'

My cousin drained her Prosecco.

'Sorry,' she said, 'I mean – I hope it goes well with the V-T-E.'

I smiled. Jess had about the same grasp of basic spelling as her psychic.

'So do I,' I said, pushing back my chair and leaving the money for my lunch under the rim of my plate.

'And I'll see you back at the hotel? Promise?'

I kissed her on the cheek.

'Yes,' I said, 'you will. I promise not to go anywhere – for the time being at least.'

Chapter Six

I made my way across the square and down one of the larger side streets where, I'd been informed by our waiter, there was a veterinary practice. Luckily for me the nurse on duty and the vet both spoke excellent English and – even more luckily – they happened to be having a slow afternoon and were able to see me without too much of a wait.

I carried the little dog through into a consultation room at the back of the building. It contained a sink and an examination table as well as the all-pervasive, overpowering reek of disinfectant.

At least that meant it was clean, I supposed.

Placing the pooch carefully on the table, I watched as the vet, a small man with huge bushy black eyebrows and an equally bushy moustache, began his examination. I learned that the dog was a Jack Russell and that it probably (unlike any of my relations) had an impeccable pedigree; was a he rather than a she; and that he was likely to be little more than a year old. After checking him over and pronouncing him disease-free, the vet squeezed a few drops of anti-flea treatment onto the back of his neck and forced a worm tablet between his resisting teeth. Then the nurse reappeared, carrying a device that looked like a bar-code reader from a supermarket and ran it over the little dog's neck and shoulders.

'This,' said the vet, his moustache blowing out walrus-fashion as he spoke, 'is a microchip scanner. Many owners have a chip injected into their pets' neck, so that if the pet gets lost the chip can be read and the animal and owner can be reunited.'

'Blimey.' I was impressed. 'It all sounds a bit space age to me.'

The vet laughed and the nurse lifted the scanner away from the little dog, shaking her head.

'Give it another go,' said the vet, 'sometimes they can be a bit difficult to locate.'

As the nurse scanned the dog for a second time, I realised I was holding my breath. After a minute or so, though, she gave up and patted the little dog on the head.

'So, there is no chip. That makes things more difficult,' the vet nodded solemnly. 'You said that you found him at the Hotel Santa Lucia?'

'Sort of,' I replied, remembering Jess's words, 'although it's probably more accurate to say that he found me.'

The vet ruffled the little dog's fur.

'You might remind him of his owner,' said the vet, 'and I'm guessing he – or they – stayed somewhere locally a day or two before you arrived and he went missing then. Does anyone at your hotel recognise him?'

'No,' I replied, 'in fact, they think he's a bit of a nuisance. Not that that seems to put him off; he keeps discovering different ways to sneak in and find me.'

'Dogs are amazingly loyal.' The vet produced a treat from his pocket and held it up to the little pooch, who immediately sat up on his hind legs and begged like a pro. 'Once they bond with a human, they will follow them to the ends of the earth. I have heard stories of dogs making their way across hundreds of miles of inhospitable terrain or, in cases of avalanche, locating their owners under metres of snow and guiding the rescue teams to the exact spot. To us it seems like a miracle, but to them it is obviously no big deal. My guess is that he has decided you are his pack leader and he is doing whatever he can to stay with you.'

The vet offered me a treat and I held it out to my new pack subordinate. This time, he didn't beg but rolled onto his back and waggled his legs, barking loudly.

'At least you don't do any of that playing dead stuff,' I said, 'and don't go getting any ideas about it either – you'll give me a heart attack.'

The dog flipped upright again and thumped his tail happily on the consulting table.

'So what do I do now?' I asked. 'If there's no chip, how else can we find his owners?'

As I said the words 'his owners' a funny little feeling lodged itself in my stomach; I did my best to ignore it – I couldn't bear people who got sentimental over animals and I had no intention of becoming one.

The vet shrugged and pulled off his rubber gloves.

'I will email all the local veterinary practices and animal charities to see if anyone recognises him. I will also contact the police. I know he's not their favourite creature, but if you could persuade the hotel to mention him on their internet site too, that would be good. He may belong to a previous guest.'

'Sadly, they're a bit anti-dog,' I explained, scratching the animal behind the ears. 'Or at least, anti-*him*. I just wish you could speak, little fella – then you'd be able to fill us in on where you've come from.'

Right on cue, the dog sat up on his hind legs and barked loudly.

Twice.

'Okay,' I backtracked, 'so you *can* speak, but not in any language I can understand.'

I turned back to the vet.

'Anything else?'

'You might want to give him a name,' the vet grinned, 'and unfortunately there will be a small bill. Apart from that, I think we're on top of things. I'll keep him in for a couple of days – there are a few tests I want to run and a cut, here, that I want to keep an eye on – but unless you want me to hand him over to the dog warden, you'll need to come back and pick him up.'

I felt as though someone had hit me across the face with a wet fish.

The dog warden?

Images of a mean-looking man in a peaked cap chasing after the little dog with a super-sized net flashed through my brain. Similar thoughts presumably also occurred to the dog himself, because he put his paw over his nose and whimpered pathetically.

The vet laughed, making his moustache ripple like – well, like a hairy rippling thing.

'He's a great actor. You should call him "Olivier" – something that reflects his theatrical personality.'

'Arthur,' I said firmly. The name came from nowhere and sat in my brain like a done deal. 'I think he looks like an Arthur.'

'A very British choice.' The vet smiled and scribbled it down in the little dog's notes. 'And your name, *signorina*?'

'Ailsa Stuart,' I replied, thinking 'Arthur Stuart' had a certain, debonair ring to it.

Stop it! I was not a dog person. I would never be a dog person. And I had no intention of being this particular dog's person.

'Be careful, *signorina*.' The vet smiled at me as though he knew *exactly* what I was thinking. 'In cases like this, we do very often track down the original owner. Try not to get too attached to him.'

I glanced at the little dog. I couldn't swear to it, but I'm ninety-nine per cent certain that he winked at me.

'We're mates now,' he seemed to be saying. 'I'm not going anywhere.'

'It's okay,' I replied lightly, finding it easier not to look at my canine charge, 'I just wanted to make sure he was healthy and to help reunite him with his real owners. I'm not a dog person.'

I'm not, I'm not, I'm not!

'Okay.' The vet scooped the little dog up in his arms. 'I will finish the rest of his tests. Seeing as he's a stray, I won't charge for my time, just any medication he might need. However, as I said, he can't stay here indefinitely. I will see you soon – unless you are serious when you say that you are not a dog person?'

The little dog lifted its head and stared woefully at me.

What choice did I have?

'I'll come back,' I promised, 'and we'll see if there's been any progress with his owners. Meanwhile, I'll leave the phone number of the hotel with the nurse so you can contact me.'

'Good,' the vet nodded briskly. 'See you tomorrow then. *Ciao.*'

'*Ciao*,' I replied and, after I'd tickled him behind the ears (the dog, obviously, not the vet) I made my way over to the reception desk, where I prepared to hand across my hard-earned cash to pay the little dog's meds bill.

Huh – dog person?

Moi?

Perish the thought . . .

Chapter Seven

I decided to walk back to the hotel, a decision that I only began to regret once I had left the taxi ranks far behind me and found myself huffing, puffing and sweating profusely in afternoon sun. The heat wasn't just hot any more, if you get my drift, it was worse than that. There was an oppressive quality to it that made me feel as though I was being ground down into the pavement – and the thought that waiting for me back at the Santa Lucia was Nick didn't help.

When I finally reached my room, I wanted nothing but a cold shower and industrial quantities of aftersun. I leaned against the handle as I wrestled my key card out of my handbag – only to have the door swing open all by itself.

Anxiously, I peered round into the room.

'Hello?' I said, hoping that my credit cards were still where I'd left them. 'Anyone there?'

I peered even closer – and then clapped my hand across my mouth.

There *was* someone in there.

Someone with dark bobbed hair, just like my own.

Someone sitting in the swivel chair by the desk – and, to add insult to injury, someone smoking a cigarette.

'Excuse me,' I said, using the special scary voice they make you learn at teacher training college, 'what exactly do you think you're doing?'

Rather than be intimidated, however, the Mystery Person swung round and blew a perfect smoke ring in my direction.

'Ailsa,' she cooed, 'how lovely to see you!'

It was my sister Kitty.

My *older* sister Kitty, who had loitered at the back of the queue when tact and discretion were being handed out, and for whom the word 'empathy' was, essentially, meaningless. As ever, I didn't know whether to hug her, shout at her, or throw up my hands in exasperation and walk away. Instead, I settled for plucking the cigarette out of her fingers and throwing it into the toilet in the en suite.

'Well,' she rummaged round inside a handbag so ginormous she could have used it to smuggle whole families of illegal immigrants onto the Italian mainland. 'That's not a very nice welcome. I did *ask* you if I could use your room as a bolt-hole.'

I stared at her.

'No, you didn't,' I retorted. 'I haven't heard a thing from you for ages. Since Christmas, in fact.'

'Oh, well,' Kitty waved her hand loftily in the air as though the actual details were of very little importance. 'Perhaps I didn't actually get round to *speaking* to you – but I certainly *meant* to. This is typical of you, Ailsa – you always get bogged down by the *tiniest details*.'

She smiled as though that made everything all right and drew a packet of Silk Cut out of the cavernous bag.

'Oh, no you don't,' I replied, stepping forward and snatching it off her. 'First up, I don't want my room stinking of fags. Second up,' I gestured to a large notice written in six languages stuck to the French window, 'the entire hotel is no smoking. And third up, I am not getting bollocked for something I disapprove of.'

Kitty rolled her eyes.

'Everyone *knows* Italians don't give a flying cappuccino about rules,' she replied, 'that's just there to make sure uptight, Northern Europeans like you feel at home.'

I took a deep breath, walked over to the minibar and counted to ten.

When that wasn't enough, I tried twenty.

After I'd counted down backwards from a hundred in threes, I felt a lot better. My sister rose from her chair (or should that be 'my' chair?) and made her way over to the minibar.

'Drink?' she asked, waggling a glass at me.

'Oh, go on then,' I said, 'seeing as we're on holid . . .'

The words froze on my lips. The minibar looked as though it had been plundered by a plague of locusts.

Um, make that alcoholic locusts with a penchant for twenty-year old single malt – if the expensive-looking *open* bottle in there was anything to go by.

'Did you—?' I began.

Kitty sighed the sigh of the hard done by and topped up her glass.

'I've had an absolute bitch of a journey,' she said, 'no flights, of course, thanks to the baggage handlers, so I got the Eurostar to Paris and then another train on from there. I came to find you earlier but you weren't here, but luckily the lock on your door is dodgy, so I slipped in and availed myself of the facilities – oh, and I ate a sandwich I'd bought back at St Pancras. Ham, I think it was.'

The light dawned – that must have been the wrapper Arthur fished out of my bin.

'I knew you wouldn't mind. Hey-ho, any port in a storm.'

'Especially the ten-year-old, oak-aged variety?' I replied, spying an empty miniature languishing behind the macadamia nuts. 'Look, Kitty, don't get me wrong, it *is* lovely to see you, but I'd really rather you didn't continue availing yourself of *my* facilities – I don't want to wake up in the middle of the night and see you standing over me like the avenging angel with a glass of gin in one hand and a half-eaten Toblerone in the other.'

Kitty flopped disconsolately back into her chair and tucked her legs underneath her.

'Everything all right?' I asked, pouring myself a mineral water. 'Even allowing for the journey from hell, you don't normally drink like a pissed fish in the middle of the afternoon.'

Kitty didn't reply. Instead she ran her finger round the rim of her glass.

'I've had it with men,' she announced. 'For ever. In fact, I've decided – I'm going to become a political lesbian.'

I choked – and about twenty-five millilitres of San Pellegrino spurted out of my nose.

'Okay,' I replied calmly, as soon as I'd recovered myself and my airways were clear again, 'it's – well, it's quite a life-changer, isn't it? I can see how difficult it must have been for you to come to terms with – with your sexuality – and can I just say how much I respect your decision to come – ah – out of the cupboard and—'

'Oh for goodness' sake.' Kitty rolled her eyes. 'Don't you know *anything*? First up, it's a closet not a cupboard, and second up, I said *political* lesbian. Political lesbians don't snog girls – in fact, they sleep with as many men as they can, they just have to despise them while they're doing it. It's perfect. I can't imagine why I didn't think of it sooner.'

'So – you've decided you hate men, but you're still prepared to use them like lifeless, feelingless pieces of meat for your own selfish pleasure?'

'You say that like it's a bad thing,' my sister murmured through a mouthful of whisky.

'So, Graham's toast, is he?' Graham was Kitty's long-standing (and, to my mind, long-suffering) on/off squeeze.

'Couldn't be more so if I was spreading him with butter and looking round for the marmalade.'

I'd always quite liked Graham. I'd just never been sure that Kitty felt the same.

'I'm really sorry.'

'Don't be.' She drained her drink and clanged her glass down noisily on the desk. 'I'm not. People change, things move on. Best thing that ever happened to me.'

There was a brittle quality to her voice that told me she wasn't being entirely truthful.

'Poor you,' I said sympathetically. 'Is there anything I can do?'

Kitty glanced at me, glared and then looked away again. That would be a 'no' then.

'So,' I said, taking the hint and changing the subject, 'how come you're here? I'd have thought you'd have a million reasons why you couldn't possibly make the wedding.'

'Well, Jess kept sending me these emails telling me how important it was for me to be here – a matter of life and death, or something.'

'Really?'

Matters of life and death weren't usually pressing enough to cut any ice with Kitty.

'I didn't believe them, of course – I just put them down to Jess being flaky. But then the whole Graham thing blew up and I thought, *why not get away for a bit?*' Kitty continued. 'However – and I want to make this absolutely clear – I'm *not* upset, I don't need a shoulder to cry on and I totally, one hundred per cent do not want to talk about it. I just need a bit of R and R, a few drinks and my fags – so be a good girl and hand them over. Don't worry; I'll go out on the balcony – you won't be nicked by the Tobacco Police.'

I sighed and handed the packet back. Kitty selected a ciggie, walked over to the iron railings that surrounded my little piece of the Great Outdoors and lit up, exhaling loudly. Despite her words, she was obviously not a happy camper.

'So you and Graham,' I began softly, 'was it him – or you – or mutual – or – well, what happened?'

'I. Don't. Want. To. Talk. About. It.'

I shrugged. At least I'd tried.

Kitty didn't do sisterly intimacy, in much the same way that she didn't do free-fall parachute jumping or swimming with sharks: sure, it was out there as an option, but she would probably choose to eat her own hair rather than show me the softer side of her nature. In fact, I sometimes wondered if she had one.

'Fine,' I said, 'just so as I'm in the picture, do you want

to do the whole family bonding routine while we're here? Shopping in the afternoons, mojitos on the terrace before dinner – that sort of thing?'

Kitty took a deep drag on her cigarette.

'Bloody hell, no,' she looked at me warily. 'Why? Do you?'

I shrugged again. Why break the habit of a lifetime just because you're on holiday?

'No,' I replied, 'I just wanted to make sure. Are Mum and Dad coming?'

Kitty shrugged.

'Mum hasn't said anything to me either way, but I doubt it. You know what things are like between her and Auntie Sheila.'

I joined her on the balcony – after first making sure no sounds of life were coming from Nick's side of the wisteria.

'I don't understand it,' Kitty continued, gazing out over the Italian countryside, which was flickering a hazy blue-green in the full onslaught of the afternoon heat. 'You'd think they'd have managed to bury the hatchet by now.'

A welcome breeze rustled through the wisteria leaves.

'I know,' I replied, 'maybe it wasn't fair that Sheila got the shares, but it's only a tiny business – a microbrewery, for goodness' sake; and Uncle Dudley's hardly Richard Branson. We're not talking about blue-chip mega millions.'

'He's done pretty well for himself. You're not telling me Uncle Dudders is strapped for cash when he's shelling out for us all to come to Tuscany so that we can see Justin and Jess promise to honour and obey one another? *I* wouldn't mind having a few shares in it.'

'Money isn't everything,' I said primly, as much to

convince myself as Kitty. 'And – ten years! It's a hell of a time to hold a grudge.'

'I know someone at work whose entire family stopped speaking to each other because of a Victorian teapot shaped like a cat.' Kitty tapped her finger on the balcony railings for emphasis. 'Hideous thing it was, too. Believe me, where wills are concerned, shares in a family-owned brewery are *nothing*.'

She broke off.

Down below us was a figure in a red suit marching purposefully towards another figure wearing a large, floppy sunhat and a sarong.

'I know that's Auntie Sheila,' Kitty hissed, pointing at the figure in the sarong, 'but who's that in the red?'

'Veronica the wedding planner,' I hissed back, 'although I'm not sure she's actually human: she more of a rottweiler in heels.'

We leaned over the railings as far as we dared, feeling like children at a dinner party, hiding behind the banisters and earwigging on the grown-up conversation.

'I've sorted out the bouquets,' Veronica was ticking things off her clipboard, 'but the ice sculptures are proving tricky. I've sourced a man in Pisa who thinks he can step into the breach, but if you want swans, it's going to cost.'

We saw Auntie Sheila nod unenthusiastically.

'And speaking of cost,' Veronica stopped ticking things off and put her hands (and her clipboard) on her hips, 'I must insist that my invoice is paid. Really, Mrs Westfield, this is dragging out in a most unsatisfactory way, you've had it for over two weeks now.'

'Of course, Veronica, of course.' Auntie Sheila sighed

deeply. 'I do understand, I really do. I've spoken to Dudley and he's said that before we can pay you, he needs to transfer some funds across into our joint account. It won't take long, he says – twenty-four hours at most.'

'I would appreciate it sooner than that, Mrs Westfield,' said Veronica, 'I am not a charity. I had to turn down *three* other contracts to accompany you and your family to Italy this week – *three*; and one of them was going to have a full-page spread in *Solihull Society* magazine. It really is too bad.'

Auntie Sheila began wringing her hands.

'I'm sure it will be fine, Veronica,' she said. 'I mean, it's not as though Dudley's about to go bankrupt, is it? It's just a matter of cash flow.'

Veronica gave a brusque nod.

'Just make sure it starts flowing in my direction asap. I'll confirm the ice sculpture *once you've paid me.*'

And she stalked off down the path leaving a despairing Auntie Sheila in her wake.

'Lordy,' breathed Kitty, 'I'm glad I came. There's more drama here than you could shake an episode of *Hollyoaks* at.'

I looked at her.

'Don't,' I said.

Kitty blinked.

'Don't what?'

'Start stirring; I know what you're like.'

Kitty looked genuinely hurt.

'I'm not a stirrer,' she said.

'Yes, you are,' I said firmly, 'you're worse than a Magimix.'

'Am not.'

'Are.'

'Am not.'

'Well, then, it won't be hard for you to not do it, will it?'

Kitty didn't reply. Instead, she threw her cigarette butt onto the floor and ground it into the dust with her heel. Then she gave me a look that could have stripped nail varnish at twenty paces.

'And you,' she said, scrutinising my face for the slightest reaction, 'are you all right?'

'Yes,' I replied, taken completely by surprise, 'of course. I'm fine.'

Kitty's eyes narrowed.

'No lost love or heartbreak your side of the fence?' she asked, adding quickly. 'Not that I'm heartbroken, of course.'

'Of course,' I echoed, a terrible leaden feeling lodging in my chest, 'I mean – no. No. Absolutely not.'

My sister's expression became more thoughtful.

'So does that mean you're on the pull this week as well?'

The thought of lassoing a drop-dead waiter, snogging him in front of Nick while holding up a piece of paper with the words 'It Could Have Been You' written on it, did cross my mind. But only for about a nanosecond.

'No,' I said quickly, 'no, not at all. In fact, I'm having coffee with a guy at work when I get back. Um, Gary. Yes – coffee with Gary.'

Could it have sounded any lamer? Still, it did the trick.

'Fair enough,' Kitty clapped her hands together. 'But you can still go and get your bikini on and meet me down at reception in five. It's pool time.'

I blinked at her.

'You're going swimming?' I asked.

Swimming, like sisterly bonding, was something else Kitty never did.

Kitty shook her head pityingly and walked back through my room, draining her whisky glass as she went.

'No,' she said, opening the door, 'but I'm after a gorgeous chunk of man that I can use like a feelingless piece of meat and the pool is the best place I know to check out the talent. I hear on the grapevine that the Best Man's pretty hot.'

And, with that, she was gone.

I sighed and pulled my swimmers from a drawer in the wardrobe. The one thing you learned pretty early on with Kitty was that resistance was useless. I was as good as on my sunlounger already.

Chapter Eight

The theme of Jess and Justin's wedding was 'the Nineteen-Thirties'. The idea being that although everyone spent the day slouching round in their cut-offs and sandals, when the evening came we would all make an effort to get into the period vibe. For Jess, of course, preparing to recreate the third decade of the twentieth century in fashion had meant nothing more than taking Uncle Dudley's credit card on a tour of local vintage emporia; for me, however, it had all been a lot more traumatic and involved a series of turbulent shopping trips where I tore out my hair and ended up breathing into a paper bag as I attempted to find something that:

a. looked the part and

b. wouldn't entail me having to sell one of my kidneys in order to pay for it.

In the end I settled on a fitted, plain black maxi dress that had a vague thirties feel to it and, borrowed from Emma, the most beautiful, genuine period silk dress in a pale rose pink. It was bias-cut with tiny cap sleeves in matching pale pink satin, a band around the waist and the most plungingest of plunging necklines.

'It was my great-gran's,' said Emma, as she took it out of its tissue packaging the day before I left, 'she gave it to me when I was a student and flat broke but in dire need of a posh frock.'

'Then that settles it,' I replied, staring at its pale pink amazingness, 'I can't possibly wear it – it's far too precious. I'll spill red wine down it or trip over the hem and fall head first into the pool.'

Emma shook her head.

'Please try it on,' she urged, 'it's a good luck dress; Great-Granny wore it the night she met the love of her life, I wore it the night I met Ben—'

'I wasn't wearing it when I met Nick,' I said, stepping into the puddle of rose-coloured silk.

'My point exactly.' Emma zipped me in and then stood back to assess the result. 'Oh God, you look fantastic. Go on – get an eyeful of yourself.'

I did. The dress clung and swung in exactly the right places. The delicate rose pink gave my skin a flattering glow and I sensed a little thrill of excitement at the thought of getting dressed up that I hadn't experienced since Nick and I had parted company.

Maybe the dress had already started working its magic for me?

That similar ripple of excitement sparked through me now, as I showered, dried my hair and then wriggled into the dress's silky embrace. The faint, comforting smell of Emma's favourite perfume lingered on the fabric and, as I checked my reflection in the mirror, I realised that I actually felt *brave*. Not lion-hearted and indomitable perhaps, but not actively *nervous*.

Which was a good thing, seeing as Nick and I might well be crossing paths in a few minutes' time.

I applied a layer of lippie and then, tucking a pink silk clutch bag under my arm – also on loan from Emma

– made my way down the stairs and across the foyer to the main bar where the wedding guests were all supposed to rendezvous.

Instead of a group of extras from a Fred and Ginger movie, however, what I saw was a group of old ladies sitting round a large table with a selection of outrageously coloured cocktails, chattering away like a bunch of blue-rinsed sparrows.

'Wasn't he *marvellous?*' said one of them, carefully moving her miniature umbrella out of the way before she took a large sip of cocktail. 'Wasn't he *knowledgeable?*'

'Wasn't he endowed with lovely biceps, you mean,' giggled the lady next to her, who was wearing a silver lamé evening dress that showed off her tattooed shoulders to their best advantage, 'I could have stared at them for hours.'

'You couldn't see his biceps,' siad the first lady with a frown. 'He was wearing a long-sleeved shirt.'

'You could if you were looking properly,' giggled the Tattooed One, 'and when he started talking about the Seduction of Venus – or whatever that painting was called – I came over all light-headed.'

It took me a moment to work out who the subject of their cougarous conversation was, and when I did, it made me feel much better. If Nick had to be a part of my life for the next few days, it would be a little more bearable if he was being pursued by a bunch of lascivious old ladies. Indeed, as I made my way over to the bar I became aware of another, as old as the others, but with less of the blue rinse/tattoo thing going on. She was well groomed and had an array of overly white teeth surrounded by overly red lips, making her look like a man-eating shark that had just bitten a chunk out of the cosmetics counter at Boots.

'Oh, this is *totally* where it's at,' the woman was exclaiming in a loud American accent. 'I just *adore* old places. You know, I think if I had to live in a modern house it would just *drain* my creative flow.'

I had to crane my neck round a pillar to see who she was talking to. As I did, Shark Woman decided to sidle a bit closer to her companion and tweak his bow tie, allowing me a glimpse of the tweakee's face.

It was Nick.

My bravery wavered. For a moment I considered running back upstairs to my room, but I took a few deep breaths, ordered a gin and tonic from Liam and then lurked out of sight. Snatches of their conversation drifted over to me and it quickly became obvious that Nick was hating every minute.

'Is that a fact?' he replied, in a tone that would have communicated to any normal person that he would rather have eaten his own leg than continue the conversation.

'Sure! Old houses are just so *cool*.'

'Especially when the central heating breaks down.' This remark was lost on Shark Woman, who continued, oblivious.

'Take our house in LA. It was built almost eighty years ago – *eighty*!' she repeated in case Nick missed the significance of this architectural wonder. 'That's almost as old as my *mother*!'

Nick opened his mouth to reply – presumably something about the lady's mother having to have been a child bride – but then closed it again.

'And it's not just our place, you know. There's a whole other bunch of old stuff in the neighbourhood.'

'Your mother's friends?' Nick asked, a veneer of brittle politeness in his voice.

'Like, there's this gas station on the next block from the nineteen-sixties – isn't that amazing? I totally feel that this sort of stuff has to be saved for future generations. Hey, Professor, you know what? It's so great to be able to talk to someone like you who really *gets* this kinda thing. '

Luckily for Nick, a member of the hotel staff appeared at his elbow and said: 'Phone call for Dr Bannister.'

He didn't need to be told twice. With a desultory wave in Shark Woman's direction, he sprinted towards the door as if the hounds of hell were snapping at his heels.

'Missing you already!' she cooed after him.

Nick's route took him directly past me. Despite my best efforts to fade into the background, he spotted me.

'Still here?' he asked, raising an eyebrow.

I waited for the barb in his voice, for my chest to clench and my heart to pound, but the barb – and my reaction to it – were conspicuous by their absence. If anything, he sounded rather sad.

'Apparently so.' I took a large, courage-boosting sip of G and T.

'Your classroom okay?'

Once again, I braced myself for the sting of sarcasm, but there was none.

'Change of plan,' I said, adding pointedly, '*Doctor* Bannister.'

Nick looked uncomfortable and ran a finger round the inside of his collar.

'The tour group,' he made a vague gesture, 'they sort of assume I'm a professional lecturer – from a university or something – not just an enthusiastic artist helping out his cousin.'

'And the hotel staff?' I asked with faux innocence. 'Do they sort of assume it too?'

Nick looked sheepish.

'Look, Ailsa, do you have a problem with it? Because if so—'

'Nick, if you want to go round calling yourself Dr Bannister – or Lord Lucan – or Mr Spock or whatever you fancy – it's fine with me.'

Our eyes met and, to my amazement, Nick's mouth curled into the ghost of a grin.

'I need to get that phone call,' he said, 'excuse me.'

I stepped back to let him pass – and in doing so, nearly fell over Jess, who had sidled up behind me. She was wearing an evening gown that looked as though it had been woven out of moonbeams and shimmered and shone with every movement she made.

'Well, well, well.' There was a twinkle in her eyes. 'So you know the hunky tour guide, do you? Go on – look me in the eye and tell me he's not hotter than a jalepeño.'

I siphoned up a very large mouthful of gin. Liam had gone heavy on the Bombay Sapphire and merely shown the tonic bottle to the glass – and for that I was very grateful.

'He's not hotter than a jalepeño,' I said, my eyes following Nick to the reception desk in the foyer.

Well, maybe not a jalepeño, but even so . . .

Jess's gaze was probing my face. Despite my best efforts, I could feel myself getting flustered.

'Pants on fire,' she whispered gleefully. 'I saw how you were looking at him just now – and what's more, how *he* was looking at *you*. And did you check out that cute little bum? Couldn't you just spread it on toast and eat it for breakfast?'

I nearly dropped my glass. Nick's behind, as a breakfast condiment or otherwise, was not top of my list of conversation topics.

'I bumped into him earlier this afternoon,' Jess continued, 'and we had a nice little chat. Very informative, it was.'

Now I was anxious. I could feel sweat prick at the backs of my knees. Nobody knew about Nick. Had he spilled the beans? Had he told Jess about us?

And if he had mentioned me – what, exactly, did she now know?

'Really?' I said, trying to sound casual and debonaire.

Jess nodded and waved a finger at me teasingly.

'He's got the most amazing,' she paused, 'brain.'

'He has?' I was feeling rather dazed – not that Jess noticed.

'He's read so many books – even the ones that have been made into films. Although between you and me, why *make* work for yourself when it only takes ninety minutes to watch a DVD?'

She had a point: a warped one, but a point nevertheless.

'And he was telling me all about the paintings in the old part of the hotel – the bit that used to be a monastery, near the ruined church. They're called fresh-coes.'

'Frescoes,' I corrected without thinking. 'Yes, he knows a lot about frescoes. You paint straight onto wet plaster;

97

Italian artists used them a lot during the Middle Ages—'

I became aware that Jess had paused, mid-sip, and was staring at me.

'So you *do* know him, then.'

I had the same sensation you get when you're walking downstairs and you miss the bottom step.

'No, I don't,' I lied. 'Not at all.'

Jess's eyes narrowed.

'So how do you know about the friscos?'

I had the choice of either grabbing the cocktail stick from her glass and stabbing myself to death with it, or trying to come up with some sort of rational explanation. Think! *Think!*

'He has the room next to mine,' I said, mainlining the rest of my gin, 'I spoke to him when he was out on the balcony yesterday.'

At least that was true.

Sort of.

Medieval Italian frescoes hadn't actually been one of the topics of our bad-tempered exchange, but Jess didn't need to know that.

My cousin grinned and waved her glass at me as though it was some sort of magic wand.

'Room next door?' she said. 'You never know – that might come in handy. So what else do you know about him?'

I stared down into my empty glass.

Like what? Like we'd met after a Derren Brown gig and Nick swore that he'd been hypnotised into falling in love with me? That there had been several weeks' worth of weekends when we'd never actually made it out of bed? That whenever I thought about him now – which I tried very, *very* hard not to do – I felt as though someone was yanking my heart out of my chest, throwing it into a liquidiser and pushing the 'on' button?

'Ailsa, darling,' Auntie Sheila swept down and exhaled juniper-scented breath all over me, 'you look –' she paused as she appraised my appearance – 'you look so much better than you did last night. Did you manage to get the problem at your school sorted?'

I nodded.

'I – ah – handed over to a colleague. I don't have to rush off. Well, not immediately, anyway.'

'Oh good – Jess will be so happy that you can stay, won't you, Jess?'

Jess opened her mouth to reply, but Auntie Sheila got in first. I guessed this was usually the way of things.

'She's delighted. It means a lot to her, having her family around at a time like this, doesn't it, Jess?'

'Well, I—'

'You see she's *thrilled*. Thrilled.' Auntie S's eyes narrowed and she scrutinised Jess. 'Have you been putting on weight? Oh Lord, I hope not; Veronica will be furious.'

Jess said nothing, but gave her mother a glare. Auntie Sheila, however, opened her arms in welcome and cooed: 'Ah, and here's Kitty, my other lovely niece. You know, the pair of you remind me so much of your mother and myself when we were your age.'

My sister, in a dove-grey, floor-length dress, pulled a horrified face: given the current stand-off between Mum and Auntie S, this was not a flattering comparison.

'Now, what I want to know is, when are you two girls

99

going to find yourselves some nice young men?' Auntie Sheila's voice rang out like a clarion, silencing the chatter in the entire bar area. 'I don't want to be in a wheelchair before I get to cuddle my great-nieces and nephews, you know!'

I could feel a gaze burning into the back of my neck. I turned and saw Nick, back from his phone call, leaning against the wall at the entrance to the bar. There was a bottle of beer in his hand and his face was expressionless.

Kitty cleared her throat.

'Actually, Auntie Sheila,' she said, 'I've decided to become a political—'

'Activist,' I leaped in, 'Kitty is going to become a political activist. She's had enough of the inequalities of today's society and is starting her own anti-capitalist movement to free the downtrodden masses from their economic masters.'

'You are?' Auntie Sheila's eyes were so wide they were in danger of popping clean out of their sockets. 'But I thought you were an executive in an advertising agency?'

Kitty smiled a ghastly smile.

'Starting the revolution from within, Auntie S,' she said, 'or – or something.'

Auntie Sheila took a very large sip from her drink.

'How very – modern,' she said, and disappeared back into the throng.

Kitty turned on me with a look like thunder.

'Anti-capitalist? Downtrodden underclass? Have you gone mad?' she hissed. 'I'm going to kill you for that. And when I've killed you, I shall bury you under the nearest lawn *and then* I shall return every night and dance on your grave. What if that gets back to anyone at work? What if – *oh*, hello.'

I turned round, eager to see what (or rather who) had transformed Kitty's face from one resembling the Wrath of God Descending into something a lot more coy. Following the line of her gaze, I picked out the figure of Charles walking towards the three of us. He nodded in greeting, placing his hand lightly upon Jess's shoulder.

'Kitty,' I said, noting that Charles's hand was lingering a bit on Jess's bare skin, 'this is Charles Chapman, he works with Justin and Uncle Dudley. Charles, this is my sister, Kitty. She wants everyone to know that she's not really an anti-capitalist, she's a political lesbian and – ow! Kitty, that hurt; you're wearing heels.'

'Good,' hissed my sister, before turning to Charles, a seductive smile on her lips. 'How lovely to meet you.'

'Likewise.' Charles finally let go of Jess and leaned over and kissed Kitty on both cheeks: she looked as though all her birthdays and Christmases had arrived at once.

Then he turned to me.

'So, how are you, Ailsa?' he asked. 'I'm surprised to see you here after the break-in at your school.'

At the mention of the break-in, I glanced uneasily in Nick's direction.

'It's fine,' I said, 'my – um – colleague Gary stepped in. With the baggage handlers and everything, it would have been hell getting home.'

'*Gary?*' said Kitty, rather more loudly than was necessary. 'Is that the same *Gary* that you've just started seeing, Ailsa?'

She was obviously trying to let Charles know that she

was the only one of us currently available – but it wasn't Charles's reaction that concerned me. I looked round at Nick. He suddenly looked very small and alone and, for the splittest of split seconds, I was conscious of a sense of overwhelming loss. Then he slammed his beer bottle down on a nearby table and walked out of the room.

'Look.' I turned back to Charles who, I was vaguely aware, was speaking to me. 'I don't want to seem rude. It's just – something – I mean—'

I handed him my empty glass and set off after Nick – but he seemed to have vanished into the ether. Both the bar and the room next to it were Nick-free; so, picking up my skirts, I ran out into the main reception area. My heels clattered on the marble floor – but no one whose name began with 'N' turned to see where the noise was coming from.

I walked over to the girl on the reception desk, who was busy with a nail file.

'A man,' I said, 'with dark hair – did he come through here?'

The girl shrugged vaguely and returned to her nails.

I checked the stairs – zilch; the lift alcove – nada; then, finally, with nowhere else to try, I ran into the gardens and began to pick my way along one of the gravel paths, which led to the ruined church. Goodness knows why I chose this particular route, but I hadn't gone far when I saw him standing half-hidden in the lengthening shadows: his forehead resting against the stonework of one of the ruined pillars and his eyes closed.

'Please,' he said, without even opening them, 'please leave me alone.'

I picked up my skirts, ready to do as I was told, before a strange, empty feeling of desolation swept over me. My chest tightened and my breath started coming in shallow, painful gasps. I closed my eyes too, and tried to feel brave again.

'No.' I shook my head. 'I won't go. I know it's nobody's favourite scenario but I think we need to talk – if only to find a way of getting through the next few days without upsetting each other.'

Nick held up a hand.

'You're right; you're absolutely right. Look, I've got to do this stupid tour, there's no way out of it but here's the deal – I will do my best to get transferred to another hotel and, when I get back home to Scotland, I'll find a lawyer and tell them to start work on the divorce.'

I was glad his eyes were closed. As the word 'divorce' fell out of his mouth, I felt as though Joe Calzaghe had delivered a right hook straight into my solar plexus – a real, actual, physical blow – and I found myself staggering backwards. I was very grateful indeed that there was a wall close behind me so that I didn't literally topple over onto the ground.

Divorce.

To me, the word had always felt spiky and jagged, like a shard of shattered glass; whereas 'marriage' had a soft, absorbing quality to it, as though it would catch you if you fell and bundle you up in a comforting embrace.

Marriage or divorce.

Soft or spiky.

Breathing in . . . and then out again.

It was, of course, a perfectly sensible thing for Nick to

suggest – *if* we weren't going to get back together, then this was the obvious next step.

The only step.

I glanced at him. He was so still that the only way I could tell that he was actually alive was because I could see the buttons on his shirt moving up and down as he breathed.

That, and the fact he was still standing up, I suppose.

'I thought it's what you'd want,' he said, his voice as expressionless as if he was discussing a train timetable or the latest football fixtures. 'I've been doing a bit of research, and a divorce isn't complicated if it's done by mutual consent. We haven't been living apart for two years, which would make it even easier, but we could move forward on the grounds of either unreasonable behaviour or adultery.'

He paused.

The words 'adultery' and 'unreasonable behaviour' bounced round my brain like bullets ricocheting from a gun.

'I haven't,' I said, the syllables sticking in my throat. 'I haven't. Adultery. I mean, the last person I slept with – it was you. I wouldn't . . .'

My voice trailed off into uncomfortable silence.

'Okay, so unreasonable behaviour it is. It doesn't have to be wife-beating or neglect. We could tell them about the money: I had debts, you paid them off, I was ridiculously stupid and ran up some more. Anyway, I'm okay for you to cite me and we can come to some sort of arrangement about the fees. Then, bingo! Bob's your uncle. Or rather your ex-uncle.'

Ten minutes ago, we'd been in a bar tentatively bantering about Nick calling himself 'Doctor'; now we were getting divorced.

Next to me was the fractured base of a pillar, probably Romanesque or something – Nick would have known. I sat down upon it gratefully, my legs not feeling quite a hundred per cent.

'This is all a bit sudden,' I said.

Nick's eyes opened.

'Not for me,' he said.

I looked down at the ground. A small lizard poked its head out from behind a nearby stone and regarded me quizzically.

'I've been doing an awful lot of thinking,' Nick continued, 'particularly at two o'clock in the morning.'

I lifted my head. I was about to say sorry – to apologise for walking out and leaving him – then I remembered why I had, and my stomach clenched nauseatingly.

'I can't go on like this, Ailsa.' He pulled himself away from his pillar and came over to where I was sitting: a tumble of person upon a ruin of stone. 'If this is the end, then so be it. We made a mistake, but we're young enough to move on.'

I couldn't speak. The lizard ran out and skittered across my foot. I didn't even flinch.

Nick leaned over. For a second or two I got a noseful of him – hot, slightly sweaty and a little bit like hot buttered toast. My heart contracted still further.

'You do think we made a mistake, don't you?' he asked.

Words were utterly beyond me. Instead I buried my face in my hands. Nick threw his arms up into the air.

'Why didn't you get in touch, Ailsa? Why didn't you ring me? Didn't you care?'

There was real, raw emotion in his voice. He was hurting – badly – but then again, so was I. Splat! went my heart back into that Magimix. Whizz! went the 'on' button.

'Don't say I didn't care, Nick. Don't you *dare* say I didn't care!'

'Oh really?' Nick raised his eyebrows. 'So this is how you show "caring", is it? Walk out on me and then ignore me?'

I twisted the ring on my right hand.

'I left, Nick, yes – mea culpa, hands up. But you know why: because I couldn't take any more. I couldn't spend the rest of my life wondering where the next bill – the next bloody court summons – was going to come from. I need more from a relationship than being treated like an ATM; I deserve better.'

Nick's eyes flashed.

'I fucked up, Ailsa; I know I did. People do.'

'Nick – believe me, I'm not doing this to spite you. I just couldn't cope any longer. We met, we fell in love, we married on a whim, after what? Three months? Looking back on it, it was crazy.'

'That's why people get married, Ailsa – because they love each other.'

'Yes, Nick – but love on its own isn't enough. I didn't know that then and it looks like I found out the hard way; but I can't spend the rest of my life being miserable just to make you happy. I want a partner; I want someone who, when I've paid off their debt, doesn't go out and rack up more. I want a grown-up, Nick.'

Nick didn't reply. I continued.

'And as for not being in touch – maybe I should have done, but this hit me hard, Nick. I needed time to get my head together. Believe it or not, this wasn't easy for me either.'

Nick opened his mouth but, at that moment, in a flurry of turquoise feathers, Auntie Sheila appeared round the corner.

'Ailsa!' she trilled. 'Ailsa darling – we're just about to go into dinner.'

I went to heave myself off my pillar and stumbled, pitching forward towards the stony path. Quick as lightning, Nick's hand was there on my arm.

I might as well have licked my fingers and plugged myself into the mains.

It was still there – the fundamental, visceral, *physical* connection that had always existed between us. Three months of nothing and it hadn't gone anywhere. I looked up at Nick and knew from the expression on his face that he'd felt it too.

'Ailsa!' Auntie Sheila clapped her hands impatiently. 'They are just about to serve the quail's eggs. Come on.'

And, like an alternative (and rather miserable) version of Cinderella, I hitched up my pink silk skirts and ran back inside, leaving Nick staring helplessly in my wake.

Chapter Nine

I can't say that dinner that night was the most fun I've ever had. I pushed my quail's eggs round the plate, toyed with my veal Orloff, and made very little impression on my panna cotta. Then I excused myself as soon as it was polite to do so and made my way back to my room, where I slipped into bed and lay in the dark, listening to the laughter echoing up from the gardens below and wondering what it would feel like to be divorced.

Even though I'd never worn my ring on the correct finger, called myself Mrs Bertolini or gone on a honeymoon, the idea of a divorce made me feel as though I'd run slap bang into a brick wall.

D.I.V.O.R.C.E.

I'd barely got used to being married.

I turned over and closed my eyes – but, annoyingly, they insisted on popping open. In the end, I gave up and lay with my hands clasped over my chest, trying to convince myself that nothing would actually change: I'd still get up every day, go to work, do my best to look happy and remember that it *hadn't been my fault*.

A thought struck me – I hadn't heard from the school in Newcastle. I reached down beside the bed, pulled my phone out of my bag and realised it had been on silent since the vet's. With trembling hands, I went into my inbox and – woo-hoo! – there it was: an email offering me the job! I nearly cried with relief. Thank you, God! No more kids stealing books from the school library and trying to sell them back to me – no more gum under the desks and swearing and knives, yes, *knives* in the classroom.

And, most of all, a completely fresh start: away from Edinburgh, away from Nick, away from my failed marriage.

I typed a quick, affirmative response. Then I put my phone down on the bedside table and closed my eyes.

There. All I had to do was stagger through half a term and I'd be off. Scotland would be nothing more than a memory.

As I lay there, trying to convince myself that a move south would sort out all my problems, I heard footsteps coming along the corridor and the noise of a key card being swiped next door. I listened, my ears straining, as Nick padded into his room. There came the unmistakable sound of his French windows being opened and someone walking out onto the balcony. I stole out of bed and peeped through my curtains. Nick, a glass of something in his hand, walked over to the far side of his balcony and rested one hand on the railing. He had taken off his bow tie and rolled up the sleeves of his shirt, the white of its cotton gleaming in the twilight and giving him a faintly ghostly appearance. He stood, staring out for goodness knows how long across the little town, before turning towards me. As quick as a flash, I dived back behind my curtains and climbed under my sheets, bizarrely comforted at the thought of him just a few feet away.

By the time I struggled bleary-eyed down into the dining room the next morning, Nick and his gaggle of golden girls had left for the day. I spent the morning in the spa having my nails painted and something that looked like custard but smelled like cabbages smeared over my face and neck; then I swam in the pool and pushed a bowl of gazpacho round at lunchtime. After that, I walked into town and checked in at the vet's (who wanted to keep an eye on Arthur's paw for another twenty-four hours), before wandering round the market, looking at the fruit, veg, cheese and – yes – actual live goats that were for sale.

If anything the heat was even more intense than it had been the day before, and my T-shirt was soon sticking uncomfortably to my sweaty skin and my hair was slicking itself down onto my head – so I gave in and treated myself to a cab back to the hotel.

To step into the air-conditioned foyer was, quite simply, bliss, and I stood for a moment with one of my red-hot cheeks pressed against a marble pillar. In fact, I'm almost sure that I heard my cheek sizzle as it came into contact with the cool, smooth surface. From my position, hidden behind the pillar, I became aware of a minor drama unfolding at the reception desk. Peering round, I saw Uncle Dudley (his face an even more aggressive shade of beetroot than normal) rifling angrily through his wallet before throwing a credit card down onto the desk.

'But I know there are funds available on it,' he was saying, 'I checked the balance myself this morning.'

'It's fine, sir,' the girl behind the desk replied soothingly, 'these things happen from time to time. We recommend that you contact your bank just to make sure nothing untoward has occurred, but nine times out of ten it's only a glitch.'

'I don't do glitches,' growled Uncle Dudley, 'and my bank had better not do them either.'

The girl made a 'there-there' noise and tapped some numbers into a terminal. Uncle Dudley scratched his nose and drummed his fingers on the desk – then the girl smiled.

'That seems to have gone through for you, sir. Here is your card back.'

She ripped a receipt from the machine and handed it to Dudley along with his piece of plastic. He put both in his wallet and turned away. As he did so, he closed his eyes and let out a little sigh.

As soon as he was safely out of sight, I stepped out from behind the pillar and walked over to the bar, visions of a long glass piled high with ice cubes floating tantalisingly through my mind.

'Whatcha drinking, cowboy?' A head popped up from below the counter, making me jump out of my skin.

It was Liam.

'Water to hydrate and then something stronger to dehydrate again,' I said. 'Got anything that would fit the bill?'

Liam grinned and pulled a stainless steel cocktail shaker off a shelf behind him.

'Ever had a *really* good martini?' he asked.

I shook my head.

I'd never had a martini, good or otherwise. They didn't tend to come my way in the staffroom, no matter how much I needed them.

Liam had real difficulty grasping this.

'You've never—' he stuttered. 'You've never – how old are you exactly?'

'Thirty-two,' I admitted.

'Right,' he said, 'then grab yourself a bar stool, throw a bit of Bombay mix down your gob – I mean, throw a bit of Bombay mix down your gob, *madam*, and look forward to an experience that will change your life. Just one question: gin or vodka?'

'Which is the chef recommending tonight?' I asked.

Liam pulled a thoughtful face.

'Well, vodka is more traditional.'

'Go for it then, I'm all for keeping old traditions alive.'

I watched as he threw some ice and a measure of vodka into the shaker.

'I'm going down the James Bond route,' he informed me, putting the top on and mixing vigorously, 'you don't get stirred on my watch.'

He put the shaker down, turned to a large fridge behind him, and picked out a pre-chilled glass. He poured in a small portion of vermouth and rolled it round so that the sides of the glass were coated.

'You don't want too much vermouth,' he said earnestly. 'The trick is to keep it clean, cold and with a kick like a psychotic mule. Now, watch this – it's showtime, baby!'

He produced a tea-strainer and, holding the shaker unfeasibly high, proceeded to pour the contents into the glass with nary a drop spilled. Then he selected a fat green olive from a selection in a little dish behind him and laid it across the elegantly splayed rim of the cocktail glass.

'*Voila*,' he announced. 'There you have the best vodka martini this side of the Alps. Actually, it's the best vodka martini this side of Salford, seeing as I am the Cocktail King in the Greater Manchester Region.'

He puffed his chest out as though he half expected a medal. I took a tentative sip.

Wowsers.

Liam was right – as far as psychotic mules went, it was definitely in the zone.

'So,' said Liam, 'you enjoying your stay?'

I took another sip and, to my surprise, realised that I'd nearly drained the glass.

'Well,' I said, thinking back over recent events, 'let's just say it's been an experience.'

Liam grinned.

'You can say that again,' he said. 'The Santa Lucia – haunt of the mad, bad and dangerous to know . . . and me, of course,' he added modestly.

I put my now empty glass back down on the bar and Liam reached for the vodka, his eyebrows raised. Why not? I thought to myself – I am on holiday.

'So, what brings you here?' I asked. 'Apart from being gifted and talented with the optics, that is.'

'Money,' said Liam bluntly, 'and the hope that I'll run into someone rich and powerful who'll give me a job. I've just finished my degree and the employment market is bleaker than a yeti's bum. Even more so for me because, it may amaze you to learn, growing up in a council house in Moss Side did not give me the connections I need to get on in life.'

'It doesn't surprise me at all,' I replied. 'I teach at a school where a third of our children get free school meals, another third turn up with Skittles in their lunch boxes and the other third don't come in at all.'

But not for long . . .

Liam put down his cocktail shaker and shook his head.

'Sounds familiar,' he said. 'Where I'm from, school is basically a less cool alternative to community service, but I realised that if I got my head down and worked, it was my ticket out. I bet there's kids like that in your school – good for you for not giving up on them.'

He strained the martini into my glass and, feeling a little guilty about the shiny new academy in Newcastle, I raised it to him.

'Well, well done you,' I said, 'if I meet any millionaires, I'll send them your way.'

'Actually, I think you might know one,' Liam said slowly. 'Dudley Westfield.'

'Yes, he's my uncle,' I replied. 'But I don't think he's a millionaire.'

'Really?' Liam sounded genuinely surprised. 'But he's paying for this whole wedding – *and I've seen the tabs*.'

I shrugged.

'Seriously, Liam, I don't understand it either – maybe he won the pools? He's comfortably off, that's for sure, but he's hardly a plutocrat.'

Liam grinned.

'Even so, times are hard. If you see him in a generous mood – handing out money to orphans or patting stray puppies on the head – then remember to give me a mention.'

'Wilco,' I said, taking a sip from my martini and pausing for a moment while it stripped away the lining of my throat, 'but in a place like this, surely millionaires must be a bit like buses – miss one and there'll be another along in a minute?'

Liam laughed, threw a couple of strawberries into a blender.

'In my dreams! Anyway, speaking of your family, Jessica's out there.' He nodded in the direction of the terrace. 'She's been nursing a martini for at least half an hour. I think she might need cheering up.'

'Mission accepted,' I said, sliding off my bar stool and making my way out to the dappled green shade of the terrace.

'May I?' I asked, hovering next to her.

Jess looked up. She seemed utterly astonished to see me.

'Ailsa!' she exclaimed. 'Where did you spring from?'

'The bar,' I said, pulling out the chair and sitting down. 'I was taking a martini masterclass from Liam.'

'As far as martinis are concerned,' said Jess, nodding in approval, 'he is a god who walks among men.'

'The Martini King of Moss Side,' I said.

'Yup,' she said, 'even though I've never been to Moss Side, I'll go along with that.'

There was a pause while we both appreciated Liam's excellence in the field of martini science. Then Jess leaned in across the table and beckoned to me to do the same.

'Well, I'm pleased I've caught up with you. I've got a message.' She looked around, as though she was expecting to see earwiggers hiding behind the potted lemon trees that littered the terrace area.

'A message?' This sounded very cloak-and-dagger. 'Who for?'

Jess nodded and leaned in even further.

'For you, of course. A very important message,' she hissed.

A nasty thought shot through me. It wasn't Nick, was it? Had he given up speaking to me entirely and was using Jess as a go-between?

'Who's it from?' I asked, rather bravely IMO.

'A *man*,' she breathed.

I bit my lip. This did not eliminate Nick.

'It was a man and he had,' Jess paused melodramatically, 'a *message*.'

She made it sound as though James Bond himself had parachuted in with a secret dispatch from Her Majesty's Government.

'Yes,' I said, 'we've already established that.'

My cousin gave a little shiver of excitement and clasped her hands together.

'He's a very special man – and he is very, very much in love with you.'

I did a double take.

'Really?' I frowned and siphoned up a restorative sip of my martini. 'Are you sure?'

It felt like no one had been in love with me for an awfully long time. In fact, before Nick, it had been a good five years since I had been on the receiving end of any attention.

'Surer than sure. In fact,' Jess's smile grew so wide it looked as though her chin might fall off, 'I think he might be your soul angel. He said he really wants to get to know you better.'

I was alarmed.

Then suspicious.

'You haven't been talking to Psychic Serena, have you?' I asked.

Jess shook her head and hoovered up a mouthful of martini.

'No – although now you mention it, Serena did tell me that I am touched by the gift.'

It was a close thing, but I managed not to laugh. Touched by the gift? Just touched, more like.

'It's so romantic,' Jess clasped her hands together. 'Last night, after dinner, I went for a wander by the sea – you know, the rocky bit where we were the other day – and *I wasn't alone*. There was . . .' cue another dramatic pause '. . . a *man*!'

'Yes, yes, yes.' I was becoming impatient.

I was also, however, beginning to feel intrigued. I leaned in over the table and almost knocked myself out on Jess, who was doing exactly the same thing.

'So, this man,' I said, doing my best to sound casual and unconcerned, as though men who said they were in love with me approached my cousins on rocky beaches every day of the year. 'Does he have a name?'

'Ah-*ha*!' said Jess mysteriously.

'Is it someone you know?'

'Ah-*ha*!'

'Is he someone *I* know?'

'Ah-*ha*!' said Jess again.

It was starting to get just a tiny bit irritating.

'Hurry up,' I wriggled in my chair. 'Spill the beans.'

Jess continued: 'I went over to him and sat down next to him.'

Okay, I thought, this means she knows him. She

wouldn't have pitched up next to a complete stranger in a deserted spot.

'And he was looking miserable – and I mean *really* miserable.'

'Oh.' My spirits sank. I wasn't sure I wanted to be admired – even from afar – by someone really miserable. My own life was hardly a bundle of laughs as it was.

'Although he's normally very happy indeed,' added Jess, picking up on my anti-misery stance. 'Really, terribly cheerful – but not in an annoying way – just normal and not depressed or suicidal or—'

I held up my hand.

'Okay. So he's mentally stable. I like that in a man.'

'Anyway, I asked him what was wrong and he said he was just getting over a serious relationship.'

'Really?'

'In fact, he said his heart had been broken. And – what was the word he used? He said it wasn't just broken, it was – "ob" something. Ob – ob—'

'Obscene? Obsessive?'

'Obliterated! That was it.'

'Really? That doesn't sound good. I mean, I know how I feel—'

I hastily corrected myself.

'I mean, I know how *other people* feel when their hearts get broken. Falling in love when you're not over your ex is usually a disaster.'

'No – his heart is – um.' Jess was trying very hard to find a way out of this one. In fact, I could almost hear the cogs grinding away inside her head. 'Well, when I say broken, I mean broken in the sense of *not* being broken. Tricky old language, English.'

'I know,' I agreed, 'and you've only been speaking it since birth. Anyway – go on. This guy with his not-broken broken heart.'

Jess drew her almost invisible blonde brows together into a frown.

'Look, Ailsa, please start taking this seriously. There is a gorgeous chap, here, in this hotel, who fancies the pants off you and – *he wants to meet you. Tomorrow night.* But (and this is really important) you are not to breathe a word to anyone else.'

That was what decided me (not that I'd been particularly stoked by anything else she'd come out with); but this was the icing on the cake – the mozzarella on the thin crust, hand-stretched pizza – the Marmite on the thickly buttered toast – that told me I should say 'no'.

'He's not some sort of weirdo stalker, is he, Jess,' I asked, 'wanting to lure me onto a remote corner of the beach so that my dismembered remains can be found at dawn by an early morning dog walker?'

Jess threw up her hands in exasperation. My concern for my own physical safety was obviously too nit-picky for words.

'No – we've been through all this. He's perfectly normal.'

'How can you be sure – do you know him?'

'Yes – I mean, no – I mean, a little bit.'

'Then how do you know he's not a stalker?'

'Because – because – I just do, okay?'

She took a deep breath.

'Look, if it bothers you that much, I'll come along too.

Not to the actual rendezvous, of course, that would be a bit of a passion killer; but I'll walk over with you and hang around in the background for a bit. Discreetly.'

I took a restorative sip of my martini. It didn't make things any clearer, but it gave me a fuzzy warm feeling in my tummy which was a definite plus.

'Look, I don't want to seem ungrateful, Jess; I mean, obviously you've put a lot of thought into this; but, if I was going to meet him – which in itself doesn't seem like the best idea I've ever heard – why couldn't we just hook up in a bar like normal people?'

Jess looked alarmed.

'No,' she said quickly, 'that won't do at all. No – it has to be out there, under the cedar tree. You know the one – it's down near the ballroom where the wedding ceremony is going to be on Saturday.'

'That's very precise,' I said.

Jess flipped her sun specs up onto her head and looked straight into my eyes. Gone was any flippancy: this was serious.

'Ailsa,' she said, 'I know it sounds weird. Actually, scrub that – I know it sounds totally loopy – but please, *do this* – be there at midnight, tomorrow, under the cedar tree. Really, really – you won't regret it for a moment and it might just change the rest of your life. Do it. Do it for me if you won't do it for yourself.'

I narrowed my eyes.

'Jess, he's not some friend of yours you feel sorry for? It's not someone you've invited to the wedding on the promise that you'll set him up with your cousin? Some sort of sympathy shag?'

I groaned as a thought hit me.

'He's not got a "great personality", has he?'

Jess shook her head vigorously.

'Oh no. Nonononononononono,' she informed me. 'I mean – yes, he *has* got a great personality, but not in that way. He's clever, funny, charming, sexy and hot. Totally hot. Hotter than a flame thrower in the Sahara Desert.'

She paused.

'And he's real – I didn't just dream about him or get him mixed up with someone I read about in a novel.' She said this as though it was something that had happened to her quite a lot. 'You'll do it, won't you?'

I drained my glass. The warm, fuzzy feeling transferred from my tummy to my head. It was the only explanation for what happened next.

'Okay,' I said. 'This is the deal. I'll be there at five to midnight and do a spot of surveillance. If he looks normal, then I'll speak to him but, if he is in any way dodgy – if he turns up wearing a T-shirt saying "my other job is an axe murderer" or anything like that – then you won't see me for dust.'

'Yay!' Jess looked delighted. 'I never thought you'd agree to it in a million years – I wouldn't! Right, I'll go and set it up. Roger and wilco, gold leader!'

And she leaped off her seat and ran away before I could change my mind.

Chapter Ten

The scheduled event that night was cocktails on the terrace. A little card with scalloped edges and swirly gold writing appeared in my room late that afternoon, summoning me to the festivities, and, at about half past six, everyone retired to their rooms to don their glad rags before reconvening to get gently plastered on an empty stomach.

Hoping that Liam would be on shaker duty, I climbed into my black back-up dress and hurried downstairs. The entrance to the bar, though, was packed with Nick's little old ladies, so I decided on a quick detour out of the main entrance and round the side of the building to the rendezvous point. The hotel grounds were more or less deserted – it was too late in the day for golf or swimming and too early for an evening stroll. However, even though the sun was low-ish in the sky, the heat had not abated one jot and I was looking forward to having something with an awful lot of ice in it pushed into my sweaty palms as soon as possible.

I turned the corner that led round to the terrace, doing my best not to let my heels sink into the gravel. There ahead of me were the wedding guests: in particular I could make out Charles, his phone aloft, in the act of taking a photo. I walked on a short distance – and then stopped. Directly in front of me was a flying buttress and, on the other side of that flying buttress, shielded from view, was my Uncle Dudley. How did I know it was my Uncle Dudley?

Because I could hear him.

Even though he was using what, on Planet Dudley, probably passed for an intimate, confidential tone, it was impossible for me not to hear every single syllable.

'No,' he was saying (loudly), 'this isn't good enough. I don't want to talk to you – put the organ grinder on; I said, put the – oh, hello, Margery, how are you? Yes, we're fine. That's right – Tuscany. The wedding is on Saturday so I'll be back in the office first thing next week. Not that I'm taking any real time off, of course – more of a working holiday. Now then, Margery, about this credit—'

There was a pause.

'But that's ridiculous. How long have you been supplying us? Has there ever been a problem before?'

Another short pause.

'Well, I don't care what John says, Margery, you are putting us in a very difficult position.'

There followed a tiny, but very angry, pause.

'Don't be silly, Margery, it's nothing more sinister than cash flow. Now, I can't pay you upfront but by the time your invoice becomes due at the end of the month – what do you mean, the last one is still outstanding? Three months? That can't be right! Margery, listen, we can sort this out – it's just a minor technicality – it's – *Margery*!'

I bit my lip, waited for a decent interval and then crunched my way through the gravel to the other side of the buttress.

'Oh, hello, Uncle Dudley,' I said lightly, as though nothing at all was amiss. 'Lovely evening, isn't it? See you for cocktails?'

And I hurried on round to the terrace without waiting for a reply.

The terrace was heaving by the time I reached it – only not many of the people making it heave were wedding guests. Veronica, wearing a scarily low-cut dress, moved like an avenging angel through the crowd, pouncing on anyone she thought was trying to get their paws on free cocktails; Auntie Sheila was sitting at a table by herself nursing a clear drink in a tall glass that looked rather like neat gin; and Nick? Nick . . . was nowhere to be seen.

I allowed myself to relax a little.

'Sex on the beach?' came a voice behind me. 'Or would you prefer a long, slow, comfortable screw against the wall?'

I turned round and saw Charles grinning at me.

'Sorry,' he said, 'I couldn't help it. Aren't some of these names just ridiculous? I mean, what in the name of God is a Fluffy Duck? Or Salty Dog? It sounds more like an RSPCA convention than a cocktail reception.'

'Long Island Iced Tea,' I said to a nearby waiter, 'and tell Liam not to skimp on the gin.'

'That sounds perfect.' Charles put an empty glass back on the waiter's tray. 'Make it a pair of iced teas. So, how are you, Ailsa? Enjoying your stay? Glad you don't have to rush off home?'

It took me a moment or two to remember the fake ASBO kids.

'No,' I replied, 'everything's sorted and yes, I am enjoying myself – the hotel is amazing.'

'Isn't it?' Charles's gaze swept approvingly round the

gardens – almost as though he had designed them himself. 'I came here on holiday a while back, and when Dudley and Sheila started looking for somewhere suitable for Jessica and Justin's wedding, I immediately recommended it.'

'Did you?' I had a hazy recollection that Sheila and Dudley had themselves been married in the vacinity thirty years earlier – but, as with so much else concerning my family, I could easily have been mistaken.

'Yes,' Charles continued. 'Sheila and Dudley really value my opinions. We spend quite a lot of time together – in fact, you could say that I'm one of the family.'

'Really?' I replied, wondering why Charles was so anxious for me to know the high esteem in which he was held by my flesh-and-bloods.

The cocktails arrived and Charles handed me my glass.

'Cheers!' he said.

'Cheers!' I replied, taking a long and very welcome draught. 'You're friends with Justin as well, aren't you?'

'Oh, yuh.' Charles was quite emphatic on this point. 'I've known him for yonks. In fact, it was me that suggested he came to work for Sidebottom's in the first place.'

'Right.' I'd had no idea that Charles had been so instrumental in bringing Jess and Justin together. He was practically their fairy godmother.

Or father.

Or something.

'Two more of those.' He drained his glass and turned to a waiter who was hovering at a respectful distance. 'Just what the doctor ordered.'

The waiter nodded and buzzed, returning a remarkably

short time later with two more Iced Teas. Goodness, I thought, I could get used to this – teams of servants waiting to cater for my every whim. If it wasn't for Nick doing his fly-in-the-ointment trick, it would be perfect.

'The thing is,' Charles took a sip of his cocktail and then leaned in towards me, 'I do worry about them.'

'About who?'

'Sorry – bit of a leap there, blame the cocktails – Jess and Justin.'

'Really?' I felt my brow furrow into a puzzled frown. 'Why's that?'

'Well, don't you think they're rushing into things? They haven't known each other long.'

I opened my mouth to tell him about Justin being Jess's soul angel, but I quickly changed my mind. It seemed a really weird thing for Charles to want to discuss with someone he'd only just met – even if he did think of himself as family.

'I can't say I've thought about it,' I replied, choosing my words carefully. 'They certainly seem happy enough.'

'That's just it,' Charles glanced over his shoulder and whispered: 'They *seem* happy.'

I frowned; where was he going with this? So, Jess and Justin *seemed* happy – maybe that's because they *were*? Newsflash: soon-to-be-married couple in loved-up bliss shock!

Charles gave an enormous, world-weary sigh.

'Jess is a sweet, sweet girl but, well . . . *Justin*?' He trailed off with a small, sad smile and a shrug of his shoulders.

'Mmmmm,' I replied, deciding Charles's Iced Teas must have loosened his tongue – not to mention affected

126

his brain. 'I'm sure it will be fine, Charles. They've had loads of time to get used to the idea of marriage, and you only have to look at Jess to know how happy she is.'

'But are they?' Charles persisted. 'Are they *really*? Or are they just going through the motions to please Sheila and Dud – and oh, hello there—'

'Charles!' My sister appeared from nowhere and planted a kiss on Charles's cheek. 'I wanted to say how much I enjoyed our round of golf this afternoon.'

'Golf?' I asked. 'When did you take up golf, Kitty?'

My sister waved a half-empty martini glass at me.

'Oh, it's always been a hobby of mine,' she replied airily. 'Gets me out, keeps me fit – and there's always time for a quick drink in the clubhouse bar afterwards – eh, Charles? Such a shame I twisted my wrist on the first hole and couldn't actually play.'

She waggled her left hand at him.

'Ouch!' she said pathetically. 'Anyway, Charles, I was thinking I'd better rest it tomorrow, so why don't you and I try a spot of sightseeing? We could wander through the old town, try out one of the bistros down by the marina, gawp at the yachts and then chill on the beach afterwards? It's going to be hot tomorrow. Really *hot*.'

The implication of 'hot' was unmistakable. Charles ran his finger round the inside of his collar. He gave a slow smile.

'Well, I do have a prior engagement,' he said. 'Dudley's keen to try the golf course up in the mountains and—'

'I think you'll find me keener,' purred Kitty.

'Actually,' I said, 'I think I can see Jess over there. If you'll excuse me—'

And I slipped away before I sprouted hairs, turned green and morphed into an actual gooseberry.

As it happened, I did spot Jess. She was arm in arm with a thin bald man and beckoned me over.

'Ailsa,' she said, pushing Justin forward, 'I don't think I've properly introduced the pair of you. Justin, this is my cousin Ailsa and Ailsa, this is—'

'My fluffy soul angel,' I thought to myself, before saying out loud: 'Good to meet you, Justin. Any news on the baggage handlers? I heard on the grapevine that your folks are stuck back in the UK.'

Justin nodded.

'Sadly, yes. They've tried calling Eurostar and the ferry companies, but everyone's fully booked. Sod's law, really. Never mind.' He flashed a smile at Jess who instantly smiled back. 'I've got my little baby lamb and that's all that matters.'

Jess went all gooey at being called a little baby lamb and kissed him tenderly on the cheek.

'Pop off and get us a couple of mojitos, there's a love,' she said, and we watched as Justin trotted off to do her bidding.

'So,' I sipped at my own drink, 'did you track down my mystery admirer then? Is he up for our moonlit tryst?'

'Actually,' Jess whispered, 'I've not been able to find him yet but I've left a note with reception telling him I need to see him urgently.'

'Oh?' I raised an eyebrow at this piece of information. 'So he's staying at the hotel, is he?'

But before she could reply, the opening bars of 'Barbie Girl' rang out across the terrace.

'Excuse me,' Jess said, and reached into a teeny-tiny evening bag, 'that's my phone.'

She lifted a bubble-gum-pink mobile to her ear.

'Hello?' she said and waited. 'Hello?'

There was another pause.

'Look,' she hissed into the receiver, 'I know there's someone there. You might think that this is funny but it's not, so fuck off before I call the police.'

Then she switched her phone off and threw it into her bag.

'Jess,' I asked, 'are you okay?'

Jess's eyes flashed angrily.

'No, I'm not.' She ran a hand through her hair. 'Bloody hell! I thought I'd be all right in Italy. I didn't think it would happen here!'

She reached out, removed my glass from my encircling fingers, and knocked back a large gulp of LIIT.

'Prank call? Did someone ring and then hang up?'

'No,' Jess drained the glass. 'Whoever it is stays on the line but doesn't say anything. It's horrible, Ailsa – so, so creepy. All I can hear is the static hum of the phone line and the occasional rustle of a person moving and that's it. Whoever it is doesn't even have the courtesy to be something interesting – like a heavy breather. It's just silence and it bloody freaks me out.'

'It's not a bum call, is it? You know, when someone has their phone in their pocket and they don't even know they're dialling you?'

Jess looked longingly at my now empty glass.

'Nope, this is deliberate. It's been going on for, what – a year? Maybe longer? It doesn't normally happen on

129

my mobile; it's more often the landline.'

I was appalled.

'It's been more frequent since Justin and I moved in together,' she said, 'and it only seems to happen when he's out for the evening – isn't that weird? I don't think it's ever happened when we've been in the house together.'

She frowned.

'Except – except once when he wasn't very well and didn't go to football training – as though the person *expected* him not to be there. Oh, Ailsa, it's horrid – I've tried everything: taping the calls, doing ring back, but whoever it is is clever and does that thing where you can't trace the number. I've no way of finding out who it is.'

'Have you told anyone?' I asked.

Jess nodded.

'I told Mum – and Justin, of course – and Justin mentioned it to Charles. Charles suggested going to the police – in fact, he rang them for me, but they said short of putting a tap on the line and tracing the calls, which they wouldn't because there weren't any threats being made, there was nothing we could do.'

'But it's still frightening,' I said, 'and the person doing it knows that. They *want* to upset you, that's the point.'

'I know.' Jess's fragile little body drooped like a fading flower. 'Justin says Charles got really cross with the police, but they stuck to their guns and said it wasn't a police matter.'

'And there's nobody you can think of who would want to freak you out like this?'

Jess shook her head.

'I haven't insulted or upset anyone – at least, not that

I'm aware of; and my friends are all nice people, not creepy stalker-types who'd want to scare the bejaysus out of me on a regular basis.'

'Pleased to hear it,' I said. 'I always find it's best not to have a bunch of psycho crims as your mates.'

'The only thought that's occurred to me,' Jess went on, 'is that it could have something to do with Pop's phone call. What if there *is* a problem with Sidebottom's and someone is trying to get at him through me – a journalist maybe?'

I bit my lip; I didn't want to mention the angry phone call *I* had just overheard.

'It doesn't sound much like journalists,' I replied. 'After all, silent phone calls don't get you very far in terms of column inches.'

I'd meant to soothe her, but Jess looked even more distressed.

'Well, if it's not journalists, then what if it's a proper stalker? What if they've followed me to Italy? And they're here – at the hotel – watching me? What if they try to ruin the wedding? What if—'

'Jess,' I linked my arm through hers and pulled her in close. 'It's going to be fine. No one is going to ruin your wedding. Look, is there anyone here who shouldn't be? Is there anyone you didn't invite but has turned up anyway?'

My cousin shook her head.

'No. We had to cut down the guest list quite considerably when Pops saw how much the whole thing was going to cost. We kept it to family and some of the Sidebottom's crew. I wasn't even allowed to invite my friends. But there's no one here who would do something like this.'

131

'Okay, so if the only people here are ones you can trust, that probably means whoever is responsible for the calls is miles away back in England.'

'I suppose so,' Jess managed a ghost of a smile.

'I know so,' I replied.

'Sorry, Ailsa,' said Jess, 'you must think I'm bonkers. First I get upset because I think Sidebottom's is up the spout, then I tell you about a load of silent phone calls—'

'It's fine, Jess,' I gave her one last squeeze. 'It's all going to be fine.'

'Sorry about the delay,' said Justin, bustling up, 'I had to go to the bar and you wouldn't *believe* the queue; it's packed with those old ladies – the ones on the coach trip – all drinking like a bunch of pissed newts. I feel sorry for that guy with them. Whatsisname – Neil – Nigel—'

'Nick,' said Jess and I simultaneously.

'Nick,' echoed Justin, throwing most of his mojito down his throat in one go. 'Well, I think Nick deserves the MBE for Services to Elderly Ladies with Tattoos Who Go on Coach Tours; and if no such award exists, then I think it should be created especially for him. The man is obviously a saint.'

I looked down at my mojito. I was beginning to feel a little woozy and the thought of siphoning up yet more units of alcohol was less than appealing. Thankfully, Veronica saved the day by clapping her hands together and bellowing in a very loud voice: 'Dinner is served.'

And, without needing to be asked twice, we disappeared into the air-conditioned cool of the dining room.

Chapter Eleven

I have to say that I felt an awful lot better once I'd had something to eat and some of the Long Island Iced Teas had been absorbed. Kitty engineered herself into the spot next to Charles and did everything within her power to attract his attention. This was not carried out with any subtlety or discretion; in fact, if she had tattooed her forehead with the words 'Look at me, Charles, look at me!' she would have been less in-your-face. Charles seemed to be enjoying the attention – at least, he wasn't running wild-eyed and terrified in the opposite direction. I just hoped Kitty knew what she was doing: she liked to think of herself as hard as nails, but I knew that, deep down, the whole Graham scenario had shaken her badly, however much she tried to deny it.

I wondered if I should mention something about the Graham situation to Charles. I felt slightly uneasy, having warned Kitty about not stirring; but, I reasoned, this was completely different. Stirring was something *the rest* of my family did. I merely intervened when necessary in a discreet and helpful way.

After the meal, my sister slipped away to the ladies and I spotted Charles loitering by himself out on the terrace. I went over to have a (discreet and helpful) word but, before I could get a word in, Justin trudged past the bottom of the steps that led down into the gardens, hands in his pockets and a harassed expression on his face.

'Everything all right, mate?' Charles leaned over the low wall that bordered the edge of the terrace.

Justin ground to a halt.

'I'm looking for Jess,' he called. 'There's a wedding emergency and that hideous old bat – I mean Veronica – has gone into a tailspin. I've been dispatched to find the blushing bride. It's about string – or is it twine? I really have no idea; something completely pointless anyway.'

'Oh,' I, too, leaned over the edge of the terrace wall. 'I think I saw her go that way, down towards the old church. Do you want us to help you look?'

'It was only about two minutes ago,' Charles added. 'She was walking fast – she looked as though she was on a bit of a mission – but even so, she can't have gone far.'

Justin ran a hand through his blond hair.

'Thanks, guys,' he said, 'I'd appreciate a couple of extra pairs of eyes. It's probably only Veronica throwing her weight around, but apparently Jess's input is vital.'

Charles and I ran down the steps and then we all three crunched our way along the path. The towering archways of the ruined church loomed darkly ahead of us.

'You know, if Veronica ever gets fed up with arranging weddings, she could probably find work with the CIA interrogating terrorist suspects,' said Charles.

Justin snorted with laughter.

'You're right! Oh God, the woman's hideous,' he said. 'If I didn't know that, after Saturday, I never had to speak to her again, I think I'd kill myself. Or possibly just kill her.'

'You say that like it's a bad thing.' Charles flashed a smile.

'There isn't a jury in the land that would convict me, mate.' Justin looked round, as though he expected Veronica to leap out from behind a pillar crying 'Boo!' 'But I wish she'd give us a break. She's supposed to lift the burden of the wedding from our shoulders, not turn the bride suicidal and the groom into a gibbering wreck.'

We had reached the end of the hotel buildings proper and came to a halt next to the enormous curving double archway that marked the entrance to the ancient church. The arches, like the rest of the church, had been worn away by time and were missing a large chunk of connecting masonry right at the very top, giving them the appearance – to my eye at least – of a broken heart.

'Jess?' Justin called out doubtfully into the gathering gloom. 'Jess? Can you hear me?'

'It's pretty dark now, Justin,' I said. 'I don't think she's likely to be out here by herself. Maybe we should try inside the hotel?'

'Isn't her room somewhere around this end of the building?' Charles pointed to a smart modern extension a few hundred feet away.

Justin shrugged.

'I think so – but I find the whole place a bit of a rabbit warren, I'm afraid. All I can remember is that she's the third floor, fourth room along.'

He pointed at the side of the building and counted along the windows.

'No,' Charles stepped forward and shook his head. 'You're counting from the wrong side. Hers is the fourth room along if you're *in*side; but we're *out*side so you'll need to count the other way.'

'Has she got one window or two?' I asked, peering up at the side of the building and trying to make a contribution to the debate.

'Two,' said Justin, 'plus a balcony with a large flower pot thing on it and – yes – there – that one there. It has to be. Right. Thanks, guys.'

He began to make his way over to a door half hidden by a large lemon tree.

Charles gave a little cough.

'Justin,' he said, 'the light's not on. She either out or asleep. I wouldn't waste your time.'

'Oh bother,' groaned Justin. 'I hadn't thought of that.'

'No,' I stared up at Jess's window. 'Someone *is* in there – the curtain just moved. Look!'

We stood on the path, our necks craning backwards, and watched as the curtain twitched again and the unmistakable sound of Jess's laughter drifted through the open French window.

But there was another noise, too: the low hum of a deeper, male voice.

I began to feel a little uncomfortable.

Jess laughed again and the person with her – undeniably a man – spoke again.

'Look,' I gestured in the direction of the bar. 'I might just – I think I might sort of—'

But the others stayed exactly where they were.

More talking – and another peal of laughter from Jess.

'I'm sure it's all perfectly innocent,' I said – and immediately wished I hadn't.

What if Justin *did* think it was perfectly innocent? Had I gone and put a load of toxic ideas into his head? I glanced at his face, or as much of his face as I could see, given that it was pretty dark: he was not happy. His eyes were big and bulgy and his mouth was twisted into a painful grimace.

Above us, there was the rustle of curtains and a light was switched on. Silhouetted against the window as though they were projected up on a cinema screen, were the unmistakable images of Jess wearing her long evening gown – and someone else.

I didn't want to look. I really, really didn't want to look. But my eyes were fixed to that window as surely as if they'd been spot welded there.

The man said something which I couldn't make out, and then came the clincher: with a squeal of delight, Jess threw her arms round him and kissed him – I could not tell whether on his lips or cheek – just as a gust of wind forced its way in through the French windows. The curtains blew wildly for a moment or two inside the room and the scene vanished.

There was a cry. A heart-rending sound of abject misery that made my blood run cold.

For a moment I thought it was an injured creature calling out from somewhere in the hotel gardens, but I looked round and saw Justin, his eyes fixed on the window, his mouth open and his breath coming in heavy gasps.

'Justin,' I said, 'Justin – are you all right?'

'Of course he's not all right.' Charles turned on me angrily. 'Didn't you see that . . . that . . . that . . .'

Words failed him. Instinctively I sprang to Jessica's defence.

'You don't know what was going on,' I cried. 'You weren't in the room.'

Jess was sweet and loyal – she wouldn't cheat on her angel soulmate.

Would she?

'I – I – I –' Justin was still staring up at the window.

Charles slipped an arm round his shoulders.

'Come on, mate,' he said, 'let's go and get a drink in you. You're in shock.'

'No,' Justin shook himself as though he was coming out of a trance. 'No, I need to speak to her. Jessica! Jessi-*ca*!'

He broke free from Charles and headed towards the door. We ran after him.

'Not now, mate – not now. Don't go barging in there,' Charles said, 'whatever it is they're up to, you don't want to see it. It will only make things worse. Keep your dignity and confront her later.'

Charles's continued insistence that Jess was up to no good was starting to make me feel cross as well as deeply confused.

'They might not be up to anything, Charles,' I said. 'You've got as much idea as I have who that man was – you don't have a clue why he was there – you don't know *anything*.'

Justin turned to me, his face a study in tragic despair.

'She kissed him,' he said simply. 'I saw her – she kissed him.'

'I know, Justin,' I replied as soothingly as I could, 'but there could be a perfectly rational explanation.'

'Yes,' Charles stuck his oar in once more. 'Like she's having an affair.'

'No!' Frustration rose within me. 'Not that sort of rational explanation.'

'But she kissed him!'

'I know! But it could have been – it could have been,' I prayed for inspiration to strike, 'Uncle Dudley!'

Inspiration was obviously having an off-day. The man in the room patently hadn't been Uncle Dudley: Uncle Dud's shadow would have looked like Jabba the Hutt's, whereas whoever-he-was-in-there's had been lean and athletic.

'Ailsa,' said Charles crossly, 'leave this to me. I'm sure you mean well, but this isn't helping.'

'She kissed him!' said Justin again to no one in particular. 'She. Kissed. Him.'

'I know, mate,' Charles re-established his arm round his friend's shoulders. 'I saw it too. Now come with me, I'm going to buy you a good strong drink.'

They turned and began to make their way back towards the main area of the hotel.

For a second or two, I watched them go; but the feeling that something was seriously, fundamentally wrong was so overwhelming that I picked up my skirts and sprinted after them, almost twisting my ankle as my heels sank into the soft gravel.

'Justin,' I panted, 'think about it! Don't you reckon you'd be better off talking to Jess? I'm sure it's all very straightforward and, once you know that for certain, everything will go back to normal.'

Justin looked woefully from me to Charles and back again.

'I think he's seen enough for the time being,' Charles answered for his friend, 'and my priority is Justin. He's had a nasty shock and he needs a drink. I'll take it from here, thank you.'

And, leaving me standing alone in the gathering gloom, they shuffled off together. As they went, I caught Charles's voice saying: 'I can't believe it, mate. I never thought she'd do anything like this – not to you.'

And they were swallowed up by the gathering gloom.

Chapter Twelve

Feeling very upset, I climbed the stairs to my room.

It wasn't right.

None of it.

It was all very, very not right.

Something was nagging away in my brain – something I couldn't put my finger on, no matter how hard I tried.

I paused, key card in hand, ready to swipe and let myself in; however, at the last second I changed my mind and swung round on my heel: I was going to see Jess. Whatever the sight that might greet me on my arrival, it was better that I found her before Justin and Charles did. If she could give me a straightforward, non-cheaty explanation for what I had just seen, great – and if not, she needed to know that her moment of indiscretion had not been acted out in private.

Justin was right about one thing – the hotel was a rabbit warren. It took me ages to negotiate the miles of corridors and flights of stairs that led to Jess's wing, and, by the time I reached her landing and remembered to count the doors from the right-hand side to left, rather than the other way round, I was completely puffed out. I raised my hand and knocked gently on her door.

'Jess?' I whispered. 'Jess? It's Ailsa. Are you in there?'

I pressed my ear to the door and listened – but there was nothing.

'Jess,' I said again, slightly louder, 'if you are in there, can you open the door – it's really important.'

I paused, but the silence was undisturbed.

What else could I do? She was obviously not at home.

After a quick sweep of the main public areas of the hotel – including the bar where I saw Justin and Charles, sitting in a corner nursing large glasses of whisky – I dragged myself back to my room and got ready for bed. Not that I felt in the least like sleeping, but hey, it was almost midnight and my options were pretty limited.

I opened the French windows (the smell of Kitty's cigarette smoke still lingered on the curtains), slipped into my jim-jams and curled up on the bed. A funny, squishy feeling settled itself in my tummy and the beginning of a headache started to make its presence felt around my temples.

I closed my eyes.

What the hell was going on?

Was Jess really seeing another man? Was she intending to marry Justin on Saturday but keep this other guy revved up on the side?

Did it have anything to do with those creepy silent phone calls?

And Charles – there was *something* going on with Charles. Something so obvious that I couldn't actually see it; something so simple that I couldn't understand it – but all the same, I knew that it was *there*.

The mind boggled.

I opened my eyes. What was that out in the corridor? Footsteps? Voices?

I lifted my head and listened, but the sound died away

142

and all was quiet again: it was probably Nick returning to his room after an evening dodging the lascivious attentions of the little old ladies. Or worse, Nick coming up to his room to do a bit of web surfing and find a set of divorce lawyers in Edinburgh so that he could start proceedings the moment he got back onto Scottish soil.

Thoughts of Nick and our impending divorce thumped round my brain, trumping even my fears for Jess and Justin. I lay there for goodness only knows how long, staring into space and thinking about the future. Despite my fresh start in Newcastle, it all felt terribly bleak. The idea of severing my connection permanently with Nick had a crushing, choking quality to it that was so intense that, in the end, I couldn't bear it any longer. Notwithstanding the fact that I was wearing nothing but a pair of pink gingham pyjama shorts and a white strappy top, I locked my French windows, slipped my feet into my sandals and padded softly down the stairs and out into the gardens beyond.

I have no idea how long I walked, or quite where I wandered to, but I crunched my way along one of the labyrinthine gravel paths until I found a bench under a blossom-laden tree and sat myself down with my feet on the seat, hugging my knees tightly against my chest.

Scenes from my life with Nick flashed through my brain like a series of photographic stills: Nick kissing me; the cocoon-like intensity of our first weeks together; the pair of us running through the driving rain and up the steps to the grey registry office; the illicit thrill of our secret wedding; me hurrying home after school to play house with my gorgeous man. Then came the other side: the shouting, the pain, the stinging words – until finally I saw myself, tears running down my face, grabbing my handbag and running out of the flat into the freezing damp of a March evening. And after that . . .

Nothing.

Nothing but the stars up above, the sound of the sea and the damp, earthy smell of a hotel garden on a warm Italian summer's night.

Slowly – very slowly – the crushing sensation in my chest began to ease and I felt my muscles start to relax. I focused hard on the rhythmic sound of the sea as the waves washed up and down the beach, then, from somewhere nearby, an owl hooted. Life goes on, it seemed to say – there will always be the sea, there will always be stars; the world will keep turning from darkness into light and back again: keep the faith.

I tiptoed back down the corridor to my room (which, like all hotel corridors the world over, was much more loud and creaky at night than it ever was during the day) and, as I approached my door, I was astonished to see that it was open.

Was this Kitty? I wondered. Availing herself of my facilities once again? Or was it something (or even someone) else?

I gave the door a little push.

'Hello?' I called softly, sticking my nose – but nothing else – into the room. 'Kitty? Is that you?'

There was no response.

I stepped over the threshold, walked the few paces into the centre of the room and stopped dead.

Cushions from the armchairs were strewn all over the floor; a heap of towels had been dumped next to the minibar and, most alarmingly of all, my bedclothes seemed to have been dragged from the mattress and piled up unceremoniously under the window (apart from one lone sheet which was – bizarrely – tied to the end of my antique wrought-iron bedstead).

For a moment I wondered if I'd taken the wrong turning somewhere and ended up in the 'Hit by a Bomb' room, or the 'Turned Over by Burglars' suite.

The hairs on the back of my neck stood to attention: *oh my God! Burglars?*

Had somebody broken in while I'd been getting my head together down in the garden?

I glanced at the French windows that I had been so careful to lock and saw that they were wide open and the curtains were blowing in the sea breeze.

My heart leaped into my mouth and every atom of my being began screaming as loudly as it could for me to get the hell out of there.

I took a step backwards.

Nothing moved, leaped out at me or threatened me with an offensive weapon. (This, I decided, was a plus.)

I took another step.

And a third.

And—

'Argh!'

I slipped on a cushion which the intruder had randomly redistributed across the floor, and fell down smack on my bottom.

'Argh!' came an answering cry from the other side of

145

my bed and a head – presumably that of my burglar – popped up above the level of the mattress.

I screamed again.

So did the burglar.

And I was about to scream for a third time when, backing as quickly as I could out of the room, I missed the door and struck the light switch with my shoulder.

'Holy Nora, Justin,' I cried, as I recognised the terrified face staring at me over the edge of my bed, 'what the hell are you doing in here?'

I paused and peered again, more closely.

'You *are* Justin, aren't you?'

The last time I had seen Justin, he had been in the bar with Charles, looking upset but reasonably normal. Now, however, he looked as though he'd been buried, dug up and then chewed by badgers: his hair was all over the place, his shirt was ripped and something that might have been lipstick but was more likely to be blood was smeared over his trousers – and he looked just as shocked to see me as I did him.

'Is this your room?' He was aghast.

'Of course it's my room.'

Justin crawled out from behind the bed and staggered to his feet.

'I'm sorry,' he said, 'I had no idea. I saw the door was ajar and came in. Did you know you'd left your room open?'

I threw the armchair seat cushions back where they belonged and then sank heavily down on top of them.

'The lock's faulty. In fact, my room is starting to feel

146

like a drop-in centre for waifs and strays. But what are you doing wandering round at gawd knows what time of night? I thought Charles was looking after you?'

'Oh,' Justin sounded bewildered. 'Is it late? I've no idea. It's all become rather a blur.'

'It's about as late as it can get before it starts being early again.'

Justin sank down weakly in the other armchair. He looked less like a thrusting young captain of industry and more like an apprehensive rag doll.

'I'm trying to find Jess. I *have* to speak to her,' he said. 'Charles kept telling me not to, so I waited until he went to bed.'

'I absolutely agree that you need to talk to Jess,' I said, 'but maybe you should try looking in a place you'd be likely to find her – like her room, for example?'

'The thing is,' he said, staring doggedly at his feet, 'I can't.'

I yawned and rubbed my eyes.

'Justin,' I said, 'you're not making any sense. Of course you can go to Jess's room. You know where it is: fourth door along—'

'No I can't,' he cut me off, a note of desperation creeping into his voice. 'I can't *go* anywhere: Dudley's looking for me.'

'But that's okay,' I replied soothingly. 'You never know, he might be able to tell you where you can find Jess. You should try asking him.'

Anything so that you bugger off out of my room and leave me in peace, I added silently.

Justin shivered.

147

'I can't,' he said, 'it's – oh, fuckadoodle doo, it's the wedding – it's off.'

Up until that point, I'd thought it would be impossible for me to be any more shocked than I had been already that evening.

But I was wrong.

So totally wrong that I could have got a PhD in Wrongness from Professor Wrong at the University of Ineptitude.

'I'm sorry, Justin,' I said, 'I don't think I heard you properly; for a moment there, I thought you said that the wedding was off.'

Justin let out a low moan.

'It is,' he replied.

'But why?'

He looked as though he might be about to burst into tears and eyed the minibar longingly. I opened it and handed him a whisky miniature; he downed it in one.

'Justin,' I said firmly, 'I know you've had a nasty shock but, seriously, you can't call the wedding off without speaking to Jess first.'

'It's not like that,' he muttered, 'you don't understand.'

I began to feel a little cross. My own emotional situation, the mixture of drinks I'd sunk that night and my lack of sleep were beginning to take their toll.

'I understand only too well, Justin: my cousin is about to have her heart broken by you, her soul angel, just because – oh, I don't know – you saw her taking a fly out of the eye of the room service man. Now stop all this nonsense about calling off the wedding, get over to her room and find out what is really going on.'

Justin looked even more tragic than before.

'But I keep telling you, *I can't go and find he*! Haven't you been listening? And it's not me who called the wedding off, it's Dudley – and he's after me.' He gestured to the carnage around the room. 'I'm really sorry about the mess; I was trying to escape from him out your window.'

He said this as though it was a perfectly rational thing to be doing.

'I was down in the bar and, even though time was getting on, Charles suggested I call my brother. I went upstairs and I was just standing in the corridor making the call when Dudley overheard me on the phone saying I thought Jess was having an affair, and he went mental. And when I say mental, I mean totally, psychotically bonkers. Thankfully, I managed to escape his clutches, but then he started yelling for Roberto the manager – and now he's got the entire hotel staff out looking for me. There's a doorman guarding the lift and another one at the bottom of the stairs – I had no idea how I was going to escape until I spotted your door open and decided that the thing to do would be to come in here, tie the ends of the sheets together and abseil down the outside of the building.'

'Are you serious?'

'Deadly serious – only there weren't enough sheets. So, I thought about throwing the cushions and the towels out of the window and jumping down on top of them, but as we're quite high up here, it might have been a bit dangerous.'

A bit?

I felt as though I'd just walked into the plot of a Marx Brothers' film.

'And you were just going to run off into the night,' I

cried, 'and abandon Jess and all your wedding plans? I mean, bugger Uncle Dudley, this is your life we're talking about – were you really going to throw all that away?'

Justin opened his mouth to reply, but before he could get any words out of his mouth, there was a pounding noise on the door.

'Chilmark!' bellowed a deep, male voice. 'Chilmark – are you in there?'

Justin gave a gurgle and dived back under the bed. I, however, was made of sterner stuff and went to open the door.

I immediately regretted it.

Outside stood Uncle Dudley, holding a large golf club and looking about as happy as a hippo that has just spotted an embarrassing picture of himself that some other hippopotami have put up on Facebook for a laugh.

However, worse – much worse – than his expression was what he was wearing. He must have been on his way to bed when he encountered Justin on the phone and he was clad in slippers and a silk dressing gown that was stretched almost to breaking point over his enormous pot belly. Every time he breathed, the knot in the belt strained that little bit more. It was surely only a matter of time . . .

I gave an involuntary gasp of horror.

'Where is he?' cried Dudley. 'Where the bloody hell is he? I'm going to rip him limb from limb. I'm going to pull his legs off. I'm going to make sure he never walks again.'

For a moment or two I was unable to reply. My eyes were drawn irresistibly to the inadequate coverage offered by his dressing gown. It was even more terrifying than his threats of retribution.

'Where is he?' demanded Uncle Dudley again, his bushy eyebrows almost exploding off his forehead. 'One of the staff said he was seen heading this way.'

'I – I—'

He went to barge past me, but I stood my ground. This wasn't just a matter of Dudley pushing me around, this was crime prevention: even though Justin was behaving like a total fathead, I didn't want him dispatched to meet his maker in my hotel room – and Dudley looked as though he was in full-on dispatching mode.

'I'm sorry, Uncle Dudley,' I said firmly, 'but you can't go round walking into other people's rooms.'

These were brave words.

Uncle Dudley drew himself up to his full height – which I think right then was about eleven foot ten.

'I,' he said in a growl that resonated up through the floorboards, 'am paying for this room, young lady.'

I tried drawing myself up to my full height too – although at only five foot four, I couldn't really compete.

'That still doesn't give you the right to come in uninvited.'

Uncle Dudley looked as though he was about to explode – and the belt on his dressing gown strained ominously.

'Why?' he thundered. 'What have you got to hide?'

Just your next victim – I mean, future son-in-law . . .

He craned his big, fat neck over the top of my head and did his best to peer in through the doorway. Short of jumping up and down and waving my arms around (which I did consider), my options were pretty limited.

'What the heck has been going on here?' he cried. 'It looks like someone's ransacked the place.'

151

Oh, bloody hell – think! Think!

'I – ah – I went out for five minutes and left the balcony windows open,' I lied. 'I think I might have been burgled.'

Uncle Dudley's eyes narrowed and he brandished the golf club menacingly. I shrank back into the room.

'Oh you do, do you?'

'I wouldn't worry – they don't seem to have taken anything. I'll sort it out, you can go back to bed.'

'Don't be ridiculous, they might still be in there – they might be,' Uncle Dudley's eyes gleamed: he liked a challenge, 'armed and dangerous.'

Before I could stop him, he had pushed past me and was on the hunt for lurking miscreants. It was surely only a matter of seconds before Justin was dragged out by the ear from under the bed and subjected to summary justice at the hands of Uncle Dud.

Holy crap! What could I do?

Uncle Dudley headed first for the wardrobe. When that proved to be a burglar-free zone, he then slammed the doors shut and went into the bathroom, where he peered behind the shower curtain and had a good look under the sink. I had only zepto-seconds before he made his way over to the bed—

'Uncle Dudley,' I went and stood between the bed and my uncle. 'There's something you need to know.'

'Yeeees?' One hairy eyebrow arched upwards.

I took a deep breath and plunged in headlong. Inspiration had struck – but it was far from being her finest moment.

'I wasn't telling the truth about the burglar.' I paused.

'I'm sorry, but this mess was – um – the bedclothes and cushions and things – this was me.'

Uncle Dudley stopped. He stared at me so hard his eyes went all bulgy and boggly.

'You,' he said at last, 'you did this? Why?'

'I did it,' I replied, feeling the fire of embarrassment creeping across my face, 'because I was here with – um – *someone.*'

Uncle Dudley blinked.

'Someone?' he echoed.

Oh God, I was going to have to spell it out for him.

'Um, someone,' I scratched the back of my neck awkwardly. 'A man. And – ah – he suggested that we should perhaps – um – try a few – um – *things*. Have you read *Fifty Shades of Grey*, Uncle Dudley?'

I pointed at the sheet still knotted round the bedpost, my cheeks hotter than an industrial blast furnace. Uncle Dudley narrowed his eyes in thought.

'I think Sheila may have done,' he replied, 'it's not really my cup of tea. I prefer to go to bed with a copy of *Fermenting Weekly.*'

For a moment, I felt sorry for Auntie Sheila, before realising that *Fermenting Weekly* probably saved her an awful lot of hassle in the bedroom department.

I mean – Uncle *Dudley*? You just wouldn't, would you?

For the first time since entering the room, my uncle lowered the golf club.

He took a few deep breaths; his cheeks faded from puce to sunset red and, for a moment – for one glorious, exultant moment – I actually thought I was going to get away with it.

But no – even as my blood pressure was returning to normal and my jangled nerves were beginning to heave a sigh of relief, a muffled groan wafted out from under the bed.

Until that moment, I'd always assumed that the phrase 'his ears pricked up' was purely metaphorical. However, I am as sure as I can possibly be that Uncle Dud's ears did, literally, move as the sound reached them. In fact, I wouldn't have been surprised if they'd rotated full circle like a pair of radar dishes.

'What,' he said, 'was that?'

I closed my eyes.

If Uncle Dud found Justin in my room, it would not only seal Justin's fate, it would place me squarely in the firing line too, as a person who fooled around with her cousin's fiancé.

Ex-fiancé.

Whatever.

I swallowed.

'It's – ah – it's the man I was trying a few things with. He's – um – well, I left him under the bed.'

'Is he all right?' For a moment something that looked like genuine concern flashed across Dudley's face. 'He sounds like he's in pain.'

'Yeah, well, he might be. You know that *Fifty Shades* stuff . . .'

Inside I was dying. Okay, so I might have saved Justin's sorry arse – but what if Dudley told Auntie Sheila about the bondage stuff? What if Auntie Sheila got over ten years of silence and told Mum and Dad I tied men to bedposts? What if—

Don't think about it. Just don't think about it.

'Anyway, he's under the bed and it's probably getting a bit uncomfortable for him. So, if you wouldn't mind, I should probably be – um – getting back to it . . .?'

I pointed in the direction of the door. Uncle Dudley looked quite relieved to be going and, golf club in hand, lumbered out into the corridor.

'Good luck with finding Justin,' I called, bolting the door after him. 'If I see him, I'll deck him one on your behalf.'

I waited, my back pressed against the bolted door, as Uncle Dudley's heavy footsteps retreated down the passageway. Then I walked over to the bed, grabbed Justin by the collar and hauled him out. He had turned whiter than an arctic fox in a bucket of bleach.

'Sorry,' he whispered, 'sorrysorrysorrysorry. I tried to stay quiet but I got cramp in my foot – but thank you, Ailsa, thank you. I owe you.'

'Too right you owe me,' I replied, folding my arms, 'now will you please get out of my room and go and sort things out with Jess before Uncle Dudley comes back, finds you here and decides that you and I are having a sado-masochistic affair.'

'I can't leave,' he warbled, 'I just can't. He'll hunt me down like a dog.'

The temptation to say 'good, bring it on' was almost overwhelming, but I resisted.

'Then what's the plan?' I asked. 'You can't spend the rest of your life hiding under my bed.'

'I think I could,' countered Justin. 'I could sleep on the floor and live off nuts and Toblerones and whiskies from

155

the minibar until I grow a beard as big as Brian Blessed's so that no one recognises me and—'

'Oh, don't be absurd. This is serious, Justin.'

'I *am* serious. If I can't marry Jess then my life is over.'

He picked up a cushion and threw it moodily into a chair.

'Your life is not over,' I reminded him, 'but if you don't go and find Jess then your relationship with her certainly will be.'

Justin threw his hands in the air.

'What if Charles is right and she's having an affair?'

'I wish you'd stop bringing Charles into this,' I said. 'What's he got against Jess anyway?'

Justin's eyes flashed angrily. It was the first bit of spirit I'd seen in him all evening.

'Charles is a really good friend,' he replied, 'to both of us.'

'I'm sure he is,' I replied, 'but this isn't his life we're talking about here.'

There was a pause.

'Justin,' I said softly, 'do you love Jess? I mean, really, truly, soul-of-my-soul-type love her?'

Justin hesitated. He looked down at his feet and ran his hand through his unsmoothable hair.

I held my breath. An awful lot depended on what he was about to say next.

'Yes,' he nodded his head sadly. 'Yes, I do.'

'Do you love her more than you respect Charles's opinion?'

Justin rubbed his face with his hands; he looked exhausted.

'It doesn't make any difference what I think, Ailsa. As far as Dudley is concerned, I'm dead meat. He overheard me suggesting that his precious, beloved, beautiful, only daughter is a cheat. Do you think that he's about to start slapping me on the back and talking about "simple misunderstandings"? No! He says the wedding's off; and if Dudley says the wedding's off then it's off, and I don't see it ever being back on again.'

He was right; Dudley was infamous for his steely single-mindedness. Even so, I wasn't about to admit defeat.

'You're going to have to trust Jess,' I said. 'You're going to have to tell her what's happened this evening and, if she loves you – which I'm sure she does – you'll work something out.'

Justin gave a huge sigh that seemed to come all the way up from his Italian leather loafers.

'God, I hope you're right. But doesn't that bring us back to where we started? I *can't* speak to her with Dudley out there on patrol. How do I even find out where she is? How . . .? Oh, God, it's a helluva mess.'

He shuddered.

'Stay here,' I said, offering him another whisky miniature. 'I've got an idea.'

'Don't leave me!' he cried. 'What if Dudley comes back? What if he still has that golf club with him?'

'I'm only going next door,' I said. 'If it makes you feel any better you can hide under the bed again.'

And, thinking that I would rather have root canal work than knock on his door, I went to make a nocturnal call on Nick.

Chapter Thirteen

It would be an understatement to say that Nick was
unhappy about being disturbed. I don't think he had been
asleep (it would have been hard to kip with Uncle Dudley
doing his impression of the Wrath of God Descending
next door) but he had certainly been lying in the dark
with the light off. The thought flashed into my brain – *had
he been thinking about me? About us?* But I quickly pushed it
away again. I needed to put all my energies into Jess and
Justin, rather than dwelling on the lost cause that was me
and Nick.

'I hope this isn't going to take long,' he muttered as
we trailed back next door. 'I've got to be up in five hours
to say coherent things to a bunch of half-deaf old ladies
about Giotto frescoes.'

A faint scrabbling noise came from under the bed.

'What's that?' Nick looked at me in alarm. 'Rats?'

'An asylum seeker,' I replied, before calling to Justin:
'You can come out; the coast is clear.'

Slowly, Justin's face appeared, then his shoulders, then
finally the rest of his body. He stood up and brushed the
dust off his trousers.

'Justin, Nick,' I did the introductions. 'Nick, Justin.
Justin is the man who is going – was going – whatever – to
marry my cousin Jess; and Nick is, well, Nick is—'

'I'm an old friend of Ailsa's,' Nick said tactfully,

extending a cautious hand in Justin's direction. 'What can I do for you?'

'Can I,' asked Justin doubtfully, 'can I trust you?'

'Yes,' I said instinctively, 'you can. Both of us.'

Nick's eyes met mine. He looked taken aback.

I do trust you. I thought, the realisation hitting me with the clarity and shock of a cold bucket of water. *I trust you with anything at all in the whole wide world – apart from my heart.*

And my money.

Then Justin and I both started talking at once.

'Uncle Dudley—'

'Wants to kill me—'

'He tried to make a rope with the bed sheets, only it didn't work—'

'I've got to get away—'

Nick held his hands up.

'One at a time – please!' he begged. 'It's late and I've had quite a lot to deal with recently.'

Justin sank down onto the bed.

'Dudley thinks I've slandered Jess,' he intoned mournfully. 'And there's a chance that she might be having an affair. In short, I've lost my wife-to-be, my job and my self-respect. My life is pretty much over.'

'I'm sorry, mate,' replied Nick. 'I'm really, really sorry, but I don't see how I can help.'

Justin groaned and fell onto the bed, rolling himself up into a little foetal-shaped ball. It was going to be up to me to deliver the explanations.

'We need to get him out of the hotel,' I said to Nick. 'Uncle Dudley wants to kill him and has already been in here with a golf club looking for him. It occurred to me that he could climb down that fire escape between our balconies. Do you reckon it would be easier to reach from your side, Nick?'

Nick sat down in one of the chairs and rubbed his eyes. He looked absolutely knackered.

'I'm not going to pretend that I understand what's going on, but surely, even if Justin gets out of the hotel, there are still a million things to consider. Where is he going to go, for a start? You can't have him roaming the streets of San Antonio in the middle of the night. And what about poor Jess? Someone needs to find her and tell her what's been happening. Believe me, having the love of your life vanish into the night with no idea if you'll ever see them again is heart-wrenchingly traumatic.'

The meaning of his words was all too obvious.

My chest gave an encore of its clenching trick and a lump appeared in my throat.

'Nick, you know you were going to look for a room in town?' I did my best to disguise the wobble in my voice. 'Well, did you find anything? It doesn't have to be palatial, just somewhere Justin can set up camp for the night.'

Nick fiddled with a stray thread on his bathrobe.

'There was only one place and I'm afraid it looked as though it had hot and cold running bedbugs; everywhere else was fully booked. I didn't take it – hence I'm still next door.'

'I'll try it,' said Justin. 'It sounds perfect. Well, actually it doesn't; but it's got to be better than being beaten to death by Dudley. Where is it?'

160

'It's the Casa Penseroso, opposite the church in the market square. I'll write the address down for you.'

'Thank you,' Justin went to hug Nick, thought better of it and then patted him on the back. 'Thank you thank you thank you! You have just saved my life!'

Nick scribbled something on a sheet of hotel notepaper, folded it in half and handed it over. Justin pocketed it.

'Ailsa,' he turned to me, 'would you – would you speak to Jess for me? Try and explain what's happened and get her to give you her side of the story? She trusts you – she was saying only yesterday how wonderful it was to have you here.'

I almost smiled.

'All right. First thing in the morning. I promise.'

'Now show me this fire escape of which I have heard so much,' he said, 'and I'll be on my way.'

'I'll come and find you tomorrow and let you know what Jess has to say for herself,' I told him.

Justin nodded. He was almost on the verge of looking perky.

But Fate, yet again, went and stuck her size nines into the mix. Just as I thought we were home and dry, someone hammered on my door. In fact, the word 'hammering' doesn't do justice to the sound levels generated – I'm almost sure I saw actual blast-waves fan out across the room.

'Chilmark!' came a voice that sounded horribly like Uncle Dudley. 'I know you're in there. Roberto saw you!'

Justin's jovial expression vanished. He gave a whimper and pawed at my duvet cover.

'Come out and face me like a man,' Uncle Dudley

demanded. 'And if you don't, I shall have no alternative but to break down the door!'

A voice I recognised as Roberto's raised itself in angry protest at this suggestion.

'Oh, right you are, Roberto,' Uncle Dudley sounded disappointed. 'What I meant to say was: come out and face me like a man, and if you don't, I shall have no alternative but to ask the staff to use the skeleton keys!'

I ran across to the French windows, dragging Justin with me.

'Look,' I said, pointing down to his right, 'there's the fire escape. It's on this side of Nick's balcony.'

Justin, pale of face and unsteady of foot, joined me. He didn't look in any fit state to be walking and breathing at the same time, let alone shimmying down fire escapes.

'But it's miles away,' he said, peering uncertainly over the railings of the balcony, 'I can't jump that far.'

'Let me in!' roared Uncle Dudley from the corridor. 'I've given you every opportunity to do the decent thing, Chilmark, and I've had enough. I'm going to count to five. One . . .'

Justin leaned over the balcony and did his best to reach the fire escape. It was tantalisingly about a foot and a half beyond his reach.

'Two!' cried my uncle. I could almost hear his foot scraping along the ground and smell the smoke pouring from his nostrils.

'Look,' Nick was behind me. I could feel the warmth of his body hovering just inches from my bare skin. 'Grab hold of the wisteria, Justin. It's strong enough to take your weight.'

He paused.

'I think.'

'Three!'

Justin covered his face with his hands.

'Holy cripes,' he moaned, 'I don't like heights.'

'I think it's fair to say you'll like what Dudley has in mind for you even less,' observed Nick succinctly. 'Want a leg-up over the railings?'

'Four!'

With another whimper, Justin allowed himself to be hoisted up over the railings and lowered down onto the wisteria branch.

'For shit's sake, open your eyes,' I told him, 'you may not want to look at the ground, but it'll be a lot better than missing your footing and having it rushing towards you at great speed.'

'Five!'

There was the rattle of keys on the landing outside and the sound of the lock opening. I glanced back at Justin – he had a drop of a foot or so down onto the fire escape but was still clinging onto the wisteria for dear life. The door opened and, at the same moment, I reached over and gave the branch an almighty shake, sending him crashing down right on target. Then there came the sound of footsteps and—

Smack!

A hand inserted itself into the small of my back and shunted me into a warm, solid chest. At exactly the same moment, a pair of lips suctioned themselves onto mine and some fingers ran themselves through my hair. I felt as though I had jumped into the bath and thrown a toaster in after me: shocks spasmed up my spine and along my limbs; sparks flew from my fingertips and my mouth ignited. The fireworks that had happened when Nick's hand had touched my arm outside the ruined church were nothing compared to this.

Nothing.

Right then, you could have run the entire National Grid off me.

As if by magic, the lump in my throat vanished and the knot in my chest unclenched . . .

. . . and the sound of footsteps, including two extra-heavy ones I assumed belonged to my uncle, made their way into the room.

'Where,' asked my relative-by-marriage in a voice that made the glasses in the minibar rattle, 'is that miserable worm?'

Nick's lips removed themselves from mine.

'Excuse me,' he said in an icy tone, 'just what do you think you are doing?'

There was a short silence.

'I'm not sure,' I said, 'but I think you just kissed me.'

'Not you,' said Nick, '*you*. Dudley Westfield or whatever the hell your name is.'

'I . . .' Uncle Dud sounded confused, I don't think anyone had spoken to him like that before. 'I'm looking for that insect, Chilmark. He was in here, I know he was. This man,' he pointed at Roberto, 'says he saw him creeping around about an hour ago. Don't try to deny it.'

'I *do* bloody deny it,' said Nick firmly, 'and what's more I demand an apology. This is an invasion of privacy.'

Uncle Dudley's mouth opened and closed a couple of times, giving him the appearance of an overweight, belligerent goldfish.

With the last of the shocks still reverberating up and down my legs, I pulled away from Nick's embrace.

'This is Nick Bertolini,' I said, 'and he is *not* Justin. In fact, if you'd like to think back to our last conversation, Uncle Dudley, you'll remember me telling you that there was a man with whom I was busy doing – ah – well – you know – *that*.'

The idea of the pair of us re-enacting some of the hotter bits of *Fifty Shades* was enough to turn my face redder than a builder's bum in a heatwave. However, to add a bit of verisimilitude to my story, I slid my hand round Nick's waist and kissed him again; feeling, as I did so, his lips part to meet mine and another fifty thousand volts shudder through my nervous system.

Well, at least that's what I told myself I was doing. I mean, I wouldn't have kissed Nick voluntarily, would I?

Uncle Dudley's face softened. He went from looking like an overweight goldfish that was about to spontaneously combust, to one that was just very angry indeed. He muttered something to Roberto and they both turned in the direction of the door.

Then he stopped.

'What's that?' he asked, pointing to a sheet of paper on the floor that I hadn't noticed until that moment.

He had the advantage that he was standing about a foot away from it, whereas I was still out on the balcony.

'I don't know,' I said, edging slowly back into the room.

I had no idea what it was or what information it might

contain; in fact, I couldn't remember ever having seen it before – but something told me that Uncle Dudley shouldn't be getting his hands on it.

Dudley went to pick it up but, with a gymnastic leap that would have impressed Louis Smith, I got in first. I hid it behind my back just as his big, paw-like hand descended.

'It's mine,' I said firmly. 'Nothing you need to worry about.'

'Now, go,' urged Nick, coming up behind me and putting his arm round my waist.

'Walk out the door,' I added, continuing in the same seventies camp disco vein.

Uncle Dudley swallowed hard. He knew something was going on and, fair play to him, he was right – but he could prove nothing.

Just to add a bit *more* verisimilitude to the proceedings, I slid my free hand into Nick's. It was warm and firm and comforting and fitted my own perfectly.

Uncle Dudley's eyes skittered from me to Nick and back again. Roberto gave a respectful cough.

'Perhaps sir would like to try looking for the-a young-a gentleman somewhere else?' he suggested. 'When I said I saw Mr Chilmark enter the room, I may well have been mistaken. The rooms along this corridor all have identical doors. It can be tricky.'

Uncle Dudley sighed, ran his eye round the room once more and then lumbered off, followed by Roberto.

As soon as the door closed behind them, I felt Nick's hand wriggle its way out of mine and his arm detach itself from my waist.

'Is this why you always refused to introduce me to your

family?' he asked slowly. 'Some sort of hereditary madness? A genetic issue?'

I picked one of the pillows off the floor and threw it at him.

'I'm not related to either Justin or Uncle Dudley,' I reminded him, 'at least, not by blood.'

I paused. Really, once you'd said that, you'd said everything: certainly as far as my female relatives were concerned, he wasn't too far off the mark. Nick's expression remained utterly inscrutable but he shrugged.

'It's okay, I already know you're nuts,' he said simply, 'and I wouldn't have it any other way.'

I opened my mouth to protest at his use of the present tense but Nick held out his hand for the piece of paper.

'Did Justin drop this?' he asked, as I passed it over. It was covered with numbers and had the name 'Justin Chilmark' emblazoned across the top.

I stooped down to collect another cushion.

'It's got his name on it. Why? What is it?'

'Well, I'm no expert, but I'd say it's the printout of some sort of account – only there's a lot of money going out and not much going in. Look – the amounts leaving the account aren't big in themselves, but there are an awful lot of them.'

I walked over and did my best to focus on the sheet, but I was too tired to make any sense of it.

'It's probably to do with his Italian distribution deal. Put it back on the minibar, Nick,' I said, stifling a yawn, 'I'll have a butcher's at it in the morning.'

'I hope for his sake it's not his current account,' he said

and stopped before changing tack. 'Ailsa, do you think he's right? Is the wedding off?'

I paused before committing myself but, despite the events of the evening, my instincts were firm.

'No,' I said, 'Jess thinks he's the bee's knees, the dog's pyjamas and the cat's underpants all rolled into one. They are genuinely crazy about each other. Vomit-inducingly crazy.'

I began to pick up the scattered bedclothes. If the procession of random people through my bedroom had finally ended, I intended to try and get some sleep in the not too distant future.

'Although, having said that, if she's heard he thinks she's been cheating on him, I reckon she's likely to punch him in the face before she does any kissing and making up,' I continued. 'Maybe it would be better if the first move towards reconciliation came from someone she trusts.'

'Like you.'

I heaved my sheets back onto the bed and began smoothing them out.

'Yes, but not right now, I think we all need some sleep.'

Suddenly, out of nowhere, I felt a wrenching, gut-churning sense of loss. The thought that, not so long ago, the ideas of 'Nick' and 'Bed' had been more or less interchangeable in my mind tore through me and I felt achingly alone.

I hauled the duvet back onto the mattress and shook it down.

'Would you like me to go and check up on Justin now?' said Nick. 'He doesn't look like the sort of bloke who should be left to his own devices at one o'clock in the morning in a foreign country. I could track him down and make sure he's safely stowed away at the hotel. I might even take the precaution of sharing a room with him – if that's not going to start another batch of ridiculous rumours among your nearest and dearest.'

I sat down on the bed and kicked my shoes off. It was the end of an unnecessarily long day.

'Would you really?' I was touched. 'I'd be very, very grateful.'

'It's fine.' Nick hesitated by the door. 'Shall I see you tomorrow?'

'If I don't see you first,' I threw back. 'And, Nick, thank you. For everything.'

The faintest hint of a smile flickered across Nick's mouth.

'No worries,' he said, 'it's fun – or it would be if there wasn't so much at stake.'

Nick opened the door and was about to step into the corridor when, quicker than it took my mind to process the fact that there was someone outside, Charles materialised in the centre of the room.

'Will people,' I forgot my fatigue and felt quite annoyed, 'please stop coming in here uninvited? This is *my* room and *I* want to go to sleep.'

Charles didn't seem bothered that I was cross. Instead, he smiled one of his ingratiating smiles, revealing a greater number of perfect teeth than I would have thought it possible for one human to keep inside a normal-sized mouth. However, his smile didn't seem to be echoed in his eyes. Nick must have sensed something, because he made his way back over from the door and hovered halfway between us.

'Well?' I said.

'I just wondered if there was any news?' Charles's voice was smooth and easy, like honey flowing over hot buttered toast. 'No one knows where Jess is; I can't find Sheila; and Dudley looks as though he's about to keel over with apoplexy at any moment – but I saw your light on and thought I'd pop in for a minute. Have you heard anything?'

'No,' I said, hoping I didn't sound as though I was lying.

Then Charles noticed Nick for the first time – or at least pretended to, given that Nick had been standing in full view since he'd entered the room. He held out his hand and Nick shook it.

'Nick Bertolini,' said Nick.

'Charles,' drawled the other, 'Charles Chapman. I'm on the board at Sidebottom's.'

This was clearly meant to impress Nick – and quite possibly intimidate him as well.

'Good for you,' replied Nick, in a voice that was almost – but not quite – sarcastic.

Charles shot him a sideways look, before relaxing back into his MO of effortless superiority.

'Isn't it an awful state of affairs?' Charles went on. 'I mean, how will this affect Justin's position in the company – not to mention the family? Quite a catastrophe all round.'

'*If* your interpretation of events is correct,' I said, folding my arms defensively in front of me. '*If* Jessica is having an affair.'

'Which we can't know for certain, because no one has spoken to Jessica,' Nick finished off my thoughts perfectly.

Charles rocked back on his heels and smiled again. Another teeth-only effort.

'Well,' he said pleasantly, 'it's late. I'd better let you get on. Nice to meet you, Mr Bertolini. What line of work did you say you were in again?'

'I didn't,' replied Nick. 'You'll see yourself out, won't you?'

'Yes, of course,' replied Charles, slipping through the door and closing it quietly behind him.

As soon as it had shut, Nick ran his hand through his perennially untidy hair.

'Who the hell was that?' he asked.

I yawned. Across the room, my bed was calling loudly to me and I didn't have the strength to resist its siren voice for much longer.

'He's a boardroom crony of Uncle Dud's who's being pursued by my sister, God help him,' I replied.

'Kitty? The scary one who looks exactly like you?' said Nick.

'No, she doesn't.' I was indignant: my entire existence was spent trying to be as unlike my family as possible. 'Kitty and I have absolutely *nothing* in common – looks or otherwise.'

''Course you don't,' Nick's face relaxed into a grin. 'I only said it to wind you up.'

I narrowed my eyes and gave him a Hard Stare.

'So, if he's after Kitty,' Nick continued, 'what's the story with him and Jess?'

I continued to stare at him, but this time in puzzlement.

'What do you mean, "him and Jess"? Jess is with Justin – or she will be, when all this has been sorted out.'

'Well, I think someone should mention that to Charles.'

'What?'

'Don't tell me you haven't noticed? He's all over Jess like a cheap suit: a hand here, another hand there – on her shoulder, her waist, her arm – all lingering just that little bit too long. And if he's not touching her, he's staring at her.'

I shook my head. I couldn't process this just now.

'Don't be silly, Nick. He's an old family friend: a slightly odd one, maybe, but, as we've already established my family are a bunch of loopers, it stands to reason that they'll get on with other people who are equally weird.'

I gave another, truly enormous yawn.

'Go away,' I said, 'and let me get some kip. Or I might go mad through sleep deprivation and kill someone – like you.'

'Seeing as you asked so nicely.' Nick opened the door, glanced both ways down the corridor – casing the joint for sneaky brewery executives, marauding uncles and renegade bridegrooms – and stepped outside. 'Sleep well.'

And he closed the door behind him, leaving me alone with the last echoes of his kiss flickering round my body.

Chapter Fourteen

Almost the next thing I was aware of was coming to with my body splayed across my mattress, my cheek on a wet patch of pillow where I had been dribbling, and the first grey fingers of dawn winding themselves in through the undrawn curtains at the French windows. My feet were cold and my neck was stiff and, even though I tucked the former in under the duvet, and tossed and turned and did my best to get back to the deep and dreamless, it was impossible: the birds were singing away with gusto and memories of the night before began poking and prodding my brain into wakefulness.

Suddenly, I sat up in bed, eyes wide open.

Jess! I'd promised Justin I'd talk to Jess.

I blinked at the clock: it was still only half-past sparrow fart, but I wanted to get to her before anyone else did.

I threw back the duvet, hopped over the few cushions and towels still littering the floor and pulled on some clothes. Then I went downstairs in search of my cousin.

The foyer was deserted apart from a couple of night porters staring glassy-eyed at a telly behind the reception desk. It was the replay of a football match and they didn't blink as I made my way across the marble floor, helped myself to coffee from a lovely Gaggia machine in the corner and took my cup out into the garden.

Night was fading fast. Indigo clouds streaked across the

horizon, and an arc of gold over in the east showed where the sun would shortly be putting in an appearance; the gravel beneath my feet was damp with dew and, annoyingly, the birds didn't seem half so loud once you got outside.

Bastards. Did they do it on purpose?

I crunched my way along the little path that led towards Jess's end of the hotel. I intended to scan the windows to see if there were any signs of life inside her room and, if she too was up to greet the dawn, go and speak to her. Wrapped up in what I was going to say, I rounded a corner and saw, seated on a bench ahead of me, a crumpled and bedraggled-looking figure.

'Jess?' I enquired softly.

The figure lifted its head.

From my earliest memories, Jess had always been immaculate – the sort of child to whom dirt was alien. She was always dressed in the loveliest clothes Auntie Sheila could find and I seemed to remember some sort of debate as to whether or not she should to be allowed to join the Brownies, because it would mean her having to *wear the same as other girls*.

But not today.

The girl on the bench had rats' nest hair, a grubby gown and mascara tracks making their way relentlessly down her cheeks. It was fair to say that she bore only a passing resemblance to my cousin.

'Sod off, Ailsa,' she said, in a voice that spoke of utter exhaustion rather than annoyance. 'Please, just sod off and leave me alone.'

I crunched over to her.

'No,' I said, sitting down on the bench too, 'I won't.'

174

Jess hung her head once again and stared at her shoes. Beautiful, high-heeled, strappy sandals that probably cost more than I earned in a month, but which were now dirty and scuffed, the toenails peeping through the leather showing more than a few scrapes and chips in their varnish.

For a moment there was silence.

'Did you see him last night?' asked Jess at last, lifting her head and staring hard into the distance.

'Justin?' I replied. 'Yes, I did.'

Jess plucked at one of the ruffles on her grubby gown.

'I guessed as much. Roberto told Daddy he'd gone into room A-one-one-three – and I know that's yours. So tell me – what happened? What did he say about me?'

Her voice was high and brittle.

'He didn't plan to pitch up in my room – he saw the door was open and dived in. Your dad was after him,' I replied.

There was another, even more uncomfortable silence.

'Justin saw – I mean *we* – me, Charles and Justin – saw someone in your room last night. I'm sorry, Jess, we weren't prying; we just happened to be outside and you had the light on and, well, let's just say it didn't leave an awful lot to the imagination. Justin was gutted.'

Jess didn't move, but her body stiffened.

'Jess,' I said softly, 'I don't have a clue what went on in there last night, but I don't for one moment believe that you would cheat on Justin.'

Jess turned to look at me. I swear there were sparks flashing from her eyes.

'Then why doesn't Justin think that too? Why did he call off the wedding? Why did he simply assume the worst?'

'He didn't call off the wedding,' I replied. 'When I saw him last night he wasn't in any sort of state to be making decisions like that.'

The sparks vanished and Jess's brow furrowed with despair.

'But he still thought the worst of me, didn't he? He believed I'd do that to him! Oh God – how could he? He's not my soul angel any longer! In fact, I hate him for not trusting me. Do you hear that? IhatehimIhatehimIHATEHIM!'

Then her face crumpled and her bottom lip began to wobble.

'I hate him,' she wailed, 'but he's also lovely and perfect and sooooooooooooooooo wonderful. I hate – I hate, I lo–ve hiiiiiiiiiiiiiim.'

Painful, shuddering gasps shook her tiny frame. As far as poor Jess was concerned, this was the utter and wretched end of the road. However, from my point of view, it was some of the best news I'd heard in a long while.

'He loves you too, Jess.'

Jess paused in the middle of one her huge, hiccoughing in-breaths.

'But he-he-he-he-he-he-he-he-he-he—' she stammered, as a tear the size of a five-pence piece squeezed itself out of the corner of her eye, trickled down her cheek and splashed onto her hand.

'No,' I repeated, 'he loves you.'

'How-how-how-how-how-how-how-how-how-how—'

'How do I know?' I interpreted. 'Because I asked him, and he told me.'

'And you – and you – and you—'

'And I believe him? Yes, I do, actually.'

Jess gulped back a few more monster tears and stared at me.

'But – but – but—'

'But he was shocked, he got drunk, your father overheard him on the phone to his brother and it all kicked off. Nick,' at the mention of the name, the ghost of an electric shock trembled down my spine, 'Nick and I helped him get out of the hotel using the fire escape, but I promised him I'd come and speak to you first thing to let you know he loves you and to find out what was really going on.'

Jess gave an enormous gulping swallow and wiped the back of her hand across her eyes.

'So-so where is he?'

'At the Casa Penseroso in town,' I said. 'It's a place Nick found when – well, never mind. Nick gave him the address and he's gone to ground there. In fact, Nick followed him over last night to check he was okay.'

Jess put her face in her hands. For a moment I thought she was going to start crying again.

'Thank God,' she mumbled. 'Oh, thank God. I just thought – I assumed – Justin and I were over. '

She lifted her head and yawned. She opened her mouth until her entire face was consumed by it; then she rubbed her eyes.

'How much sleep did you get?' I asked.

'None.' Jess shook her head. 'I was way too upset. When I found out about Justin I may have got the teensiest bit hysterical, and Mum called this odious little doctor from the local hospital who wanted to have me sedated – but I ran away, and I've spent most of the night out here. There's a sort of boat hut thing, down by the beach. I went and hid in it for a few hours. I did try to nod off there, but every time I closed my eyes, all I could see was Justin packing his bags and getting a cab to the airport and it made me cryyyyyyyyyyyyyyyyyyy even more!'

There was another gulping, hiccoughing intake of breath.

I reached out and hugged her.

'Justin isn't going anywhere,' I told her, 'apart from back to the Santa Lucia as soon as we get this sorted out. Why don't you just tell me what was going on last night, then I'll go and tell *him* and we can draw a line under the whole thing once and for all?'

Jess sniffed. Then she bit her lip and looked up at me. There was something steely and determined in those baby-blue eyes.

'I know this is going to sound dodgy,' she said, 'but I can't.'

'You can't what?' I asked.

'I can't tell you what was going on last night.'

'Why not?'

Jess paused.

'Because if I tell you, then you'll know,' she replied.

'Yes,' I nodded my head encouragingly, 'and when I know and I tell Justin so that *he* knows, we can get this show back on the road.'

'But you *can't* know,' said Jess, 'that's the point – *you* can't know so I can't tell you.'

'But you have to,' I said, conscious that we were starting to go round in circles.

A little breeze floated through the garden and Jess gave a violent shiver.

'Would you like me to take you back upstairs?' I asked. 'I'll get room service to bring up some hot chocolate and toast – to warm you up properly?'

Jess gave a brave smile.

'No thanks,' she said, 'a hot shower and a change of clothes are in order – I don't want to frighten the horses – and then I'm going to find Justin and tell him the thing that I can't tell you. I just hope he'll believe me.'

Her already pale face went even paler than before. Virtually transparent, in fact.

'You don't think – you don't think he'll have changed his mind about marrying me, do you?' she asked.

I grinned.

'I think he's more worried it's the other way round.'

An answering smile twitched at the edges of Jess's mouth.

'Well, if you're sure,' she said, heaving herself off the bench.

'You can trust me,' I told her, 'I'm family.'

'And bloody lucky I am to have you.' She reached down and pecked a kiss on my cheek. 'See you soon. I'll let you know how I get on.'

A couple of hours later, I made my way into the dining room, scanning it for signs of intelligent life – or, if none of that was available, for signs of my family. Squirrelled away in a corner was Kitty, tucking into the fullest of full Englishes. I decided to do the sisterly thing and join her.

'Hello,' I said, indicating an empty chair on the opposite side of her table, 'is this seat taken?'

'What?' Kitty's gaze snapped back from the middle distance and focused upon me. I may have been wrong,

179

but I think she jumped – I'm sure her bottom lifted a good few millimetres off her chair.

'This chair,' I repeated, 'is anyone sitting here?'

Kitty rolled her eyes.

'All right,' she replied grudgingly, 'if you must.'

In Kitty-speak, this was a warm and heartfelt invitation to join her.

'So,' I said, smiling gratefully at a waitress who had materialised silently by my side with a fresh pot of coffee and a second cup, 'what are your plans for today? Looks like it's going to be another scorcher.'

'Oh?' Kitty replied, blinking a couple of times. 'Oh right. Yes. Today. It is indeed today. Yes.'

I frowned.

'Are you all right?' I asked. 'Or have you been at my minibar again?'

'For goodness' sake,' Kitty muttered, stuffing a combination of egg and bacon into her mouth, 'don't start. If you're going to be annoying, go and sit at another table.'

Then, as though she was under the influence of a very powerful spell, she flipped her gaze back to the middle distance. So intense and trancelike was this stare that I began to wonder if it wasn't a hangover so much as an unscheduled lobotomy that was causing her problems. I followed the line of her sight to try and work out what it was that was exerting such a magnetic hold over her, but there was nothing, apart from an ugly, renaissance-style painting of an obese cherub. However, just at the point when I'd decided she must have finally cracked, a smile crept over her features. A slightly woolly, goofy smile – and I knew immediately what was up.

'You're in love,' I said.

Kitty didn't react, instead she glanced down at the table and popped half a fried tomato into her mouth. The evidence was stacking up: ever since adolescence, the big indicator that Kitty had fallen head over stiletto heels for someone was the fact that she immediately started stuffing her face. To be honest, it said a lot about her relationship with Graham that she was currently as thin as I had ever known her. *She* put this eating frenzy down to nervous energy causing an increase in her metabolic rate; I put it down simply to her being a weirdo.

'I said you're in love,' I repeated.

Kitty's expression changed. It was a look which, on anyone else, would have made them look coy and bashful, but on Kitty just made her slightly less scary.

'What makes you say that?' she mumbled through a mouthful of tomato-y mush.

I grinned, pouring myself a cup of coffee.

'Can I have a cigarette?' I asked.

My sister stopped looking bashful and frowned.

'You don't smoke,' she replied.

'I know,' I said, 'but can I have a ciggie?'

Kitty scowled. She knew when she'd been outmanoeuvred.

'I've given up,' she announced loftily.

'I knew it!' I cried triumphantly, helping myself to a slice of toast from a rack on the table and watching as Kitty took two. 'I bloody knew it! You fancy someone.'

Kitty bit into her toast.

'Might do,' she replied indistinctly.

Even though I had a pretty good idea of who her latest victim was, I wasn't going to waste the opportunity of

181

getting her to admit it herself. 'Is it someone here? Or did Graham spend some of his hard-earned cash and fly out here to woo you back?'

Kitty's face turned bright scarlet. You'd have got a similar effect if you'd placed a chameleon on top of a postbox.

'Graham is dead to me,' she announced, 'deader than a cremated doornail. More history than the Battle of Hastings. More over than spandex.'

'So?' I was agog.

'It's just – it's just – someone I've seen around, that's all. Political lesbian activities have been stepped down. Now bugger off and mind your own business.'

'Is it one of Justin's friends?' I continued innocently.

Kitty didn't reply.

'One of the other guests?' I was enjoying this. 'Go on, you can tell me; I am your sister, after all. Your only sister. Oh, hello, Charles,' I added, as the man in question walked past on his way to the hot buffett.

Kitty, caught in the act of trying to swallow a hash brown, made a strange strangulated noise as though she was trying to gulp down a live frog.

'It's Charles, isn't it?' I whispered happily. 'Charles, Charles, Charles, Charles, Charles.'

Kitty looked away and fiddled with the tablecloth.

'It might be,' she said, before blushing a little, 'but, like I said, this is nothing to do with you and – yes, Charles, of course you can sit here. I think Ailsa was just leaving.'

'No,' I replied, 'I'm fine for a few more minutes yet.'

Charles, a plate of scrambled eggs in one hand, pulled up the chair next to mine and smiled a smile so dazzling they could have used it to signal across the galaxy and contact alien civilisations. I checked his eyes – but once again there was no warmth in their blue depths. It all felt – I don't know – a bit predatory.

'How are you today, Charles?' Kitty glowed visibly in his direction.

'Really good,' replied Charles before a thought struck him, 'at least – really good apart from being desperately worried about Jessica and Justin, of course.'

'Of course,' I said pointedly. 'Is there any news?'

Charles shook his head sadly and forked up a mouthful of egg.

'Not yet,' he said, 'but I don't see how the wedding can go ahead now – not after what's just happened.'

'Why?' interjected Kitty, sniffing a good story from ten paces. 'What has happened?'

Charles sighed again.

'Jess was seen kissing someone who wasn't Justin—'

I cut him off.

'No, Charles – *you* think Jess was seen kissing someone who wasn't Justin and you've immediately leaped to all sorts of conclusions. I still reckon there is an entirely innocent explanation.'

Charles put his knife and fork down.

'Really, Ailsa, it would be better for everyone if you kept your opinions to yourself. After all, it's not as though you are close to either of them, is it?'

Miaow!

'Perhaps Jess and I haven't always been bosom buddies,' I retorted, 'but I care an awful lot about her and I'm not prepared to judge her without hearing her side of the story first. You seem desperate to convince everyone that their relationship is dead in the water.'

Charles gave me a glare that could have stripped wallpaper at fifty paces. It was a good job I'd grown up with Kitty as my older sister, or it might have unsettled me. As it was, the feeling – yet again – that Charles was not quite what he should be, shot through me.

'Anyway,' the glare vanished and Charles turned back to Kitty. 'Back to other matters. I was speaking to Roberto just now and he told me the hotel arrange boat trips out to the islands in the bay. Very secluded, some of them. Very . . . private.'

'Sounds fabulous,' I stuck my oar in, 'count me in.'

They pointedly ignored me and Kitty considered his offer for a moment or two.

'That sounds amazing,' she purred, 'when were you thinking of?'

Charles's smile switched from 'brilliant and dazzling' to 'lazy and seductive'.

'I'm entirely at your disposal,' he said.

There was something in his tone that made this sound very suggestive indeed. Kitty's eyes twinkled and she opened her mouth to reply.

'Kitty,' I said loudly, pushing my chair back and standing up, 'you know that thing we have to do. The thing.'

Kitty blinked up at me, uncomprehending.

'The really important thing,' I replied, tugging at her reluctant hand, 'the really, really important thing that we have to do *right now.*'

Kitty turned to Charles.

'I'm sorry,' she said, 'my sister seems to be having a nervous breakdown. Please excuse us.'

184

Charles shrugged and helped himself to the last slice of toast from the rack.

'Be my guest,' he replied between chews, 'just let me know about the boat trip.'

Kitty flashed a smile in his direction before allowing me to march her off to the ladies' toilets.

'This had better be good,' she growled, 'this had better be bloody good.'

I took a deep breath and lowered my voice.

'Kitty,' I said in what I hoped was a serious, level tone, 'this thing you've got – with Charles – I don't think it's a good idea.'

It was Kitty's turn to raise an eyebrow.

'Oh really?' she queried. 'And who asked you? Last time I checked, I didn't need my baby sister's permission before I started spending time with someone.'

'But it's not spending time, is it?' I sensed doom around me but pressed on regardless. 'It's a trip to an island. Just the pair of you. I mean, things might happen.'

'Ten points for observation,' she replied. 'And, seeing as I am well over the age of consent and this is not Victorian Britain, what's your problem?'

I bit my lip. What could I say? That he seemed determined to think the worst of Jess while at the same time going on about how much she meant to him? That he didn't smile properly? That Nick didn't like him?

'He's in business,' I said at last, 'with Uncle Dudley. He might not be very nice.'

Kitty's eyes blazed.

'I'm not bothered about *nice*,' she cried. 'In fact, from where I'm standing, nice doesn't come into it: he's bloody hot. Frankly, I don't care if he's one of Uncle Dud's cronies – he's young, he's fit and he's on a collision course with my libido and, as far as I'm concerned, that's that.'

Then she turned on her heel and walked away.

And, to be fair, I can't say I blamed her.

I washed my hands and then left the loos, crossing the foyer just as the girl on the reception desk (who had replaced the football-watching night porters) called me over.

'Message from the veterinary surgery in town,' she said, passing a piece of paper over, 'they want you to ring them as soon as possible.'

Suddenly I forgot Charles and my heart lurched with anxiety – Arthur? Had he taken a turn for the worse? Had he succumbed to an unexpected but terminal illness? With my fingers trembling, I hooked my phone out of the bag and dialled.

'*Buon giorno! Sant'Antonio veterinari; parlando Giulia.*'

Even though I knew (of course) that I was in Italy, somehow this rush of speedy Italian so early in the morning took me by surprise and I found myself replying in loud, deliberate English.

'Hello, this is Ailsa Stuart – Arthur's . . .' I hesitated, the desire to say 'mother' was almost overwhelming.

The receptionist switched immediately to fluent English.

'Hello, Signorina Stuart, this is Giulia. How are you today?'

Oh, sleep deprived, confused and totally bewildered.

'Fine, great, never been better. You wanted me to ring?'

'Yes. Just to tell you that Arthur's paw is much better

and he will be ready for collection this morning. What time would be convenient for you to pick him up?'

I had to pause while my mind readjusted itself from a doggy death-bed scenario to something not as unhappy but far more complicated.

'The thing is,' I began, hoping that a plan or an idea or something would begin to form in my mind as I spoke, 'the thing is, I'm staying at a hotel at the moment and they're not very fond of the guests having pets.'

Actually, that wasn't strictly true – I was pretty certain some 'pets' were welcome. I had seen more than one furry, beribboned little face peeping out of an oversized handbag. Arthur, however, was a completely different kettle of Bonios.

'This is fine,' the receptionist replied, 'we understand your situation is a bit difficult. I have the phone number here for some very nice kennels where he can stay.'

'Oh,' I said, the image of row upon row of wire cages filled with barking, circling mutts filling my guilt-ridden mind.

'They are good – but is not cheap,' she continued.

'Ah,' I said slowly.

Row upon row of *expensive* wire cages, etc., etc.

It was not a happy thought.

'I am sorry, Signorina Stuart,' Giulia did sound genuinely sorry, 'but Arthur cannot remain here. He is a healthy dog and we need the accommodations for our patients who are sick.'

'I know,' I said, 'I understand.'

There was a pause.

'If you are unable to look after Arthur yourself

'– and we do understand that your situation puts you in difficulties – there are charities who might take him in,' Giulia continued. 'I can ring them for you. They will try to rehome him.'

I bit my lip.

I didn't want him to go to a charity and I didn't want them to rehome him. And if they couldn't rehome him – well, frankly, I didn't want to know what we were talking about there.

'I don't suppose there has been any progress in finding his owners?' I asked – even though I already knew the answer to my question.

'I'm sorry, Signorina Stuart,' came the expected reply, 'Signor Valencio, the vet, he has been drawing the blanks.'

I hesitated.

What choice did I have?

'I'll come and fetch him,' I said. 'How about eleven-ish?'

'Perfect,' replied Giulia. 'The vet will be free, so he can sign Arthur off for you and talk to you a little about caring for a dog long-term.'

Long-term?

'Well, I, I mean,' I began – but Giulia cut me off.

'We will see you at eleven,' she said brightly, 'or a little earlier if you can. It looks like there is a storm heading our way. You do not want to be caught walking back to the hotel in the rains.'

Indeed I did not.

'Eleven then. Or before.'

And I put my mobile away and walked back up to my room wondering how on earth I was going to ace this one.

Chapter Fifteen

At about ten o'clock there was a gentle tapping on my door. Opening it, I was surprised to see Jess standing there.

'I thought you were off to find Justin,' I said. 'What's the matter?'

Jess bit her lip.

'I'm scared,' she said. 'What if he's changed his mind and doesn't want me any more? What if he doesn't believe me?'

'And what if he really loves you and you miss out on marrying your big fluffy soulmate—'

'Soul angel – he's my soul angel. It's a completely different thing.'

'All right, your soul angel – just because you're too frightened to go and see him?' I put on my best teacherly voice. 'And what if that means you have to spend the rest of your life alone with nothing but sixteen cats for company?'

'Not cats; I'm allergic to cats.'

'Well, whatever – cats, dogs, the shopping channel – the point is, you won't be with Justin. Whatever Physic Serena says about his name supposedly beginning with "K".'

'Will you come with me?' Jess's eyes were as huge and pleading as I had ever seen them. 'Into town, I mean – hold my hand, moral support – that sort of thing?'

How could I refuse?

'All right,' I said, 'you're on. And, actually, if you don't mind, you can do me a bit of a favour while we're at it. Can you keep a secret, Jess?'

'Ooooh!' Jess's expression changed from 'tragic' to 'intrigued'. 'What is it?'

'Well,' I replied, 'you know that dog that isn't mine? Well, there might have been a slight change of plan . . .'

Jess and I made our way through the arched gateway of the hotel and along the winding streets of the little medieval town in silence. She had a lot on her mind, as did I: not least about how I was going to smuggle an unwelcome and very boisterous dog into a top-class hotel.

The cool of the early morning had long since evaporated and the air draped itself around us: hot, heavy and humid. Out towards the mountains, towering pillars of cloud were starting to build. At the moment, they were white and fluffy, but something told me that it wouldn't take long for them to develop into something darker and much more threatening.

As we entered the vet's surgery, Arthur was being led down the corridor from his sleeping quarters by Giulia. As soon as he saw me, he gave an excited little bark and my heart melted. God, I must be a real meanie to have ever countenanced the thought of not picking him up.

Giulia handed me the lead and I bent down to pet my newfound responsibility. His tail thumped loudly on the lino and his tongue covered my hands in doggy drool as I cuddled him.

It felt great.

'I did one last check with the local police this morning,'

the vet leaned over the counter and tapped at the computer keyboard, 'but there have been no dogs reported missing in the area. However, they said they will keep Arthur's details online for a while longer. Would you like me to pass them your contact information, or would you like the entry on their website to stay as it is, with our phone number and address?'

I extricated my face from a particularly enthusiastic doggy snuffle.

'Would you mind if we kept things as they are?' I replied.

The vet grinned and nodded.

'Fine. We will let you know if anyone contacts us – with the utmost discretion, of course. Now, on to the next thing. If you have now decided you are a dog person after all and you want to take Arthur back to Britain, you will have to start thinking about quarantine procedures, and I'm afraid it's not a simple process.'

A heavy, uneasy feeling lodged itself in the pit of my stomach. Of course I had known that if I chose to take Arthur home, it wasn't simply going to be a matter of buying an extra ticket for the flight and picking up a few tins of Pedigree Chum. But quarantine – that was six whole months. In a cage. Being looked after by customs people.

It didn't seem fair.

'Do you think he would be easy to rehome over here?' I asked, putting Arthur down on the floor.

The vet crouched down and tickled him behind the ears. Arthur rolled over and waggled his legs in the air. He was clearly in doggy heaven.

'Well, he's an intelligent, amusing, pedigree animal

– I'm sure someone would want to have him. But if not . . .'
He let his voice trail away pointedly.

'I'll give you some time to think about it,' he went on,
'meanwhile, here are the cross-border animal regulations
for the United Kingdom. Let me know what you decide to
do, and we will help in any way we can.'

'Thanks,' I said, pocketing the sheaf of papers.

We dealt with the small matter of the bill, then the vet
handed me a plastic bowl and a small bag of dog food.

'Compliments of the house,' he said, 'have a good day.'

Jess and I walked out of the surgery, Arthur gambolling
around our feet like a week-old lamb.

'Can I take him?' she asked.

I handed over the reins (or rather, the lead) and she
tried her best to navigate through the town square while
an overexcited Arthur did *his* best to tie us both up in
knots.

'He's very cute,' she said, stopping for the umpteenth
time to tickle him under the chin. 'Do you really think
you'll take him back to Scotland with you?'

'I don't know,' I replied, trying to ignore the lead weight
that settled on my heart whenever the idea of Arthur's
long-term future was mentioned. 'It would be a big ask for
him to have to spend months and months in quarantine.
Plus, I'd be looking at renting a house rather than a flat
so that he would have a garden to play in, and that would
be expensive – and what would he do while I was out at
school during the day?'

'But he's such a lovely-buggley baby!' cooed Jess,
picking him up and giving him a full-on cuddle.

'He is,' I agreed sadly, 'a lovely-buggley baby. Anyway,

first things first, Jess: I'm going to have to keep him hidden at the hotel. Are you up for helping me?'

'Of course,' said Jess, 'anything for this gorgeous little bubba-boy.'

She was clearly besotted. Did animals do this to everyone? I wondered. At what point would I go soft and start calling Arthur 'my gorgeous little bubba-boy'?

And how long after that would it be before the men in white coats came and carried me off to a secure facility?

'Okay,' I got down back to brass tacks. 'When we get back, I'll need you to distract the girl on reception so I can smuggle him past the desk. Second up, will you go on ahead to my room and make sure housekeeping aren't in there? Oh, and third up, please don't breathe a word to *anyone.*'

'Of course,' Jess still had Arthur in her arms. 'I'd do anything for this little boy. He's so squidgely and booootiful. Oh, Ailsa, if you don't want him, can I have him?'

'You're going on honeymoon to the Maldives,' I said firmly. 'If it's going to be difficult taking him to Britain, think what it would be like trying to fly him out to the middle of the Indian Ocean and back.'

Jess buried her face in Arthur's fur.

'That's if there is a wedding,' she said, 'because if there isn't, then there certainly won't be any honeymoon.'

I opened my mouth to tell her not to be so silly, but, as we rounded a corner, we both stopped dead in our tracks.

And so did the man who had been walking towards us: Justin.

Jess went white and her mouth fell open. For a moment,

I thought that she was about to drop Arthur. We stood there staring at each other, until Arthur scrambled out of Jess's arms and ran towards Justin, barking happily at him as though he was a long-lost friend. Justin crouched down and rubbed him behind the ears and Arthur showed his appreciation by biting Justin gently on the knee.

'Hello, buddy,' said Justin cheerfully to Arthur. Then, less certainly, 'Hello, Jess. How are you?'

Jess gave a stiff little nod of her head.

'Good,' she said, 'you?'

Justin gave an identical incline of the bonce.

'Good,' he said – then he paused. 'Actually, no, I'm not. I'm awful – I feel awful, I look awful . . . hell, I *am* awful. I ran away, Jess; I ran away from you when what I should have done was the exact opposite.'

Jess still looked as though someone had just hit her round the back of the head with a steel pipe.

'Really?' she said.

Justin nodded.

'I should have come to find you immediately,' he continued. 'I should have listened to what you had to say. Only I didn't.'

'No,' Jess replied, 'I know you didn't. I was there. Or rather, I wasn't there. Where you were, I mean. I was somewhere else. Obviously, otherwise we'd both have been in the same place and—'

'Yes, okay,' Justin held up his hand. 'But we're both here now, Jess. Together. In the same place at the same time. And we need to talk.'

Jess bit her lip. This was obviously going to be a make-or-break moment and she was gearing herself up for it.

'I need to know what happened, Jess,' he continued. 'I need to know the whole story.'

Jess twisted the hem of her T-shirt between her fingers then she looked him dead in the eye.

'Last night,' she said, 'I did have a man in my room and I did kiss him. But – before you start getting upset – it wasn't *that* sort of kiss.'

Jess looked at me and then back at Justin. Her cheeks were flushed and she seemed very uncomfortable indeed.

'So,' Justin was just as flushed as Jess. 'If it wasn't "that sort of kiss", what was it?'

Jess looked at me again, then down at her feet.

'I can't tell you that. Not right now. You're going to have trust me on this one, at least for a couple of days.'

Justin shook his head.

'No,' he said. 'This goes both ways, Jess. If I trust you, then you have to trust me too – with whatever it is that you think you can't tell me. You are my life partner, the person I want to be with – and it's really important that we don't keep anything from one another. Particularly something as important as this.'

Jess's cheeks fired up even more.

'Justin, I can't – and please don't ask me why I can't, because that's something *else* I can't tell you.'

Justin stepped forward and took her hands in his. Jess avoided his gaze and scuffed her toe along the edge of the pavement.

'Is it that you can't tell me – or that you won't?' he said in a low voice.

'Can't,' she replied, her voice so quiet that I had to strain to hear it, 'I *will* tell you but I *can't* now. I'll tell you soon, I promise. Now, can you trust me? Can you live with that?'

I held my breath. *Could* he live with that? And if he couldn't, what was the alternative?

Justin stared down at the ring on the third finger of Jess's left hand: it glittered outrageously in the morning sunshine. Then Jess's alabaster forehead crumpled into a frown. She pulled her hands away from his and balled them up into tightly closed fists. For a moment or two, I thought she was going to deck him, but instead she flung her arms around his neck and buried her face in his shoulder.

'Oh bloody hell, Justin,' she cried, 'I love you. I don't want us to fight. Just tell me it's okay between us!'

For a moment, Justin looked as though he didn't have a clue how to react. Then, very slowly, a smile began to make its way across his face and he hugged her back.

'It's my fault,' he said, 'absolutely one hundred per cent totally my fault. I know you'd never cheat on me.'

'No, it's my fault,' Jess howled back, 'totally mine. Will you forgive me?'

'No, really, it was me,' Justin countered, as Arthur leaped excitedly round their legs, barking. 'If I hadn't—'

I held up my hands.

'Stop it,' I told them, 'enough of the self-flagellation, please! I can't bear it. Just tell me – are the pair of you back together?'

Jess snuggled deep into Justin's arms and gazed up adoringly into his face.

'I've missed you,' she said, 'I didn't know what I was going to do last night when it all blew up. I don't want us to spend another moment apart. Ever.'

Justin smoothed her blonde hair and kissed her tenderly on the nose.

'That may be a bit difficult to manage,' he said, 'seeing as we both need to go to work and I hate shoe shopping, but yes, I basically feel the same.'

Suddenly, Jess looked at me.

'Ailsa,' she said, 'would you mind . . . just for a moment? Could you look over there?'

I had no idea what the heck was going on but I took myself and Arthur through a hundred and eighty degrees.

'Fingers,' Jess demanded, 'fingers in your ears, please. And hum – something loud. "Bohemian Rhapsody" – that'll do.'

Bemused, but frankly beyond arguing, I did what I was told. When I turned round, Jess was grinning and Justin gave me a large wink.

'Let's just say, that's sorted that one.'

'What has?' I asked.

Justin sighed heavily, as though he was dealing with a bear of very little brain.

'I can't tell you,' he said, parroting Jess's words of a few minutes earlier, 'and I can't tell you why I can't tell you, otherwise I'd be telling you – but Jess explained everything while you had your fingers in your ears.'

'And you're cool with it?' I asked.

Justin's grin became as expansive and as cheesy as Jess's.

'Oh yes,' he said, 'cooler than a cucumber that's been cooled in a cooling tower.'

'Brilliant,' I said, 'so the wedding is back on?'

Justin's face fell once again.

'It wasn't me who called it off,' he said miserably.

197

'That was Dudley. He chased me round the bar last night yelling, "*No daughter of mine is going to marry a man who calls her a cheat.*" Only he didn't say "man", he said "creeping miserable worm", and there was quite a lot of swearing, too. He really wasn't happy.'

'Okay,' I said, 'so, Jess, you need to go and find your dad and tell him that the whole thing was a horrible misunderstanding and bingo! You can rebook the vicar and we get to toast the pair of you as planned.'

Jess lifted her head.

'Oh, Ailsa, you really don't know Pops at all, do you? Once he gets an idea into his head he never changes it back. And if he thinks Justin is a miserable worm—'

'A creeping, miserable worm,' Justin reminded us. 'A creeping miserable worm who is not fit to marry his daughter—'

'Then we've had it!' Jess's shoulders slumped and her face fell. 'He'll cancel the wedding, we'll all have to fly home – and I expect he'll give you the sack, Justin.'

'I didn't even think of that.' Justin was horrified.

'And he won't let us marry. Ever. Ever ever ever.'

They clung to each other like a pair of rabbits facing down an oncoming juggernaut. As far as they were concerned, this was pretty much the last word in doomsday scenarios.

'Okay,' I took a deep breath. 'Jess, how old are you?'

Jess frowned. She was having to concentrate.

'Twenty-nine,' she said after a short pause.

'And you, Justin? How many times have you celebrated your arrival on this planet?'

'Thirty-two,' he replied, shuffling awkwardly. 'Why?'

'Because,' I replied, 'you are both adults. *You* should be deciding if you get married, not Dudley.'

Jess stared at me as though I'd just spoken to her in Swahili. I was obviously making no sense whatsoever.

'But he's livid, Ailsa – he's absolutely gone into orbit.'

'So what? Don't live your lives by what Dudley says, make your own decisions. If you want to get married, then get married; if he gives you the sack, Justin, then go out and get a new job. It's simple.'

'But—' began Jess.

'Jess – do you want your life ruined?'

'But—' Justin protested.

I was beginning to lose patience.

'And you, Justin: you managed perfectly well without Dudley for most of your thirty-two years. Are you going to let this ogre – no offence, Jess – stand in the way of you marrying a beautiful princess?'

It was an unreconstructed bundle of fairy-tale schmaltz, but hey – it seemed to work. Justin puffed out his chest and threw back his shoulders. Male pride had clearly been invoked.

'No, I'm bloody not,' he replied. 'Especially not this princess. Have you ever seen a girl so enchantingly beautiful?'

Jess gazed up admiringly at him.

'Oh, Pixie,' she said, 'that's so sweet.'

Pixie?? I think I'd have decked Nick if he'd ever called me Pixie.

Justin curled his arm round her protectively.

'But it's true, Baby Lamb; I couldn't stand life without you by my side. It wouldn't be living. It would be – I don't know – something that *wasn't* living. And I'm not having that.'

Not the most eloquent declaration, perhaps, but it came from the heart.

'Oh, Pixie,' Jess melted into his arms.

'Oh, Baby Lamb.' Justin turned equally molten.

Their eyes closed and their lips came together in a kiss worthy of the most block-busterish of films. All they needed was a sunset in the background and the screen fading to black before the credits came up.

Arthur barked excitedly and tried to jump up at Jess's leg, but they didn't take any notice. I gave a discreet little cough.

'So, I'll see you back at the hotel then, Jess?'

No reply. They didn't even look as though they were going to come up for air. Was there, I wondered, any precedent for Death by Snogging?

A passing group of school children began to giggle and whisper things that sounded as though they might be an Italian version of 'get a room'.

'I'd – well,' I said, picking up Arthur and deciding that to linger any longer would be bordering on the voyeuristic. 'I mean, I'd better be – I mean, I'll leave you to it.'

And, dog under one arm, I began to walk back to the hotel, hoping that, for once, the course of true love might be about to run smoothly.

Chapter Sixteen

As Arthur and I approached the entrance to the hotel, I began to think that getting Jess and Justin back in each other's arms had been the easy part of my morning. I now had to attempt to smuggle a noisy and energetic animal (already well known as a troublemaker and an outlaw) into a busy and well-staffed hotel. If I wasn't very careful, there was every possibility that he might yet meet his doom at the hands of the angry doorman – or even the vengeful chef and his collection of meat cleavers.

I paused for a moment just outside the hotel grounds: partly to get my breath back and partly in order to come up with a Plan B. Plan A, of course, had involved Jess distracting the door staff and the girl on reception but, as she was currently fully occupied with Justin, that particular option was off the table. I looked around for inspiration but all I had in the way of dog-smuggling accessories since the demise of the beach bag was my handbag (barely capable of concealing an emaciated gerbil), my maxi dress and a cardigan, which I'd tied round my waist due to the heat.

I looked round again and this time, my gaze focused on Arthur, who was barking happily at a lizard.

I narrowed my eyes and scrutinised him: he was quite small; he could stay still.

Sometimes.

Would it work?

Was it at least worth a try?

I quickly untied my cardigan, slipped it on and buttoned it up.

Then I scooped up Arthur and, stretching the cardigan as far as it would go, shoved him in.

As I did so, a rotund, elderly lady clad from head to foot in black and with her head covered by a scarf, came out of a cottage nearby and stared at me.

'*Bambino?*' she said, gesturing to the bump under my cardigan and patting her own stomach.

I nodded and tried to smile. Arthur, not fond of his new and rather cramped lodgings, gave an experimental wiggle and my bump moved alarmingly. The lady gave a groan of fellow feeling.

'Ah,' she said knowingly, '*bambino*. He kicking. You must rest.'

And, before I knew what was happening, she had taken me by the shoulders and pushed me down onto a set of sun-bleached steps outside her cottage door.

'No,' I tried to stand up, but she immediately pushed me down again, 'it's not a baby. Er, no *bambino*.'

'*Bambino*,' the lady insisted.

'No *bambino*,' I replied.

'*Bambino!*' She was getting cross with me now.

'No *bambino* – is *canine*!' I bared my teeth and gave a dog-like growl.

'*Stupida signorina!*' the woman cried, and put her hand on my bump.

This was not a good move. At the precise moment her hand came into contact with my cardi, Arthur decided

202

to stick his nose out of a gap he had been working on between the buttons. She shrieked as though she had been bitten by a nest of vipers and there was a spattering of very angry Italian.

I couldn't understand a word, but none of it sounded particularly complimentary. Arthur, however, always keen to make a new friend, wriggled free from his makeshift hiding place and tried to jump up at the lady but, with a speed that belied her age, she grabbed a broom and began to chase him with it.

This was obviously Arthur's role in life – to cause mayhem at every turn. Just as the broom was about to descend on his head, I dived down, caught him up in my arms and walked off as quickly as I could.

'*Stupida signorina!*' yelled the lady again.

I had to admit, she was probably right.

We trudged the final couple of yards up towards the gates, the old lady's cries still ringing in our ears. The humidity was making me sweat like a pig with a perspiration issue, my legs ached from the long walk from the town centre, my head was beginning to do the same – and I still hadn't solved the problem of how to get Arthur back onto hotel premises.

However, just as we were about to cross the car park, I stopped. Somewhere, deep in my brain, an idea was brewing. I seemed to remember someone saying that if you wanted to hide something, the thing to do was to put it in full view of everyone: so, if it's a letter you're trying to conceal, the best place for it is a letter rack . . .

Hmmm . . . and if you want to hide a dog who is not welcome in your five-star luxury hotel, the best way to do it is to . . . march it right in at the front door.

Really?

There was only one way I was going to find out.

I clipped on Arthur's lead, took a deep breath and, if I'd known what it meant and I'd happened to have any girds with me, I'd have girded my loins as well. Then I held my head high and walked purposefully along the path towards the revolving main door.

It wasn't far from the car park to the entrance but it felt like miles. You know those dreams you have where you are running and running and you never seem to get anywhere? Well, this was exactly like being in one of those – only it took *even* longer because Arthur insisted on stopping to sniff every bit of gravel we passed.

The first danger point was Auntie Sheila over by the terrace, wearing a bathing suit that could best be described as 'ill-advised'. I slid my sunglasses down over my eyes and slumped forward in a vain attempt to look like someone else – luckily, she was having a shouty conversation into her phone and didn't pay me any attention.

About twenty metres on and – oh, blimey, there was Charles, striding across the lawn with a golf club in his hand and looking (I followed the line of his gaze) . . . thank you, God . . . looking at a girl *behind* me, who was wearing a bikini top and hot pants and had legs up to her eyebrows.

Good luck with that one, Kitty.

With the backs of my knees sweaty and prickly, I turned towards the shallow steps that led up to the main door. This was the bit I had been dreading. I could see the doorman with his claret-coloured coat and hat lurking just inside the air-conditioned cool of the foyer. But I had come too far to turn back now.

I swallowed.

Hard.

And put my foot on the bottom step.

It turned out that luck was with me after all because, at the crucial moment, the girl at the reception desk waved him over and I was able to dodge inside and, looking neither to the right or the left, I stalked through the marble foyer. I could have done without Arthur's claws making a loud 'tip tap, tip tap' on the floor – but I'm sure the noise was more than drowned out by the sound of adrenalin pumping through my veins.

As soon as we had turned the corner by the stairs and were out of view of the main desk, I scooped Arthur up and dashed up the stairs as fast as I could, back to the safety of my room, thanking my lucky stars and Gods of Dog Smuggling for giving me a clear run.

I put Arthur down and closed the door behind me. He ambled off into the bathroom and began to drink noisily out of the toilet, so (gagging a bit) I offered him some mineral water from the minibar in a saucer. He lapped it up furiously and I swigged the remainder out of the bottle.

I'd done it. I'd made it back to my room and *no one* had seen me.

I untied my cardi, walked into the bedroom and threw it on the bed – and, as I did so, a figure appeared, silhouetted by the French windows, making me jump a good three feet into the air.

'Kitty,' I said crossly, thinking I really had to get round

to speaking to maintenance about the crappiness of their key cards. 'What the hell are you doing? I specifically asked you not to keep letting yourself into my room.'

My sister didn't reply. Instead, she in stared in disbelief as Arthur trotted out from the bathroom and began to chew a pair of my trainers.

'What on earth's that?' she asked, as though she half-expected my reply to be 'a hammerhead shark' or 'a double-decker bus'.

'It's a dog,' I replied.

'I can see that,' Kitty replied. 'But what's it doing here?'

'It's not an "it", it's a "he", and *he* seems to have adopted me,' I replied. 'I've just brought him back from the vet's.'

'Oh?' Kitty arched an eyebrow. 'Nothing trivial, I hope?'

'Just a check-up,' I replied lightly.

Kitty walked over to the minibar and helped herself to a packet of shortbread biscuits: Charles was obviously having quite an effect on her metabolic rate.

'You can't possibly take it home with you,' she told me, 'think of the hassle – all that paperwork, time and expense, and for what? A furry flea bag.'

'He's not a flea bag,' I bristled at the accusation, 'and yes, I just might, actually.'

At that moment, I would have liked nothing more than to take Arthur back to Edinburgh – simply because it would really, really, *really* have annoyed her.

'And in the meantime, do you seriously think you're going to keep him here, in your room?'

Arthur stopped chewing my trainer and looked at Kitty, before emitting a low growl. He'd obviously formed some pretty clear views on my sister.

'Why?' I asked cautiously. 'Are you going to grass me up?'

'No!' Kitty sounded shocked at such a suggestion. 'Of course not. If you want to keep livestock in your room, then it's nothing to do with me. Just make sure he doesn't sleep on the chairs, though, Ailsa – I don't want his hairs all over my clothes.'

I folded my arms.

'Is there anything I can actually do for you, Kitty, or did you drop by just to wind me up?'

Kitty's expression became serious and she put the packet of shortbread down.

'I wanted to have a word,' she took a deep breath, 'a *civilised* word about this morning.'

'You mean Charles?' I asked.

Kitty checked the nearest armchair for dog hair and then sat down, crossing her legs.

'Yes,' she said. 'I wanted to make sure that you and I understood each other.'

She took a very deep breath.

'I don't know what impression you got about me and Graham,' she said, 'but I didn't leave him, he broke up with me and, before he did, it was pretty much hell on earth. I think he was having an affair, but frankly that was the least of our worries.'

'Oh, Kitty,' I said, sitting down on the bed, 'I'm so sorry, I had no idea.'

'No,' she said, 'I know you didn't. No one knows – not even Mum and Dad – and I'd like to keep it that way, thank you.'

'It's all right,' I replied, 'I've had a lot of practice at keeping secrets recently.'

Kitty gave me a bit of a funny look but continued.

'So – I turned up here a bit of a wreck and hoping for a bit of a holiday fumble to take my mind off things and I met Charlie.'

Charlie? *Charlie?*

'Now,' my sister continued, 'I know what I said at breakfast about it just being physical, but, actually, there's more to it. This morning we went for a walk along the beach and really got to know each other. There's a connection between us, Ailsa, a real connection. It's almost as though we met in a previous life.'

'You haven't been speaking to anyone called Psychic Serena, have you?' I asked.

Kitty frowned.

'Don't be absurd. Anyway, I know you don't rate the man, but *I do*. Very much. We're going on the boat trip to the island tomorrow, then he's coming to stay with me *next* weekend – the one after we get home – and we're talking about a holiday together later in the summer and then, for Christmas—'

'Kitty,' I spoke in a low voice, warning bells going off all over the place, 'isn't this happening rather quickly? I mean, you didn't even know he existed a week ago.'

She shrugged.

'I don't care,' she said. 'I spent years with Graham feeling as miserable as sin; I deserve a break. As far as I'm concerned, it can't be happening fast *enough*. And the amazing thing is that he feels the same – he was let down very badly by someone too, you know, and he's desperate to move on.'

For a moment, Jess's words about my mystery admirer

having just escaped from a painful relationship rang through my brain but I did my best to ignore them. There was no way my moonlit tryst could be with Charles, particularly if he was carrying on like this with my sister.

But still . . . I had this weird feeling about him . . .

'Kitty,' this was going to be difficult, 'I'm pleased for you – really I am, but there's something about Charles. I don't know what it is, I can't put my finger on it and—'

There was a bleeping sound and Kitty pulled her phone out of her pocket.

'It's him,' she said, a huge blush creeping over her face, 'he keeps on texting to check up on me; it's so sweet.'

What could I say? I had no evidence against the man – other than his bizarre behaviour concerning Jess and Justin – but that had nothing to do with Kitty. The grown-up thing to do would be to go along with my sister's wishes and butt out.

'Okay,' I said, holding up my hands in surrender, 'I agree. It's nothing to do with me. I hope you're very happy together.'

The phone bleeped again. Kitty blushed even more and typed something in on her keypad.

'Good,' she said breezily, pressing the 'send' button. 'I'm glad we understand each other. But that's enough about me, what about you?'

'What about me?' I tried to sound light and carefree too, but I'm not sure I succeeded.

'I think,' she said slowly, 'that there's something *you're* not telling *me*.'

Don't ask me how, but I knew immediately that she meant Nick. My cheeks flared redder than a lobster on

209

a sunbed and, from that moment, any denial was useless.

'That tour guide,' Kitty said. 'There's something between you, and it's serious.' She paused. 'Or it *was* serious.'

She had me. I was going to have to say something – even if it didn't quite count as the truth.

'If you ever mention this to anyone, you're dead,' I said.

'Yes,' said Kitty, 'and . . .?'

I took a deep breath.

'He's called Nick. We were together. For over a year. We – we lived together.'

My sister's eyes bulged.

'You *lived together*?' she echoed.

I could feel the words 'and now he wants a divorce' forming in my mouth but, with a huge effort of will, I managed to stop them from actually coming out.

'You lived together?' Kitty repeated. 'As in – *not* flatmates?'

'Not flatmates. Not even flatmates with benefits,' the words tumbled out. 'He moved in because we couldn't stand being apart. We didn't plan it, it all just sort of happened. I met him – at the theatre, a hypnotism show, and we had dinner and I invited him back for coffee . . . and he never really left. It was intense; it was powerful stuff – like getting hit by a truck; but an amazing, captivating, sexy, wonderful truck that you know you can't ever let out of your sight again because if you do, you'll crumble away to dust and nothingness. Does that make any sense?'

'None at all,' said Kitty, 'but then again, you've met Graham.'

'It was mesmerising,' I went on, not really hearing her,

'entrancing. I called in sick for an entire week because I couldn't bear to be apart from him.'

Kitty's mouth dropped open. I'd never managed to say anything before that could shut her up. It was a shame that it had taken over thirty years and the subject of Nick to render her speechless.

'And you kept him a secret? I mean – does Mum or anyone know about him?'

I shook my head.

'I know – I know. I couldn't even tell the olds. It's hard to explain, but it was just me and him in our own little loved-up world – if I'd told anyone else, it would have felt as though I was bursting our bubble. But it's over now. There were rows – really nasty ones – and I left. It's pure coincidence that he's here, he's working for his cousin who runs a tour company in Auchtermuchty.'

There was a pause, then Kitty spoke.

'Do you – do you want him back?'

'Why?' I was suddenly fearful. 'You're not sizing him up as a fall-back position in case things don't work out with Charles, are you?'

'No,' she shook her head. 'Nonononononononono. Of course not.'

I relaxed. A little.

'No,' I said firmly, shaking my head. 'Things happened – things involving money and courts and stuff – and I don't know if I can trust him again. Anyway, I've just accepted a job in Newcastle, a deputy headship, so it's the perfect opportunity for me to get away and make a fresh start without him.'

I paused.

'I mean it, Kitty,' I said, 'please don't tell anyone about me and Nick. Apart from the fact that this week is about Jess and Justin, there really is no point: it's over. As the police say: move along, nothing to see here. Do you promise?'

Kitty continued to stare at me for a few moments more before heaving herself out of her chair.

'Just as long as you keep your nose out where me and Charles are concerned. Deal?'

'Deal.'

Her eye alighted on the piece of paper that Justin had dropped the night before.

'What's that?' she asked, picking it up from its resting place on the minibar and smoothing it out.

'Nothing,' I said. 'At least, I don't know – I haven't had the time to look at it properly.'

I went to take it from her grasp but she snatched it away and peered at it.

'I've seen this before,' she said at last.

'You can't have,' I replied, reaching for it once again only to have it spirited away out of my reach. 'It's been here all night.'

'Well, maybe not this exact sheet but something very like it. I found it lying on the floor just outside the bar this morning. It was figures, some sort of accounts, I think – like a bank statement. Only it wasn't one I would want to have anything to do with. There was a lot of red ink involved. Oh, look – this one says "Justin Chilmark" at the top. Whatever can it be?'

'I don't know but I think it needs to go straight back to Justin.' I made another grab, but Kitty lifted it high out of my reach. Curse her extra two and a quarter inches. 'And the other one – the one you found downstairs.'

Kitty shrugged.

'I haven't got it. That one said "Sidebottom's" on it, so I handed it straight to Charlie,' she replied. 'Don't worry, I can drop this one off too if you like – I'm seeing him later.'

I shook my head

'No, give it to me, Kitty; it belongs to Justin.'

'No, really, it's no trouble – Charlie can pass it on to him. They do work together after all.' Her eyes flashed. 'Unless you think there's something dodgy going on that Justin wouldn't want Charlie knowing about?'

For a split second, the idea that Justin might be siphoning money out of the Sidebottom's company account sped through my brain but I quickly dismissed it. If Justin didn't have the gumption to stand up to Dudley over Jess, he probably didn't have the presence of mind to diddle his father-in-law's brewery out of large amounts of cash either.

'No, I don't. In fact, I think it's likely to be highly confidential – I know Justin's working on some sort of deal at the moment. It needs to go straight back to him.'

Kitty sighed as though I was spoiling her fun. Then her phone bleeped for the third time and she brightened.

'Oh, it's Charlie again,' she said, a girlish squeal in her voice, 'he wants me to meet him down at the pool!'

'Sounds great,' I said, sliding the paper from her unresisting hand, 'a long, slow dip in a lovely cool pool. Don't hurry back.'

'I won't.' Kitty was busy texting back – with, I noticed, a large number of x's at the end of the message. 'Oooh!

Shall I ask him to order cocktails? The ones we had last night were lovely, weren't they?'

'Spectacular,' I agreed. 'Good idea. Lots and lots of cocktails.'

'Right,' she grinned at me. 'I'd better go. Shall I mention this other sheet of paper to him?'

'No,' I said, 'best not spoil a romantic afternoon with work stuff. See you at dinner.'

'If Charlie doesn't make me a better offer,' she cooed, and shut the door behind her.

I waited until she was safely down the stairs before I stepped out onto the landing myself. *Charlie's* text couldn't have come at a better time: for the next couple of hours at least, he was going to be occupied with my sister down by the pool – meaning his room would be empty.

And that gave me the perfect opportunity to try and get Justin's other paper back.

For about eight of the ten minutes it took me to walk to Charles's room in the Da Vinci wing, I didn't meet a soul. In fact, it was going much too well until, when I was finally in sight of his door, I heard footsteps. I flattened myself against the wall in the manner of Shaggy and Scooby Doo and two men, engrossed in conversation, came past.

'. . . so Joe said it was all about extra bandwidth when it came to taking the deliverables to the next level, so I asked if he wanted me to conversate with Judy in HR . . .' the first was saying.

The second man sniggered.

'Wouldn't mind giving Judy some of my bandwidth, if you know what I mean.'

Hidden in the shadows, I silently pitied Judy in HR.

'So, Archie, I'll need you to be proactive not reactive . . .'

To my immense relief, they continued down the landing, round another corner and down the stairs, taking their management-speak arsewittage with them. I breathed again and, with a quick glance each way along the corridor, tiptoed the final few steps.

I assumed that if people kept getting into my room because the hotel key cards were a bit crap, there was a chance I would be able to do the same myself. Crossing the fingers on my left hand, I lifted my right, inserted my own key card into Charles's slot – and swiped.

Nothing happened.

I swiped again.

Still nothing – trust me to have the only rotten lock in the entire place.

From the direction of the stairs, I heard more voices. With my palms hot and sticky with fear, I lifted my hand for a third time, swiped – and my ears picked up the tiniest possible click: the lock had opened.

I slid through the door, closing it silently behind me, just as whoever it was came round the corner.

Right. To work.

If I was a junior executive from a brewing firm who had just been handed a piece of paper covered in all sorts of dubious figures, where would I put it? As there was nothing visible on any of the surfaces, I walked over to a large wooden chest of drawers next to the bathroom door and looked inside.

Pants, pants, pants and pants.

Oh dear – *rub gently and genie will appear.* Er, thanks but no thanks.

The next drawer: socks and neatly folded T-shirts.

The last – jumpers. Nasty yellow golfing ones with big orange diamonds knitted into them.

Yuk.

The drawer in the bedside table? Zilch.

The bathroom – nothing.

Under the bed? (Not so much as a dust bunny).

I was just about to give up when I remembered the minibar. Very carefully, I opened the glass door and – bingo! I struck gold. There, hidden behind a half-bottle of red wine and a large packet of Bombay mix, was a wallet.

Ah-*ha!*

The fact that it was lurking behind the wine and the snacks seemed to indicate that whoever had put it there had not wanted it to be immediately visible. With trembling hands, I picked it up, opened it and pulled out some euros, a couple of platinum cards – and two folded-up photos printed onto old-fashioned shiny paper.

I put my haul down on the top of the minibar and carefully checked all the remaining flaps, openings and card-holder-type places in the wallet – but there were no account printouts; just a few pennies, an old button and a Tesco receipt.

And even *that* was for nothing more interesting than dental floss.

With a heavy heart, I put the money, the button and the receipt back where I had found them.

If the paper *was* here, which I was starting to doubt, it was very skilfully hidden indeed.

I glanced down at the folded photos and picked them up, ready to place them back within the confines of the wallet as well. However, as I did so, my thumb skidded across the shiny paper and the first one flipped open. I gave a gasp and very nearly dropped the wallet onto the floor.

It was Jess.

Jess looking very glamorous indeed, in a backless evening gown, with a magnificent up-do and a glass of champagne in her hand.

I immediately unfolded the other one: it was almost identical, except it seemed to have been taken from a slightly different angle.

As I stared at them, a rather creepy feeling came over me. Jess was with Justin; what on earth were pictures of her doing in Charles's wallet? Had they once been an item? Had Justin snatched Jess away from Charles and left him sobbing into his pint of premium quality Sidling Stoat?

I peered at the pictures again, looking carefully for any clues they might be able to give me as to what was going on: Jess, stunningly beautiful, turning away from the camera, her mouth half open as though she was speaking to someone else and—

The penny dropped.

And a shiver ran along the entire length of my spine.

Jess hadn't known the pictures were being taken. If she had, she'd have been smiling into the lens and saying 'cheers' with her glass of fizz. No, this was a sneaky, stalker-type pic and it made me go all goose-bumpy just to think about it.

I quickly refolded the pictures, shoved them back where I'd found them and replaced the wallet itself carefully behind the wine bottle. A nasty, claustrophobic atmosphere had descended on the room and I wanted to get out as quickly as possible. As for Justin's sheet of paper, if it was in here, then this was where it would have to stay – I would confine myself to damage limitation when the time came.

Like a shadow, I opened the door and slunk back out into the corridor. Then I hurried as quickly as I could down the stairs. The creepy feeling persisted, though; following me down into the foyer and hovering round me like an intrusive, unsettling fog. I felt strangely tarnished, as though some of Charles's sleaziness had rubbed off onto me, and I had an almost overwhelming desire to wash my hands.

I made my way as quickly as I could back into the bustle of the foyer, then I paused and leaned against one of the cool marble pillars and thought about what I should do next. Should I tell Jess? It would be a pretty delicate operation seeing as he was her fiancé's best friend – not to mention the stand-in Best Man at her wedding. And what the hell did I say to Kitty? Especially now I'd promised to keep my nose out of her love life.

With no simple solutions rushing to present themselves, I made my way out into the garden and walked down to the sea to consider my options.

Chapter Seventeen

It was midnight.

Dinner that evening had been a sombre affair. Jess and Justin were conspicuous by their absence; Auntie Sheila ordered room service, Uncle Dudley had a sandwich in the bar; and Kitty and Charles were nowhere to be seen (which was probably just as well, because his nasty little photographs made my skin creep so much that I couldn't have brought myself to be polite to him).

Rather than be Billy-no-mates in the hotel dining room, I had grabbed my bag and my novel and walked a little way down the main road to a restaurant I'd noticed earlier that afternoon and spent a pleasant couple of hours in the company of a good book, a bottle of Chianti and some local scallops.

Then I stole back to my room through the thick, humid darkness of the Italian night.

I let myself in and gave Arthur (who had been hiding out in the bathroom) his supper. While he was noisily wolfing it down, my phone rang.

'Hello?' Jess's voice came on the line. 'Is that you, Ailsa?'

I smiled, bit back the words 'of course it's me, you rang my mobile, didn't you?' and instead replied: 'Hi, Jess, how's things? And by things, I mean Justin.'

There was a happy sigh from the other end of the line.

'Oh Justin's *amazing*. After we left you, we went back to his hotel room and spent the entire afternoon—'

I cut her off.

'Teeny bit much information, Jess – but I'm happy for you, really I am.'

Jess made a sort of purring noise.

'Anyway,' she said, 'speaking of true love, I'm ringing to remind you that you have a hot date tonight under the cedar tree.'

'Yes,' I was having second – and even third and fourth – thoughts about that hot date; and the more thoughts I had, the dodgier it sounded. 'About me saying that I would—'

'No buts,' said Jess firmly, even though I hadn't used the word 'but', 'you are going. You need to do this. It's the key to the rest of your life. You've got to trust me.'

'You sound like Psychic Serena,' I muttered.

'As I said,' replied Jess, 'Serena told me I have the Gift. And that gift is yelling at me *right now* to make sure you're under the tree at midnight.'

'But—'

'No.'

'Look—'

'No.'

'Jess—'

'Just do it,' she sounded exasperated, 'or, or, or, or – I don't know – just do it. Pretty please?'

'All right, all right,' I said, as much to stop her from going on at me as anything else, 'okay, I will. Promise.'

I paused.

'Look, Jess. I'm glad you rang. You see, something

220

happened this afternoon,' I was cautiously trying to work out how I could bring up the subject of the photos without totally freaking her out, 'something to do with Charles.'

But Jess wasn't listening. She had started giggling and then, without warning, she let out a shriek that set my eardrums ringing.

'Jess?' I said. 'Are you all right?'

There was the noise of a hand going over the mouthpiece and the muffled sound of kissing. Then another giggle and a clatter, presumably as Jess dropped the phone.

Justin was obviously making his presence felt.

'Jess?' I called, 'Jess? Are you there?'

There was more shrieking and the sound of bedsprings. I sighed and hung up.

Fifteen minutes to midnight.

A quarter of an hour before I was due to stumble through the darkness to a rendezvous under an isolated tree and get mauled to death by a random madman.

I slid off the bed and walked over to the French windows. The sky was blacker than a black cat being sucked into a black hole in the middle of a coal cellar and, try as I might, I couldn't make out a single star. I glanced again at my watch. If I was going to make my tryst on time, I'd need to think about leaving soon.

But – the nasty little thought popped into my head once again – what if the mystery man was *Charles*? After all, hadn't he told Kitty that he was suffering from a recently broken heart.

I bit my lip and tried to be rational about what was a very irrational situation.

Lots of people had their hearts broken every single day, I told myself – the fact that Charles had been dumped didn't mean anything. In fact, if it *was* him, maybe it was actually the opportunity I needed to tell him that I had found some creepy photographs of my cousin in his possession and ask him to explain himself? Maybe I could even use them as leverage to get Justin's missing sheet of paper back?

'Arthur,' I whispered, pulling his lead out of a drawer and clipping it on, 'it's time for walkies – and if I say "kill", I want you to do just that, is that clear?'

Even with the residual light cast by the hotel buildings out across the grounds, it took longer than I'd imagined for Arthur and me to make our way along the gravel path that wound down the hill to the lawn where the cedar tree was situated. The air was warm and oppressively humid. My cotton top was sticking to my skin and the soles of my feet clung damply onto the inside of my sandals – although, to be fair, this could have been down to nerves rather than the weather. Even so, the night air pressed in on me like a damp, heavy blanket, slowing my pace down from my usual brisk walk to a weary trudge.

I was relieved when, rounding the final corner by the ballroom, the gravel track came to an end and there before me, in the middle of a neatly kept sward, stood the magnificent cedar tree, spreading its branches out against the last faint glimmers of light in the western sky. I paused for a moment as the faintest of breezes whispered across my perspiring skin – and did a quick reconnaissance job.

I was alone.

To my amazement, a little tingle of disappointment zipped through me.

Oh well, I sighed, my hopes hadn't been high. It had been a crackpot scheme hatched by my well-meaning but nonetheless crackpot cousin – and at least it meant I didn't have to have a showdown with Charles.

I stepped onto the lawn and walked slowly across the closely cropped turf. I could hear the sea close by, dark and restless, and from across its wide expanse came a strange sensation that things were on the move – change was coming – and that it would arrive, unheralded, from the most unexpected quarters.

Suddenly, I heard footsteps crunching their way along the gravel path behind me.

I froze.

Was it the person Jess had set me up with?

Or was it someone else entirely – the much-feared axe-wielding homicidal maniac of my worst imaginings, perhaps?

Picking up Arthur and 'shhhing' into his ear, I stole back across the lawn and crouched down next to a hedge on the far side of the tree. I would wait and see who emerged round the corner and then – if I felt like it – I would step forward and introduce myself.

Crunch! Crunch!

The noise of the footfalls grew nearer and then stopped. Someone, silhouetted against the light from the hotel, stepped from the path onto the lawn. With my ears straining so hard, they practically lifted away from the sides of my head, I detected a soft 'pad-pad-pad' as whoever it was made their way across the turf towards the dark bulk of the tree.

Unable to breathe, I saw the outline of a man (yes, definitely a man – I could trace the line of his neck and the shape of a pair of broad shoulders) come to a halt beneath the canopy. He seemed to be about six foot – my preferred height – and, so far as I could make out through the darkness, very nicely proportioned indeed.

He walked all the way round the trunk before stopping and, I presumed, listening for my approach. His face was in profile, so that I could just about see a neat nose, a strong jawline and a fine pair of cheekbones. Whoever he was, he wasn't Charles: Charles's nose had an aquiline quality to it and, I had noted earlier, he also had the beginnings of a double chin.

No, this chap was a superior specimen of his sex.

Also – I did a double check – he didn't seem to have brought an axe with him.

Phew.

The mystery man walked over to the tree and leaned against the trunk, his arms folded, staring in the direction of the path. With one hand round Arthur's muzzle to keep him quiet, I stood up and tiptoed away from my hedge and across the lawn – making sure I stayed safely out of his line of sight. Then, as soon as I reached the tree, I made my move.

'Pssst!' I said.

I think he leaped a clear three feet into the air.

'Who's that?' he whispered back.

'Me,' I replied.

Before deciding I'd better be more specific.

'I mean, it's me – Ailsa Stuart.'

I wondered if I should add something else like 'pleased to meet you' or 'do you often hang out under deserted trees in the middle of the night?', but thought better of it.

'Really?' the man replied, sounding puzzled.

My heart sank again. This wasn't anyone exciting and mysterious. This was simply a random bod who happened to like inspecting the trunks of ancient trees after dark. What a waste of a decent pair of shoulders.

I slid my mobile out of my bag and switched it on, holding it up so that it would illuminate my companion's face. The man put up his hand to shield his eyes from the glow and—

I almost dropped the handset.

'What the bloody hell are you doing here?' I demanded indignantly.

Nick frowned and the phone cast strange, looming shadows across the lawn behind us.

'I could ask you exactly the same thing.'

There was a very uneasy pause.

'I – I – look, Nick, I know this sounds a bit odd, but – um – I would really appreciate it if you would go and hang out somewhere else. How about the pool? A midnight dip in this heat might be just what you need!'

Nick folded his arms.

'No,' he said.

'What do you mean, "no"?'

'I mean, I'm not going anywhere.'

I was starting to feel a bit agitated. I didn't want whoever it was I was supposed to be meeting turning up and finding me mid-row with my soon-to-be ex-husband.

'Complicated' didn't even *begin* to sum that one up.

'I mean – look, Ailsa,' he continued, 'when did you get here?'

'A few minutes ago,' I replied cagily. 'Not that it's any of your business.'

'And was there anybody here when you arrived?'

I shook my head.

'Are you sure?' he was insistent on this point. 'Very, very sure?'

'Of course I'm sure. The only person who's pitched up has been you. Only, I'd like you to leave now, please, in case the person I've arranged to meet does actually turn up.'

In the feeble glow from the phone, I could see Nick's eyes open as wide as they could go.

'You're *meeting* someone?' he asked.

Oh crap.

I scuffed my toes through a little drift of needles at the foot of the tree.

'Yes,' I admitted, adding quickly, 'it wasn't my idea – but yes, I am.'

Nick nodded.

'So,' I continued, grateful for the darkness so that he could not see the colour of my cheeks, 'you'll go, then?'

'No.'

'Why not?'

'Well, for a start, Jess was very insistent,' he said.

I froze. 'Jess?'

'Yes, Jess your cousin. She – ah – passed on a message.'

This was all starting to feel horribly familiar.

'And this message,' I asked, 'what did it say exactly?'

226

Nick looked down at his feet – well, as best he could given the lack of daylight.

'Was it something along the lines of: a really gorgeous girl has seen you from afar and would love to get to know you better, yadda yadda yadda?' I suggested.

My phone screen switched itself off. However, before it did, I was pretty certain I'd seen a look of incredulity spread over Nick's face.

'How did you know that?' He sounded aghast.

'Because—' I paused, conscious that I needed to be careful about how I phrased this next part, 'because she said exactly the same thing to me.'

A low 'huh?' of incomprehension reached my ears.

Arthur started to wriggle under my arm and I put him down onto the ground. He sniffed round the base of the tree for a moment or two and then sat at my feet, looking up at us. He knew something big was playing out and he had the air of someone who had just bagged the best seat in the house.

'You mean,' Nick was struggling, 'you mean she told *you* there was a gorgeous girl who wanted to meet up under a cedar tree?'

'No, you muppet, not a girl. A bloke. A man. All crazy stuff, obviously. And I very nearly didn't come.'

There was a pause.

A long pause.

'Did you,' I said, doing my best to make sure that I sounded light and carefree, 'did you very nearly not come too?'

Divorce or no divorce, at that moment, I really needed him to say 'yes'.

Nick's eyes were scanning the horizon. The blue tinge in the western sky had been gobbled up by the darkness. We were alone in the night.

My heart thumped – but instead of an answer, I got another question.

'What exactly did Jess say to you?'

'That there was a man who really liked me and wanted to meet me in secret under the cedar tree.'

Through the darkness, I could sense Nick starting to smile.

'And this didn't strike you as peculiar because—?'

I leaned against the tree and folded my arms.

'I don't know! Because I read too many novels? Because I see too many chick flicks? Because I have an inherently romantic nature and want to believe in a world where men ask women to meet them in picturesque locations at clichéd times of day and tell them they are the most beautiful creatures they have ever seen?'

Nick gave an almost inaudible chuckle.

'And I also bet that you were hiding over there by the hedge in order to check this secret admirer out – just in case he was a bit of weirdo,' he said. 'Like an axe murderer, perhaps?'

'No,' I retorted. 'Don't be silly.'

'Really?' Somehow, I could tell that Nick had just raised his eyebrows. 'Would that be the type of "no" that actually means "yes"?'

I paused – before surrendering to the inevitable.

'All right,' I conceded, 'I did. That's why I brought my killer hound along – one word from me and the guy would have been dead meat.'

Arthur's tail thumped happily on the ground.

'You know what,' Nick said, 'I *like* that. It reminds me of when you used to have to get out of bed about fifteen million times before you went to sleep to check you'd locked the door.'

'You used to tell me I was being silly,' I reminded him.

'You were,' Nick confirmed. 'But it was also rather endearing. Make sure you don't stop doing it.'

'I'm just going to change,' I murmured, remembering a cheesy line we used to throw around between us.

'Don't ever change,' Nick threw the reply back without even thinking. 'I love you exactly as you are.'

The words hung heavily in the air between us. They couldn't have been any less intrusive if they had been written in six foot high, orange neon letters. Nick was the first to recover himself.

'Ailsa,' his voice was low. 'Why did you come here – I mean, what was it that you really wanted out of tonight?'

I opened my mouth to tell him about Jess nagging me, about Psychic Serena – even about Charles, the photographs and the missing sheets of paper.

But the words didn't come.

There was a deeper, more fundamental reason why I was standing under a tree in the darkness of a June night with the heat and humidity pressing down upon me like a steam iron.

'I'm lonely,' I said at last. 'I've been lonely since we finished and, even though I know that meeting a total stranger under a tree at midnight is a bonkers thing to agree to, a tiny part of me thought, "What the hell, it might be nice to be with someone who fancies me, even if it is just for a couple of hours."'

From somewhere a long way off – probably back at the hotel – I could hear the sounds of people enjoying themselves; the chink of glasses and cutlery. It made me feel even more isolated.

'What about Gary?' Nick asked, his voice hinting at injured male pride.

Despite the gravity of the moment, a smile crept across my face.

'I'm not actually seeing Gary,' I said. 'He works at my school and he keeps asking me out for a coffee but I haven't agreed to go yet.'

I sensed Nick relax.

'Right,' he said, 'yes – ah – right.'

'Nick,' I said, changing the subject and feeling a familiar tightness return to my chest, 'I need to say something about you and me – I want to get at least one thing straight. I didn't leave you because I wanted to, I left because it wasn't working and I'd done everything I could to try and fix things. I did my best, I really did, but I'd reached the end of the line. I didn't do it to hurt you and I don't deserve to be painted as the bad guy.'

There was a pause.

'No, that would be me.'

'No – really – please – I'm not here to throw accusations about. God knows we did enough of that and look where it got us. I was miserable, Nick, scared even, wondering where the next bill, the next court summons was coming from. Do you think I'd have grabbed my toothbrush and

230

my handbag and run away if I'd been deliriously happy?'

Nick sucked in his breath as though someone had punched him in the stomach.

'Yes – I was *that* desperate, *that* upset.'

I paused.

'I went through those last few months hoping, Nick: hoping that tomorrow it would be better, that we'd be able to get back to that amazing place we'd started from. And when it *didn't* get better, I hoped for the day after – and the day after that. Only finally, that night, I realised that all my tomorrows had run out; and the idea of a lifetime with nothing in it apart from you and me shouting at each other was more than I could bear.'

'We didn't shout at each other all the time!'

'Yes we did!' I cried, desperately wanting him to acknowledge the truth. 'And we're still doing it *now*!'

Nick turned away and gave a groan of frustration. As he did so, an ominous flash of light lit up the inky black sky. The humid air pushed against me even heavier than before and I felt myself fighting to get the air into my lungs.

'You left me,' he said, his voice low and angry, 'you left me, Ailsa, and it hurt – it hurt *here*,' he pounded his fist against his chest. 'It would have been better if you'd finished me off with a kitchen cleaver and shoved my body under the patio.'

'Don't be so melodramatic; and anyway, we didn't have a patio, Nick, we lived in my flat.'

'Jesus, Ailsa, that is not the point. This point is—'

There was another flash of light and an enormous drop of rain landed on my nose. I brushed it away angrily. I was too busy to worry about the weather right now – it could go and rain somewhere else.

'The point is what, Nick? That you expected me to support you financially – to support *us*? No one has *ever* made money as an artist and you are no exception. I was stupid not to see it coming.'

Apart from the fact that the night was hot, and the sweet smells of an Italian summer garden were wafting up into our nostrils, this could have been any one of the rows we had had back in Edinburgh. It was exactly the same pain, the same resentment – just parcelled up and hurled at each other through the scented darkness of a Mediterranean night.

'I ran a business!' Nick was practically yelling at me. 'My paintings were my business. I had a problem with cash flow.'

'It wasn't cash flow, Nick, it was cash *stop*. Any flowing that might have happened went strictly from my bank account into yours.'

Out at sea came the low growl of thunder. Above us, the branches of the cedar tree creaked and groaned ominously as a gust of wind rattled through it.

'And you revelled in it, Ailsa. Have you any idea what it was like for me – having to ask you for money to go to the pub, money for a haircut, money for a pair of shoes? What do you think that felt like?'

This was a declaration of war.

'Don't try to make out you were the victim in all of this, Nick – if anyone gets to feel sorry for themselves here, that's me. Me who fell for your ridiculous charm; me who paid off debt after debt – yes, even the ones you tried

232

to hide away. You want to know part of the reason why I didn't introduce you to my family? Because I was ashamed of you! Ashamed of the fact I went out to work all day while you spent your time playing with your paintbox – and no, that is *not* a euphemism.'

'I was putting together a portfolio, Ailsa – a bloody good one!'

'I didn't want a portfolio, Nick – I wanted *a husband*!'

I heard him inhale sharply, but before he could reply, the heavens opened and a deluge of biblical proportions descended. It was incredible. In a matter of seconds, I felt as though I had tripped and fallen into a swimming pool.

Directly overhead came another flash of lightning and the most enormous crack of thunder, followed by a thousand fluttering wings as the birds roosting in the tree above us burst out of the branches, thinking someone was taking potshots at them.

Arthur let out a piteous whine – and there was another flash.

In that split second of illumination I looked out to sea and saw the water had turned a livid green; swollen, angry waves were pounding their way onto the rocks down by the shore. I also saw Nick, drenched and gasping. We glanced at one another and then looked up into the brooding sky, just as another bolt of electricity tore across it.

We were under a tree. A huge, enormous tree. The tallest thing in the hotel garden and . . .

. . . where was it again that you weren't meant to stand during a thunderstorm . . .?

Nick grabbed my hand.

'This way,' he yelled, half-pulling, half-dragging me towards the shore as Arthur yapped at my feet.

'What the hell do you think you're doing?' I shouted over the roar of the thunder. I tried to drag my hand back, but his grip held firm and I found myself propelled in the direction of the pounding sea. 'Now is not the time for a spot of paddling.'

Down a shallow incline we scrambled, across the slippery grass and then across some even slippier rocks.

'Nick!' I yelled again, as a dark shape, a couple of metres high, loomed up in front of us.

A hut of some sort? No! My memory clicked into action – it had to be the boathouse down near the shore where Jess had spent most of the previous night.

Nick let go of my wrists and fumbled with the door. Spray from the waves drenched our already sodden feet and the wind howled round us, chilling our bones to their very marrow and making us shiver violently – including Arthur. Nick shook the door even harder and then, in a fit of desperation, barged at it with his shoulder. Finally, with a rattle and a bone-curdling squeak of wood, it swung open – just as another clap of thunder rolled overhead.

I blinked and stuttered, momentarily rooted to the spot by the noise, but Nick pushed me inside, pulling the door to as another flash of lightning tore the sky apart.

'Arthur!' I cried. 'You left Arthur out there!'

There was a howl from the hapless pooch and the scrabbling of doggy claws on the other side of the door. Without a second's hesitation, Nick opened it and bundled Arthur inside. Arthur ran to me and wrapped himself as best he could round my legs, shaking and dripping water onto my already wringing feet.

Inside the shed, the air was a trifle warmer. I switched on my phone and by the light of the screen was able to make out ropes, life jackets and a couple of plastic buoys strewn across the floor. In one corner, half covered by a green plastic sheet, loomed an outboard motor, and the pungent smell of salt and seaweed hung in the air.

'Don't say I never bring you anywhere nice,' Nick said, his voice raised to carry over the drumbeat of the rain on the tin roof overhead.

I sank down on the edge of a large wooden crate full of manky old lobster pots, mentally, physically and emotionally exhausted.

'How did it come to this, Nick? What went bloody wrong so that we end up screaming at one another under a tree in the middle of a thunderstorm?'

Nick slithered down the wall opposite. He picked up the end of his shirt and wrung it out. Water trickled onto the floor, mixing with the sawdust and engine oil already there.

'I have no idea.'

'Back there – in Edinburgh – did you,' I hesitated, 'did you love me?'

Immediately, I regretted my words.

There was silence. For a moment or two I thought he might not have heard me over the wind whistling through the cracks in the door and the rain pounding overhead.

'Yes,' he said at last, 'of course I loved you.'

'At the start?'

'At the start – in the middle—'

'At the end?'

There was another weighty silence.

'Yes,' he murmured, 'at the end. But my end was different from your end.'

He paused and the sound of a smile flickered, momentarily, through his voice.

'Only that sounds wrong. I mean – I think you stopped loving me long before I stopped loving you. I was terrified when you left. I felt terrible about the court thing, I didn't know where you'd gone, if you were all right, why you didn't call or reply to my texts – I didn't sleep for a fortnight.'

For the first time, my perception of events swung through one hundred and eighty degrees and I saw things from Nick's point of view. Whatever his crimes, he had suffered too – and the thought was not a happy one.

'I didn't stop loving you, Nick. I might have hated you at times – or rather, the things that you did – but I never stopped loving you.'

The lightning flashed and, instantaneously, the thunder roared. The storm was virtually overhead. Arthur tried to burrow under my legs and let out a pitiful whimper.

I picked him up and buried my face in his wet fur. He smelled a bit rank – like wet dog, funnily enough – but he was warm and comforting and that was what I needed right then.

'Actually, do you know what I really hate, Nick?'

'You mean – apart from me?'

I shuffled closer across the filthy floor, hoping that I didn't come a cropper on any boat hooks or other assorted nautical detritus.

'I've just said – I didn't hate you, Nick. What I hated was

236

the way you refused to take responsibility for yourself and the fact that we were trapped in this cycle of blame: going over the same old chewed-up ground again and again and again.'

The words tumbled over one another. I reached out and found his hand.

'You need to know that *that* was what I was running away from,' I said, 'the thing our marriage had become; and, even though I needed a bit of headspace – and yes, I could have cheerfully killed you over that final debt – I never stopped loving you.'

He wasn't moving. In fact, I couldn't even tell if he was breathing. It was as though he had been frozen by some sort of cosmic 'pause' button.

'Nick,' I put Arthur down gently on the floor and then knelt in front of him. 'Nick, are you okay?'

Slowly, very slowly, through the darkness, I sensed Nick's arm stretching out towards me and, a moment later, the edge of his thumb grazed my cheekbone. I closed my eyes as the thumb tracked its way across my face and came to rest at the corner of my mouth. Without even being conscious that this was what I was doing, I tilted my head slightly and rolled my lips across it, pulling gently against his skin. My first taste of Nick in more than a quarter of a year; prosaic in its execution but searing, visceral and painfully intimate.

'I'm lonely, Ailsa; so fuckingly, painfully lonely.'

I reached out a hand and pulled him to his feet. At that exact moment, we were illuminated by a blinding flash of lightning. Almost as though he couldn't believe what was happening (which, to be fair, may actually have been the

237

case,) Nick ran his eyes over my body. He might as well have used his hands, because I could literally feel the heat of his gaze sweeping through my wringing wet clothes, scorching my skin.

I took the single step towards him. I was so close, I could feel his breath on my skin and the pulse of his heart through my ribcage. I became aware of a source of heat on my thigh. In the dark, I groped my way along my leg and grasped it. It was his other hand.

'Your hand,' I said, 'is on my leg.'

Nick sounded genuinely surprised.

'It is?' he said. 'I mean, is it?'

I was about to move away, but at the last nanosecond, I leaned in even closer to where I knew his face to be. His breath was hot and damp on my already soaking skin and he smelled of earth and rainwater.

I knew perfectly well what was going to happen next: my Nick sixth sense.

Nicksense.

There was the barest flicker of a connection between our lips before his mouth opened and pressed down on mine – just as I had known it would – and his fingers grasped my arm and pulled me on top of him. I slid my leg over his and ran a hand across his chest while my lips worked hard against his. The heat of his body slunk through the clinging, wringing folds of his shirt and transferred through to mine, and somewhere, a pulse was pounding like a heavy metal bass line – although, for the life of me, I couldn't have told you which one of us it belonged to.

His hands were in my hair, under my wringing wet shirt, running across my back. I pulled my mouth away from his

238

and flickered it over his ear, his jaw and down his neck. His skin was wet and stubbly and had a musky taste that I had entirely forgotten about but which ran along my nerves and zapped into my brain. I felt his hands explore the shape of my breasts and then fumble with the buttons on my shirt.

Mouth on mouth, body against body; I knew as surely as if I had been handed a script of the evening's proceedings that the encounter was not going to end here.

Nick had given up with my buttons and instead slid his hands under my shirt, and released my bra from its clasp. I found myself gasping for breath and, with trembling fingers, I undid my shirt buttons myself, before slipping the sodden garment off my shoulders and dumping it unceremoniously on the ground.

Then I leaned forward and, slowly and deliberately, undid his buttons too, planting my mouth on his chest as I went. His skin was damp and goose-pimply – although whether that was due to the rain or the physical intensity of the moment, I didn't know.

As I reached his navel, Nick let out a sound that was half-groan, half-gasp, before levering the shirt off, dumping it on the floor next to mine (another bolt of lightning) and kissing me once again.

My fingers were across his body, under his belt, squeezing and caressing and feeling their way. Instinct took over and I found myself doing those things that I knew would elicit the most powerful response. With the weight of his body pressing against mine, I took a step backwards and nearly tripped over a stray wooden oar, ending up with my naked back pressed hard against the wall of the shed but I hardly noticed: my senses were consumed by Nick. I could feel his low murmurs as I kissed his throat, taste his skin, feel his mouth as it flickered across my body, down my neck and over my breasts. I was saturated by him and still I wanted more: the man was like a class A drug.

His hand wound its way down inside the waistband of my jeans. I wanted to cry out – but no sound came. From somewhere that felt a long way off, I could hear Nick's voice murmuring: 'I want you, Ailsa, I bloody want you.'

Me too, Nick, me too.

I wanted him so much, it hurt.

I fumbled with the zip on his jeans but, before I could undo it, a noise that sounded as though someone had detonated a bomb tore through the lock-up, making the walls shudder and the roof groan ominously. It was so loud and terrifying I think the fillings in my teeth rattled.

And it brought us up short.

'What the hell was that?' I cried.

'I don't know,' Nick bent down and scooped up Arthur, 'but we can't stay here.'

'But – but –' I protested, 'if we don't stay here we have to—'

'Go outside, I know.'

There was another, horrendous creak.

'Come on,' Nick picked up my shirt and threw it across my back and put his arm round my shoulders, before opening the door and, with Arthur under one arm, half pulling, half pushing me through the driving rain back to the hotel.

Chapter Eighteen

I came to rather slowly the next morning. My eyes fluttered open and I registered that the sun was already up and about. Then I turned over, pulling the duvet back over my head to ward off the light – not to mention the blasted birdsong – and paused. As my hand slithered across the sheet next to me, it felt warm.

And the pillow above it felt warm and ever so slightly damp.

Almost as though someone had been sleeping there *with wet hair* . . .

Feeling dazed, I struggled up onto my elbow and, blinking away sleep, looked around.

This was not my room. This room was much smaller, with only one armchair, no desk and a decidedly inferior minibar.

Then the memory of the night before zipped through my brain like a bolt of Tuscan summer lightning – and the whole episode flashed before me.

Me.

Nick.

Soaking wet and in total darkness, doing our best to scramble into our clothes.

Running back from the boatshed in a howling gale; thunder crashing round our ears and a general feeling that if this was actually the end of the world, we wouldn't be at all surprised.

And after that . . .

I snapped back into the present as a flurry of movement over by the French windows caught my eye: it was Nick, in a bathrobe.

I clasped the duvet coyly about my person.

. . . As though Nick didn't know what I looked like naked . . . as though, even if he had forgotten, he hadn't had enough opportunities to remind himself last night . . .

'Hello,' I said.

Awkwardly.

Nick smiled back; not awkward in the least.

'I hope I didn't wake you. I was just – I was just . . .' he waved his hand vaguely in the direction of Outdoors, '. . . making the most of the sunshine.'

He sounded on top of the world – any happier and he would have been whistling a merry little tune. I struggled further up the bed, still clutching the duvet. I looked round the room for my clothes but, even though my eyes were nowhere near as blurry with sleep as they had been, I could not see them anywhere.

Nick followed the line of my gaze – and the train of my thought.

'You left everything you were wearing in the bathroom,' he said. 'You were soaked. First, you put Arthur in your room, then you dumped your clothes in my shower. Not that you needed them . . .'

His voice trailed off and another smile, this one rather rakish, crept over his features.

'No, I suppose I didn't,' I said, my heart giving a funny, uneasy little wobble.

'Anyway, seeing as you're awake, would you like some

breakfast?' Nick continued happily, 'I'll ring through to room service – what do you fancy? Coffee? Croissants? Fry-up?'

He looked chipper, untroubled and (if I was being honest) more than a little bit pleased with himself: as far as he was concerned, last night had obviously been A Good Thing.

I, on the other hand, wasn't feeling quite so upbeat.

'Nick,' I began and then stopped.

He paused, the telephone receiver in his hand.

'What?' he said.

There was a pause.

'Is – is everything okay?' he asked.

I met his eye and then quickly looked away.

'I don't know,' I replied slowly, 'look, about last night—'

What could I say? Did I even understand what had happened myself?

That we'd both been lonely; we'd both been emotional; we'd both been set up by Jess and, into this tinder-box of feelings, we'd allowed the ever-present spark between us to ignite. My brain flashed back to a few hours earlier, as the pair of us had fallen onto the bed – mouths on lips, mouths on skin, mouths on – well, everywhere you could think of.

Had that really been me?

I focused on my aching thighs.

Yes, it had been me; and boy, was I out of practice.

But sex on its own didn't change anything. Nothing had been resolved by a night of mattress surfing – in fact, it had made things a hundred times more complicated. But how was I going to explain that to a happy, slightly smug Nick?

243

I wriggled to the edge of the bed, still clasping the duvet to my bosom. The atmosphere in the room was so thick you could have cut it with a teaspoon. I was practically suffocating with guilt.

'About last night,' I said again and paused. 'I – um – think I got carried away.'

Nick put the phone down. Oh God, I thought; he must have reckoned last night was about us getting back together – he must have thought that if we slept together we were back on again: a tumble under his duvet and we were good to go.

Immediately, my chest tightened and words fell out of my mouth, tripping over one another as I tried to explain.

'I don't want to hurt you, Nick, I really don't; but what happened – us – you and me – it can't undo what happened in Edinburgh. We can't just sleep together and expect everything to go back to normal.'

Nick didn't reply. He looked absolutely dumbstruck.

If I'd had a button I could press so that the floor opened up and swallowed me alive, right then would have been the optimum time to use it. However, in the absence of any floor-swallowing devices, I slid off the bed and, still enveloped in the duvet, hobbled pathetically towards the door.

Escape!

Then I saw my key card on the table next to the bed and hobbled – even more pathetically – back to get it.

'You left your handbag in the boatshed,' Nick said quietly, his thumb picking at the skin round the edge of his fingernail – something I knew he only did when he was very agitated. 'But luckily your key card was in your pocket.'

I picked up the card and then turned back round to

face him. I'd never thought that heartache was a real, physical condition – until then. My chest had tightened even further and every beat was agony.

'I'm sorry,' I cried, 'I'm really, really sorry. I shouldn't have slept with you. I know I shouldn't. I'm sorry if you'd hoped for more; but it doesn't change anything – life doesn't work like that.'

Nick blinked.

'So, last night meant nothing to you?' He spoke with some difficulty, as though he was having trouble understanding what I'd said. 'And when you said – when you said you'd never stopped loving me you were – what – lying?'

Oh God, this was hideous.

'No, no – I did – I do – but—'

'But what?'

'Feelings – love on its own – just aren't enough. I can't go back to how it was, Nick; it wasn't good – not for either of us. I'm sorry, I shouldn't have got your hopes up.'

Nick didn't reply. I hesitated for a moment, before gathering the duvet round me once more.

'I have to go.' I shuffled painfully towards my exit, praying that I could avoid tripping over the edge of the duvet and leave with what scraps of my dignity I still possessed. 'I'm really sorry.'

'So am I, Ailsa,' his reply was so faint, I almost couldn't make out the words, 'really sorry.'

And, as the door closed behind me, I burst into tears.

I showered, fed Arthur and climbed into some fresh clothes – trying to forget about the ones I had left festering in Nick's shower. Then I made my way down one of the steep, twisting paths that led to the shore. This was a different route to the one I had used last night to reach the cedar lawn, and it gave me the most magnificent view of the bay that horse-shoed around the edge of the hotel grounds. The sea remained a deep, stormy green with white waves heaving and pounding restlessly against the rocks, even though the sun was shining brightly and the sky shone a clear, translucent blue. But none of this could distract me from my thoughts.

Oh, why had I gone and slept with Nick? Why, oh why, oh why?

Because I still loved him? Because he did things to me that no one else could? Because I was weak and spineless and ripe for a comfort shag?

One thing I was sure of, though, was that it didn't change anything – our last months together had been a nightmare; an empty packet of condoms could not, on their own, make that good.

I slid my way down the sharp incline of the path until, there ahead of me, half hidden by pine trees, was the boathouse. To my horror, there was a branch resting precariously across its roof.

Had that been the cause of the horrendous noise last night?

With my heart in my mouth, I scuttled as fast as I dared over to the door of the hut. It was open and inside was an elderly man, his balding head inadequately covered by wisps of white hair and a dark blue yachting cap, stroking his chin and surveying the damage.

'Excuse me,' I said, any Italian I might once have

246

known deserting me entirely, 'is there a bag here – um, a handbag? Red?'

The elderly man inside stared at me for a moment as though I was crazy, then bent down and picked up my bag, hidden from sight by a pile of fishing nets.

'Thank you,' I received it gratefully. A quick check inside told me everything was just where I had left it.

'The storm,' the elderly man declared, pointing out to sea, 'is not safe out in the bay today. The boat is in a harbour a few miles round the coast. I will do the island trips tomorrow or day after. Okay?'

'It's fine,' I said, deciding not to argue the point about whether or not I had come to enquire about boat trips. 'Really, it's really fine. Thank you. And I'm sorry about your roof.'

The man shrugged.

'Is okay,' he replied, 'could have been-a worse.'

It could?

He lifted his hand in farewell and then returned to whatever it was that he had been doing – fussocking with his self-bailers or whatever nautical types like him got up to after a big storm.

I turned and made my way back along the path, crunching across the wet gravel. Despite the personal complications it had brought, the storm seemed to have been welcomed by the hotel gardens: raindrops sparkled in the morning sunshine and from all around me came the sharp, pungent smell of damp earth and growing, living things making the most of the summer rain.

This, I thought, must be the calm *after* the storm.

Suddenly, the path forked. The path to the right, I

knew, would take me back to the main entrance and the dining room; the fork to the left was a longer, more scenic route that led round by the ballroom, where Jess's nuptials were due to be celebrated. My stomach rumbled – I was hungry – but I decided to take the longer path, to enjoy the freshness of the morning for a few minutes more. Duly, I began to make my way round the bend and along through the shrubbery. Then I stopped.

Dead.

There was the ballroom, standing as it always had done, slightly away from the rest of the hotel complex; but it was surrounded by a crowd of people, most of them in normal clothes, but a few in the unmistakable uniform of the local fire service. They were all talking in low voices and shaking their heads. I spotted Liam, fully dressed, on the outskirts of the throng and tugged at his waistcoat.

'What's happened?' I asked. 'Is there a fire?'

Liam stepped back and shook his head. He was white and visibly shaken.

'Not any more,' he replied. 'Come and see.'

Together we pushed our way through the sea of people until we reached the front. Then—

Oh. My. God.

Omigod.

Oh, my GOD!

Where yesterday there had been bleached stone walls, set with narrow windows filled in turn with brilliant, vibrant eight-hundred-year-old stained glass, there now stood something resembling the set of a disaster movie. The sun streaked in through an enormous hole that ran like a flesh wound right through the middle of the

248

building. Roofing felt flapped gently in the breeze and here and there an orange tile jutted out against the clear blue of the sky, giving the gap the appearance of a mouth in need of some serious dental attention. Rubble, wooden beams and plasterwork lay in huge mounds both inside and out, while clouds of masonry dust swirled round the interior, lifted by the sea breeze and lit by shafts of summer sunlight.

Finally, right in the middle of the room, lay the author of this destruction: the ancient cedar tree under whose canopy Nick and I had met not twelve hours earlier.

This, not the minor branch incident down at the boathouse, must have been the noise that prompted our midnight sprint back to the hotel.

Bizarrely, what amazed me more than the totality of the devastation was the tranquillity that surrounded it. Normally, I assumed, accidents on a grand scale would be accompanied by blue flashing lights and people with megaphones controlling crowds of rubber-neckers. However, apart from a bit of murmuring from the assembled onlookers, it was quiet and respectful. If it hadn't been the case that a magnificent medieval building had been beaten up and left for dead, it would have been almost beautiful.

Liam broke the silence.

'We knew the tree was dying and the manager had booked the tree surgeon for next week, but the storm beat us to it. I was up when it happened. Actually, I was raiding the fridge down in the kitchen after my shift finished – and I heard the crash. All the alarms on this side of the building went mental. There was a small fire where the trunk came through the wiring but it had burnt itself out before the fire brigade got here.'

I covered my face with my hands.

'This is awful – what's Jess going to say?'

'Jess?' Liam blinked uncomprehendingly at me.

'It's where she and Justin are going to get married on Saturday; where the ceremony is due to take place. If there *is* going to be a ceremony . . .' I trailed off doubtfully. The obstacles in the way of Jess and Justin ever getting round to tying the knot seemed to be stacking up in a pretty emphatic way.

I wondered what Psychic Serena would have made of it.

'And not just Jess, but Auntie Sheila too. She's going to go into orbit when she sees this. Does anyone else know?'

Liam shook his head.

'I don't think your lot are up yet. Most of the guests on the far side of the hotel were oblivious. This area is well away from the bedrooms.'

I nodded. I hadn't heard the alarms either – but then again, I might not have been in the hotel when they'd gone off.

Me and Nick.

In the boathouse.

With the fishing nets.

It almost sounded like some sort of X-rated Cluedo game.

'Don't worry,' I said, 'I'll find Sheila and tell her. Break it to her gently.'

Liam nodded.

'Thanks,' he replied. 'We've got a structural engineer coming out asap to make an assessment, but I'm sure

Roberto would be grateful if you could find her. Fingers crossed it's not as bad as it looks.'

We both surveyed the scene of chaos.

'And then again,' I said, 'it might be even worse.'

'We'll sort something out for the wedding.' Liam held up his hand to shield his eyes from the glare of the morning sun. 'Meanwhile, I've got a couple of hours to kill and I was about to pop into town. I'll slip into the church and offer up a couple of prayers to St Lucy on your family's behalf. It looks like you could do with them.'

I made my way back across the lawn towards reception. Breaking the news that the wedding of the century had now been hijacked by a half-dead tree and an electric storm was not going to be easy. I was also not looking forward to reacquainting myself with Uncle Dudley and his silk kimono. There are times, though, when a girl has to do what a girl has to do – but I was still mightily relieved when I saw Auntie Sheila standing at the bottom of the stairs fully dressed.

'How are you, Ailsa dear – did you sleep well?'

I thought back to my adventures the preceding night.

'No,' I replied, thinking that the bags under my eyes would probably speak for themselves. 'Not terribly well.'

'I'm not surprised,' Auntie Sheila sighed, 'all that thunder and lightning. It would be enough to wake your Granny Sidebottom, and she died a decade ago.'

I ran my eyes down her face, from the arch of her brows to the scoop of her chin, and noticed, for the first time, her resemblance to my mother – only Mum looked like a teenager by comparison. Poor Auntie Sheila: since the start of the week, she'd aged at least twenty years.

'Come on,' I said gently, 'let's go and get you something to eat.'

She allowed me to slip my arm through hers and steer her in the direction of the dining room. Once inside, Sheila paused by the sideboard to pour herself a glass of orange juice.

'You might as well know,' she said, taking a sip, 'this is the strongest stuff I'll be drinking from now on. I've given up alcohol. After the day I had yesterday, you'd think the first thing I'd want to do would be to reach for the bottle, but I don't. For the first time in decades I've realised that a large glass of gin isn't going to solve anything.'

I hesitated. It was hard to say anything that didn't either sound patronising, or indicate that we all knew she was a bit of a lush and talked about her behind her back.

'That's a brave thing to do,' I said, my words feeling clunky and awkward, 'if I can help in any way—'

Auntie Sheila squeezed my hand.

'You are helping, darling,' she said, 'just by being here – although I could have done without you bringing that dog who likes tampon holders with you to the do on Monday night – but you are helping.'

'I am?' I said.

'Jess called me last night,' said Auntie Sheila, 'and told me you had sorted things out between her and Justin. And that friend of yours – the lovely man staying here with the tour group – he saw me as I was coming downstairs just now and asked how I was – he sounded genuinely concerned.'

My heart twisted.

Nick had done that?

Although why was I surprised? It was one of the things I loved – I mean, I *used* to love about him: his generosity of spirit. Auntie Sheila took another sip of juice and closed her eyes.

'You know,' she said sadly, 'I'm to blame for all of this.'

I open my mouth to contradict her, but she continued before I could get the words out.

'Jess didn't want all this fuss. She asked for a no-frills wedding at our local church – you know, the one where Granny and Grandpa are buried – just with the family.'

Auntie Sheila sighed.

'But Dudley wouldn't have it: from the word go he was determined that this was going to be the last word in weddings. It's typical Dudley – everything he does always has to be bigger and better than everyone else, it's like a permanent competition. If you've been to Tenerife, he's been to Eleven-erife. It drives me crazy but I gave up trying to talk sense into him long ago.'

She gave me a weak smile.

'I'd assumed Jess wanted to get married here because this was where you and Dudley had your wedding,' I said.

Auntie Sheila shook her head.

'There was no way we could have afforded this place back in the eighties,' she replied. 'It's true that we were on holiday in the town here, though, and we did want to get married, but Granny Sidebottom – my mother, of course – had all these ideas about a huge ceremony and an enormous reception—'

She laughed as the irony of the situation hit her.

'So Dudley and I decided we'd tie the knot while we were away – all very spur of the moment and just the two of us. It was quite funny: we found the priest from the church in the town square, only his English was as bad as my Italian, and Dudley thought that so long as he spoke VERY LOUDLY AND VERY SLOWLY everyone could understand him. Anyway, after much shouting and waving of arms and a bit of miming, we eventually got our message across and he married us. Your grandmother nearly went into orbit when we told her.'

A little smile danced over her lips.

'As far as Dudley's concerned *now*, of course, our wedding wasn't grand enough, so he's mentally Photo-shopped it into this great big production number. I don't know what he's said to you – probably that the Pope himself did the honours – but in actual fact, it was just me, him and the priest. It was all over in ten minutes and we didn't even sign a register. I know – isn't it awful? I don't actually have a marriage certificate – Dudley thought it would be sent on after the event but it never arrived. I suspect it got lost in the post.'

Even though my experience of Italian weddings was less than extensive, this still sounded a bit odd.

'You *are* married though, aren't you?' I asked.

'Of course I am, dear,' Auntie Sheila waved vaguely at me. 'I've never really bothered too much about the marriage certificate – after all, it's only a piece of paper, isn't it? It's how you feel about someone that really matters.'

My aunt paused.

'Although, having said that, I do hope Jess and Justin manage to make it to the altar on Saturday. Dudley's still storming around like a bear with a sore head; I don't even want to think about what he'll do to Justin when he gets hold of him.'

I reckoned it was time to let her know what I thought about Uncle Dudley throwing his weight around.

'With the greatest respect, Auntie Sheila, I think someone needs to tell him to stick it.' I poured myself a glass of juice too. 'He needs to understand that this is none of his business and that he should let Jess and Justin run their own lives.'

Auntie S looked as though I'd just suggested she order a slice of whale pie with some baby seal fritters on the side.

'You mean – stand up to him? To your uncle? Me?'

'Somebody has to. And if you don't want to lose Jess – who I suspect will be marrying Justin with or without anyone's approval – it might be the only way.'

Auntie Sheila bit her lip.

'Maybe,' she said unconvincingly. 'Perhaps.'

Then she paused.

'Look,' she said, 'if I wanted to talk to Jess, where would I find her?'

'She's in town,' I said, 'but she has her phone with her. Why don't you text her and ask if you can meet up? I'm sure she'd jump at the chance.'

Auntie Sheila leaned over and gave me a huge hug.

'Thank you,' she said, giving me a very wet auntie-style kiss in the middle of my forehead, 'I will. And if you speak to her in the meantime, will you pass on a message for me? Tell her that I'm sorry if I've let her down – and that I want to try and work things out. Justin is such a lovely man, I do hope we can get this wedding back on track.'

'No problem. Look, Auntie Sheila' – a thought about

a less-than-lovely man had struck me – 'did Charles ever have a thing for Jess?'

'Why yes, he did,' Auntie Sheila looked a bit cagey. 'He and Jess went out with each other for about six months.'

'Really?' I don't know what answer I'd been expecting, but it certainly wasn't that.

'And then she met Justin and, well, let's say that Charles became surplus to requirements.'

Blimey – she'd dumped Charles and hooked up with his best mate.

Auntie Sheila lowered her voice.

'Although she wasn't happy with Charles; not for a long time. He was very – how can I put it? – *controlling*. I think she found it flattering to begin with, but after a while the constant texts and the checking up to see where she was and who she was with was a bit much. I was very glad when she started seeing Justin. There's just something about Charles . . .'

She gave a huge sigh, before snapping back into action mode.

'Right,' she drained her glass and put it down on the sideboard. 'I want to go and ring Jess. If you see her before I do, tell her I'm trying to get in touch. Goodness, I do hope we can pull it all together in time for Saturday.'

Oh Lord – Saturday – the ballroom!

'Um, Auntie Sheila,' I began. 'About Saturday. Something's sort of come up. In fact, it might be a good idea if you sat down because—'

'Tell me later,' she said, swinging her enormous handbag over her shoulder. 'I need to find Jessica – anything else will just have to wait.'

Chapter Nineteen

I ate some breakfast (a yummy, sugary bun thingie) and then set out to find Charles.

I was not meddling, stirring or interfering, I told myself – in fact, given what Auntie Sheila had just said, I was on a mission of the utmost importance. Any deals I might have done with Kitty about keeping my nose out were well and truly void.

I tracked him down to the front lawn where he was practising his putting with the help of a golf club (obviously) and a teacup. Checking that Kitty was nowhere to be seen, I walked across the grass and scooped up his golf ball, just as he was about to pot it into the cup.

'Hey!' Charles looked up. 'What do you think you're doing – oh, Ailsa, it's you. What can I do for you?'

I chose my opening shot carefully.

'I thought you'd like to know that Jess is fine,' I said, watching carefully for his reaction, 'and that she and Justin are sorting things out. Isn't that good news?'

This was a deliberate test and – yes, something that could indeed have been dismay flitted over Charles's face.

'Wonderful news,' to the casual observer he would have sounded pretty convincing, but I suspected he would have rather stuck forks in his eyes than be told the wedding was back on again, 'however, I'm sure you didn't track me down just to tell me that.'

He regarded me with a steady, even gaze. The sort of gaze that said, 'You don't scare me; bring it on, lady.' I sent one back that I hoped said, 'Don't worry, mate, I will.'

I looked round again. As much as I disliked the man in front of me, I didn't want the rest of the world knowing what he had done to my cousin.

'I've seen the photographs, Charles,' I lowered my voice, 'the ones of Jess that you keep in your wallet.'

He gave a nervous laugh and flashed one of his humourless grins in my direction.

'Well, you know what I said about me and Jess,' he replied without missing a beat, 'like brother and sister.'

Ewwwww! This was so wrong – on so many levels. I had to wait for my skin to stop crawling before I could reply.

'No,' I said firmly, '*not* like brother and sister. In fact, I'd put money on it that Jess didn't even know they were being taken – and I'd put even more money on it that there are a hundred others like them on your phone that you take out every so often to leer over.'

The image of Charles snapping away on his mobile on the night of the cocktail reception flashed through my mind. Had he been getting a few shots of Jess on the sly? Very likely.

Charles scowled at me and tapped his club against the edge of his shoe; he was clearly rattled but not about to admit defeat – not yet, anyway.

'So I have some photos. For what it's worth, Jess and I used to be an item; I must have taken them when we were together and then forgotten they were in my wallet. You know how it is.'

No, Charles, I thought, I *don't* know how it is – and I'm bloody glad I don't, either.

'Whatever.' I wasn't here to argue the toss. 'I don't care what justification you have in your grubby little mind for those snaps, or how you treated her when you were together – but it's over. Is that clear? In the future you steer clear of not only Jess but my sister as well. I do not want any more members of my family becoming ensnared in your dirty clutches.'

Charles was looking horribly pale and leaned in towards me, his voice low and venomous.

'You little witch,' he hissed, 'are you threatening me? Is it money you're after?'

He was towering over me and I could almost feel the anger coming off him in waves. I'm sure that if I'd been a bloke he would have decked me. However, I could be as stubborn as anyone else in my clan, and I wasn't about to back down.

'I wouldn't stoop so low,' I hissed back. 'Just stay away from us from now on, or I'll make sure you live to regret it, is that clear?'

Then, after treating him to an extra-special Sidebottom family glare, I turned on my heel and marched back to the hotel, my hands and legs shaking, but my head held high.

It took a couple of moments back in the safety of my room to regain my composure. For all my bravado, Charles had been really angry – and something told me that he wasn't the sort of person who would be happy to leave the score at Ailsa – 1; Creepy Charles – 0. But what else could I have done? I wouldn't have been able to sleep at night knowing he was perving over pictures of my cousin; and the thought that my sister – annoying though she was – might be his next victim was more than I could bear.

To take my mind off Charles and his nasty ways, I collected a bottle of water from the minibar, found my bikini and some factor thirty, rolled Arthur up in my beach towel and headed back down to the shore. The sea was calmer than it had been first thing that morning, but it still wasn't back to its normal millpond state – the water glass green rather than azure blue, with white horses breaking noisily onto the rocks.

While Arthur barked loudly at the waves, running towards them as they ebbed and then running even faster in the opposite direction as they chased him back across the sand, I set up camp in the shade of one of the remaining pine trees that clung perilously to the edge of the turf above me. I poured Arthur a drink of water and, while he happily worried and growled at a few large stones, I settled down on my towel and did my best to read my holiday novel.

But it was no good.

Thoughts of Charles, Kitty, Nick, Jess, Justin and the rest of the shemozzle buzzed round my brain like moths in a lampshade, and I found I couldn't focus on the book for more than a few seconds. Defeated by the written word, but still determined to relax, I lay down and pulled my sunhat over my eyes – but this time, rather than the follies of young love, it was a weird niggling feeling about Auntie Sheila and Uncle Dudley's wedding that took hold of me and wouldn't let me rest.

Waves – listen to the waves. Let your breathing synchronise

with the sound of the sea on the beach and feel your tension ebb
away like the tide . . .

There was something about Auntie Sheila's secret church wedding and the marriage certificate getting lost in the post that didn't seem quite right.

Ebb and flow . . . ebb and flow . . .

I flipped over onto my front, but the niggling wouldn't leave me alone – it darted round my brain like a slippery thing; always there but always just out of reach.

The ceremony: whatever it was that was worrying me was absolutely to do with the ceremony and—

A wet nose planted itself right in the small of my back and I leaped into the air.

I obviously wasn't going to be allowed to sunbathe in peace.

'Come on, boy!' I called.

Braving the post-storm chill of the water, I dived into the sea and pulled myself through the rolling green waves while Arthur stood on the sand, barking anxiously in my direction, like a short, hairy lifeguard. The cold of the water must have kick-started my brain, because I suddenly knew what I had to do: I needed to speak to someone who knew far more than I did about Italian weddings.

And, even though I would rather have eaten my own hair than ask for it, that person was Nick.

To Arthur's enormous relief, I emerged like Venus from the waves and wrapped myself in my beach towel, rubbing my hair into a semblance of dryness and feeling sparkier and more refreshed than I had for a long time.

'Come on, Arthur,' I called, 'we've got to find your

Uncle Nick. I hate to say it, but he's the only person round here who can help sort this out.'

And I walked back along the path to the hotel crossing my fingers that he and his charges had got back from their morning outing – and that he was willing to talk to me.

Nick and his old ladies were, however, nowhere to be seen.

I enquired at reception and was told that they had gone to visit a local vineyard and weren't due back much before teatime. Thus, with my hopes dashed, I changed both my clothes and my tack and headed off into town with Arthur.

We wound our way through the late morning crowds in the market square, which seemed to be even busier than usual. The place was heaving, with stalls offering brightly coloured fruit and veg, glistening local fish, including lobsters on blocks of ice with their claws taped shut, and wooden crates full of live chickens and ducks. As I watched, a toothless Italian grandmother, who must have been a hundred years old if she was a day, selected a grey speckled hen and walked off towards the bus stop with the bird squawking and flailing under her arm. I sampled some cheese, some bread, some olives, some more cheese and then, just as I was trying to dodge a man with a very smelly goat who really, really wanted me to try *another* type of cheese, I heard a commotion. On the other side of the square was Kitty; and ahead of her, looking very much as though he was trying to escape, was Charles.

'What do you mean, you haven't got time to see me?' she was yelling at his retreating form. 'We agreed: the boat trip was cancelled, so we were going to spend the afternoon on the beach. It was a *date*.'

'I'm sorry,' Charles called over his shoulder, 'some-thing's come up. I told you.'

'You're on holiday!' Kitty looked angry and upset in pretty much equal measure. 'What the hell comes up when you're on holiday?'

Charles gave a heavy sigh and ground to a reluctant halt. He didn't turn round, but kept his eyes fixed doggedly ahead of him. Kitty stamped her foot.

'I want the truth!' she cried. 'And *look* at me when I'm talking to you!'

Charles did not do as he was told. Instead he sighed again.

'You want the truth?' he said. 'Well, here it is: I don't actually know if you and me are such a good idea after all.'

Kitty looked as though someone had just whacked her over the head with a length of lead piping.

'No,' she shook her head. 'Don't be ridiculous. You said last night that you'd fallen in love with me. You said you'd never felt like this before and that we had something special – really special. You're coming to Manchester to visit me in a couple of weeks' time and you're going on holiday with me in August and at Christmas—'

'Actually, I'm not.' Charles started walking away from her. 'Like I said, something's come up.'

Kitty stood for a moment, rooted to the spot. Then she unfroze and let rip with the full power of her vocal cords.

'You bastard!' she screamed so loudly they could probably hear her back up at the hotel. 'You total, shitty bastard! I hate you!'

And she picked up an over-ripe orange from a nearby

stall and hurled it at him. Charles dodged and it hit a crate of chickens, making them squawk like crazy.

'Is this sudden change of heart anything to do with my sister?' she shouted. 'Has my sister been speaking to you?'

Charles didn't reply, but Kitty had already made her mind up.

'I bet she has – this has got her fingerprints all over it. I'll bloody kill her. I'll—'

I didn't wait to find out what else Kitty had in mind for me. I slunk quickly (if you can slink quickly) over to the church, lifted the latch on the heavy oak door and pushed it open, slipping inside just as a second rotten orange made contact with the back of Charles's head. The musty gloom of the interior was cool and soothing, but it took a while for my eyes to adjust to the tiny amount of light that filtered in as best it could through the narrow arched windows – and I almost took a tumble down a set of three steps hiding behind the doorway.

Once I became attuned to the gloom, however, I started to cast my eye around the interior of the building. It was not the familiar cruciform of an English country church but more like a sort of high-ceilinged, oblong box with a round domed bit at the far end. A gleam of gold on a nearby wall caught my attention and I walked across the dusty, flagged floor to peer at it. It was an enormous wall painting – a magnificent beast, a good ten feet long and another eight or so high, rich reds and lapis blues mixing vividly with the glinting gold. On the right-hand side, it depicted angels with trumpets who were helping frightened-looking people scramble out of graves, while on the left, another – even more terrified – group of individuals were being prodded by fearsome-looking demons holding super-sized barbecue forks.

I noted with a degree of resignation that I was not standing on the side of the angels.

Feeling strangely disillusioned, I turned and trudged back across the expanse of the nave towards a rack of flickering votive candles. I was just about to throw a bit of change into the collection box and place my own little light in a holder next to the others, when I heard the latch lift and the base of the heavy main door shudder across the floor.

I stiffened and sent up a quick prayer that the newcomer was anyone other than my sister.

'Hello,' said a familiar voice, which seemed to reverberate off the walls and echo up through the stone flags beneath my feet as well.

'Nick!' I spun round and shhh-ed Arthur who was barking enthusiastically at him. 'What are you doing here?'

Nick trotted down the steps into the main body of the church and came to a halt in the middle of the nave, illuminated by a shaft of sunlight. Even though there was several hundred cubic feet of air between us, not to mention some chairs and a couple of racks of votive candles, he felt dangerously close. I don't know what I thought could possibly happen between us in a church, but I sensed my heart rate pick up and my stomach start to fizz. Or maybe that was just an after-effect of that cheese I'd sampled in the market . . .

Nick raised his hand in greeting. I relaxed – fractionally. At least he hadn't tracked me down solely to tell me what a bitch I'd been for leading him on the night before.

'Um – how was the wine-tasting?' I asked, thinking this was safe, neutral conversational ground.

'Well, there was quite a lot of wine, only most of the ladies didn't really understand about *tasting* as opposed to *swallowing*, so we came back early to allow them time for a lie-down before dinner.'

'Oh,' I couldn't help smiling at the thought of a busload of little old ladies off their trolleys from too much vino.

'So, as I've got an afternoon free, I thought I'd take the opportunity to pop into town and have a look round the church – Liam says that the medieval wall art is quite spectacular.' He paused. 'You?'

'I'm hiding from Kitty,' I said a little sheepishly. 'I think she wants to kill me. Only please don't ask, it's a long story.'

This time it was Nick who was obviously trying to smother a smile.

'You know,' he said, 'the pair of you are more alike than you think – and I bet the same goes for your mother and Sheila: all four of you popped out of the exact same mould. Just be careful you and Kitty don't end up at daggers drawn too.'

'Don't be ridiculous,' I retorted, 'I am *nothing* like the rest of my family. Not in the least.'

'No, of course not,' said Nick, the smile finally breaking through despite his best smothering efforts.

Then his expression changed.

'Look, Ailsa, I'm glad we bumped into each other. There are a few things I want to discuss – about last night.'

I bit my lip. There were a few things I *didn't* want to discuss about last night. Like . . . well, all of it really. I decided to move the conversation onto a less excruciating tack – namely Auntie Sheila.

'Nick, I need some advice: marital advice.'

Nick gave me a sideways look.

'Not about us,' I said quickly, feeling my face light up like a maritime distress flare, 'about – look, it doesn't really matter who it's about – what do you know about Italian weddings?'

Nick shrugged.

'They tend to be loud, noisy affairs and we throw rice. And the dresses – meringue doesn't even come into it.'

'No, I mean *legally* – what do you have to do to be legally married in Italy.'

Nick rubbed his face.

'Now you're asking. Well, I think if you're *British* and getting married in Italy there are all sorts of hoops you need to jump through concerning passports and banns and that sort of thing. Once you're over here it's usual to get married at the town hall or possibly in a Catholic church – like this one – but you must make sure that you comply with the civil rules for weddings as well as any church ones, or the marriage won't be valid. You'd be better off asking Jess; after all, this is exactly what she's had to do for her own wedding.'

This wasn't looking good for poor Auntie S.

'Can you remember any details? About church weddings? From ones you've been to over here – or your family discussing it – or anything, really.'

'Well, from what I *remember*, you'll need two witnesses and you'll have to complete a whole load of paperwork beforehand. The Vatican doesn't approve of people just

267

rocking up at random to a place like this, for instance, and tying the knot.'

He looked me dead in the eye and the silence that hung suspended between us felt like a lead weight.

That is, if lead weights *can* hang suspended in mid-air.

Which I doubt.

'Would you mind?' he began. 'I mean, can I ask what this is about? I'm sorry, I hope you didn't think you could find a loophole of Italian law that would let us walk away from our marriage. I know I'm half-Italian, but we married in Scotland and the law there is clear: our wedding was entirely binding.'

The corners of my eyes felt hot and itchy: this wasn't supposed to be about me and Nick; but then again, it was starting to feel as though everything *was* about me and Nick, whichever way I turned. It was true what they say – you can't run away from your problems because they will always come and find you. And they do; even in a dark, medieval church in a sleepy seaside town in Italy.

'No, Nick, it's not about us.'

'Then who? Jess and Justin? Or are you keen to start a career as an Italian matrimonial lawyer?'

Even as I took a deep breath and prepared to tell him what had happened, I knew I could trust him. Just as I had over Justin. Just as I once had with my heart. How had it all gone so spectacularly and painfully wrong?

'My aunt told me that she and my uncle came to this town when they were on holiday a million years ago, walked into *this* church and, after a bit of linguistic difficulty, got the priest to marry them. Except, after what you've just said, I'm pretty sure that he didn't – at least, not in any legally binding sense. Only, they don't know that.'

Nick's eyebrows shot up so fast they nearly became detached from his head.

'Seriously?'

'Seriously.'

He made a whistling noise.

'As soon as she told me, I started to become suspicious – and everything you've just said has confirmed it. The problem is, do I say anything to Auntie Sheila? I mean really and truly, deep down, does it make any difference? Auntie Sheila *wants* to be married to Uncle Dudley; she just doesn't have the marriage certificate to prove it, whereas – whereas you and me – well, our piece of paper actually means *nothing*.'

The words were out of my mouth before I even knew they were forming in my brain.

Nick took another few steps towards me until there were only two rows of rickety-looking wooden chairs between us. Arthur pressed protectively against my legs and the atmosphere was so intense I could barely breathe.

'About that piece of paper—' Nick began.

His eyes were dark and serious and they held mine as surely as if our sightlines had been superglued together. Slowly, he made his way round the chairs and stood in front of me. Then he reached out and took my hand.

'Like I said,' he continued, 'there are a few things I want to discuss. I need to know, Ailsa, was any of what happened last night for real? Or were you trapped in a shed in the middle of a thunderstorm and it came down to a choice between sex or charades?'

I swallowed. I needed to be very careful about how I phrased the next few sentences. I didn't want to hurt him any more than I already had.

'Last night, Nick, like I told you, I got carried away.'

'Right. Okay.' He wasn't any more impressed by my explanation now than he had been at nine o'clock that morning. 'So it was just a physical thing.'

'No – no it wasn't. I didn't mean it like that.'

'So, how do you mean it?'

'I mean – I mean I'd missed you. I'd forgotten how much I fancied you – how much I felt for you. Like I said, I got carried away.'

I looked down at my feet, which seemed to have rearranged themselves so that they were inside Nick's. My left leg was leaning against his right. Our hips were almost, almost touching . . .

'But fancying each other isn't enough, Nick. I can't go back to how it was, and, if you're being honest, neither can you. You were as miserable as me. If last night is going to mean anything at all – if we decide we want to think about getting back together permanently – things are going to have to change. Really, seriously change.'

I paused, waiting for him to speak or nod or make any indication that he understood what I was trying to tell him.

'No more rows,' I said. 'No more shouting. Just talking – absolute bloody shedloads of talking. Taking responsibility for equal shares of the bills. No spending what we can't afford. Being partners for each other – equals. It's a huge shift for both of us, Nick. It's not going to be easy.'

But he still didn't reply.

Instead his mouth brushed mine and the taste of Nick

– savoury, sweet and with a lingering hint of locally grown Chianti – spread out through my waiting body.

'Believe me,' he said. 'I've learned my lesson. Just give me another chance; you won't regret it, I promise.'

And he kissed me again, my body curving into his and my lips pulling at his just as hungrily as they had done the night before.

It was only the start, but it was a good one.

We would sort out the details later.

No, really – we would.

Chapter Twenty

Somehow we made it back to the hotel.

Somehow we managed to pay the taxi driver.

Somehow we managed to get halfway down the path to the main door – when Nick pulled me into an alcove behind a flying buttress and kissed me again. My mouth opened to receive his and, suddenly, his hands were on my back, in my hair, stroking my face. I kissed him back – hard and passionate – and felt his hand slide from my jawline to my hand, which he proceeded to tug. Hard.

'Shall we get a room?' he murmured, his voice low and hoarse.

I hesitated.

'What's up?' Nick's breath was on my cheek.

'I want to take things slowly,' I whispered.

'We're not rushing into anything,' he replied, homing in once again. 'We're married. It's practically compulsory – especially in Italy.'

I ran a hand down his arm. Flesh against flesh, my bare fingers on his bare skin. It was almost unbearable.

'Let's talk first, Nick: lay down some proper ground rules, find out if we really can make this work – for the long-term.'

'So,' he went to kiss me again but I dodged to one side. 'Come to my room and we'll talk.'

I smiled.

'I know the sort of talking you're on about,' I said, 'and it involves wearing not many clothes and lying on a bed.'

Nick gave a sheepish grin.

'Am I that transparent?' he asked.

I nodded.

'Pretty much,' I said.

Nick shook his head.

'Okay,' he said, 'so the *other* sort of talking – the one where we try and sort things out – shall we do a bit of that now? And then maybe afterwards we could . . .?'

He was gazing at me in much the same way that Arthur did when he knew there was the possibility of food: all huge, pleading brown eyes. I'd heard of people looking like their pets – but an animal that reminded you of your ex . . . ?

'All right,' I said, running a finger along the edge of his jaw, 'but let's steer clear of bedrooms for the time being; I think the temptation would be too great.'

'Then we'll walk.' Nick grabbed my hand and pulled me back onto the path. 'Come on – this way.'

We made our way along the path in silence for a short while.

'The first thing I need to do is apologise,' he said solemnly, 'I behaved badly. I took you for granted financially *and* emotionally and, worst of all, I wasn't honest with you – although none of it was deliberate. You see, I thought I'd be able to pay off that loan, but then I found I couldn't. I kept waiting for the right time to tell you I'd run up another debt – to ask for help – but that time never came: you were always too busy or too tired or too angry. It's not an excuse, I know, but it's what happened. Anyway, the longer I left it, the harder it became to broach the subject; until in the end, I panicked. I put the letters in the bin so you wouldn't see them and pretended nothing was wrong – it was ridiculous and childish, of course it was, but I swear to you I've changed and nothing like that will ever happen again.'

He paused.

'I was so frightened of losing you – sensing it was all going horribly wrong but thinking I was powerless to stop it – that I turned into a different person. The man you spent those last few months with wasn't me, Ailsa. Me, the real me, is the guy you fell in love with at the start. I don't ever want to meet that other chap again.'

My chest did its tightening thing again, but this time in a good way. Why couldn't we have spoken to each other like this months ago?

'Me too, Nick,' I said, 'that girl, Ailsa – the shouty, angry, sarcastic one – I'm not her and I never want to go back to living in her skin. You behaved badly, yes, but so did I – I nagged and yelled and made it impossible for you to talk to me. I'm sorry too.'

I leaned in against his chest and he kissed me softly on the top of my head.

'Ailsa,' he said, 'all I want is to be with you. Tell me what I need to do to make it happen.'

'I want to be with you too,' I replied, 'and all you need to do is work with me, Nick. Earn your keep and above all, be honest – even if you think I'll go ballistic. Is that a deal?'

I took a step back and Nick squeezed my hand.

'It's a deal. Actually, on the "earning my keep" front,

I have some news. What would you say if I told you I've applied for a job? A really good job, too. One that means I still get to draw, but that brings in a decent amount of cash.'

I stared at him.

'Seriously? A job?'

'Aye. It's more or less official: I'm going to be a wage slave. You remember the portfolio I told you about? Well, this is what it was for. Contrary to appearances, I do listen to you, Ailsa. I did actually take on board what you were saying – or even screaming – at me.'

I could barely believe my ears.

'And?' I was beside myself. 'Tell me – tell me everything.'

But he just grinned and brushed my lips with his.

'All in good time,' he said. 'But you *can* trust me, Ailsa; I'm not going to let you down. When you left, it brought me up sharp and – holy cow!'

We had rounded the bend that brought us within view of the ballroom. Or rather, what had been the ballroom before nature had intervened and given it a good kicking. The gawping crowd and firemen of earlier had gone and the area was now festooned with yellow tape. Gangs of men in hard hats were busy erecting a forest of scaffolding.

Nick turned to me, his mouth hanging open in astonishment.

'Shitting Nora! That noise – last night? Oh, bloody hell.'

But I didn't have any spare capacity to deal with his shock: I had failed to do something very important indeed.

'Oh no, Auntie Sheila!' I cried.

Nick looked horrified.

'Why – was she in there?'

'No.' I put my head in my hands. 'I was supposed to break it to her gently that the wedding venue had had a bit of an accident. Only she went off to find Jess; and I – well – I got a bit distracted.'

'Look.' Nick pulled my hands away from my face and looked down into my eyes. 'Here's what we'll do. I'll go and ask that chap over there what the state of affairs is and then you can go and find your aunt and give her an up-to-date report. Okay? Does that sound like a plan?'

I nodded. Nick gave me a quick smile and then walked over to a chap in a blue hard hat and a yellow high-vis jacket. I followed, keeping a wary eye open for any relatives.

'*Dimmi, cosa è successo?*' asked Nick.

The chap lifted up his hard hat, scratched his hair (which was plastered down onto his head with sweat) and replied with a stream of fast-moving Italian.

'Nick?' I pleaded for a translation.

'The tree's out but they need to secure the structure,' he replied, before turning back to the workman. '*Tercento, questa stanza? Quattrocent?*'

The man shrugged and wiped a bead of perspiration from the tip of his nose before replying.

'Really?' Nick nodded. 'The monastery dates from the thirteenth century – wow.'

My heart sank: Nick had found something of historical interest. I knew from experience that we could be here for hours – only, we didn't have hours.

We had minutes, if we were lucky.

The sound of a taxi pulling up outside the main entrance reached my ears and I spun round.

'Nick,' I said, craning my neck to see who was getting out of the cab, 'I'm just – oh buggerfuck, it's Auntie Sheila! Find out how long it's going to be before they can make the walls safe. I'll try and head her off. Please, Nick, hurry!'

'No, young man,' Auntie S's strident tones cut through the midday air, 'I have just seen my daughter and she wants me to double-check the number of pillars in the ballroom. She says there are six and I say eight. We need to give the florist the final order for the garlands. *Will you get out of my way!*'

'But – *Signora* – you must not – until the workmen have finished—'

'Workmen? Don't be absurd. It's a wedding, not a building site.'

I picked up the skirts of my dress and ran down the path as fast as I could without turning an ankle, and almost collided with my aunt, who was marching in the opposite direction, an expression of steely determination on her features.

'Auntie Sheila,' I panted, 'did you find Jess?'

'I did,' Auntie Sheila smiled. 'And the good news is that it's all going ahead. Jess and Justin are going to be married here on Saturday. Everything has been sorted out.'

'Even Uncle Dudley?' I was so gobsmacked that for about thirty seconds I forgot about the ballroom.

Auntie Sheila's eyes narrowed.

'I gave Dudley a choice,' she said, 'I told him they were getting married and he could either like it or lump it.'

'What did he say?' I was agog.

'There was a lot of spluttering and he started talking about money and the hotel bill and that sort of thing, but I held up my hand and told him that it was his choice whether or not he showed his face at the ceremony, but it was going ahead with or without him.'

Respect for this new, improved, no-nonsense Auntie Sheila spread through me.

'I don't know whether he'll come,' she continued, 'but as far as I'm concerned it's chocks away. Now, I need to count those pillars!'

'How about we have a nice sit-down and cup of coffee first?' I suggested.

I linked my arm through hers and tried to swing her round, back towards the main entrance.

'Later, dear,' Auntie Sheila patted my hand. 'Veronica's not answering her phone and the florists are most insistent. Speaking of Veronica, you haven't seen her anywhere, have you? She isn't in her room and I can't find her anywhere else in the hotel. Really, it's most infuriating.'

'I'll count the pillars,' I said, 'I'll go and do it right now and then come and tell you the answer.'

'Don't bother, dear, it won't take two seconds.'

And with a nimbleness that belied her middle-aged spread, she dodged round me and continued marching down the path for all she was worth.

'No, really, Auntie Sheila – I mean—'

But it was too late. She rounded the bend and, there before her, lay the ballroom.

Or, rather, the ex-ballroom.

I had expected her to go very pale, stop dead in her

tracks and possibly keel over. However, she just kept on going. She marched straight up to the nearest workman and put her hands on her hips.

'What do you think you are doing?' she cried.

The man took a step back. He was a big chap, in fact, he could probably have given Uncle Dudley a run for his money in the hippopotamus stakes – but I don't think he had ever met anything like Auntie Sheila before.

'Is tree,' he said, a discernible quaver in his voice.

'Is not tree,' she said, 'is ballroom. Is where my daughter be married on Saturday.'

She was so angry she'd lapsed into broken English with a bad Italian accent.

'No – is tree!' the man insisted, somewhat bravely in my opinion as the tree was nowhere to be seen.

Auntie Sheila was so angry she didn't even bother to reply. Instead she whacked the poor man across the back of the shoulders with her handbag. He staggered forward and almost pitched headlong onto the gravel path.

'Is daughter's wedding,' she yelled, in broken, fake-Italiana. 'Where is manager? Where is Veronica? Somebody is-a going pay for this!'

She swung her body round and prepared to give the builder a second dose of her handbag. I looked at the distance between us – there was no way I could reach her in time.

'Nick!' I yelled. 'Nick – stop her before she injures someone!'

Nick broke off his conversation with the other workman and sprinted as fast as he could towards my aunt. He put up his arms to try and ward off Auntie Sheila's second blow but – doooof! The handbag caught him across the shoulders and along the side of his cheek and he wobbled for a moment before toppling gracefully to the ground.

Auntie Sheila immediately dropped the bag and fell onto her knees beside him.

'Nick!' she cried. 'Nick – are you all right?'

Nick struggled up onto his elbow. There was a red mark underneath his chin and another running the length of his neck.

'Walking wounded,' he said, sitting up and running his hand across a nasty graze on his elbow, 'I'll live.'

'Oh, Nick,' Auntie Sheila was almost in tears. 'I am so sorry, I had no idea it was you. Goodness – are you all right?'

'You crazy lady,' said the first builder and, turning to Nick added, 'you keep your *mamma* under control.'

'She's not,' said Nick through gritted teeth, 'my mother.'

The builder shrugged and went back to his scaffolding. I slid down onto the gravel and put my arm under Nick's shoulder to help lever him up.

'Oh dear,' I said, kneeling down next to him, 'that looks sore.'

And without thinking, I pressed my lips lightly on to his chin.

Immediately, Auntie Sheila's gimlet gaze was upon me.

'Ailsa,' she began, 'are you and Nick—'

Luckily, she was cut off by the sound of pounding feet on gravel and the arrival of someone in an orange hard hat, whom I took to be the foreman. Auntie Sheila scrambled to her feet and I made a point of relieving her of her bag before she was tempted to assault anyone else with it.

'Are you in charge here?' she demanded, with not even the merest hint of an apology for handbagging one of his staff.

'I am,' replied the foreman.

'Then do you mind telling me what is going on?'

'It is a tree,' replied the foreman.

Auntie Sheila gave a huge, exasperated gasp.

'Will you all *stop* saying that,' she told him, 'there is *not* a tree, there is a ballroom – only now it is a ballroom with no roof and only three walls.'

'There was tree,' the foreman insisted, 'tree fell through ballroom roof.'

Auntie Sheila was firmly in denial.

'There is *not* a tree,' she repeated. 'Ailsa – tell them there is not a tree.'

I touched her gently on the arm.

'There was,' I said softly, 'it was that one, look.'

I pointed to the blackened remains of the cedar, half hidden behind the truck carrying the rest of the scaffolding.

Auntie Sheila went pale.

And a bit wobbly.

I put my arm round her waist and felt her lean against me.

'This isn't happening,' she murmured, 'this really, really isn't happening. I can't find Veronica – and now this.'

'It's fine,' I said comfortingly, 'we'll sort it out.'

Auntie Sheila shook her head.

'It isn't fine,' she whispered, 'it's really very completely absolutely not fine. I don't know – I can't – oh, *where the bloody hell is Veronica!*'

'Look, Auntie Sheila,' I said, in what I hoped was a bright, positive tone, 'they've shored up the building and removed the tree.'

'Is it safe?' asked Auntie Sheila. I could hear the hope in her voice – what were a few scaffolding poles just so long as the wedding went ahead?

The foreman shook his head.

'Will be weeks,' he said, 'possibly months. Is—'

He searched for a word.

'Conservation. Very expensive.'

Auntie Sheila covered her mouth with her hand. For a moment, I thought she was going to be sick.

'But the wedding is on Saturday,' she said, 'we need it for Saturday.'

The foreman shook his head again.

'Not Saturday,' he said, 'is impossible.'

Slowly, very slowly, my aunt turned away.

'It will be fine, Auntie Sheila,' I said, putting my arm round her shoulders. 'We'll use another room. The hotel will come up with something.'

Sheila bit her lip.

'It's the licence,' she said. 'The ballroom is licensed by the town hall for weddings – *only* the ballroom – the licence doesn't apply to any other part of the hotel. If Jess doesn't get married there, then she won't actually be married. There *is* nowhere else.'

Nick and I exchanged glances, but said nothing.

'Come on, Mrs Westfield.' Liam appeared as if by magic

and slipped his arm round her waist. 'You've had a nasty shock. I'll take you inside.'

Auntie Sheila nodded and leaned against him. I took my arm away.

'Here,' I said, pushing the handbag into Liam's free hand, 'I'd keep this away from her until you get inside if I were you.'

But Auntie Sheila was a long way from bopping anyone else with her Radley. Held upright by Liam, she hobbled down the path towards the main entrance. If there was ever a dictionary definition of a broken woman, it was her.

As soon as she was safely out of earshot, I turned to Nick.

'What are we going to do, Nick? It's a disaster.'

Nick was dabbing cautiously at his face with a tissue.

'It's not looking good, is it?'

'You heard what Auntie Sheila said about the licence: it's the ballroom or nothing. Unless – Nick, would the town hall license another room in the hotel, do you think? As it's an emergency?'

Nick shrugged and put his tissue away.

'It would probably take too long. I suppose they might be able to get married at the town hall itself, though – that's not a bad option. The building looks quite nice and they could always have the photos taken outside the church in the market square – that's what real Italians do.'

'Mmmm,' I murmured thoughtfully, 'and Jess did say she'd have preferred a church to be involved somewhere along the line.'

Nick nodded in the direction of the ancient monastery church with its decaying rose window.

'Shame that one doesn't have a roof, she'd have loved that.'

I looked from Nick to the ruin and back again. Then I flung my arms round him and planted an enormous kiss on his lips.

'You genius!' I cried. 'You total genius!'

'Ow!' Nick winced in pain.

I kissed him again, more gently this time.

'The church,' it was *so* obvious, 'we can use the church! Come on – I'm going to need you to translate. Come *on*!'

I took him by the hand and began dragging him (and Arthur, who had somehow managed to fall asleep in the middle of all the excitement) back down the path.

'She is crazy!' yelled the handbagged builder to Nick. 'Just like the older one!'

'Maybe – but she's the one I want to spend the rest of my life with!' called back Nick.

My heart leaped. I didn't care how crazy I was – I had my husband back!

Chapter Twenty-One

It was seven o'clock that evening. I'd had a very busy but productive afternoon, a lot of which had involved Nick and the king-sized bed in my room – but it had also included a visit to the town hall and another to the local registrar.

I showered, washed my hair and slid into the vintage evening gown Emma had lent me. As I checked my reflection in the mirror, a pair of tanned arms reached out from the bed and grabbed me round the waist, pulling me, shrieking, down onto the mattress.

'You think I'm going to let you go this evening?' Nick, wearing nothing but a strategically placed hotel sheet, manoeuvred his (naked) body next to mine (fully clothed) and ran a hand up under the layers of film and froth that constituted my skirt.

I grinned.

Or rather, I continued the grin I had been wearing since we had finished dealing with Italian officialdom earlier in the day. I bent down and kissed him on the lips.

That kiss took longer than I'd anticipated, but it was worth it. I'd forgotten that kissing Nick was such a satisfying and compelling thing to do.

'I have to be there,' I said, running my index finger across the side of his face, down his neck and then right along the full length of his body. 'It's the pre-wedding dinner, remember? It's a three-line family whip. Even Jess and Justin are turning up.'

'But we still don't know that there's *going* to be a wedding,' Nick's hand travelled a little further up my leg. 'We haven't heard back from Jess and Justin yet. Why don't you just avoid any acrimony and unpleasantness and stay here with me? I think we could find one or two things to do to while away the long, dark winter night.'

I kissed him again, even more lingeringly, while his hand continued its journey along my leg until it reached the very top of my thigh. There was absolutely no doubt about what he had on his agenda.

'Dark winter night? It's thirty-five degrees and broad daylight, Nick. And you've had me to yourself all afternoon.'

Nick's other hand made its way up my back and began to tug at the zip on my dress.

'But it's been months, Ailsa,' he gave up with the zip and simply pulled me down on top of him. 'I might have learned some new tricks I need to show off.'

'Show me when I come back.' I pulled away, laughing and smoothing out the silk of my skirts.

'Don't be too long.' He grabbed my wrist and pulled me back down for one last, lingering kiss. 'I could – I could even come with you if you like?'

I hesitated.

Nick on my arm – at a family dinner?

Auntie Sheila had already seen me kiss him; Kitty knew we'd been living together – and Jess was the one who set us up on our thunder-and-lightning date under the ill-fated cedar tree. Was it really all that secret any more?

'No, not now, Nick.' I pulled myself away. 'It's going to be difficult enough this evening as it is, without you and me throwing our piece of craziness into the mix.'

Something that might have been disappointment, but didn't hang around long enough for me to properly decode, flashed across Nick's face.

'Okay,' he said, 'it's fine. I really should be going over my notes. We're off to Pisa tomorrow and I need to swot up on leaning towers.'

His words brought me up with a jolt. It said something for the level of shock surging through me that I completely failed to make any sort of Freudian joke about towers, leaning or otherwise.

Nick was going?

So soon?

He raised his eyebrows.

'I told you I was only here till Friday,' he said. 'A couple of days ago, you couldn't wait to get rid of me.'

'I know.' I sat up and smoothed down my skirts. 'I just – well – things change, don't they?'

'I don't change,' he said. 'I love you, Ailsa. I always have done. This tour lasts for two more weeks – that's all – then I'm home again for ever.'

His hand wound its way back up my thigh.

'I'll be as quick as I can.' I tried to wriggle free of the hand and kissed him again, savouring the taste of his mouth and the smell of his skin, moving my lips slowly and meaningfully against his. 'Meanwhile, why don't you work in here? Then, as soon as I *do* get back, we can—'

Nick's finger began to tug at my knicker elastic. The temptation to say 'to hell with it' and spend the evening reacquainting myself with my husband was almost overwhelming.

Almost . . .

'I'll see you soon.' One last kiss – really, it *would* be the last. 'Get yourself some dinner from room service – oh, and don't let the dog out.'

Arthur, who had been relegated to Nick's room for most of the afternoon, gave a pitiful whine. I felt guiltier than an armed robber caught with one hand in the till and the other round the barrel of a sawn-off.

'Okay, I'll see you *after* dinner and *after* I've walked the dog,' I corrected, causing Arthur to thump his little tail loudly on the carpet. 'Although it won't be a long walk, I'm afraid, Arthur, it's clouded over again and it looks like it's going to be raining cats and dogs at any minute.'

At the sound of the word 'cats' Arthur's lips pulled back in what I could only describe as a huge, doggy grin. Not for the first time I wondered if he could actually understand what I was saying.

Nick sat up and rubbed the back of his head.

'I'll take the little chap out,' he said. 'It won't be any trouble. I'll squeeze him into my rucksack and sneak him past the SS people on the door. You'd like to come out with me, wouldn't you, buddy? We'll see if we can find some rabbits for you to chase.'

Arthur leaped off the floor with enthusiasm and barked excitedly, but I felt less thrilled about the plan. Call it a premonition, call it boring old pessimism – I don't know which – but I had a strange, lurking feeling that Arthur should be enjoying a quiet night in. At least until I got back.

'Shhh!' I kissed Nick again – *quelle surprise.* 'Don't get him excited. I don't fancy having to lie to the hotel staff and tell them you do this thing to me that makes me bark like a dog. Please don't take Arthur out of the room – even in a rucksack. It's too risky. Let me take him for his walk as usual; that way, if anything *does* go wrong, I'll only have myself to blame. *Capisce?*'

'Mmmmmm,' Nick's hand was now inside my knickers. 'All right. But as for the barking thing – I think I could have you making a whole range of noises you had no idea you were capable of.'

Using the most astounding amount of willpower, I stepped back out of hand/finger reach and checked I had everything I needed in my bag.

'Maybe,' I smiled. 'Meanwhile – both of you – be good. And if you can't be good, be careful.'

And I slipped out of the door, closing it softly behind me.

Down in the anteroom next to the bar I paused, checking my reflection one last time in one of the art deco wall mirrors before I stepped forward into the throng.

The party was in full swing. Teams of waiters and waitresses wound their way through the guests carrying trays laden with elegant flutes of champagne. There was a jazz band – yes, an entire band with a double bass and a grand piano and *everything* – at the far end of the room and, standing next to them, was a lady in a long shimmery dress doing a microphone check.

I removed a glass of champagne from the tray of a passing waiter and scanned the assembled scene. The first person I recognised was Kitty. Taking a large sip of champagne for Dutch courage, I began to make my way over, thinking that I would give her an edited version of Charles's crimes in the hope that sisterly murder would not be committed. However, as soon as she saw me, she gave me a glare that would have turned anyone else to stone and walked off, nose in the air.

I was about to follow her when, out of the corner of my eye, I saw a figure silhouetted in the doorway. It was Auntie Sheila, looking decidedly pensive.

Kitty could wait five minutes.

I picked up a glass of orange juice and walked across to her. She took the juice and kissed me lightly on the cheek.

'How are you?' I said.

Auntie Sheila ran the tip of her tongue over her lips before replying.

'I think I can safely say I've had better days,' she said. 'I found out after lunch that Veronica has walked out on me after Dudley's stupid cheque bounced. But on the other hand, I've got my daughter back – so I've decided to treat anything positive that happens from now as a bonus.'

She took a sip of her juice.

'How's Nick?' she asked.

A thought of Nick wearing not much more than a smile and a handbag-inflicted bruise flashed through my brain and I felt myself blush.

'He's fine, Auntie.'

Auntie Sheila closed her eyes.

'I am so sorry about the bag. I don't know what came over me.'

'Please don't give it another thought,' I replied. 'Really

– it's okay. We both know the amount of pressure you've been under.'

'Jess told me that you and he are – how do you young people put it? An *itinery*?'

I grinned. A wicked, lascivious grin. I simply couldn't help it.

'An item,' I corrected.

'And – is it true?'

For about a nanosecond I thought about denying it – but I quickly realised there was no point. My face had erupted in a pyroclastic extravaganza so intense they could probably see it from space. And it wasn't just my face – my ears, neck, cleavage . . . in fact, every atom of my being was glowing redder than a sunburnt tomato covered in strawberry jam and wearing a Manchester United home strip.

Even though we had a lot of the nitty-gritty stuff to iron out, it was pretty clear where we were heading.

'Yes,' I said, 'I think you could safely call us an item.'

Auntie S gave me an indulgent smile.

'That's wonderful, Ailsa. Jess mentioned she'd given the pair of you a shove in the right direction.' She clasped her hands together. 'Oh, I do love a good romance – especially in such a beautiful setting: the castle, the sea, the moon – it would be almost impossible not to fall in love in a place like this. And Nick – goodness: I wouldn't kick him out of bed for eating biscuits, I'll tell you that for nothing.'

I almost dropped my champagne.

'Auntie *Sheila*!' I cried.

My aunt smiled.

'You young people like to think you invented sex – well, let me tell you, when I was young—'

Argh! There's no place like home! There's no place like home!

'Actually,' I said quickly, 'I need to talk to you about Jess. You see, I've had an idea for an alternative venue for the ceremony.'

Auntie Sheila's smile broadened.

'I'm one step ahead of you there,' she said. 'Jess rang me and said she'd spoken to Roberto and, as far as he is concerned, the hotel is all systems go!'

I was just about to ask her whether Jess had mentioned anything else, when I looked up and saw that we were no longer alone. There were two men standing just a few feet away: one was Uncle Dudley and the other was none other than creep-meister extraordinaire Charles.

'Hello,' said Charles, nodding brusquely at Auntie Sheila and flinging an especially mirthless smile in my direction.

Before that moment, I'd always thought that the idea of one's skin crawling was just a very vivid metaphor – but, no! As he walked towards us, mine literally felt as though it was trying to remove itself from my body and slink off into a dark, Charles-free corner.

Uncle Dudley followed. Only he wasn't smiling – mirthlessly or otherwise.

'Would you two mind going somewhere else?' he said to Sheila and me, completely ignoring the fact that we'd been there first. 'Charles wants to have a chat in private.'

I had to bite my tongue. I was itching to tell him that it wasn't the brewery they should be discussing, but Charles's slimy attitude towards his daughter.

Auntie S, however, stood her ground.

'I wanted to bring Ailsa up to date on events concerning

292

Jess and the changes we've made to the wedding ceremony, somewhere quiet. The noise in the bar is deafening.'

'Jess?' Charles's smile did not waver but I noticed his voice was a little unsteady. 'Are they – I mean, is the wedding back on?'

'It is,' I said, 'although it's none of your business, Charles.'

'Is that so?' The smile was still in place, although it seemed even more mirthless than before. 'Because I beg to differ.'

Even before he had put his hand into his pocket, I knew what was going to happen next. What with one thing and another, I still hadn't found time to study the crucial piece of paper, but I was certain that Charles meant to cause trouble. The time for damage limitation had arrived.

'Uncle Dudley,' I said quickly and firmly, 'you don't need to worry about anything Charles has to show you; the only question you need to concern yourself with is whether Justin is the right man to marry your daughter.'

Charles couldn't resist a self-satisfied smirk.

'I couldn't agree with you more, Ailsa,' he said, 'and I think I'm about to give Dudley all he'll ever need to know about Justin's credentials.'

Even though I could quite happily have grabbed Auntie Sheila's bag and clonked him round the head, I managed to remain calm.

'*Actually*,' I countered pointedly, 'all that piece of paper will tell him is that *you* are prepared to sell your best friend down the river just to stop him marrying Jess – which is another matter entirely.'

'We'll see, won't we?' He smirked. 'And anyway, what are you going to do about it?'

He narrowed his eyes and, if looks could kill, I would not only have been dead, but six foot under with the grass growing over my grave.

But I'd grown up in a family where deadly stares were de rigueur.

'There are two things in your wallet,' I said, narrowing my eyes too, 'things which *you know* I know about and which *you* do not want me revealing to the rest of the world. And, before you say it, if it comes down to a question of your word over mine, don't you think that Uncle Dudley is going to prefer that of his niece to a mere employee who is basically out to shaft his daughter?'

Okay, so that was an unfortunate choice of words but I hoped it would do the trick. My mouth went dry as I waited to see if this was enough to stop him. I really hoped I didn't have to go into detail – Auntie Sheila had enough on her plate without finding out about those horrible pictures.

But it was Uncle Dudley who got in there first.

'What do you mean, "shafting" my Jessica?' he asked, a bushy eyebrow raised and his face turning from dark pink to a deep claret colour. He and Jess might not have seen eye to eye recently, but it was obvious from his tone that she was still his little princess – anyone who crossed Jess would do so at their peril.

'I have no idea what Ailsa's talking about,' Charles replied, a little too quickly to sound entirely truthful.

Uncle Dudley swelled to about three times his original size. He scared me – and I wasn't the one he was angry with.

'Chapman, something's going on and I want to know exactly what it is.'

Charles swallowed nervously.

'Or do you think I should find Jessica and ask her?' Uncle Dudley was practically quivering with rage.

Charles did his best to look unconcerned and carefree. It wasn't very convincing.

'Look, Dudley – these things that Ailsa's going on about – it's just a minor misunderstanding. Jessica is a lovely girl and you know how fond I am of her. However, having looked at this piece of paper,' he produced it from his pocket with a flourish, 'I really wonder if Chilmark is the sort of chap you want in your family – or your business.'

If he'd been looking for buttons to push to get a reaction from my uncle, he couldn't have done better if there had been a huge, red one fastened to Dudley's forehead.

'My business!' he yelled. 'My *business*? Are you trying to tell me who I should and shouldn't have in my business?'

'I think,' said Charles, 'that you are not in possession of all the facts, Dudley.'

'Charles,' I said angrily, '"the facts" have got nothing to do with what is or is not written on that piece of paper – the bottom line is that you don't want Jess and Justin to get married and you have done everything in your power to try and stop them.'

It felt like a speech from a low-budget American soap opera – but what else could I say? It was the truth. Or at least one of the many versions of it that had been swirling round the hotel for the last few days.

And things were about to get even more complicated.

'What's that about me and Jessica?' A familiar voice floated across the room. It was Justin – thankfully without Jess in tow.

Charles, at the arrival of his supposed best friend, hesitated for a moment, but he wasn't about to throw in the towel now. Slowly, with the air of a stage magician revealing a particularly impressive trick, he began to unfold the sheet of paper.

'Good timing, Justin,' he said, 'just the man we were talking about.'

'No,' I cried, reaching over and snatching the sheet of paper from him. 'It's lies! It's not the truth, it's—'

But Charles reached over and snatched it back.

'It's not lies,' his voice was calm and unbelievably menacing, 'it's something Dudley needs to be aware of. Something that affects him. And me. And the rest of the company. And how does it affect you again, Ailsa? Oh, that's right – it doesn't. So back off.'

I thought of Jessica. Of Auntie Sheila. Of the consummate havoc that could be unleashed the moment Uncle Dudders clapped his eyes on the sheet of paper.

It did involve me.

Very much indeed.

'Justin! Nab it!' I cried, making a grab for it myself.

Charles, however, was too quick for the pair of us. With a twist of his wrist he dodged my lunge, sidestepped Justin and managed to throw the paper in Uncle Dudley's direction. Uncle D, however, wasn't quite up to speed and missed – and it fluttered gently towards the floor.

For a moment there was complete stillness and all five of us stood transfixed, watching it float gracefully downwards; almost as though the whole event was playing out in slow motion.

Then an extraordinary thing happened.

With a happy bark, Arthur bounded in between Uncle Dudley's legs, causing him to sit down heavily in a potted palm. Arthur made a beeline for the sheet of paper and picked it up between his teeth, before turning tail and running off across the room.

Charles, Justin and I stared at each other in momentary disbelief before we unfroze and pounded after him.

I had a head start but was hampered by my long, flowing vintage skirts, not to mention the fact that Charles's legs were at least twice the length of mine. Justin put in a valiant effort, but the soles of his shoes were rather slippery and he skidded into a sofa and winded himself badly.

Not that any of us were a match for Arthur.

The little dog thought it was a brilliant game. With the sheet of paper dangling tantalisingly from his mouth, he dodged round the chairs and plant pots in the main foyer. Charles pounded after him, his initial cries of 'good dog!' and 'give!' deteriorating quickly into: 'I'm going to kill you, you little bastard!'

In and out of sofas, coffee tables and even behind the reception desk they ran, until Arthur, barking merrily, made for the stairs. Presumably intending to cut him off at the pass, Charles struck out across the foyer – and collided heavily with a waiter carrying a large tray of champagne-filled glasses. Flutes, fizz, tray, collider and collidee hung suspended in mid-air before crashing back down to earth with a noise that could probably have woken the medieval monks buried under the floor of the ruined church.

Arthur paused to get his breath back (or possibly laugh at Charles) and I saw my chance.

'Arthur!' I called. 'Here, boy!'

At the sound of my voice, Arthur looked round – but rather than obediently trotting over to me, he gave a low growl and set about savaging the paper. Justin and I sprinted across the foyer but, by the time we had reached him, Arthur had reduced the page to a pile of shreds. Just for good measure, Arthur swallowed a few; leaving the rest in a heap on the floor.

Nothing Uncle Dudley would want to look at.

'Good boy.' I patted him on the head and picked him up for a celebratory cuddle.

With Arthur in my arms, I turned round to see Nick pushing his way in through the main door of the hotel. He clocked the scene of devastation that greeted him and stopped.

'What the—?' he began.

'Arthur,' I said, gesturing to the chaos around us, 'Arthur's done it again.'

Nick rolled his eyes.

'I'm sorry,' he said, 'I left a book I needed in the lounge and went to look for it, but when I opened your door to get back in he slipped out. I've been in the gardens searching for him for ages. I should have known he'd have come to find you. I'm obviously a very poor substitute.'

'It's okay,' I said, ruffling Arthur's furry chest. 'In fact, it's a good thing he did escape, isn't it, Houdini dog?'

Over by the reception desk, Charles was heaving himself to his feet and picking bits of shattered glass out of his hair. There was a cut on his left hand and champagne was dripping from his hair down onto his collar. It was fair to say that he was not, in any shape, manner or form, a happy camper.

And neither was my uncle by marriage.

With the glass crunching underneath his size twelves, Uncle Dudley made his way across to the source of the destruction.

'What the bloody hell do you think you are doing, Chapman?' he roared. 'What on earth do you mean by this?'

Charles pulled a handkerchief out of his pocket and wrapped it round his bleeding hand. He clearly wasn't impressed by Uncle Dudley's apportioning of blame.

'It was the dog,' he whined. 'It was that bloody dog. If I ever get my hands on it, it'll wish it'd never been born.'

Arthur stiffened in my arms and growled in a way that clearly meant 'bring it on if you're hard enough'.

'I don't care about the dog – I mean this,' Dudley indicated the shattered glass, the pools of champagne and the waiter, who was now holding an ice pack against a rapidly expanding lump on his head.

Roberto the manager appeared, accompanied by one of the girls from the reception desk, talking excitedly and very loudly in Italian. He cast an angry eye round the foyer and then marched straight up to Uncle Dudley.

'Mr Westfield,' he said in clipped and authoritative tones, 'what is the meaning of this?'

Uncle Dudley wheeled round as quickly as a man whose build resembles that of an unfit sumo wrestler could reasonably manage.

'I deny all responsibility,' he spluttered. 'It's all down to him.' He pointed at the unfortunate Charles.

Roberto shot his cuffs in an alpha male sort of way.

'I am fully aware that Mr Chapman is one of your party, sir, mainly because Mr Chapman has been adding bottles of vintage champagne to the bill being underwritten by yourself, together with numerous room service requests for foodstuffs including beluga caviar, lobster and pâté de foie gras.'

Charles stopped looking angry and began to look sheepish.

Uncle Dudley turned to him.

'You've been doing *what*?'

The manager continued.

'We have passed daily copies of these bills to yourself, Mr Westfield. Are you saying that you were unaware of these expenses?'

'I didn't think to look at them – I – well . . . Chapman, you *idiot*. Did you think I would be prepared to keep you in luxury booze for a week? Just how much of a fool do you think I am?'

Charles shrank back against the wall.

'I'll pay,' he whimpered, 'I'll make sure you don't get charged a penny.'

'Too bloody right you will,' growled Uncle Dudley, his face so red and swollen with rage, he looked like a giant lump of acne.

'And the damage here?' added Roberto in a steely tone. 'I think a couple of hundred euros at least.'

'At least,' replied Uncle Dudley. 'Go on, man – get your wallet out. Pronto.'

Biting his lip, Charles reached into his inside jacket

pocket and pulled out his wallet. He went to take out his credit card but, fumbling because of his injured hand, he dropped the lot, sending cards, cash and other wallet-related detritus down onto the floor.

Including the pictures of Jess.

They landed face up in a pool of spilled champagne. Like an iron filing drawn to a particularly arresting magnet, Uncle Dudley's eyes fixed on them straight away and he bent down and grabbed them before Charles even knew what was happening.

Uncle Dudley went puce.

Then he went white.

Then he went green.

Then he turned yellow.

Then he opened and closed his mouth a few times, but no sound came out. For the first time in his entire life, my Uncle Dudley had been rendered speechless.

But another voice, deep, authoritative and very dangerous rang out instead: 'You bastard. You treacherous, two-faced bastard. This is what it's all about, isn't it? You wanted me out of the way so that you could get it back on with Jess – well, I've got news for you: she thinks you're a Grade One creep, Charles! And those photos agree with her!'

Charles didn't reply. He had run out of words – weasel or otherwise. He stood in the middle of the carnage looking from the photo of Jess, to Justin, and then back again. Then, before I had time to realise what was actually happening, a well-aimed right hook had landed itself on Charles's jaw.

'That,' Justin growled, 'is for Jessica. And that,' he took

another swing at Charles, this time connecting squarely with his nose, 'is for me. And this is for those silent phone calls. You utter, utter bastard.'

He threw a third and final punch that caught the unfortunate Mr Chapman right in the mouth. Charles fell against a potted palm. Pulling a white handkerchief out of his trouser pocket and holding it against his face, he struggled to his feet.

'You little shit, Chilmark,' he snarled, 'there's no way you're getting away with that.'

And he squared up to Justin, who had a strange, un-junior-brewing-executive glint in his eye.

'Bring it on, Chapman,' he said. 'Bring it on and I'll give you another one.'

Auntie Sheila, who had been down on her hands and knees sifting through the shreds of paper left by Arthur, straightened herself up and came over to see what was going on. I watched as her mouth dropped open in disbelief.

'You took this?' she breathed. 'You took this picture of my lovely girl! You nasty, *nasty* little man.'

There was something in her eyes which was even scarier than Justin's. She had the fire of an enraged tigress that sees its cub in danger coursing through her veins and she was spoiling for a fight.

'You,' she said, the glass crunching ominously under her high heels, 'you have had it in for her – and Justin too – ever since she dumped you. Oh yes, my boy – I know all about you. She's my daughter – don't you think she *talks* to me?'

'But,' Charles spluttered, 'but – but – but—'

Auntie Sheila narrowed her eyes until they were nothing more than tiny slits.

'I've never liked you,' she said. 'Never. But because of Dudley I had to be polite to you. I invited you to dinner parties, Sunday lunches – and all the while you were spying on my little girl, leering at her like some stalker, making silent phone calls to upset her. Well, you know what, Mr Chapman? It ends. It ends here, it ends now and it ends for the rest of your life. Get out – and don't ever let me set eyes on you again.'

Charles turned to Uncle Dudley.

'Please, Dudley, Mr Westfield, sir – I didn't mean it. I didn't mean any of it. It wasn't about Jess, really, it was about Chilmark – I wanted Chilmark out. He's no good for the company. He hasn't got my experience. It's me you want, not him. Let me explain—'

But Uncle Dudley didn't get a chance to reply. Justin began rolling up his sleeves while Auntie Sheila gripped the handle of her handbag. The pair of them were ready for action.

'You don't give a shit about the company,' said Justin, 'or me or Jess; in fact, the only person you care about is yourself. Well, I'm telling you now, Chapman, that if you don't sod off far and sod off fast, I will personally see to it that you spend the rest of your life singing soprano. Do I make myself clear?'

Charles opened his mouth and then thought better of it and closed it again, before taking to his heels and sprinting right out the door of the hotel.

Arthur barked ecstatically. You'd have thought it was what he'd been planning all along.

The manager cleared his throat respectfully.

'The matter of the bill and the damage to hotel property remains, sir. If you would be so good as to indicate how you intend to pay?'

Uncle Dudley gave a heavy sigh and mopped his brow with a large spotted handkerchief.

'Put it on the tab, Roberto,' he said wearily, 'put it all on the bloody tab. You've got my card.'

The manager cleared his throat again. This time not quite as respectfully.

'I'm afraid, sir, that we attempted to process a transaction on your credit card earlier this evening but it was declined. Twice. Do you have an alternative means of payment?'

Uncle Dudley stared at Roberto as though he had just suggested we added sweet and sour panda to the menu at the wedding reception.

'That's impossible,' he said, his face beginning the transformation from red, through to puce, yellow and green all over again. 'That is quite impossible.'

'Mr Westfield, your card provider refused to honour the payment,' Roberto repeated, in a slow and deliberate voice, as though he suspected Uncle Duds was having trouble understanding him.

'Which card did you use?' Auntie Sheila walked over, her achingly high heels crunching through the glass that still littered the floor.

Roberto went to hand the offending credit card to Dudley but Auntie S got in there first. She turned it over in her hands and let out a shriek.

'Dudley!' she shrieked. 'This isn't our credit card – it's

the business one. What the hell do you think you are doing paying for our daughter's wedding out of the company accounts?'

Uncle Dudley began to sway slightly. One of the waiters pushed a chair towards him.

Auntie Sheila, however, looked as though she couldn't have cared less about his wellbeing.

'Like I said,' she repeated, her hands on her hips in the traditional 'I am taking no more nonsense from you' posture that women have used for centuries when telling off their menfolk, 'what the bloody hell do you think you're doing using the company credit card to bankroll the bloody wedding? What are you? A moron? This is fraud. Do you hear me? This is fraud – you're stealing from *my* company.'

She brandished the card accusingly at him.

'Actually,' Justin gave a respectful cough, 'it's not just the credit cards. Myself and some other members of the board put a stop on the company bank account yesterday. I expect that's why Veronica's cheque bounced.'

Everyone spun round and stared at him.

'That piece of paper – the one that the dog has been eating – well, it's a printout I authorised from accounts and had them email over. I needed to check the figures before my meeting with the Italian distributors earlier in the week. It seems that someone has been transferring money out of the Sidling Stoat export fund for quite a while now. I have the hard copy on my phone if you'd like to have a look and—'

'*Dudley!*' shrieked Auntie Sheila. 'Was that you?'

Uncle Dudley shuffled uncomfortably.

'Keep your voice down, you stupid woman – do you want everyone to know?'

That was the wrong thing to say. Auntie S narrowed her eyes and gave him a stare so deadly it should have come with a government health warning. I was impressed – or I would have been if I hadn't been so utterly horrified by the revelation that my Uncle Dudley was a fraudster.

'Don't you ever,' she said, slowly and menacingly, 'speak to me like that again. I am *not* stupid and I have been keeping my voice down for the last thirty years – the news is that I won't be doing it any longer.'

She signalled to Roberto.

'Here,' she said, 'put it all on this. Except whatever that idiot Chapman owes. I'm not paying for him.'

She delved into her handbag and pulled out something suspiciously like a platinum card.

Uncle Dud looked as though he'd just been hit round the head with a wet fish.

'What's that?' he asked, aghast. 'Where did you get that? We don't bank with them.'

'No,' agreed Auntie Sheila, typing a pin into a handheld terminal offered to her by Roberto, '*we* don't bank with them – but I do.'

'We have a joint account,' insisted Uncle Dudley.

Auntie Sheila took her card back and popped it in her bag.

'Yes, we do,' she agreed, doing up the zip and throwing the bag back over her shoulder, 'but you're very much mistaken if you think it's the only money I have access to.'

'But – but – but –' Uncle Dudley was now spluttering like an astonished walrus, 'but – but – no.'

306

'But yes, actually,' replied Auntie Sheila. 'It's my escape fund, Dudley, in case I've ever had enough of you. And you know what? I'm starting to think that time might just have arrived.'

Uncle Dudley made a noise like a walrus struggling to swallow a live fish. I would have loved to know what he was trying to say, but at that moment, something *else* happened.

Something really not very nice at all: Roberto spotted Arthur.

He marched over and, without a word, snatched the little dog from my grasp. Then he handed him to a nearby waiter, before launching into a stream of angry Italian. The waiter turned and, holding Arthur by the scruff of the neck, ran towards the main doors. As I watched, something that may just have been a smirk of triumph crept across Roberto's face.

I don't think I have ever hated anyone as much as I did Roberto at that moment – and I wasn't the only one.

With a cry of outrage, Nick set off after the waiter – and I ran after Nick. Outside the main door, I paused and glanced round, first in the direction of the gardens and then over towards the arched gateway that marked the entrance to the hotel grounds. There, in the middle of the car park with all its neat rows of Ferraris and Porsches and – yes, admittedly – one or two Fiats, I saw Nick and the waiter having a very heated discussion.

The waiter was holding Arthur close to his chest, while Nick was valiantly trying to snatch him back. They were both yelling loudly in Italian and, even though I couldn't make out any of the actual words, they both sounded furious.

As I watched, Nick tried again to grab Arthur out of the waiter's clutches but the waiter swung him high up out of Nick's reach. Arthur gave a plaintive whine – the waiter had obviously hurt him – before twisting his head round and sinking his terrier teeth into the man's hand. With a yelp, the waiter let go; Arthur hit the ground, righted himself and ran towards Nick. However, before he could reach safety, the waiter aimed a powerful kick in Arthur's direction. It came home on target and, with another pitiful whine, Arthur scooted off as fast as he could in the direction of the archway.

My heart lurched. I went to run after him but my legs felt as though someone had replaced them with tubes of extra-heavy blancmange.

'Arthur!' I yelled.

And then, even louder: 'Nick!'

But to no avail.

Arthur kept on running and Nick, shouting and waving his arms at the waiter (and generally looking more Italian than I'd ever seen him before), did not hear me.

I was on my own.

'Arthur!' I yelled again.

Picking up my skirts, I did my best to put my blancmange legs into action, but it was too late: Arthur was already through the archway and running as fast as he could down the road towards the town. I followed, my high heels sinking into the gravel and my legs struggling to match the four-legged whirlwind that was Arthur. As I reached the gateway, there was a flash from a set of headlights and the screech of brakes – followed by another yelp and then silence.

I ran as I have never run before. My shoes came off and my bare feet pounded onto the tarmac, onto stones and shards of rock – but I felt none of it. A figure flew past me – it was Nick. Stronger and faster, he reached the car first. It had ground to a halt, its engine still running, and as Nick drew level, the driver opened his door and got out.

I stumbled on, while the driver (who obviously assumed Nick was Arthur's owner) began shouting loudly. Nick did his best to remain calm.

I looked around for Arthur – fully expecting the worst – but to my astonishment, he was nowhere to be seen.

'Where is he?' I cried, hoping that the driver would feel sorry for me and give me some clue as to which direction Arthur might have taken. 'Where is he?'

'*Adato!*' the driver yelled. '*Pazza, e? Pazza!*'

'Nick – what's he saying?' I was almost on my knees with panic and fear for Arthur. 'Did he hit Arthur?'

Nick took a deep breath.

'*El cane, lo ha colpito?*' he asked the driver politely.

The man threw his hands up into the air in exasperation.

'I do not know if the dog is okay,' he yelled in English, 'I do not care. You English are crazy. He is a dog. He is just a dog. Do you know how much my car is worth?'

By now, there was quite a scene building. Guests from the hotel and residents of the nearby houses were gathering to see what all the fuss was about. A woman from one of the cottages produced a screaming baby and thrust it at the car driver, yelling at him in loud, excitable Italian. Next, a man wearing pyjama bottoms and pulling out a pair of earplugs joined the crowd and began hollering indescribable-sounding things and waving his arms (and

309

earplugs) around energetically. The motorist ripped his panama hat from his head and threw it onto the ground in a fit of temper, but the crowd took no notice. They pushed in around him and Nick, closer and closer, until me and my dog were entirely forgotten.

Ignoring my feet, which had now begun to bleed, I ran once more. I sped along the road calling for Arthur, ducking down alleyways and back streets and chasing across patches of waste ground littered with old tin cans. I raced through narrow streets where lines of washing still lingered and yelled his name until my throat hurt.

As a last-ditch hope, I ran to the vet's, thinking that he might have been drawn there by some sort of homing instinct. But the building was dark and shuttered and the door firmly locked. Nevertheless, I hammered loudly on the glass and rattled the handle for quite a few minutes until, with a heart like lead, I sat down on the stone threshold, still warm from the afternoon's sunshine, and buried my head in my hands while fat, tear-like raindrops began to fall.

Chapter Twenty-Two

I don't know how long I sat on the step at the vet's, only half-conscious of the light levels dropping away into darkness, a steady drizzle beginning to fall and the bustle of people coming and going from the bars and restaurants that surrounded the market square. Eventually, the gathering gloom of the dusk, the chill from my rain-damp clothes and the fact that I could no longer feel my left leg led me to stir myself, and I began the long pull back to the hotel.

Strangely, I wasn't upset. I was in a bizarre place where I was aware of no emotion whatsoever. It was as though a kindly passing surgeon had amputated my heart and replaced it with a large lump of ice-cold granite – a feeling I remembered from the days immediately after I'd left Nick. Even my internal monologue was almost the same as the one as I'd had then:

It's not your fault, I found myself saying (just as I had with Nick).

It's just a dog (which I hadn't).

There was nothing more you could have done (Nick again).

It is out of your control (ditto – Nick).

But it didn't make me feel any better now than it had then, and the freezing lump of granite in my chest weighed heavier and heavier as I trudged homewards.

To my relief the angry, baby-waving crowds had gone by

the time I reached the hotel, and I walked alone through the stone archway and across the car park, picking up my shoes en route. I went to slip them back on, noticing the cuts and bruises that scarred my poor, aching feet for the first time. Limping now, as my adrenalin rush wore off and the pain flooded over me, I made my way over to the main door and peered cautiously in through the glass.

The foyer was almost empty. The glass, champagne, tray and general chaos of earlier had been cleared away, and it was as though the hiatus had never happened. One or two guests sat in armchairs, sipping drinks, while members of staff flitted to and fro replenishing them. The flicker of the screen behind the reception desk told me that there was another football match on.

The rest was silence – or at least it seemed to be.

I pushed at the door and hobbled in. I was just about to turn left and creep up the stairs to my room when one of the perfectly attired girls on the desk saw me.

'*Signorina!*' she called.

My heart sank. Was I about to be upbraided? Presented with a demand to pay for the carnage caused by Arthur? Or worse – a message from my uncle that he didn't have any more money and we were going to have to settle our own hotel bills, which would have cost at least one, if not two, months of my teaching stipend?

But – no.

'*Signorina*, the veterinary surgery in town, they called.'

This didn't make any sense. I'd been at the vet's for what felt like hours: it had been closed.

I blinked uncomprehendingly in her direction. The receptionist held out a sheet of paper.

'A message for you. The vet would like you to ring as soon as possible, please.'

From a position of crushing despair, my heart leaped.

Arthur! He had found Arthur!

Of course he had – what other possible reason could he have for ringing?

With shaking hands, I took the paper and unfolded it – but there was no message, just a number that I presumed was the vet's home line.

'May I?' I gestured towards the phone on the desk.

'Of course,' replied the girl, smiling. 'I do hope your little dog is all right. He is such a cutie – I do love him.'

The words 'he's not my dog' began to form yet again on my lips, but I scrubbed them. I might not own him in any legal sense of the word, but I loved him. And in my book, that made him as good as mine.

'Thank you,' I replied with true feeling, 'so do I.'

I dialled and waited what felt like a couple of aeons before the receiver at the other end was picked up.

'Hello?' I said, as relief broke over me in huge tsunami-like waves. 'It's Signorina Stuart here. Arthur's – well, the person who has been looking after Arthur.'

'Oh, *signorina* – good evening!' It was the vet, sounding very jolly indeed. 'I am sorry to bother you so late on a Friday night.'

'No problem, no problem.'

'How are you? I hope the preparations for your cousin's wedding are progressing well.'

I clenched my fist in anguished frustration. Why didn't he just tell me he had my dog? Why didn't he just put me out of my misery?

'Fine, good, it's all fine – you wanted to speak to me?'

He paused. *Come on – tell me!*

'I have some good news for you – at least, I hope it is good news.'

He paused again, and my knees went weak.

'I have had a phone call – about half an hour ago – from a family who were touring in the area at the weekend and lost their dog. I think from the description that it could very well be Arthur.'

'Pardon?' I said.

I had a feeling he'd just said something about Arthur's owners ringing him – but that couldn't be right, could it?

'An American family,' the vet continued, 'called the Hendersons. They live near Rome and were up here last weekend. They went for a walk on the beach just before they left and their terrier – Boodle – ran away. Their little girl has been absolutely hysterical ever since and they are more than happy to pay a large reward.'

I meant to say something in reply; honestly I did. However, my mouth felt as though it had been stuffed with cotton wool. Arthur's family had traced him – only at the exact same moment he had gone missing again. The timing was incredible, not to mention cruel.

'I'm sorry,' I said. 'I'm really, really, sorry, but I don't know where he is. There was a commotion this evening and he got frightened and ran off. I've looked everywhere, honestly I have, but he's vanished. Please tell the Hendersons that I am so very, very sorry.'

There didn't seem much else to say.

'It is one of those things,' the vet replied philosophically, 'you must not blame yourself.'

But I did.

I blamed myself very much: I blamed myself for not putting up more of a fight when the manager had wrestled him from my arms; I blamed myself for not snapping out of it and giving chase sooner; and I also blamed myself for allowing Nick to use my room as a study when I'd had a weird feeling that something bad was going to unfold.

I replaced the receiver and walked slowly up the stairs. All I wanted was Nick – not in the way I'd wanted him that afternoon – but in an altogether more comforting capacity, where I crawled into his arms, he held me tight and made everything seem a little better. He couldn't bring Arthur back, but he might be able to make me feel it wasn't quite the end of the world, and tomorrow morning before he left, we'd launch another search – together – so that the errant pooch could be reunited with his proper family.

Even this thought didn't do much to cheer me up. With my heart still firmly in my boots, I rounded the corner onto my landing. As I did so, a figure rushed up the stairs behind me, almost sending me flying. It was Jess – and she was looking absolutely elated.

'Hi,' I said, trying not to sound as miserable as I actually was.

My cousin threw herself at me and hugged me so tightly all the breath left my body.

'Thank you,' she said, 'thankyouthankyouthankyou.'

'What for?' I asked, disentangling myself from her embrace. 'What's happened?'

Jess blushed and bit her lip, her smile growing wider

315

by the second. Then she pulled her left hand out from behind her back with a flourish.

Instead of the glittering boulder which had previously adorned the fourth finger, she wore a plain gold band.

'I'm married,' her voice was low – almost as though she didn't dare say the words out loud. 'Justin and I went to the town hall today, just like you and Nick suggested – and we got married. We didn't want to tell anyone beforehand because we had no idea till we got there whether or not they would be able to fit us in, but apparently all the paperwork was in order and we went for it. I'm not Jessica Westfield any more, I'm Jessica Chilmark, and I *love* it.'

'Oh Jessica!' I threw myself at her. 'That is fantastic. The best of the best. I am so pleased for you.'

Jessica gave me a python-like squeeze before releasing me.

'I knew you would be. I had to tell you. We made a formal announcement at dinner but you weren't there. Oh, Ailsa, without you, none of this would have happened. I am the happiest girl in the whole wide world and every bit of it is down to you.'

'Well, I don't know about that,' I began modestly. 'I'd say most of it was down to you and Justin. After all, it was the pair of you who decided not to let anything stand in your way. This happy ending is your own doing.'

Jess shook her head.

'No,' she said firmly, 'it's down to you – you and Nick. God, I love him. In fact, if I wasn't so head over heels with Justin, I'd be doing my best to get my hands on that Signor Bertolini of yours. And not just on him – but all over him!'

She giggled.

316

'Although it looks like that's what you've been up to. I saw him earlier today: his shirt was on backwards and his hair was all over the place and he had this smudge of lipstick right here.'

She pointed to a spot just under her left earlobe. It was one of Nick's more sensitive spots and I remembered I had spent quite a lot of time focusing my attentions on it while I got dressed for dinner.

'I'm so happy for you, Ailsa. It's perfect, isn't it? Me and Justin, you and Nick.' She paused, clasping her hands together in the manner of a heroine in a silent film, and looked at me with glittering, hopeful eyes. 'You know, Ailsa, I was wondering – although tell me to shut up if I'm saying the wrong thing – wouldn't this be the *perfect* opportunity for you and Nick to come out as a couple? Imagine – everyone waiting for me and Just to shimmy down the aisle and then – whammo! Nick and Ailsa join us at the front as a surprise extra bonus attraction.'

'You mean, make an announcement at *your* wedding that Nick and I are already married?'

Jess's hands fell limply down by her side and she blinked at me.

'You mean – you're *married?* You and Nick? Mr and Mrs Bertolini?'

'Yes,' I said. 'I'm sorry – I shouldn't have said anything. It sort of slipped out.'

Then Jess's eyes lit up with an extra-bright sparkle as an even more exciting possibility popped into her brain.

'Oooooooh!' she squealed, emitting the sort of noise people do when they step on a wasp. 'Oooooh! Don't be sorry – it's amazing news and it's given me an even better

317

idea! You should renew your vows! It would be amazing – almost like a double wedding – and Justin can do a speech about how we wouldn't be getting married at all if it hadn't been for you and Nick – and then *you* can do one about the power of love triumphing over adversity or whatever it is – and ooooooooh! Please say yes, Ailsa! Don't you think it would be the perfectest thing ever?'

I hesitated. This was a big step. A huge step.

Jess raised her eyebrows.

'You know,' she said softly, 'you're going to have to tell people at some point. You can't hide him away like a guilty secret.'

She was right. Of course she was right: Nick and I were husband and wife. We still needed to work through things, to make sure we never hit the skids in such a spectacular way again, but I loved him and he loved me and, with a bit of luck and a following wind, we could rock this marriage thing.

'All right,' I grinned. 'But this isn't a decision I can make by myself. Nick is supposed to be in Pisa tomorrow, so I doubt he'll be able to, but I'll speak to him and, if he can blag a bit of time off – and he says yes – I don't see why not.'

Jess nudged me.

'Of course he'll say yes. He's mad about you – you can tell; whenever you're together he can't take his eyes off you!' She paused. 'You know the chap you and Justin saw with me in my room?'

I nodded.

'That was Nick. I was trying to persuade him to meet you under that tree. I was so happy when he said yes that I kissed him on the cheek – nothing else, I promise. I hope that was okay?'

I almost laughed with relief.

'Of course, Jess. And you did the right thing not to tell me who it was – if I'd known, I don't think I'd have gone.'

Jess grinned back at me.

'So tomorrow . . .?' she asked.

I put my arms round her and hugged her tight.

'Tomorrow I will watch you and Justin promise to obey each other till death do you part – or whatever it is – and I will be outrageously happy on your behalf. Nick and I may or may not be part of it but, whatever happens, I will be very, very proud of you. Of both of you.'

'Good.' Jess disentangled herself from my arms and kissed me lightly on the cheek. 'As I am of you.'

'I'll see you tomorrow,' I replied. 'I'll see you tomorrow in the sunshine – and I can't wait.'

'Me neither.' Jess, turned and ran lightly back down the stairs.

I continued my limp down the corridor towards my room. Telling my entire family that I'd been married for well over a year was going to take a hell of a lot of guts, and I wanted Nick's reassurance that we were doing the right thing; then there was poor Arthur – more than ever, I simply wanted to fall into Nick's waiting arms and stay there until some of the stress and trauma melted away. However, when I reached our adjacent doors, I could see no welcoming flicker of light coming from the gap underneath Nick's. I assumed this meant he would be in my room – but that was in darkness too and there was no dozing figure on the bed drowsily awaiting my return. My heart sank still further as I threw my bag down on top of the minibar and poured myself a large whisky. The thought occurred to me that maybe he was still out searching for Arthur, so I tried his phone – but it was switched off. For a moment, I considered scouring the hotel grounds to find him, but my feet were too sore and swollen to fit into my shoes. So, in the end, I lay down on the bed, fully clothed, intending to wait up for him, but my exhaustion got the better of me and I felt my eyelids getting heavier and heavier.

And the next thing I knew, it was daylight again.

Chapter Twenty-Three

The day of Jess and Justin's wedding dawned clear, bright and sunny. The rain of the previous night had brought the temperature down to a comfortable level and washed the dust out of the air, leaving it as clear and sparkling as a jewel. It was just a shame that my feelings had more in common with the heavy drops and cloudy skies of yesterday evening.

As the daylight blazed in through the French windows, I struggled up onto my elbows, wondering why I was fully dressed and the bedside light was on. Then I remembered – I'd been waiting up for Nick. I looked round the room, in case he had come in during the night and, not wanting to disturb me, had done the gentlemanly thing of kipping in an armchair – but the chairs were entirely empty of dark-haired, good-looking, half-Italian Scotsmen.

My heart sank afresh and something new – a strange, niggling feeling that something was very much amiss – washed over me and then vanished again. It would be fine, I told myself; nothing to worry about. We'd just been ships in the night, that was all. He was probably downstairs *right now* wondering if he should start breakfast without me. In fact, I'd better get a move on – if we were going to look for Arthur before he left, we'd need to get started soonish.

I slid off the bed and staggered into the bathroom, but

the first thing I saw was Arthur'sbowl on the floor, still half-filled with food, and I just couldn't help myself.

Parking my bum on the edge of the bath, I burst into huge, horrible, hiccoughing tears – poor little Arthur: alone, frightened, hungry and very possibly injured. Then there were his owners, who would now never see him again, their hopes of a reunion raised, only to be dashed by an uncaring Fate. And, finally, I wept for myself – the non-pet lover who had given her heart away to a stumpy-legged, splodgy-coloured menace of a mutt only to fail in the most basic duty of keeping him safe. What happened last night was entirely my fault, I told myself mercilessly; the buck stopped with me. If he hadn't come to find me, if he'd just stayed quietly in my room with Nick, none of this would have happened.

The flow was so terrific that it seemed nothing would ever staunch it. Even as I tried to brush them away with my hands, rivers of tears ran down my arms, dripped off my elbows and soaked into the fabric of my dress.

I was a dog person after all; only I'd waited until it was too late to admit it to myself.

Suddenly, I heard the sound of someone moving around on the landing outside my room.

I wiped away yet more tears and ignored it. It was probably housekeeping, coming to change the towels and make the beds.

But no – there was no discreet knock and the sound of a key card being swiped. Instead, there was another noise – one that sounded like a piece of paper being pushed under my door.

I held my breath and listened: there was a pause and

then (I could just make it out) the sound of footsteps retreating along the landing. Gulping and hiccoughing, I uncurled myself from the edge of the bath and padded on still-swollen feet across to the door. There was a scrappy bit of paper peeping out from underneath it. I picked it up and unfolded it: *Good luck in Newcastle*, it said. *Shame you didn't have the guts to tell me yourself. Have a nice life.*

Reason told me that the handwriting was Nick's, but beyond that, it didn't make any sense. Why should I feel ashamed? What was this about not having guts? In short – what the hell was he on about?

I continued to stare at it for a moment or two. Then I read it backwards – and even tried turning it upside down in case it made more sense that way.

But it didn't.

Then I remembered – shit! Newcastle! The job!

Nick thought I was moving to Newcastle.

Oh God – I should have said something, of course I should, but everything had happened so quickly it had entirely slipped my mind. I mean, one moment we'd been heading for the divorce court and the next we could hardly drag ourselves out of bed. New jobs in Newcastle had been pretty far down the list of my priorities.

But where—? How—?

Nobody here knew about it. Nobody at the Santa Lucia knew I was thinking of moving apart from—

Kitty.

Of course! Bloody, bloody, bloody Kitty! She was the only one I'd mentioned the job offer to – and she was certainly the only one capable of sticking her nose into my life and stirring in such a spectacularly nasty way.

As quickly as I could, I showered, dressed and then, after knocking at Nick's door and getting no response, I limped my way, barefoot, downstairs. I had to clear this up *now*, before he left for Pisa. I couldn't risk him going back to Edinburgh thinking I'd led him on, or worse, out-and-out lied to him.

'Excuse me.' I went up to the girl on the reception desk (it was the nice one, I noted; the one who liked Arthur). 'Is Dr Bertolini around? I've tried his room and he seems to be out.'

'He had to pop into town,' she smiled at me. 'If I see him, I'll tell him that you are looking for him. The tour group is due to depart at around nine-thirty so you've got a bit of time.'

'Thank you,' I said. 'Please let him know that it's urgent.'

With sweaty hands, I pulled out my phone and tapped in Nick's number. Yet again it went straight to voicemail. (Why couldn't he be like normal people and keep his mobile *switched on*? Didn't he realise that was the whole *point* of having one?) I rang off without leaving a message. I'd go and have something to eat – I was starting to feel a bit wobbly – and then try again. He wouldn't be going anywhere for an hour or so and, anyway, he *had* to come back to collect his gaggle of little old ladies – I would just have to make sure I caught him then.

My stomach was adamant that it didn't want any food, but I was determined not to take any notice of it. I hadn't had any dinner the night before and my legs were feeling more than a little shaky – although, to be fair, that could have been the cumulative effect of a missing Arthur and an AWOL Nick. As I walked into the dining room, I saw Roberto leafing through seating plans for the wedding reception later on and noted that he avoided my eye as I went past. Shame on you, dog murderer, I thought. sending some suitably evil and unforgiving thoughts his way.

I sat in the plushest seat I could find and ordered the largest breakfast on the menu, then I picked up one of the English newspapers and began to flick through it to try and take my mind off things. It wasn't overly helpful. There was an article about Crufts (cue: desolate thoughts about Arthur) and another on the rocketing divorce rate – something I sincerely hoped I wouldn't soon be contributing to. Then my breakfast arrived, a plate the size of a manhole cover full of fry-up. My stomach wasn't happy at the thought of having to deal with this greasy feast and twisted nauseatingly. I took a sip of coffee to try and settle it – and, at that exact moment, the door to the dining room swung open and Kitty walked in. I immediately raised my newspaper so that she couldn't make eye contact. Any normal person would have understood this meant I did not want to talk to her. However, I should have known it wouldn't have any effect whatsoever on Kitty.

With a growing sense of doom, I could hear her making her way determinedly across the polished parquet of the floor. I raised the newspaper even higher in front of my face and willed her to turn round and bugger off. But psychic powers failed me.

The footsteps stopped.

'Hello, Ailsa.'

There was a pause.

I probably should have replied – engaged in a grown-up, rational conversation – but I was so angry with her then that I literally couldn't speak. Kitty, however, didn't need me to tell her what my problem was.

'I've noticed the way you've been leading Nick on, so I thought I'd do the poor boy a favour,' she said, an almost pitying tone in her voice. 'After all, if you're moving to Newcastle, he has a right to know. I mean, it's not as though you were serious about him, is it?'

I couldn't help myself. I threw down my newspaper in frustrated rage, catching the handle of my coffee cup as I did so, tipping it over and sending a warm brown slick flooding over the snow-white cloth.

'I'm sorry,' I said, my voice so icy it was a wonder Kitty didn't freeze solid in its blast, 'I didn't quite catch that.'

Kitty blinked. She knew she'd overstepped a line, but she'd done that so often in our shared sisterly past that she probably had difficulty working out which line we were dealing with.

'I said,' she repeated (although with less conviction), 'that it's not as though you were serious about him. Even if you weren't about to move back to England, you've got your eye on Gary or whatever he's called. Nick is pretty much surplus to requirements.'

'This has got nothing to do with Gary or my job or even Nick.' I mopped half-heartedly at the mess on the tablecloth with my napkin. 'This is about Charles, isn't it? You think that because I interfered with your relationship, you now have carte blanche to do the same to me. Only, first up, Charles was a nasty little creep who was going to hurt you in ways you couldn't even begin to imagine, and second up, you've messed up something much more serious than you could ever understood and I have every right to be mad with you. Now push off.'

Kitty didn't move. In fact she rooted herself even more firmly to the spot and put her hands defiantly on her hips.

'No, I won't,' she said. 'I'm talking to you.'

'Well, I'm not talking to you.' I folded up my coffee-stained newspaper and placed it on the chair next to me. 'I'm not talking to you now and I have no intention of speaking to you again at any point in the future. Go away.'

The last thing in the world I wanted to do was eat, but I made myself shove an enormous forkful of bacon, sausage, tomato and fried bread into my mouth. There was no way Kitty was going to know how much she'd upset me. I valiantly chewed and, with quite an effort, managed to swallow.

'You are moving to Newcastle,' she insisted. 'You told me. All I've done is bring Nick up to date.'

'Newsflash, Kitty: I *am* allowed to change my mind about a job *without* informing you first. Nick and I were getting back together. And, just so that you are absolutely clear on this one, Nick and I didn't just live together, we were – we *are* – married. That's right – man and wife, who no man should put asunder. And for your information "no man" means "no woman either", Kitty.'

There was a little gasp from my sister. She shook her head vigorously.

'No, Ailsa, you've got it wrong. You and Nick – you said you don't trust him – you said you want a fresh start – you—'

I picked the newspaper up from the chair and pretended

to scan it.

'Go away.'

'What?' Kitty sounded bemused.

'You heard me,' I turned a coffee-sodden page over. 'Go away. I never want to see you again. You know that thing called a life – well, you've just done a pretty good job of ruining mine. Now go away. Sod off. Scram.'

Out of the corner of my eye, I saw her stand there, picking at her nails, for what felt like aeons; until finally, with a sigh, she turned on her heel and exited the dining room.

I did my best not to watch her leave and continued forcing forkfuls of food into my face until I was sure she had well and truly disappeared – but it was hard work. Then I put my cutlery down and pushed the plate away. I had reached my lowest point. I'd come to the wedding of a cousin I hadn't much liked – and I had grown to love her. However, for the cousin gained, I had also (potentially) lost a husband and now a sister. It wasn't a very good ratio.

Then I saw the clock – nine-fifteen. There was no time to lose.

Leaving the remains of my breakfast congealing unappetisingly on the table behind me, I made my way out of the dining room via the French windows. Bacon, mushrooms and a bit of black pudding rumbled around unhappily in my digestive tract, but I didn't have time to worry about them now – I needed to find Nick.

I could hear the chugging of a diesel engine coming from the front of the hotel. With my heart in my mouth, I half-ran, half-walked on my poor, painful feet until I saw a coach parked outside the main entrance, its door open and its seats full of little old ladies clutching canvas shopping bags and offering round bags of boiled sweets to one another. I stumbled over to it, tiny stones squeezing their way into my cuts and grazes – but there was no time to stop and hoick them out – and peered in at the open door. Standing at the top of the steps was a girl in a navy-blue uniform ticking off names on a clipboard.

'Excuse me,' I hauled myself up onto the bottom step. 'Excuse me, is Nick Bertolini on board?'

The girl paused in her clipboard activities.

'Sorry?' She smiled.

'Is Nick here?' I asked again. 'It's rather urgent.'

'Are you with the party?' she asked. 'I didn't know we had anyone new joining us today.'

I took a deep breath. I was going to say it – to admit it – in public.

'No, I'm not with the tour group,' I replied. 'I'm his wife.'

She looked as though someone had poked her unexpectedly in the rear with an unexpected poking device.

'Crikey!' she said, before remembering her manners. 'I mean, he's at reception signing out.'

For all her smiliness, I can't say that I took to her. It might have been because she was giving me a very funny look – the sort of look that clearly says, 'I think you are sectionable' – but it could also have had something to do with the fact that she was a very attractive girl in a figure-hugging uniform who was going to be spending the next week in close proximity to my husband.

There, again – those words: *my husband.*

There was a crunching sound on the path behind me

and I turned to see Nick making his way across to the bus. He had his rucksack slung over one shoulder and his expression, as he caught sight of me, was pretty much overtly hostile.

I jumped back down from the coach and hobbled over. Nick looked the other way.

'Any news on Arthur?' he asked, his voice brittle and angry.

I shook my head.

'No, nothing on Arthur.'

The atmosphere between us was as tense as it had ever been. I didn't need Psychic Serena to tell me that we were not going to get over this with a few easy words and a quick laugh about silly misunderstandings. His demeanour, his tone – everything about him – told me that he was very upset indeed.

My stomach gave a huge, terrible lurch and I took a deep breath.

'I spoke to Kitty,' I said.

Something flashed across Nick's face.

'Yes,' he said, 'me too. Lucky I did, wasn't it?'

From inside the coach, the girl in the navy uniform waved at Nick and he waved back. She was obviously anxious to be off as soon as possible.

'She's wrong – I mean – about me going to Newcastle.'

Nick's face was stony.

'Oh, she is, is she? Did she make it up? Pull it out of the air?'

I clutched at the handrail that led up onto the bus.

'No – I did get an offer of a job there, a deputy headship. I had the interview for it last Friday.'

Nick paused.

'But what – you didn't accept it?'

I began to feel distinctly nauseous.

'No, I did,' I replied, 'I accepted it as soon as I got it.'

Nick pursed his lips as though he'd tasted something unpleasant.

'Okay then – so you rang them up and told them that things between you and your husband had changed and you wouldn't be moving to England after all?'

'No, no I didn't—'

Nick gave a curt nod of the head.

'Then Kitty was right: you've taken a job that means you're going to move miles and miles away to Newcastle and not even *mentioned* it to me.'

Suddenly, the world around me, which had been doing a good job of staying still up until that point, started whirling and spinning like a merry-go-round. The girl on the bus put her clipboard down and stared at us.

'Let's get down to brass tacks here, Ailsa,' Nick continued. 'If you want to know what really upset me, it wasn't the job; it was all the other stuff – how I'm untrustworthy, how it was never serious between us – that's the shit that bothers me. So it's fine – you go to Newcastle and I'll stay out of your life. Sounds like a plan.'

Oh, bloody hell – why had I told my wretched sister *anything*?

'Look, Nick,' I said, trying hard to keep my cool, 'I'm sorry. When I spoke to Kitty I was still very upset – you'd just asked me for a divorce and – look, the point is, I—'

'No, the point *is* that you have been using me,' Nick's voice cracked as he spoke. 'You say you don't trust me?

331

Well, Ailsa, that's how I feel about you right now.'

I looked down at my feet, raw and bruised, as the implication of his words sank in.

'It was different when I said those things,' I protested, 'a hell of a lot has changed since then.'

'No, it hasn't.' His voice was soft, almost to the point of inaudibility, but its tone was steely and unyielding. 'Feelings – really deep feelings – don't change: either you love me or you don't; either you trust me or you don't. You can't have it both ways.'

He paused.

'I have my faults, Ailsa, of course I do – huge, bloody big ones – but so do you. And the difference is that you won't admit it.'

I didn't dare look up because I could feel the telltale itchy heat in the corners of my eyes that told me tears were getting their act together and there was no way – no way at all – that I was going to cry in front of Nick.

'It's very simple, Ailsa.' I couldn't see his face because I was still staring hard at the ground between my feet, but I could hear the emotion in his voice. 'We have to be able to believe in each other, without that we've got nothing.'

I blinked and bit my lip. I was struggling to find words – any words – to contradict him. But they just didn't come.

'Anyway,' he continued briskly, 'I'm glad we've sorted everything out. I wouldn't have wanted to waste any more of my time thinking that we had a future together.'

The sound of someone clearing their throat respectfully floated down from inside the coach.

'Nick,' it was the girl with the clipboard, 'we're running behind schedule. Do you think you could . . . ?'

I risked a glance upwards as Nick nodded in her direction. My heart twisted and I pulled at the ring on my right hand.

His eye followed the line of my gaze.

'It's not valuable,' he replied. 'Keep it. Give it away. I don't care.'

I swallowed hard. He sounded as though he actually meant it: *he didn't care.*

The girl gave another cough. One of the old ladies called out, 'Come on, Dr Bannister. What are you waiting for – Christmas?'

'I've got to go.' Nick's gaze rested on me once again. 'I'll speak to a solicitor when I get back to Scotland.'

He walked round to the luggage compartment on the side of the coach, opened it and stowed away his rucksack. Limping, I followed. It was the last-ditch attempt to end all last ditches – but what else could I do?

'Do you want it to end?' I said, forcing the words into my throat and out through my lips. It was almost physically painful to speak. 'Is this honestly what you want?'

It was Nick's turn to look down at his feet. He scuffed the edge of one of his shoes through the gravel.

'No,' he said, turning away and taking the few steps over to the door of the coach, 'no, I don't. But what's the point? It's over. We're over. The sooner we both get used to that, the better.'

I wanted to run after him, grab his hand, pull him back – but my legs were as unobliging as my voice. I tried to move one foot – to take even the tiniest step that would bring me closer to his disappearing form – but my legs were lead weights and refused to take any orders from my brain.

Like one of those horrible dreams when you can't run or scream for help, I stood in the bright Italian sunshine and watched the man I now knew was the love of my life walk to his waiting coach, pull himself on board and talk briefly to Clipboard Girl before settling himself down in the front seat. The girl did one final head-check and sat down next to him. Then the doors swung closed and Nick and the rest of his tour party swept under the arch and off down the road towards Pisa.

Chapter Twenty-Four

I stood there like a lemon, watching the coach until all that remained was a trail of dust. I didn't want to cry – I simply didn't have the energy for it. My heart felt as though it had swelled to nearly ten times its original size and was pressing against the walls of my chest, making it very difficult to breathe.

And the pain – *the pain*.

I couldn't move.

With my limbs heavy and my eyes dry and sore, I stood staring into the empty space where the coach had been, trying to come to terms with the fact that I was never going to see Nick again.

Well, unless we ended up glowering at each other from opposite sides of a divorce court – which probably didn't count.

I have no idea how long I remained glued to the spot like that, but at some point, a hand came to rest against my back.

'Hey you,' said Jess softly, 'your shoulders are starting to go red. Is everything okay?'

I shook my head, still unable to look anywhere except the coach-free space in the archway entrance to the hotel grounds.

A hand slipped round my waist and Jess hugged me, her long hair flowing down over my shoulders and the smell of her perfume covering me like a warm, soft blanket.

'Nick,' I managed to articulate, covering my face with my hands, 'over. Nick. Over. Me.'

Just saying the words out loud made it all seem ten times more terrible. However, the swelling in my poor old heart reduced slightly and I managed to take a shaky breath in.

Jess didn't reply immediately. Instead she gave me another hug and kissed me on the top of my head before prising my hands away from my face and looking me dead in the eye.

'Do you love him?' she asked, scanning my face for all available clues.

I nodded.

'Yes. Only. He. Thought. I'd. Taken. This job. In Newcastle. And. That. I. Don't. Trust. Him.'

I paused and did a bit more hiccoughing. My heart swelled again as the memory of Nick climbing onto the coach and driving out of my life seared through me like a knife.

'Only. I. Do. And. Now. He's. Gooooooooooooone!'

Jess scrunched her face and stamped her foot down onto the gravel.

'Shit shit shit and double crapping shitty shit,' she said. 'Oh, Ailsa, I am so sorry.'

Just like me, then. Very, very sorry indeed.

'Can you ring him?' asked Jess. 'Can you text him? Can you explain?'

I shook my head.

'I tried,' I was still having difficulty getting words out, coherent or otherwise, 'just now. You know, to say . . . to say . . . to say . . .'

The words trailed off.

'Go on,' Jess urged.

'To say – that I *do* trust him – that I'd been upset when I said yes to the job in Newcastle – that things had changed now. But he said there wasn't any point. '

A huge wave of grief swept over me.

'He got his act together,' I said. 'He found a job in Edinburgh and everything – only I went and bitched about him to Kitty and she told him what I'd said. It's all my fault.'

Jess's face took on a stony expression.

'No, it's not. You're never going to get anywhere if you blame yourself.'

I sniffed.

'But isn't he right?' I protested. 'If I'd loved him – really, really loved him – wouldn't I have immediately cancelled the Newcastle job and not spoken to Kitty? Wouldn't I have known?'

Jess shook her head.

'You saw him for the first time in months on Monday,' she said, brilliantly matching the speed of her speech to the pathetic processing capabilities of my brain. 'The time before *that* you were probably throwing a large saucepan at him. This is real life, you know – not a film or a novel where you sort it all out in five minutes and live happily ever after. Give him some time, let him cool down and then see how you both feel.'

I wiped my nose on the back of my hand. Not the most gracious of moves, but hey – needs must and all that.

'Okay,' I said, 'but I'm not holding out much hope.'

Jess took a deep breath.

'Now,' she said, 'I've got something to ask you. I meant to ask last night but I was so excited, it slipped my mind. Anyway, please say no if you don't feel up to it, but would you consider being my bridesmaid?'

'Bridesmaid?' I echoed. 'I didn't think you wanted any bridesmaids?'

'I want you – if you would like to,' replied Jess. 'You and Nick, although we won't dwell on him too much, are the reason that Justin and I are here today and I would love you to be the one who helps me get down the aisle this afternoon.'

'But what about your mum and dad,' I asked, 'and Veronica? I mean, it's all been planned down to the last hatpin, hasn't it?'

'Maybe,' Jess smiled, 'but now Veronica's gone, I'm back in control; and more than anything, I'd like you in pole position, cheering me on. Will you think about it?'

Despite the circumstances, I found myself smiling too.

'There is nothing I'd like more,' I said. 'I may not be the biggest fan of weddings, but I have a feeling this one's going to be rather special.'

'Thank you,' she said. 'If you change your mind, I understand; I know that with Nick and everything that's happened this morning, it might be hard but . . .'

'You know what, Jess? I'm glad I married Nick. I love him and it was the right thing to do at the time. I will do my best to turn things round with him but, at the end of the day, Nick and I have nothing – do you hear me, Jess? – *nothing* to do with your wedding and I would be honoured to be your bridesmaid. It'll be a laugh. We'll get our make-up bags out, have a glass of fizz, dress up, put on some music . . . what do you say?'

Jess nodded. 'I can't think of anything more perfect. Thank you. Thank you so much.'

And off she went back to the hotel, a spring very much evident in her step. I turned and made my way to one of the benches that lined the lawn opposite and sat down, my head once again in my hands: how could so much happen before lunchtime? It was all very exhausting.

But the day had not yet delivered its quota of surprises.

There was the sound of a taxi drawing up outside the main entrance of the hotel and footsteps on the gravel as the occupant got out. I took my head out of my hands and stared: walking towards the revolving door that led into the foyer was a short lady with dark, bobbed hair and a very determined expression on her face. She looked like an older version of Kitty – and then I realised that that was *precisely* who she was: my mum.

At that exact same moment, the revolving door began to turn and an almost identical woman stepped out, blinking, into the sunlight and stared at her: it was the first time Mum and Auntie Sheila had seen each other for – goodness, I didn't want to think how long.

'Deborah!' Sheila was taken aback. 'What are you doing here?'

My mother stuck out her chin in the defiant manner my family have been doing for generations.

'It's my niece's wedding,' she replied, 'and she has asked me to be here. Don't worry, Sheila, I'm staying at another hotel down in the town and I've left John at home fussocking over his runner beans – I wouldn't dream of expecting Dudley to fork out any of his hard-earned cash on me.'

She said the words 'hard-earned cash' in a rather sarcastic way. I don't think it helped.

Auntie Sheila's chin immediately jutted out every bit as far as my mother's. If it wasn't for the fact that they were wearing different-coloured sundresses, they would have been mirror images of one another.

'Actually,' she said stiffly, 'it's my money, not Dudley's, and I'll spend it how I see fit. I suppose you'll be expecting to come to the reception, though, won't you? I mean, I can't have you turning up to the church and then everyone asking why you're not eating with the rest of us.'

She gave a heavy sigh. My mother, meanwhile, put her hands on her hips and pursed her lips.

'Ten years and nothing changes,' she replied sourly. 'It always comes down to appearances with you, doesn't it, Sheila? Not to worry that I came out here at Jessica's specific and repeated request – no, the only thing that matters to you is what *other people might think*.'

Even though Auntie Sheila didn't have her handbag with her, she looked as though she was spoiling for a fight. It was time for me to step in.

'Hello, Mum,' I said, hobbling over and kissing her on the cheek. 'What brings you here? Apart from the obvious.'

Auntie Sheila bit her lip and stalked off in the direction of the pool.

'Well,' Mum produced a pair of ridiculous-sized sunglasses from her bag and slipped them on. 'Apart from Jess insisting I came, I thought it was about time that all

340

this nonsense between Sheila and myself was knocked on the head once and for all. Dad says he's sorry to miss you and Kitty, but we agreed it would be better if I came alone – plus he really is worried about his beans.'

I couldn't have been more surprised if she'd told me she was opening support act for the Rolling Stones on their next world tour.

'Really?' I said. 'I mean, about you and Auntie S?'

Mum tilted her head on one side in a thoughtful manner.

'Yes,' she said, 'I've decided that ten years is too long to be in a huff with her. After all, apart from you and Kitty, Jess and Sheila are the only blood family I have. So, when the wretched baggage handlers finally sorted themselves out this morning and I had *another* email from your cousin Jess begging me to be here, I thought, okay, I'll have a weekend in Italy and talk to Sheila while I'm at it. Not that round one has been an overwhelming success, as you saw for yourself.'

'Well, full marks for trying,' I said. 'It must have taken a lot of guts to get on that plane. I'm sure Auntie Sheila will come round to the idea. I'm afraid she's a bit stressed at the moment – quite a lot's been happening this week.'

'Oh?' said Mum. 'You can fill me in on that later. Meanwhile, I hope that you and Kitty are behaving yourselves.'

I sucked my cheeks in and looked at the ground, something I could remember doing from when I was knee-high to a particularly small grasshopper.

'We're not talking,' I replied. 'In fact, I've decided that I don't have a sister any more.'

'Oh for goodness' sake.' My mother folded her arms

in a no-nonsense manner. 'The pair of you are the bloody limit – why can't you just get on nicely?'

I bit back my reply, which was something along the lines of 'just copying you and Auntie Sheila, Mother dear'. Instead I muttered: 'It's all her fault.'

'That's as maybe,' came my mother's reply, 'but she's still your sister – and, in case you hadn't noticed, she's the only one you've got.'

Instantly, I was no longer in my early thirties with a responsible job, a degree and a hefty credit card bill – I was six and a half again – and Kitty had just pulled the head off my Tiny Tears.

Mum's expression softened.

'Look,' she said, 'I have no idea what Kitty is supposed to have done to you – or you, for that matter, are supposed to have done to Kitty, but don't write her off: it's not worth it. Meanwhile, before you can say anything to *me* about not practising what I preach, I'm off to find Sheila again and see if we can't come to a truce, at least for Jessica's wedding.'

And she too crunched off in the direction of the pool.

As I watched her go, her dark hair swinging in exactly the same way that mine, Kitty's and yes, even Auntie Sheila's did, I had the most bizarre realisation. Nick had been right – we were all cut from the same mould and, however much I wanted to deny it, however far I moved to get away from them, I was part of this crazy, loony clan and I wouldn't have it any other way.

It was turning out to be a very strange morning indeed.

Chapter Twenty-Five

As soon as I had finished speaking to my mother, I limped as quickly as I could back to my room and thought about what to do next. My conclusions ran something like this:

1. I needed to speak to Nick.
2. But Nick did not want me to ring him.
3. However, if I didn't, he would never know how I felt.
4. If I rang him too soon he would still be cross with me.
5. If I left it too long, he'd think I didn't care.

Again.

It was one of those horrible times in life when you simply can't work out what the right thing to do actually *is*, because whichever way you jump, the chances of landing up to your neck in something unpleasant are very high indeed.

In the end, I took out my phone and rang his mobile number. Knowing Nick, I guessed he'd have his phone switched off and I wouldn't actually have to speak to him directly. To my immense relief, it didn't even ring but clicked immediately to voicemail.

Hello, came an automated female voice, *the person you are calling doesn't want to be married to you any longer but please leave a message after the bleep. BLEEEEEEP.*

Actually, it didn't say that. But it might as well have done.

'Nick? Hi, it's Ailsa here.'

(Excruciating pause.)

343

'I'm really sorry about what happened this morning and what I said to Kitty and—'

BEEEEEEEP – I was out of time.

With my fingers still trembling, I redialled.

'Nick, it's me again. The thing is – you see, the thing is – I mean, the thing *is* – I do trust you; absolutely. That's sort of the point. I was so shocked when you said you wanted a divorce—'

BEEEEEEEP.

Oh fuckety-fuck.

I stamped my foot in sheer frustration.

Redial. Come on, come on, connect, you bastard.

Hello, the person you are calling really doesn't give a shit, but if you want to pretend they do then please feel free to leave a message . . .

'ThatIwastryingtoconvincemyselfourmarriagehadbeen rubbishonlyitwasn'tandweneedtositdownandtalkthings outandgettoknoweachotheronceagainandaweekinItaly withmyinsanefamilyisnotenough—'

You have ten seconds of battery remaining.

No! No! Nooooooo!

SopleaseringsowecantalkandIneedyoutoknowthat—

Click.

My heart sank.

'I need you to know that I really want to work this out.'

I threw my phone back into my bag.

There. I'd done it.

If he was just pissed off, but deep down he still loved me, he would ring. If not – well, I didn't want to consider the 'if nots'.

Please God, please don't let it be a not.

Three hours, a full face of make-up and four glasses of Prosecco later, I was standing in the shade of the magnificent medieval ruins of the abbey church. The sky was a faultless blue and there was a cooling breeze blowing in from the sea, taking the edge off the mid-afternoon heat.

Just as Jess had predicted, it was perfect.

No, it was better than perfect.

In place of the forests of lilies and swags of ribbon as per Veronica, there were instead just a few simple ivy-leaf garlands wreathing the ancient pillars. A mismatch of wooden chairs borrowed from the dining room and the terrace stood on the closely cropped turf, and at the head of the nave where the altar would once have been, two huge church candles stood in large, twisted pewter holders, their flames burning bright and strong in defiance of the breeze. Gone were the planned choir, the legions of clergy, the officiators from the town hall, the orchestra and all the rest of the faff. All that was left was a single priest and the sun-bleached stonework of the church blazing white against the soft green of the grass and the blue of the sea.

As settings for romantic weddings went, it was pretty much unsurpassable.

Jess was still in her room, putting the final touches to her dress. Like the ceremony, this too was a pared-down version of the original – but it was what Jess had wanted all along. Instead of the cathedral-length train and the enormous bouquet, I had left her looking radiant in a simple sheath dress with cap sleeves and a plunging neckline, a pair of plain cream court shoes, Granny's pearls round her throat and a white peony in her blonde hair. Needless to say, she looked amazing.

I'd had no idea what I should wear, it being a bit late in the day to run up any official bridesmaids' outfits. Jess, however, had scrutinised my wardrobe for mere seconds before pulling out Emma's vintage gown.

'You looked amazing in this,' she said, 'it could have been made for you.'

I bit my lip.

'The friend who lent it to me said that it was a lucky dress,' I told her. 'Her grandmother was wearing it when she met her husband.'

Jess gave an approving nod.

'Then you *definitely* need to wear it,' she replied, 'husband-meeting luck is my favourite sort.'

The fact that I already *had* a husband who was currently in Pisa and unlikely ever to speak to me again seemed to have temporarily slipped her mind.

But I let it go and allowed myself to be zipped into its soothing folds with nary a protest.

So, there I was: pink heels, pink floaty dress, hair teased into good behaviour and piled on top of my head, peering through the ancient doorway of the church. Looking straight down the aisle I could see Justin and the priest – a friend of his who'd come up from Rome for the occasion – standing next to one of the candles, chatting. Settled into seats immediately in front of them were a tiny blonde lady and a smartly dressed man. The woman looked round, a beaming smile on her face, and I knew immediately that she was Justin's mum, taking her place to proudly watch her son wed the love of his life.

346

The church was a lot fuller than I'd expected – it looked as though a lot of people had taken advantage of the baggage handlers' strike settlement and flown out at the last minute. On the bride's side, I picked out Uncle D and Auntie S. Although both were done up to the nines, Uncle Dudley's expression was decidedly mutinous, making Auntie Sheila look as though she was sitting next to an active volcano.

Behind her was my mother, still looking like Auntie Sheila's doppelgänger, and next to *her* was Kitty.

I hesitated. I was still so angry, I could have happily laid my sister out cold, but my mother's words resonated with me: even if I couldn't forgive her, I would have to find a way to live with what she'd done. I couldn't have Jess's big day marked in my memory by the birth of yet another family feud.

Taking my courage in both hands, I walked over to Kitty, touching her lightly on the shoulder. She looked round and I pressed my index finger to my lips: I wanted a word – but I didn't want to have it in front of everyone else.

She followed me to the back of the church, and when I was sure we were alone, I took a deep breath.

'Kitty,' I said, 'I need to talk to you about Nick.'

Kitty, who had been fiddling with a stray thread on the hem of her dress, slowly raised her face and looked at me. She looked very uncomfortable indeed. There was a truly terrible silence, and for a moment, I wondered if she was about to take to her heels and run away. At last, she spoke.

'I need to apologise,' she said, glancing away again. 'I didn't mean to ruin your life – really, I didn't. But, if I'm being honest, I was out to cause trouble.'

347

Her words hit me like an actual, physical blow.

'So I was right – you really wanted to hurt me?'

Kitty swallowed.

'No, not that; not hurt you. Look, you hit the nail on the head this morning. I spoke to Nick because of what happened with Charles. I was *beyond* livid with you for sticking your oar in and I went a bit mad. The thought that you'd told Charles to dump me, whilst at the same time getting yourself all loved up, was more than I could bear. Honestly, Ailsa, I've never been so angry in all my life; so while you were out looking for that dog, I found Nick and told him exactly what you'd said to me.'

She paused.

'It's no excuse for what I did, I know that, but, if it's any help, I didn't think for one moment that it would cause so much heartache.'

There was the sound of approaching footsteps. Jess, with the help of the dark-haired, smiley girl from reception, was making her way over the grass towards us. She had a grin so enormous plastered over her face that it was a wonder her jaw didn't dislocate, and a curl had escaped from her up-do, wisping in front of her face in a slightly dishevelled, cheeky way. The hotel staff – or the more friendly elements of it at any rate – were forming a guard of honour, and as she passed, they clapped and stepped forward with extra flowers to add to her hastily put-together posy.

Kitty smiled faintly.

'Jess spoke to me at lunchtime and told me all about her and Charles and what a disgusting creep he is. I just wish I'd known earlier; I'd have taken great pleasure in helping give him his come-uppance. Oh, Ailsa – I'm so, so sorry about you and Nick.'

Her voice tailed off into nothingness.

'So am I,' I replied. 'And I'm sorry that I didn't tell you what I knew about Charles. I should have just given you the information and let you make your own mind up.'

Kitty gave me a watery smile.

'Is there any way we can get back to where sisters should be,' she asked, 'or at least, how you and I normally are? Attainable goals and all that.'

'I don't know,' I said honestly, 'I hope so. But there is so much going on at the moment that I don't know how I feel about any of it.'

Kitty nodded.

'If I could go back and change everything,' she said, 'I would – you know that?'

I touched her hand.

'Me too, Kitty, me too. I think we're far more alike than either of us were prepared to acknowledge.'

Our time was up. Jess stepped onto the grass, taking care not to let the heels of her satin shoes sink into the turf, and made her way towards us. I nodded briefly at Kitty and then walked over to meet her, kissing her lightly on the cheek.

'You look amazing,' I said, 'really beautiful.'

'Ditto,' she said, picking some freesia stems out from her posy and handing them to me. 'I'm so glad you're wearing that dress. My gut is telling me it's about to work its magic again. That's the thing about instincts – they're beyond bonkers, but you've still got to go with them.'

I nodded. I didn't believe her gut for one moment, but

it was her big day and I was prepared to humour her.

'All okay?' She inclined her head in the direction of Kitty, who was making her way back slowly to her seat.

I shook my head.

'Not really,' I confessed, 'but I know the truth now, so I suppose that's a step forward of sorts.'

'Good,' she replied, taking my hand in hers and squeezing it, 'clean slates, bottom lines. Remember, real love doesn't just happen overnight – you have to work at it.'

Tell me about it.

'Anyway, are you ready?' Jess whispered, tugging at my hand. 'It's showtime!'

Together we walked across the grass to what was left of the broken-heart-shaped doorway, ready to begin our progress along the remains of the aisle. Even though the doors themselves were long gone and the rest of the building no more than a few pillars and crumbling rows of weathered stonework, I sensed that the ceremony we were about to embark upon was approved of by whatever force it was that watched over the ancient church.

Jess peered in between the stone pillars and gave a little gasp.

'Oh my goodness! It's even more lovely than I'd imagined.'

I pulled a tissue out of a cunningly concealed pocket in the seam of my bodice and ran it carefully under her eyes to catch possible mascara leakage.

'It *is* lovely,' I agreed, 'and if I ever get married again, then this is pretty much what I'd want. I don't really recommend register offices in Scotland in the middle of a howling gale. Your way of doing things is much more civilised.'

Jess gave a happy little shiver.

'I don't know,' she said, 'at the end of the day, it's the person you're getting married to that counts, not the venue.'

She paused. 'Besides, I don't think you'll be getting married again.'

'Oh?' I wasn't entirely sure how to take this. Surely Jess wasn't suggesting I was so intrinsically unlovable that no one would want me?

She gave a mysterious smile.

'But we really ought to get going; I think I've tortured poor Justin long enough. I know it's the bride's prerogative to be late, but I don't wanting him thinking I've left the country.'

Then she winked at the smiley girl with dark hair who was positioned behind the pillar opposite with a CD player. The girl pressed a button and the unmistakable strains of Barry White rumbling 'My First, My Last, My Everything' rang out across the nave. Everyone in the pews – sorry, mismatched wooden chairs – turned round expectantly.

Everyone.

Including a man at the front with unruly, dark hair and chocolate-brown eyes.

'Come on,' Jess nudged me. 'This is it.'

And before I had time to say, 'But what the blooming heck is my estranged husband doing in the congregation?' Jess had glided serenely through the lichened portals of the church, stepped lightly down the two steps into the nave and was heading for Justin. I hurried after her, although I'm sure I stepped much less lightly and did not, in any shape, manner or form, glide.

Holy matrimony, Bat Girl.

Nick?

He should have been miles away in Pisa, helping his pensioners take amusing pictures of themselves trying to push the tower over.

Ahead of me, Jess made her way along the path of chipped but still-colourful floor tiles that marked the way to the altar. Even though I couldn't see her face, I knew that she was smiling. I also knew, from the occasional shake of her shoulders, that she was crying – but I didn't blame her. As we progressed down towards the candles, just about everyone in the congregation welled up in sympathy. Even my mum and Kitty had a wobbly lip apiece – and if they could succumb to the magic and emotion of the moment, then nobody was safe.

As we walked – a walk, by the way, which seemed to take about fifteen million bazillion times longer than any other walk I've done before or since – I kept my eyes focused firmly on Jess. This was partly because she was wearing vertiginously high stiletto heels and I had visions of one of them becoming lodged in the medieval floor tiles – but mainly because I didn't want to look at Nick.

However, my eyes refused to obey orders, and as we approached the front of the church, I couldn't help but trace the familiar line of his body. As I did so, a familiar wobble reasserted itself in my stomach and I, too, found myself blinking back tears as well.

Jess and I took the final few paces towards Justin. Then Jess turned and handed me her bouquet. I took a step back and watched as she held out her hand so that Justin could grasp it in his. Their eyes met and an instant, identical smile wreathed their faces. The girl from reception pressed the 'stop' button on Barry White, Justin's priest friend cleared his throat, and we began.

'Good afternoon and welcome to this unique setting for the marriage blessing of two people very dear to all of us. Although Jessica and Justin have already married in a civil ceremony, this is their opportunity to celebrate the love that they have for one another in front of the people who are dearest to them. Marriage – whether it happens at a town hall in Italy, an English country church, a ruin in Tuscany or a rainy register office in Edinburgh . . . '

I couldn't stifle the astonished gasp that flew from my mouth. One or two people – including my mother – stared at me and I did my best to turn it into a cough.

'. . . is a solemn and binding commitment. The English Book of Common Prayer puts it like this: "The union of husband and wife in heart, body, and mind is intended by God for their mutual joy; for the help and comfort given one another in prosperity and adversity; and therefore marriage is not to be entered into unadvisedly or lightly, but reverently, deliberately, and in accordance with the purposes for which it was instituted by God."'

A nasty little mind-worm wriggled into my brain. Was that what I had done? Entered marriage lightly? And what price was I about to pay for doing so?

But my thoughts were interrupted by a noise on my right. I looked round and saw Uncle Dudley purse his lips together and shuffle in his seat. Auntie Sheila gave him a Sidebottom glare and the priest continued.

'So, in the holy setting of this ancient church, I would now like to ask Jessica and Justin to come forward and recite – not the vows that we are all used to hearing at wedding ceremonies – but a more intimate, personal set that they have written themselves.'

There was a snort. Again, I looked round and saw that Uncle Dudley had a certain puce-ness about him. Luckily, Jess and Justin were too wrapped up in each other to notice. Jess gave Justin her other hand and they looked into one another's eyes.

'Justin,' began Jess, clearly blinking away tears as she spoke, 'I love you more than life itself. I love you more than words can say. I love you with everything that I own, everything that I am and everything that I will become and I shall love you like that for ever.'

'Jessica,' Justin was doing a fair bit of blinking himself. 'I love you from the bottom of my heart. I love you with a passion that is never ending. When I met you, I discovered what it is to be truly happy.'

Jess bit her lip and took a moment to compose herself before replying. I was so bound up in what they were saying that that I hardly noticed as a large, fat tear rolled down my own face and splashed onto the tiles at my feet.

'I promise that for the rest of our lives, I will always be there for you, Justin. I don't care if you are a multi-millionaire or out on the streets, because I will go with you wherever the road of life leads you.'

There was a third, even louder snort. This time the whole congregation spun round and stared. Jess clenched her hands into fists and gave her father a look every bit as deadly as the one her mother had just delivered.

'What exactly,' she said, in a loud, clear voice that echoed round the pillars and rebounded from the archways, 'do you think you are doing?'

Uncle Dudley looked thoroughly taken aback. The puce colour slowly diluted down to a pale pink.

'I said,' Jess picked up her skirts and took a few steps towards her father, 'what do you think you are doing?'

Dudley shifted uncomfortably in his seat but said nothing.

'Is it the vows?' asked Jess, her hands on her hips. 'Is there something wrong with the vows?'

Dudley remained silent.

'Go on,' Jess commanded, 'spit it out. If you've got a problem with them that is so important it is worth disturbing my wedding for, then I want to hear it.'

She continued to stare at him. I swear that Dudley began to grow smaller in the heat of her gaze. Rather than being a huge hippo of a man, he seemed to be shrinking down to normal proportions.

'It's all,' Dudley began, recovering his poise as he spoke, 'it's all rather – modern – is perhaps the right word. Yes, that's it. If you really want to know what my problem is, it's all this modern nonsense.'

Jess gave a brief, sharp nod.

'Right. Let me get this straight – because I want to make sure everyone is absolutely clear on this – you think that it's okay to growl and grumble away while Justin and I are speaking because you don't approve of the vows?'

Just as Dudley seemed to be shrinking, it occurred to me that Jess seemed to be doing the exact opposite.

'You are here as a spectator, Pops – nothing more,

nothing less. What I say at my wedding is up to me and no one else.'

'Apart from me,' added Justin, looking nervously but admiringly at Jess, as though he could not quite believe the crusading Amazon standing beside him.

'And Justin, obviously,' Jess didn't miss a beat. 'I am grateful to you for everything you have done for me, Pops – everything that money could possibly buy and a whole lot more – but that does not give you the right to dictate like this.'

'But—' Dudley began but Jess held up her hand.

'Bag it, Pops.'

The words had an immediate and impressive effect. I decided to file them away for future use myself. Jess's face softened.

'The bottom line is that I love you: you're my dad and I don't doubt that in some slightly bizarre way you have wanted the best for me all along. But you need to stop being a bully – and that includes making sure you sit quietly while Justin and I say what we want to say to each other.'

'Um,' the priest held up his hand, 'do we perhaps want to think about carrying on with the service now?'

'Actually,' Auntie Sheila stood up, 'While there's a little break in proceedings, there's something I want to say – if you don't mind, Jess.'

All eyes flipped from Sheila to Jess to Dudley and then back again. It was a bit like watching Andy Murray in the finals at Wimbledon.

Only even more nerve-wracking.

'I've got a bit of news,' she said. 'Particularly concerning you, Dudley.'

My uncle looked a bit uncertain.

'You know we're supposed to be celebrating our thirtieth wedding anniversary next week?' asked Auntie Sheila.

'Mmmm?' replied Dudley, looking very much like a small hippopotamus that has seen a much larger hippo approaching, and is feeling nervous about what might happen next.

'Well, we're not,' said Sheila.

'Don't be silly, Sheila,' my mother threw her two penn'orth into the mix, 'of course you are. You and Dudley buggered off to Italy – sorry, vicar – and got married at that church down in the town here and *I* had to deal with the fall-out from Mum and Dad.'

Auntie Sheila shook her head.

'We *did* find a priest, Deborah, you're right – but, as I discovered this morning when I made some proper enquiries at the town hall, our so-called wedding wasn't legal at all. So, Dudley, I'm afraid that if it's married life you're after, the past thirty years haven't counted for anything.'

Uncle Dudley opened and shut his mouth a couple of times before he could get any recognisable words out.

'Don't be absurd, woman; of course we are married.'

'I'm not absurd,' Auntie Sheila replied lightly, a half-smile creeping across her lips. 'I was going to tell you quietly once we got home, but after this little charade over the vows, I thought, why not just get it all out into the open?'

Uncle Dudley looked as though someone had hit him round the back of the head with a heavy object.

'Well, if it wasn't marriage, what the hell was it?'

Again the smile flickered over Auntie S's face.

'Well, apologies again, vicar, but the only way I can put it is to say that we've been living in sin.'

Kitty stifled a giggle. I saw her stuffing a handkerchief into her mouth to prevent any more laughter leaking out.

Uncle Dudley was finally broken.

'But I don't want to live in sin,' he cried, his face like that of a little boy at school who has just had his lollipop confiscated, 'I want to be married to you.'

Auntie Sheila raised a perfectly plucked eyebrow.

'Really?' she said.

'Yes,' stammered Dudley, 'really. Very much. More than anything. I love you, dammit.'

'That's all well and good,' Auntie Sheila waved his protestations of love to one side, 'but what if *I* don't want to be married to *you*?'

If Uncle Dudley's face was anything to go by, this was one eventuality he hadn't considered.

'You don't?' he asked, the shock etched into his features and any last remaining traces of puceness draining from his puffy cheeks.

'I'm not sure,' said Auntie Sheila, 'I'll have to think about it.'

Dudley looked thunderstruck. His gob, one might say, was absolutely and completely smacked.

'But I love you!' he protested, as though this would immediately change everything. 'I love you! Don't you love me?'

'I might love you, Dudley,' said Auntie Sheila, 'but, right now, I sure as hell don't like you very much.'

'I'll change – I'll do the washing-up – I'll make sure I

hang up my towel after I've had a shower. I'll become a new man!'

I glanced over at Jess and Justin. They were staring at the unfolding drama in total disbelief.

Auntie Sheila flicked an invisible speck of dust from her dress.

'You're right – things are going to change. Starting with your job.'

'My job?' said Uncle Dudley. 'But I'm the company chairman. I hold the controlling interest in the shares. You can't do anything about my *job*.'

'Actually,' replied Auntie Sheila, 'that's not strictly true, is it? At least not with regard to the shares. They were left to me by my mother. Sidebottom's is *my* family business and I don't think I want you involved with it any longer. I shall be calling an emergency general meeting as soon as we get home, but as far as I'm concerned, Dudley, you're fired – and not a moment too soon.'

Dudley's mouth opened and closed like a goldfish.

He was, quite simply, corporate toast.

'Don't worry, Dudley, you'll get the customary golden handshake – although,' she paused and put an immaculately manicured finger to her lips, 'I and my new co-chairman Deborah here will be requiring you to pay off the money you owe the company first, so it probably won't amount to an awful lot.'

Uncle Dudley began to splutter.

'But I did it for you – for Jess – so that we could have the life we'd always wanted. I was going to pay it back – really – it was like a loan – it was—'

Auntie Sheila shrugged.

'I don't care how it was, Dudley. You're lucky Deborah and I have decided not to take this any further. We'll have to sell our house, of course, and move somewhere much smaller, and there will be no more golf club membership or fancy holidays abroad. Think about it as a life swap – I'll have a go at running the company and you can stay at home and unpack the Tesco deliveries. Now, do you still love me as much as you thought you did?'

Auntie Sheila's eyes narrowed until they were little more than gimlets in her face.

'I do love you, Sheila, really I do. But this – but this—' Dudley was lost for words.

'Well,' Auntie Sheila smiled sweetly, 'you don't have to make up your mind right now, do you? Why don't you sleep on it? Meanwhile, we have a wedding to enjoy. So, if you'd be so good as to shut up, it's over to Jess and Justin!'

Jess grinned, took Justin's hands in hers and looked deep down into his eyes. In a flash, the magic was restored and we were back to the fairytale wedding in the romantic ruins of a medieval Italian church.

'And I promise, Justin,' Jess smiled into his eyes as she spoke, 'that I shall make you one of my special hot chocolates every Sunday morning – with sprinkles and marshmallows and squirty cream – just how you like it.'

'And I promise not to moan when you take eight pairs of shoes with you on a weekend away and I will understand that when you buy expensive perfume in duty free that you are actually *saving* money in the long run.'

Normal, slightly kooky, Jess and Justin service had been resumed.

Chapter Twenty-Six

After the vows – which went from the unusual to the frankly bizarre – we all stood to sing Whitney Houston's 'I Will Always Love You', and there was a reading from *The Tiger Who Came to Tea*, for no reason other than it was Jess's all-time favourite book. Then the rings were blessed by the vicar, dropped by Justin, found by me, and placed safely on the bridal and groom-al fingers. Finally, Jess and Justin kissed (prompting a huge cheer from all of us) and they prepared to make their way back down the aisle to the accompaniment of the *Coronation Street* theme tune.

As they turned to leave the altar (or rather, the place where the altar had stood eight hundred years ago) Jess took back her flowers and whispered to me to follow her. I did as I was told but was unnerved to see Nick rise from his seat at the front and fall into step beside me.

To begin with, I tried very hard to pretend he wasn't there: I looked down at my shoes; I raised my head and gazed at the clear blue sky; and I focused very hard indeed on Jess's back and counted the tiny mother-of-pearl buttons that ran down the length of her bodice (thirty-one in total). However, none of these activities could blot out the knowledge that Nick was there, walking beside me and matching my pace exactly with his own.

In the end I simply gave up.

'I thought you were supposed to be in Pisa,' I whispered,

keeping my eyes fixed firmly on Jess's fourth button down.

'I am,' he hissed back.

I smiled at my mum and Auntie Sheila as we went past. Mum frowned in puzzlement at Nick, while Auntie S twinkled at him in a smitten way and waved her hand coyly.

'So,' I said, staring at the fifth button for a bit of variety, 'why are you here? Did you get lost? Did the bus drive round in circles for a bit, end up back at the hotel and you decided to pop in and to see how we were all getting along with the wedding?'

'You sound cross.'

'I'm not cross.'

Uneasy and nervous, yes, but not cross.

Not yet, anyway.

'Are you sure?'

'Of course I'm sure. Are you telling me I don't know whether I'm cross or not?'

'Just throwing it out there as a possibility. Shame about the flowers.'

I looked down at my posy of freesias. I was so tense, my hands had squeezed the life out of them and they were drooping forlornly.

I gritted my teeth. It made whispering more difficult, but I gave it a go anyway.

'Stop changing the subject and tell me why you aren't in Pisa. Did someone move the tower?'

'Leah – my co-guide – took over for the rest of the day. She needs to do a couple of sections of the tour as part of her guiding exams. She's very good, you know.'

A shaft of something that felt suspiciously like jealousy shot through me.

'Oh, she is, is she?' I replied, before smiling broadly at Justin's dad who was standing at the back taking photos.

'Yes,' Nick replied, 'very good indeed.'

We followed Jess and Justin through the church doors and turned right, making our way onto another area of lawn, this one with an amazing view of the sea. The smooth, cropped turf was shaded by a large gazebo containing round café-style tables, while waiters and waitresses stood ready for us, bearing trays of brimming glasses of wine and retro-style canapés (another of Jess's fab ideas).

I took a large glass and sipped it gratefully, while the other guests drifted across after us into the comparative cool of the gazebo. Over in the far corner I spotted Mum and Auntie Sheila. As I watched, Mum put her hand on Auntie Sheila's arm and then kissed her on the cheek. Auntie Sheila gave a huge gulping sob and threw her arms round my mother's neck, almost knocking her hat onto the floor: a decade of family feuding was over – all thanks to Jess and her insistence on a proper family wedding.

I looked round for Nick. I felt steadier now and I wanted to apologise for my jibes about the Leaning Tower; then I wanted to find a quiet spot and talk. And talk and talk and talk – the kind of talking with our clothes on that we hadn't managed to do properly last time.

But he had gone.

My eyes searched through the throng in the gazebo, hoping to spot him chatting to Mum or Justin or even – God help me – Kitty, but he was nowhere to be seen. It was as though the floor had just opened up and swallowed him alive. Or, more realistically, that he'd had enough and just left.

We were short of tall, dark, half-Italian Scotsmen by a factor of one.

I took a sip from my glass, but the wine seemed to have lost its sweetness. Jess, a handful of cheese-and-pineapples in her clutches, saw my worried expression and came over.

'Wassup?' she asked, through a mouthful of seventies retro-snack.

'He's not here,' I whispered, peering behind a stack of wedding presents on a trestle table in case Nick was hiding out there. 'He's gone.'

Jess, who had been grinning like a Cheshire cat that had found some rather superior cream, wiped the smile from her face.

'But he can't,' she protested, 'he said – he promised – oh buggerpants, Ailsa, this wasn't supposed to happen.'

I stood, looking out across the Nick-less gathering, with a feeling of despair rising inside me and not much of a clue about what I should do next.

Glancing down at my right hand, I twisted the ring he had given me. It stood for so much: for hope, expectation, the future; it symbolised me and Nick when we had been at our best, when we hadn't let life interfere with our love for each other.

Out of the blue, I realised that even if it was over – even if Nick had gone back to Pisa never to see or speak to me again – I wanted to tell our story. I wanted the world to know that I had loved him.

And that he would always be a part of me.

'Jess,' I said, 'there's something I just need to – ah – say – something about Nick. Out loud. If you don't mind – it won't take long.'

Jess nodded.

'Go on,' she said, beckoning Liam over, 'go for it.'

I drained my glass – it didn't help me think any more clearly, but it did give me a nice warm feeling in the pit of my tummy, which was a big help.

It also gave me something I could make a bit of noise with.

Taking a spoon from a table in front of me, I tapped on the side of my glass.

'Hello, St Lucia,' I said.

Gradually, the babble of voices died down and fifty pairs of eyes all turned to look at me.

'Hello,' I said again, feeling rather uncertain.

Years of school assemblies complete with warnings about running in the corridors and not sticking used chewing gum on the noticeboards had done nothing to prepare me for this.

I took the deepest breath of my life.

'I have an announcement to make,' I said, 'not about Jess or Justin as is customary, I'm afraid, but about me and the man I married well over a year ago.'

'Don't be ridiculous, Ailsa dear,' my mother's voice rang out, 'you're not married! Don't you think I'd have remembered coming to your wedding?'

Out of the corner of my eye, I saw Liam running across the grass in the direction of the hotel. A mission? To find Nick? Maybe?

'You weren't invited,' I told her. 'In fact, no one was. It was all done in a hurry, in secret, up in Edinburgh.'

'But why, dear?' This was Auntie Sheila. 'Why was it all so hush-hush?'

'Because,' I paused: there were so many reasons why I'd kept it quiet that it was difficult to isolate just one. 'Because we were in love, a little bit foolish and desperate to be with one another. I know, I know, everyone these days can just move in and live with each other, but we wanted something more, you know? Something that reflected how much we felt for each other.'

'But you still could have told us afterwards,' my mother made her way into the centre of the floor, 'and Dad and I would have wanted to meet him.'

'You have met him,' I said. 'He's called Nick, and he's that chap you saw me talking to in the church just now.'

'Blimey!' Auntie Sheila's eyebrows almost shot off her head into her enormous broad-brimmed hat. 'You told me he was your itinerary, but now you're saying that he's actually your—'

'My husband, yes,' I paused. 'And he is – was – I'm not sure – an artist. You wouldn't have approved of that, Mum. That's another reason why I didn't mention him.'

My mother pursed her lips into something resembling a cat's bottom.

'You see,' I cried, 'you don't approve.'

'Well, it's not that I don't *approve*—'

'Yes, it is.'

'Well, all right, it is,' she conceded. 'I don't approve. And I'd have made sure your father didn't approve either.'

'Exactly. So I left it. Only the longer I left it, the more difficult it became. I mean, how exactly *do* you begin a conversation, "Mum and Dad, you don't know this, but I've been married for three months to this bloke you've never even heard of." Anyway, it all became rather irrelevant because we split up.'

A little gasp ran round the crowd.

'We split up because *I* didn't really approve of him being an artist either; at least, I didn't like the fact that he never had any money. We had a lot of rows and – my fault as much as his – we stopped communicating. We didn't talk about the big things, the things that really mattered, and one night in March I walked out. That was the last time I saw him until he turned up at this very hotel with a tour party of little old ladies.'

I paused. I didn't really know what to say next.

'And?' yelled out someone from the floor. 'Don't leave us in suspense. What happened?'

I glanced up and met Kitty's eye. She smiled at me and mouthed 'go on'.

'Thanks to Jess, I realised how much I still loved him,' I said. 'I began to understand that, even though we've got a lot of talking still to do, he's the man I want to be with for the rest of my life and it doesn't matter if he's an artist, or the chairman of the board, or a dustman. I love him because he changed my life. Anything else is irrelevant.'

'So what are you going to do?' asked Auntie Sheila, her eyes boggling further and further out of her head.

'The thing is,' I was stumbling over my words. 'The thing is – I don't know if he feels the same way. I don't even know if I'll see him again.'

'Oh no!' A large lady in a purple two-piece clapped her hand over her mouth.

'Can't you ring him?'

'What about a text? Here, borrow my phone!'

'Are you talking about that chap with the dark hair? Wasn't he around here a moment ago? Shall I see if I can find him?'

I raised my hand for silence.

'I will be ringing him, don't worry; and if there is any chance we can start again, believe me, I will leap at it. The point I'm trying to make, though, is that even if this *is* the end of the road, I wanted you – my family – random wedding guests and even more random hotel people – to know how I feel about him; to be aware that he and I had a moment together that was very special indeed.'

I looked down at my hand. Bizarrely, it felt wet. As I stared at it, a large drop of water fell from above and splashed on my knuckle. Instinctively I looked up, but the roof of the gazebo was dry. Another drop rolled its way down my cheek and plopped onto the tablecloth: it was me; I was crying.

I ran my hand across my face – it was either that or use one of the napkins – and sniffed.

'Anyway,' I said, pulling a chair out and sitting down, 'that's all I wanted to say: there was a man and I loved him. Please feel free to return to the cheese and pineapple on sticks.'

But no one moved.

I sniffed again.

'Go on,' I urged, 'have another drink, eat a sausage roll. Really, I've finished.'

There was silence.

'Um,' I said uncertainly, 'really, that's it.'

A thought struck me: 'Apart from this to Auntie Sheila: if you're looking for employees for your new-look Stoat

Brewery, I think Liam would be a good choice – he's hardworking, full of initiative and mixes a mean martini.'

'If you say so,' replied my bewildered aunt. 'Tell him he can come and see me first thing tomorrow. We'll sort something out.'

Jess pushed a tissue into my hand and I blew my nose, but still nobody stirred and nobody spoke.

Until, that is, a voice rang out across the gazebo.

'You might have finished, but I haven't.'

I peered across the gazebo and there, standing on the grass outside, was Nick.

'You heard . . .?' I asked, my voice trailing off.

'I heard.' Nick's face was completely expressionless.

'And?' I said, getting unsteadily to my feet.

'Well—'

Nick took a deep breath, but just as he was about to speak, all hell broke loose. There was a roar of anger followed by a crash, a shriek and the sound of running feet.

'You little—' yelled a voice I recognised as Roberto's, 'I'll teach you to eat a plate of sausage-a rolls!'

Through the crowd, dodging and diving, ducking and weaving, came Arthur; a big doggy grin on his face and quite a lot of flaky pastry round his chops. He raced in between the guests and right through the middle of Uncle Dudley's legs, before rounding the corner of my table and pawing at my skirts.

I scooped him up and clutched him to my bosom.

Roberto, his face red with rage, skidded to a halt in front of me.

'Give him,' he panted, 'to me.'

'No,' I replied, burying my nose in Arthur's fur and taking a good sniff of his lovely doggy scent, 'I shan't.'

'May I remind you, Miss Stuart, animals are not allowed on hotel premises.'

'Actually,' I replied, 'I'm Mrs Bertolini – and I've seen at least two tiny rat-dogs in here during the past week. You don't have an anti-animal policy at this hotel, you have an anti-Arthur one.'

Roberto scowled at me.

'And with good reason. This dog – he is nothing but trouble.'

'I love him,' I said simply, 'I love him and I'm not going to hand him over.'

For a moment we stared daggers at one another. But then something *else* happened.

'Boodle! It's Boodle! Mommy, I can see Boodle!'

And a small child, probably about eight or nine, with blonde curly hair and a very determined expression, charged into the gazebo. Arthur gave a yelp of delight and, before I knew what was happening, had wriggled out of my arms and launched himself at her, barking excitedly and covering her face with huge doggy licks.

So much for loyalty, then.

The expression on Roberto's face changed.

'Hey, little girl,' he said in a voice that made me want to retch, 'why don't you a-give the nice doggie to me?'

The girl stopped kissing Arthur/Boodle and stared at him.

'Nu-huh,' she replied, 'he's mine.'

Then, as an afterthought, added: 'Sir.'

Roberto took another step towards her.

'Give me the doggy,' he demanded, a little less ingratiatingly.

The little girl shook her head and Arthur/Boodle growled. His thoughts on the matter were perfectly clear.

Roberto took one final step towards them and made a grab for Arthur/Boodle. As quick as a flash, the little girl lunged forward and sank her teeth into Roberto's hand. With a yelp, Roberto sprang back, red bite marks clearly visible just below his knuckles.

'Why you little—' he began and then stopped as a wealthy-looking couple appeared, followed by the vet.

'Maddy,' said the woman sharply, 'what's going on?'

'It's Boodle,' the little girl, with Arthur/Boodle still in her arms, ran towards her mother. 'This lady found Boodle.'

'Did you?' The woman beamed at me. 'Oh, thank you, thank you – you have no idea how grateful we are.'

'And this man,' Maddy pointed at Roberto, 'tried to take him away from me.'

Arthur bared his teeth at Roberto as though he was backing up Maddy's accusation.

Maddy's father walked over to me, pulling a wallet out of his back pocket.

'I am so grateful,' he said. 'We've heard how you looked after Boodle when we lost him – you even paid for his medical care. I can never thank you enough, although maybe this will go some way to expressing my gratitude.'

He pulled out a bundle of notes so huge I could have used them as a doorstop, and thrust them at me.

'No,' I found myself backing away. 'No really. I didn't do it for the money.'

'We know you didn't,' he persisted, pressing the wad into my hands, 'but – please – this is the least we can do.'

'I don't want it,' I protested. 'Give it to the local dogs' home. I'm sure they need it more than me.'

'Well, if you're sure . . .'

I was. I'd done what I had from love – nothing more, nothing less. The only payment I wanted was to know that Arthur was safe and back where he belonged.

Maddy's mother put her arm round her daughter's shoulder.

'Come on now, sweetie. Thank the nice lady and say goodbye.'

Maddy turned to me, her face flushed with happiness and her eyes bright.

'Thank you for everything, lady,' she said. 'When we get home, I'll make sure Boodle writes a proper letter to let you know he's okay and tell you how he's getting on.'

'Brilliant,' I said, hoping that the wobble in my voice wasn't audible to anyone else. 'I'll look forward to it.'

I put my hand forward and rubbed Boodle's head for the last time.

'Go safely, little fella,' I whispered, 'and don't do anything I wouldn't do.'

Still clasped firmly in Maddy's arms, Boodle gave me a big, doggy grin, and then the family turned and walked away, followed by the vet and, still clutching his hand, Roberto.

A figure appeared at my side.

'I have to go,' Nick whispered.

I'd been so engrossed with the Arthur/Boodle end game, that I had almost forgotten he was there.

'Go?' I echoed.

'I have to go,' he repeated, 'I need to get back to Pisa. Jess wanted me here for the reception but I'm afraid I can't stay. Leah rang, apparently there's been an issue with Mrs Cribbins and the hotel photocopier – don't ask. Anyway, I need to catch a train and I'm cutting it pretty fine as it is.'

'Right,' I nodded. 'Okay.'

'I'd hoped we might be able to talk. I mean, properly.'

'Yes,' I felt my head droop slightly. 'Me too but . . .'

Argh! Nick had to go. He would be away for two weeks. I didn't think I could handle not knowing whether or not we were going to give it another go for two minutes, let alone fourteen days.

There was a pause; then he said: 'So, are you ready then?'

'Ready for what?'

'To go to Pisa. With me. Only you'll need to come straight away, the taxi's waiting.'

For a moment or two I couldn't actually speak.

'Pisa?' I said. 'But – but I'm here. I'm the bridesmaid. It's the reception. And—'

I paused. The next few words were a bit difficult for me to say.

'But you said,' my voice was little more than a whisper, 'you said you didn't care any more.'

Nick shook his head.

'The problem is that I care too much, Ailsa. Just like you, I got upset and, just like you, I said a whole bunch of stuff that I didn't really mean. Now, I know we have a lot of work to do, but will you come to Pisa with me – now – so that we can make a fresh start? I want to spend the rest of my life with you, and I'd like the rest of my life to start as soon as possible.'

I was boggling.

'But my stuff,' I said, 'my room – my clothes—'

'Um,' Jess gave an awkward cough behind me, 'I might have taken a teeny-tiny liberty and packed your case for you, Ailsa. And then I might have taken another, even teenier one, and asked Liam to bring it down to the main door for you. If you want to go, you are all set.'

'But only if you want to,' Nick's voice was low and croaky, 'really, Ailsa, only if you want to.'

I looked down at my right hand, Nick's ring still firmly on my third finger. Slowly, deliberately, and so that everyone could see, I pulled it off and handed it back to him.

'Do you want to do this properly?' I asked, holding out the ring finger.

Nick grinned and gently placed the band of white gold with its three tiny pearls onto my left hand.

Then he leaned over, kissed me gently on the mouth and said: 'I do.'

There was a lot of clapping, some cheering and a very loud wolf-whistle as well as someone (actually, my mother) saying: 'Sheila? What's happening? Do you know this Nick person? Who is he? Why does nobody tell me anything?'

Then there was a tug on my hand, Nick's voice saying 'come on', and the crowd in the gazebo parted so we could make our way through. In a daze, I followed him, my heels sinking into the soft turf. Someone threw confetti over us, someone else hurled a handful of rice and then we half-ran, half-walked across the gravel of the car park to where a taxi was waiting. It had a bundle of tin cans tied to the back bumper and the words 'Just Reunited' scrawled on a large sheet of paper and stuck to the back windscreen. Jess bundled me in, packing my silk skirts in round me to make sure they didn't get trapped in the door. Then she kissed me on the cheek.

'I took another teensy liberty and booked the honeymoon suite at your hotel in Pisa,' she grinned. 'It's in the name of Mr and Mrs Bertolini and I've texted the details to Nick's phone. Now go! Enjoy the rest of your time in Italy.'

The door shut, the engine revved and Nick turned to me, a Cheshire cat smile etched upon his face. He wound his hand into mine, while I laid my head upon his shoulder and the taxi sped through the sun-bleached stone archway of the hotel for the last time, taking us, in a cloud of dust, off towards the station – and the rest of our lives together.

Summer Nights

Allie Spencer

There's nothing quite like a holiday with your boyfriend . . .

Flora Fielding can't wait for Barney to join her in San Francisco so they can begin their dream holiday. Until Barney dumps her, leaving her stranded. Luckily, Flora's cousin Bella lives in San Francisco and, with nowhere else to go, Flora pitches up at her door.

As a singer in an Abba tribute band, Bella's life is a whirlwind of gigs, sparkly jumpsuits and nights on the town. And as Flora gets caught up in the excitement, she doesn't have time to worry about her broken heart.

In fact, she's so distracted that before she knows it she's running along a moonlit beach with a very handsome stranger...

arrow books